IN THE LIGHT OF THE DAWN
AN ANTHOLOGY OF ANTIQUITIES

IN THE LIGHT OF THE DAWN

AN ANTHOLOGY OF ANTIQUITIES

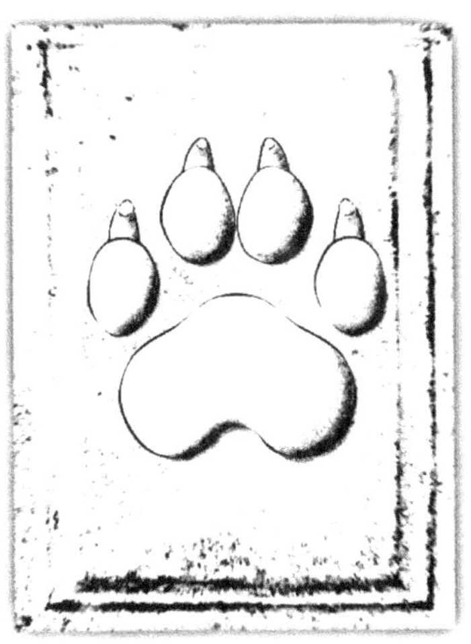

Utunu • Gar "Sahoni" Atkins • NightEyes DaySpring • Casterway • Faolan

Fopfox • Huskyteer • Thomas "Faux" Steele • Kayodé Lycaon

J.S. Hawthorne • Casimir Laski • J.F.R. Coates • Pascal Farful • Ziegenbock

Domus Vocis • Televassi • Rob MacWolf • Rose LaCroix

ISBN: 978-1-948743-37-2

In the Light of the Dawn: An Anthology of Antiquities
A project from The Furry Historical Fiction Society.

This book uses the fonts Gentium Book Plus, ABORETO, and Coelacanth.

AXIAL

CLASSICAL

The Furry Historical Fiction Society

In the Light of the Dawn is a collaborative project by the authors of the stories, with each of us chipping in to help with the process of editing, organizing, and decision-making. Thanks is given to each author in turn for their contributions, and we all hope that you enjoy the fruits of our labor.

Learn more at fhfs.ink

Content warnings: Several stories include violence or reference to violence; "...and the Sands of the Desert Wash Over the Words", "Fire and Brimstone", "To Your Own Defences", "The Satrap's Mark", "Heka", "The Lament of the Batavii", "Exile From the Land of Giant Turtles", and "Eulalius!" involve death; "The Merchant and the Martyr" and "Fire and Brimstone" involve slavery; "Fire and Brimstone" and "Go to the Road and Ask Any Passing Traveler" mention sex work; "...and the Sands of the Desert Wash Over the Words", "Go to the Road and Ask Any Traveler", "The Mouse From Mykonos", and "The Traces of Thomas Antiochus Macrotis" address sexuality; and "The Lament of the Batavii" involves depression and suicidal ideation.

AXIAL

THE PRICE OF COPPER

"Well, there it is!" stated Nas proudly. He stood with paws on hips, huge fennec ears upraised in excitement, looking down from the low hill into the basin below. The ground was sandy, reddish, and rocky, and there was a fennec-sized hole dug into the side of the hill.

That explains the smudges, thought Enshu. His friend's tunic, off-white at the best of times, was covered with red-brown stains–the fennec's sand-coloured fur even more so. Enshu crouched down and brushed some of the dust from the hem of his own tunic.

"Not much to look at, is it?" the dhole stated.

His reddish-furred friend was significantly taller, so Nas had to tilt his head up to glare at him. He rolled his eyes. "Of course not. It's a mine. Well, the beginnings of one. I checked, the seer was right, there's the right sort of ore in there."

"You put too much faith in them," admonished Enshu.

"Well, this one was right!"

"Why'd you drag me all the way out here, anyway? It must be a farsang back to the city. Does Sibi have you personally looking for new sources?" Enshu glanced back east to where Ur could barely be seen in the distance. His hyena guard, Qarradu, was watching him curiously from the bottom of the hill. He gave her a shrug—they were both used to Nas' eccentricities.

The fennec looked confused. "Sibi? The cheetah has nothing to do with this."

"What?"

"Didn't I tell you? I left his employ."

Enshu's eyebrows raised. "What?" he reiterated. "You've been with him for years! When'd you leave?"

Nas looked sheepish. "Umm, today I suppose. That's why I wanted to show you this."

The fennec was prone to rash decisions, but this was excessive, and Enshu was worried. "Why did you leave?"

"He sits there, a tick filled with blood. I do not approve of his management of his mines, his workers, or his business," said Nas emphatically. "Anyway, he delegated a lot of the administration to me, so I know exactly how everything works. And, well, it wasn't too expensive to get a claim out here. Sibi's mines are all north, he's said many times he doesn't want to worry about having multiple locations. Which makes sense, since there are so many rich veins where he digs."

"So... you bought this?" Enshu asked.

"I did! And I know where to hire labourers, I know a good smelter, and I know of a foreman who works well...and Enshu, you know I've wanted my own business since we were children causing trouble in the marketplace." The fennec kept shifting from one footpaw to the other, his excitement threatening to bubble over. "You've got yours–well, your late father's–but I need one of my own. Sibi's profiting off of my work, but I want my own name to be the thing people think of, not his."

"And Sibi's accepting of this?" asked the dhole, disbelievingly.

"Oh, probably not. I didn't tell him. I just left a tablet informing him that I quit."

Enshu pinched the bridge of his muzzle with a sigh. "That's probably unwise."

"Yes, well, I needed to do something, Enshu," Nas pleaded. "I can't sit around and manage his copper mines and ignore all the problems he causes with his decisions."

"Can you even afford this?"

"Well, let's just say I hope we refine some ore soon."

"Nas..."

"I'll be fine, Enshu! Really."

"Somehow you will be, I know. Well, you know I will support you, my friend. No matter what happens."

"I know," Nas smiled, and embraced the dhole. Enshu brushed the new stains from his previously immaculate tunic as they started down the hill to join Qarradu and begin the journey home.

Enshu's house, like those of the wealthier merchants in Ur, abutted the marketplace directly, allowing him to use his home as a storefront. It had been his father's house and his father's before him: two stories of mud-brick with a flat roof, with a simple wooden door. When displaying his goods, the dhole would set things on tables just outside the front and seat himself just within the open door, making use of the shade during the heat of the day.

He topped off the beer in Nas' cup, and the fennec nodded his thanks.

"Take one to Qarradu, would you?" Enshu asked, filling up another cup. "It's hot out there, and she's busy guarding the tables."

Nas soon returned and sat back down on his stool. His tunic was still smudged, Enshu noticed.

"It has been, what, a ten-day since I saw you last? Where have you been?"

The fennec sighed. "Busy! That's all I've been. Things are well, though."

"I've missed your visits, you know," the dhole said.

"Likewise, my friend. I'm sorry. There's just been so much to do. Teaching the new labourers, making sure that foreman of mine is organising things properly, minor adjustments to the smelting, and of course trying to find buyers once I have copper to sell. The desire to use some of my contacts there from Sibi's network is... strong, I admit, but I can't do that. Not and have Sibi leave me alone." Nas' tail and ears drooped.

"You're treading a dangerous line just by being in the same business."

"I know. But it's what I know how to do, so I don't have much option," Nas replied.

"The foreman is working out, though?"

"Yes! He's one of those reddish jackals, you know, the people that live in the mountains to the south. A lot of them are knowledgeable when it comes to mining. He's also tall, almost as big as Qarradu! But then most everyone is to me."

Enshu laughed.

"But yes, he's had experience before, and is doing well," Nas continued.

"Good. Truly, I am glad it's going well. Do not push yourself too hard, though."

"I won't. And thank you for the beer; I must be off though."

"So soon? Won't you stay for dinner?"

Nas' ears lowered. "I would, Enshu, but... I have three contacts on the other side of the city to try and persuade to buy my copper. If I finish early enough, I shall come back by?"

"Very well," Enshu replied, and softened the words with a smile. Nas grinned and set the empty cup down, raising a paw in farewell.

The heat of the midday sun hit with force as he left the dhole's house, and he winced at the brightness. Qarradu toothily smiled at him from where she stood, sickle sword visible at her side, her leather armour making her even more imposing.

"Fare you well, Nas!" she said, and he gave her a smile and wave.

All the smells outside were different too, of course. Enshu's house was redolent with varied spices—it was those and dyes that he sold—but upon exiting Nas was assaulted by the many scents, some good, some... less than good, of the marketplace as a whole. Cooking meats, earth, and sun-drenched fur mixed with the subtle fouler scents of tanning and other more undesirable effluvia.

Nas headed for the opposite end of the market. It was a busy day, but he was small, and since childhood had been adept at avoiding collisions in the crowds. He hadn't gone far before he was forced to stop short, with two black-backed jackals facing him, both in loose-fitting grey robes.

"Are you Nas?" said the leftmost one.

The fennec's ears swiveled back slightly. "Who's asking?"

"A certain cheetah we have in common," stated the other. "He wishes to speak with you."

"Well, the feeling isn't mutual, so good day to you both," said Nas curtly, and attempted to walk by them. They interposed themselves, ignored by the rest of the crowd as people flowed around them.

"We're afraid it's less of a polite request and more of a demand," said the first.

"Ah, I see," said Nas. One of the jackals had moved next to him, and he felt the prick of a dagger against his side.

"Let's go," he was told, and they began to herd him along, the dagger pressed against him a constant reminder.

Nas waited until there was a gap big enough for him and too small for jackals, and ran. The dagger pushed in and he let loose a yelp, but it didn't feel too deep. His first thought was escape, in any case, and he ran back the way he had come.

The jackals were fast. Even with the crowd in his favour, they were closing. Ahead was Enshu's place, and he darted towards it. A puzzled Qarradu suddenly loomed before him, and he managed to squeak a "Help!" as he ran past her.

There was the crunch of bone breaking.

Panting for breath at the entrance of the alley by the side of Enshu's house, Nas turned to look.

A jackal was lying in the dust in front of Qarradu, and the other halted.

"We have no quarrel with you," stammered the jackal still standing. "It is the thief behind you we're after."

"The fennec is my friend," Qarradu stated. "You are not."

"Move aside." He let the gleam of a bronze blade show, his robes still obscuring the dagger from passers-by. The other jackal staggered to his feet, cradling his broken arm.

Qarradu unsheathed her sickle sword and the jackals quickly departed.

"What is going on out here?" Enshu asked, coming to his doorway, and then took in the scene. "Nas! You're hurt!"

The fennec then noticed the blood seeping through his tunic. He was quickly hyena-handled into the house, with a worried Enshu standing by as Qarradu checked his wound. Despite his protestations, his tunic was removed, and so Nas grumpily sat naked on the floor while she tended to the puncture.

"It's not deep," she said, and the dhole breathed a sigh of relief.

"You know, I prefer seeing you like this with less blood," said Enshu, and the hyena smirked. Nas just glared. "What happened, anyway?"

"Sibi sent them to collect me, apparently," said Nas through gritted teeth. "They mentioned a cheetah, so it could really be no one else."

Enshu sighed. "Well, it was bound to happen. He won't like that you left, and he certainly won't like that you've decided to remain in the same business."

Nas grunted.

"In any case, you're not going back out there for a while. You get to stay for dinner. And the night," the taller canine said, over Nas' half-hearted protestations.

"Don't worry, I'll sleep down here," said Qarradu with a wink, and the fennec felt heat fill his ears.

"I can't just... not walk around for fear of Sibi's mercenaries," he said, frustrated.

Enshu was silent, but Qarradu spoke up. "I... have a sister."

"I can't afford a guard!"

"I can," stated Enshu firmly. "At least until you can afford one yourself. And thank you, Qarradu. Please let her know we need her services?" He eyed the fennec still seated upon the floor. "Could you also perhaps get our friend here another tunic? I think this one has seen better days."

Qarradu laughed.

It had been a good year.

Certainly it had been hard work, especially at the beginning. Finally, though, things were running smoothly and Nas had begun another excavation near his current claim. There were times he had been barely scraping by and he had felt bad he hadn't been able to recompense Enshu for paying Taraka's wages.

The fennec knew Enshu didn't mind and would never even ask for the money back, but Nas still felt guilty. It was a relief when, just last month, he had placed the coins on the table and refused to let the dhole leave until he took them. It was a good excuse for celebration, and beer and laughter had been plentiful.

But now?

Nas stared angrily at the table in front of him. The clay tablet sat there, silently mocking, its immaculately pressed wedges of cuneiform proclaiming his failure as a merchant.

Taraka stood by his side, closer than normal, perhaps sensing his distress, and her hackles were slightly raised. "Gurgu will be here soon," she said, attempting to mollify the furious fennec.

Nas jumped as she spoke, and glared up at her. "Stop looming! You're making me feel even shorter," he barked, but his voice quickly softened. "Sorry, Taraka. Just..." he gestured vaguely at the tablet.

"I know," she said, her voice gentle.

There was the scrape of paw from outside and Taraka tensed. There followed a soft knock on the door.

"Come in," said Nas, muzzle clenched.

Gurgu the foreman stepped into the room, having to duck under the doorframe—a detail that irritated the fennec all the more. Nas' house was similar to Enshu's, also mud-brick with his bedroom on the upper floor, but much further on the outskirts of the city where things were cheaper. The entry room served as his office now, and accounting tablets filled the shelves behind him where he sat at his table.

"Sit," commanded Nas. "I don't want to have to crane my neck."

Sensing the discomfort in the room, the red jackal tentatively pulled over a stool and sat across from him.

The fennec stared at him, drumming his claws on the wooden table, before finally losing his temper. "What in Marduk's name is this?" he shouted, waving a paw at the tablet in front of him.

Gurgu's eyes dipped briefly to the tablet and back up again. "What does it say? Or do you wish me to read it?"

"It's a complaint. Last batch of copper I sent to one of my new buyers was impure. Not only impure, but so much so that any bronze made from it would be brittle and useless, let alone as copper for the jewelry that was its intent! Explain yourself."

"There must have been a mis—"

"And that's your job. You're supposed to be checking the refining. And the results. I trusted you enough to do that on your own these past few months."

"Which I am thankful for, but—"

"Why did you do it?"

The pause was too long, and the jackal's scent betrayed him.

Nas sighed, and pinched the bridge of his muzzle. "I knew you were skimming off the top," Nas started, then paused to glare as the jackal involuntarily gasped. "What, you didn't think I knew? Of course I knew. I even let it slide, because it wasn't much, and you were doing good work. I was paying you well and you managed a little extra copper for yourself. So why, Gurgu? Why ruin it and send out copper that's... that's... shit?" Nas' voice was a crescendo, the last words a shout.

The red jackal was silent.

"Who paid you."

"What?"

"Who paid you to do this. Was it Sibi?"

Gurgu flinched at the name.

"So that's it. Very well. Get out. You no longer work for me and if I see you around my mines, I will ask Taraka here to forcefully remove you, along with all the various parts of you that chose to resist."

Gurgu, shoulders bowed, departed hurriedly and Taraka closed the door behind him. Nas sat, head in paws, with his elbows on the table.

The hyena came over and gently patted him. "Do not worry. It is a setback, nothing more."

"There is reputation at stake here! How will I look if my buyers think... *this* of me," he said tremulously, gesturing again at the tablet.

"Meet your buyer, tell him the truth," Taraka suggested.

"Oh, I will, and I will refund him and then gift him the copper he asked for. But Sibi tried to have me killed and now he's attempting to sabotage me. I am done; I will go tell him to back off or else."

"That... may not be the best of ideas, Nas. Sibi is powerful and has many connections," she said, brow furrowed.

"I can't just wait for the next thing to occur, Taraka. You know that," Nas said, his voice tired.

"I know."

"Well, I'm coming with you then," said Enshu.

"No, Enshu, it's dangerous," stated Nas firmly.

"Which is why I'm coming with you. And Qarradu. I am also a respected merchant, after all, so perhaps that will carry some weight?"

"I suppose," ventured the fennec.

"Well. At least your tunic is... mostly white," Enshu said with a chuckle. "Can't go calling on Sibi looking a mess, after all."

Nas glared at the dhole. "I do not care what Sibi thinks."

"I know. We'll get this sorted out. There are laws, after all."

"Difficult to prove," said Nas, glumly. "Anyway, what do I do without a foreman? I don't think I have the time to do everything myself."

Qarradu cleared her throat and Taraka, beside her, chuckled.

"What?" said Nas.

Enshu smiled. "Let me guess. You two have a sister."

Taraka spoke up. "She'd be good at this sort of thing. She's a very quick learner, and, well, similarly imposing, shall we say."

The fennec laughed. "Well, the two of you have never led me wrong, so... yes. Please."

"She does not live here in Ur, so it will likely be a ten-day before we can contact her, and another ten-day for her to arrive."

"That's fine. I can manage in the meantime!" said Nas. "That's if I survive the encounter with Sibi."

There was a moment of silence amongst the four of them, until Nas stood up and placed his cup on the table, empty now. Wordlessly, they filed out of Enshu's house into the marketplace, setting off towards the inner district where the richer houses predominated.

The early afternoon sun hung heavy in the sky, and the stillness of the air gave weight to all the marketplace scents. It was a relief when they finally entered the streets of the upper city—the houses were taller here, offering welcome shade. Nas knew the way, and quietly led the others until they all stood outside Sibi's villa.

One of the jackals standing guard outside left for the interior armed with Nas' name, and they waited. It did not take long, and soon they were led through to an opulent room with painted walls and elegant sculptures. It seemed even more ostentatious than when he was here last, and Nas distastefully glanced around before finally deigning to focus on the cheetah lounging on some cushions by a small pool.

Sibi was bare-chested, a simple white skirt clothing his slender form. Multiple earrings of gold hung from his right ear, and his ruff had been teased into ringlets and oiled.

"Well, Nas, what a pleasant surprise! And you've brought friends."

Nas was quiet and tried not to glare. He could sense the nervousness of those next to him—Enshu appeared overwhelmed, and both hyenas had their hackles raised. The jackals hadn't bothered taking the hyenas' weapons, and it was clear why—there were perhaps a dozen guards lining the room, which didn't help Nas' comfort at all.

"I thought we should speak, Sibi," he stated, with a confidence he did not feel.

"Then speak," responded the cheetah, and took a sip from the cup by his side.

"Stay away from my business."

"Why? You are a rival, after all."

"No, I am not. Yes, copper is my product, but I sell solely to jewellers. No weapons. And none of your buyers," Nas said.

"You left me in a bind, Nas," pouted the cheetah. "Just suddenly leaving like that!"

"I did not like the way you did business."

"You were part of that too, you know. You were my administrator."

Nas sighed. "Yes, I was, and I regret it. But I am doing business my way now and I wish to treat people well. So leave me be."

"What have I done?" asked Sibi innocently.

"Don't give me that. You tried to have me killed, which I decided to ignore, and for a while all was fine. But now you have sabotaged my foreman and my operation. So again, I say, leave me be."

"No," said Sibi.

"What?"

"I said no, I will not leave you be. In fact, why should I even let you leave this room? You have two... rather large guards, I will admit. But I have a dozen here and more at my call. I can just have you killed. It will be as if you just up and disappeared, no trace. Tell me why I shouldn't."

Nas felt both hyenas tense beside him, and Enshu smelled of fear. "Nas..." he whispered.

"Because I will expose you," replied the fennec.

"Good luck doing that when dead."

"Already have in fact. I left tablets with the judiciary, stating what you have done. How you attempted to have me killed and how you have interfered with my operation."

"Those accusations are hearsay and unproveable, dearest fennec."

"Perhaps. However, additionally, as your previous administrator, I was privy to quite a lot of decisions and actions that you took. Many of which were more than a touch illegal. I have, of course, deposited several tablets with said information with the same judiciary, to be exposed should something happen to me. Several that you, dearest cheetah, have personally signed. How do you think they'll respond?"

The cheetah was silent, his cup halfway to his muzzle.

"I thought so. You would be ruined. Sure, you might kill me, but is it worth it for your mercantile empire here to fall?"

Sibi said nothing.

Nas waited.

"Get out," said Sibi, voice clipped and sharp.

"Will you leave me and my business alone?"

"Yes. But have those tablets destroyed."

"I will not. They are my shield against your treachery. But I swear they shall never see the light of day should you uphold your end," said Nas, and he turned to leave, followed closely by his companions. Jackal eyes watched them go.

All four hurried silently back to Enshu's home, as if the upper city held further dangers.

Eventually, around the dhole's table as the sun set, conversation tentatively began once more. Cups held beer, bowls held a goat stew that Qarradu had concocted, and there was a sense they could finally relax.

"So, who did you leave those tablets with?" asked Enshu. "Sibi will lash out if you don't get rid of them."

"What tablets?" said Nas, innocently, eyes a-glitter.

"You were bluffing?!" asked Enshu, incredulously. "Damn you, Nas, you are playing dice with the gods."

Qarradu was laughing, having spit out some of her beer at the revelation. "I'm not surprised, to be honest," she managed. Taraka just rolled her eyes.

The dhole shook his head. "You are insane, Nas, you know that?"

"Too insane to stay the night?" he asked, innocently.

"Oh, you'll stay the night alright. Just so I can pay you back for the damage to my nerves."

"Sounds good to me!" said Nas with a grin, raising his cup in a salute.

The arrival of Na'arri, the third of the hyena sisters, was a blessing for Nas. She, like her sisters, was both imposing and clever, and quickly took up the reins that Gurgu left behind. The fennec was truly thankful, and made the appropriate sacrifices to Nanna with the moon. No longer did he need to spend so much time at the mine himself, overseeing the refining and smelting and keeping the miners in line. Na'arri managed it superbly, and Nas finally felt he could relax and let things work without him. The constant heat and dust was giving him a cough as it was, let alone Enshu mocking his constantly besmudged tunic.

But the next several years were good. Nas expanded his claims and soon had three rich veins, enough that it was almost hard to keep up. But Na'arri had it well in paw, and Nas' copper spread.

It was a good thing business went well, for it kept the fennec occupied. Enshu had departed two seasons prior, heading far east to the village from whence his family had come. He claimed it was something he had to do, to give back some of the wealth from his success. It was a noble cause and Nas, of course, wished him well, but as the moons wore on he found himself missing his companion more and more.

The knock on the door early one morning was a profound relief. For Enshu was standing there, dishevelled and dusty from the road, but alive and in one piece. Nas leapt into his embrace and held him for a long time, before finally letting him go so that he could pepper him with questions.

"Enough, enough!" Enshu laughed. "I have news, certainly. But first I would hear yours."

"Well, there's not much to tell. Business is wonderful, Na'arri is wonderful. I have labourers begging to work here—they have heard how well I pay and it hurts to have to turn some of them away. But I have missed you, Enshu."

Enshu pulled over a stool and sat down with an exhausted sigh. The fennec went to grab beer for them both and waited patiently while the dhole quenched his thirst. His eyes flicked over to the shelves with all of Nas' meticulously arranged tablets, more numerous now. But one shelf sat empty, save for a lone tablet.

"Why do you still keep that one?" Enshu pointed over at it.

"The complaint? It is a reminder. A reminder to not do as Sibi had done. A reminder to myself that my reputation and my connections will expand more readily if I am honest in my dealings. I had my fill of guilt when working for the cheetah."

Enshu nodded, and was quiet a moment. "You must come to dinner."

"Happily!"

"Tonight. So I might introduce you to my wife," Enshu said, nonchalantly.

Nas dropped his cup, then grabbed it quickly before too much had spilled.

"Wife? That's amazing news, Enshu! From your village?"

He chuckled. "Yes, a dhole like myself. I think you'll like her, Nas, don't worry."

"Worry? Ha! But yes. I shall come, and bring along Taraka and Na'arri. I'm sure they've missed Qarradu."

"A plan then! I must wash the road from my fur, so I will take my leave."

Afternoon found Nas, Taraka by his side, wandering through the upper city. The marketplace had much, but some of the most talented artisans were here, many of whom were now his customers.

He needed a marriage gift for his dearest friend's wife. Nas had money now, and so a visit to his favourite goldsmith was the best bet. He procured an elegant necklace of gold with a pendant of red amber—quite the rarity—and against her protests, bought Taraka a heavy gold earring, along with matching ones for Na'arri and Qarradu.

"Quit arguing, Taraka. Half the gold I make is as good as yours. Well, yours and Na'arri's. I couldn't do all this without you."

His own garb was as simple as it always was: the knee-length tunic, off-white, with fewer smudges than normal.

Heading back through the marketplace, he noticed Taraka stiffen, ears perked.

"Qarradu's here!" Her excitement was infectious, and at his nod she ran out ahead to meet her sisters, Nas following behind. The other two hyenas were seated at one of the larger outside tables, beer already a-flow, and their reunion was such that Qarradu didn't even notice the fennec's raised paw of greeting. He smiled and headed inside.

The two dholes within looked over as he entered, Enshu with a proud grin and, well, the other with an expectant and appraising smile. *Great, she's as tall as he is*, thought the fennec with amusement.

"Nas, this is Ru'ami. Ru'ami, Nas."

Nas bowed deeply. "It is truly an honour to meet the person who finally caught my dearest friend."

She chuckled, green eyes glittering–a striking complement to Enshu's amber ones. "Nice to meet you as well! Won't you sit?"

The first moments were of silence, and for both Enshu and Nas it was a relieved and companionable one. Ru'ami looked back and forth between the two, and Nas nodded at her, raising his cup to his lips.

"So, Enshu. This fennec is the lover you've had all this time? He's a cute one!" Ru'ami laughed.

Nas coughed beer on the table, his ears flat and heated, and Enshu grinned, patting him on the back.

"Yes, this is he," Enshu replied, barely contained amusement in his voice.

Nas could do nothing but splutter.

"It is alright, my friend! You were one of the first things I told Ru'ami when we met. Do not worry! Although I must admit I didn't expect her to be so… blunt!"

Ru'ami chuckled. "He wouldn't shut up about you, Nas. As far as mentioning the relationship you two have—well, I did that for a reason. I know of it, and it does not bother me. But I knew it would be a weight upon your shoulders, a fear that at some point you might slip and mention something. So, I assumed it would be best to just be up front that I already know. That way you're not agonising over it!"

Nas had recovered his breath, and looked red-faced over at her. Glancing to Enshu, he finally managed, "You're right. I do like her!"

"Anyway," Ru'ami continued, "what sort of person would I be to come here and separate Enshu from those he loves? You are a family in your own way and I hope to be a part of it."

Nas rubbed the wetness from his eyes, and reached for the gift within a pocket of his tunic. "I now fear I haven't gotten you a worthy enough gift, but this is for you."

It looked wonderful on her, and Nas blushed once more as she embraced him tightly.

Later, once bread was broken, stew eaten, and the beer more than enough, it turned to idle and relaxed conversation. Nas informed them of the death of Sibi not a ten-day past—he was found stabbed, face-down in his blood-darkened pool. None of the jackals claimed to have seen anything.

"Probably an unhappy guard. Or customer," Enshu suggested.

"Strangely, I don't even care," admitted Nas. "Someone else can fight for his business. I'm happy doing what I'm doing." He started to cough, and both dholes' ears flattened. "I'm alright. Just... these past few moons I've been coughing more. I think it's from being around the mines too much."

"You shou—" started Enshu, before Nas interrupted.

"I know. I don't any more, I stay at my house. I'll be fine."

There was quiet, then Ru'ami broke the silence. "Enshu says you should find yourself a wife too," she grinned.

"Enshu!"

"Well, you should," the dhole said.

"I don't know anyone. Anyway, I'm happy enough. If I bump into a wife, you'll be the first to know."

"What about one of the sisters?" Ru'ami suggested innocently, gesturing in the direction of the table outside where raucous conversation added music to the night.

Enshu laughed. "He'd be crushed!"

"I don't think it'd work," Nas smiled. "But..." and he glanced briefly outside, then spoke more quietly. "Taraka did make her way upstairs once or twice while you were away, Enshu."

Both dholes just sat and waited.

"Oh gods, it was utterly exhausting. There are apparently things I never knew about hyenas."

Enshu's laughter was unrestrained and heartfelt, and Nas savoured it, knowing his family was home again.

Nas stepped off the cart, body stiff with the two day ride. Taraka's ears flattened as he began to cough yet again, and she stood patiently until it was over.

"Well," the fennec said. Taraka looked at him sadly. "Oh, don't look at me like that, Taraka. It can't be helped. Let's go visit."

It was late morning, and they strolled leisurely through the marketplace, heading for Enshu's house. The high-pitched squeal of a pair of young dholes chasing one another was audible from several houses away, and Nas winced.

"Definitely glad I didn't find a wife," he remarked. Taraka snickered.

"Uncle Nas!" came the chorus as he and the hyena neared. Nas made as if to chase them, and they ran off, giggling. It set him coughing again, and he wiped his muzzle on the sleeve of his tunic. Taraka couldn't help but notice the red smear, but said nothing.

It had been five years. Five years of prosperity, five years of family and close friends. Five years of his cough slowly worsening. The brief trip had told him all he needed to know.

Then he was at the door and Ru'ami was embracing him. "Come, sit!"

He did, and Enshu came downstairs to greet him.

"I'll be outside with Qarradu," said Taraka, giving Nas' shoulder an affectionate squeeze. "Looks like she could use some help watching the pups."

Once all three were seated, Enshu set out the cups. "Beer?"

"Actually, could you heat some water? The healer gave me some herbs to help."

"Oh, the cough? That's good!" Ru'ami said.

"No, the pain," admitted Nas, and the dholes were silent.

Eventually Enshu asked, quietly, "What did the healer say?"

"We—" and he started to cough. It was wet and deep, and both dholes reached for him but stopped short, knowing it wouldn't help. Blood flecked his tunic even as he covered his muzzle with an arm.

"Oh, Nas," said Enshu sadly. The fennec could only shrug.

Once his breath was back, Nas spoke. "I have a favour to ask."

They waited, expectantly, for him to continue.

"Regarding my will," he continued, "and the ownership of my business."

"I've told you, Nas, we are happy with what we already have. It is plenty," protested Enshu.

Nas chuckled. "Oh, I know. You've told me a number of times you don't want it. I have no heir, but it has to go somewhere." More quietly, he continued. "I wish it to go to the sisters. All three. They deserve it."

Enshu nodded solemnly. "Write the tablets, and it shall come to pass."

"Already written. Top shelf. Only tell them once I am gone, that way they won't argue." His smile was lopsided.

Tears were flowing now, and they waited until Nas could manage some tea.

"One more thing, if I may," Nas continued. "What have I always wanted to do? Ever since we were children, Enshu?"

"Babylon," he said.

"Yes. I want to see it before I go. There are wonders there, and I would behold them."

A brief glance between dholes, and Enshu nodded. "Ru'ami must stay; it is a long trip, a moon at least, too long for the children. But yes, I will go. Of course I will. Rest, and we will leave in the morning."

Nas made as if to stand, but they bade him stay seated. "Stay here tonight. No arguments."

Morning dawned, and by the time Nas had managed to drink some tea, Enshu had already obtained a cart for the journey. The fennec winced at the thought, but then at least the journey back would be simpler—a kuphar down the river, rather than riding along a bumpy road. If he returned.

Farewells were said, and the cart rolled out, towards the northern gate. Taraka and Qarradu rode in front, chatting quietly together; Enshu and Nas sat quietly in back.

Near the gate, Nas held up a paw. "Wait, please..."

"What is it?" Enshu asked.

"A place here, a seer. I have a question. Then we can continue."

Enshu looked about to say something, but closed his muzzle and nodded. "Shall I wait here?"

"Please," said Nas, and had to pause, coughing. Once he was able to, he stepped down and headed towards a small, unassuming house.

It was not like the fancy temples with their prophets who only spoke the words their listeners wanted to hear. The fennec was too clever for that, and wanted the truth. He had heard that this seer could provide it.

He brushed the street-dust from his paws before he entered.

It was dark within, and the immediate and expected scent of incense assailed him, bringing about another coughing fit. He eventually managed an exasperated breath, annoyed at the ambience meant to impress, and bent to place coins in the offering dish.

"Ask your question." It was a female voice, and young. That was unexpected.

He paused, second guessing himself.

"Do you wish to know if you shall return to Ur?" the voice asked from the darkness, and there was a tinge of sympathy there.

"No, I already know the answer to that," Nas said, and was quiet for a moment.

The voice spoke again. "Shall I answer the question you do not wish to ask?"

Nas nodded, not knowing if he could be seen. Such a question implied the seer was a true one.

"You have done well. You are well-loved and well-respected. You will die in Babylon, as you know."

Nas felt the tears start to fall.

"But after you die, and become dust, and this city becomes dust around us, your name will live again. It will be spoken not just here in Ur, or in Babylon, but throughout the world, and you will be known by thousands, if not millions."

His breath caught as she spoke, and he felt the truth of it.

There was another, smaller bowl on the floor, barely visible in the dimness ahead of him from where he knew the seer to be seated. Overcome with emotion, he stepped forward and placed an additional coin of gold; it rang loudly in the silence.

"Thank you, O Seer."

"Go well, Ea-nasir," she said.

EXILE FROM THE LAND OF GIANT TURTLES

GAR "SAHONI" ATKINS

Author's Note: This is a magical realism retelling of a bit of an important part of Tsalagi oral history and is regarded as part of our origin as a people. The original story is a very straight-forward historical story with no grand or fantastical elements. And while it might make a dry read as a transcription, when you hear it in Tsalagi, from a language speaker, there is a level of emotion and unspoken context that can be felt in the bones. My hopes in adding the narrative beats I did, the big, fantastical elements, the personal perspective, is an attempt to capture the impressions of some of these like you would with an abstract painting. This is a story meant to be read out loud, tasting the syllables and the emotions they carry. They are the bold colors and brushstrokes of the story as it asks you to consider the perspective of the real people that made that journey. I just hope I captured just some of what this story means.

I tell this story as it was told to me...

A sudden frigid jolt rattled through the bones of The Sailor, snapping him out of his passive dream and crashing him back into reality with the wake beneath him. The Sailor hurt. Bruises bloomed onto his skin like unwanted flowers as salt ground into the bends of his body. Pale mockeries of the sweet land he left behind.

The Sailor came from a land of giant turtles, and in the future that's what he would use as its name to others.

Part of his body would always know the island. The ache in his muscle from pulling fishing nets. The longing for the taste of the tart-sweet fruit he worked the land for as a child. The way his ears picked out the songs of familiar birds and let him know home was near. The memory of its burning sun on his skin and the relief he felt as he dove into its waters to where the giant turtles play.

The Sailor wondered if the land of great and giant turtles would ever be the same. He yearned to know if the land would remember him in turn. Some bitter irrational part of him wondered if he did something to spoil the relationship he and the land had. It was all he knew and all he knew now was that he could never return. Not to the land of his birth. The place of his father and generations of his ancestors' fathers before him. This was a bond so personal and it had been pulled away from him with all the time and effort of a shaky breath.

This wasn't even the right canoe for a journey like this under the best of circumstances. A single hull vessel with a float to steady and hardly enough room for the people it held. This was never meant to leave the relative peace of the cove, let alone drift into the dangers of the open ocean.

This hadn't been a journey The Sailor had planned on making.

The Sailor remembered when the canoe was made. His Lover had made it from the trees between their houses. An unsure gift between them, an offered hand. He could practically taste the smoke on his tongue from when they hollowed the insides, though he could name other more likely reasons for that sensation other than a sweet memory.

It was something they made together between jokes and boasting. Quiet bets and teasing each other over the small things he wished he could hold in his hands once more. He remembered pulling splinters out of His Lover's hands the next day as they argued over a name. The all too warm body that felt too uncomfortable in the summer months. How it felt when they fell asleep in the canoe together. He wished he could feel it against him more than anything. To brace him against this storm. To feel him keep The Sailor warm and add his strength to his own.

He knew all too well the canoe was far too fragile for its cargo. He lost track of the times he had to repair the float after a storm.

So he held fast. He wished he had cared more about the repairs when he had had the time. He hoped the rope binding would hold.

This canoe held all of his home that was left, huddled and clinging just as tight to what they could. Family, friends, whoever could make it in time. Mothers comforted their children, stern elders stared onwards with wounded memories deeper than The Sailor's own, trying to keep watch on the other ships as they were flicked among the green foam-tipped waves.

He had no way of telling if the painted red hulls of the boats he saw were the same vessels or someone new. His body burned and struggled against him as he kept pushing forward through another wave that threatened to capsize them all to chase those glimpses of scarlet. He had to focus on keeping them upright and forward. He had to keep them together. They would die if he didn't and that was an immutable truth.

Some part of him wondered if His Lover was on one of those ships. It was impossible to tell. The silhouettes he could make out didn't give away much. Just that other fishers who had the same idea as him and gathered as many folks as they could before pushing out into danger and unknown.

It had all been so fast. So loud, when it happened. In a breath.

The island had shook underneath him. It had sunk and slipped, changing underneath the fisher as it split. Water from the ocean rushed in to fill the gaps and reclaim what slipped from its secret grasp.

But an earthquake wasn't an unknown experience. An earthquake wasn't new. The Sailor had lived through his share of tremors and major disasters. He remembered the first time he had been woken up by an earthquake. He remembered how his mother comforted him and told him that it was just the giant turtle the island was on deciding to move. He remembered being taken up the old trails and hiding out high on the mountains as hurricanes drove through their homes at the peak of every summer, as if to mark the shift of seasons. But those were the sort of things you could rebuild from, as long as you had people at your side. He remembered clearly clawing through the black dirt to help his aunts recover what precious things could be salvaged from under the mud of the landslide.

He supposed he was leaving those memories behind as well.

What had been different was what came after the turtle shifted. The mountain spit smoke and ash and soot that stuck to everything like the remnants of the ashes from the sacred fire. But there was no good luck to be found there. Just aching scalding burns. It stung his eyes and made it hard to see beyond a hazy double vision. A hateful cloud that wrapped its fingers around his throat and tried to strangle the life out of him. It had weighed him down and made it heavy to move. Sitting in his lungs until he put water between them.

He remembered seeing those collapsed on the beach, those who didn't move quickly enough, cautiously enough. Where those that were too unlucky or refused to move without making sure others were safe had collapsed. Dead or as good as dead in the moments to come. The Sailor wished he could have done more. Saved more. But a second later and he would have been another body on the beach.

Something dropped out from under his stomach as he came to the realization of what leaving all that behind meant.

When all this started, there had been five trade boats out, larger canoes made for the ocean, that had been out when the disaster had struck. They would have been out on the deep water when they were affected. Would they be okay? Would they have been safe or able to hide out from the worst of this disaster? What would they think when they saw what happened to their home? Would they be able to find home?

The stars they shared to navigate were blacked out by the cloak cast by the mountain's clouds. Seven vaults high and stretching out as far as he could imagine. All he could do was follow the others and hope for the north they knew to be there.

Seven canoes. That was all there was left. That's all that there was left of The Land of Giant Turtles. All the proof that their home existed and had been destroyed by something they couldn't stop was them and what they had been allowed to carry. The words on their lips, the clothes on their backs, and the memories they left behind.

Something happened on that trip. No matter what their relationships had been before, those had died and been washed away in those waves. Something new formed in their place calcinating friends, family, old rivals and enemies into something more unified. Maybe just because that's what they needed in that moment. An unspoken telepathic promise of shared responsibility or a simple recognition of familiarity and the comfort found within that. Why wasn't as important as what it meant.

The seven had landed someplace North and with little more direction than that. A marshland made of tall grass and slow water, and that was calm enough for the fleet's bruised bodies and bones. The marshes and swamps were home to many strangers that regarded them as strangers in turn. To the west, they met the crawfish between the reeds, fierce and bold. They showed them how to fashion darts and feed themselves. To the east, the alligators with powerful jaws, slow to act but decisive in their choice. They gave them the quiet they needed, at least for a little bit, but they knew they couldn't stay.

This was not their home and they could still see the clouds that took their home from them on the distant horizon.

So The Sailor left that name behind and became The Traveler.

The Traveler had pushed forward, leading the march through the stranger lands. They followed the old trade routes worn into the earth by people they never knew, trading what crafts they could make on the road in exchange for supplies and directions. The more they moved, the heavier the words on their tongue felt, bitter like a medicine intentionally turned poison. The Traveler's feet felt raw, leaving behind footprints of salt and soot wherever he went, black marks and blood sinking into the land.

But nowhere they rested their heads was home. Every night he would awaken to find those choking jealous clouds, just on the edge of camp, threatening to cross some unseen threshold. He could see their eyes, flickering with the embers that burned down the forest he spent his childhood running through. Smelling like the flesh of family he left behind. Whispering with the heated crack of his house collapsing in on itself. He could see it in the eyes of those he traveled with, and somehow, he knew, they could see it just as clear in his judging by the sadness they would trade.

They spoke of The Traveler like he was already dead. They feasted on the bones of all they stole while comparing him to mosquitoes and ticks. They claimed he still owed them and that he should be thankful for the burns and rattling breath. That they were gifts and a mercy. Something that made him better for knowing the curse they brought.

The Traveler found himself, despite everything, looking for the body of his lover. He didn't know what he expected to find among the grim mess and he couldn't decide for himself what would be the worse outcome. Was it better to have a longing hope they were still out there, or a grim resolution so he could mourn? The knowledge it gave him offered no answers, but he knew if he let those clouds get closer he'd join that pile of bones they dragged behind them.

So he kept moving.

He led his people through the golden grasslands where the leaves were as tall as trees and the wind raced through unfettered. Cutting, singing, telling stories of things they had yet to see. Where buffalo stood like silent guardians and weaved pretty things in the grass. But it was not home. He led them through hills and green, where spirits marched nightly between the mounds and cicadas hawked their goods. But this was not their home.

The clouds followed. Always just on the edge of camp, feeling ready to snatch and take what they could.

The Traveler didn't know what the future looked like. He had felt like that had been one of those things the clouds had taken from him too. So he focused on today and tomorrow. He knew he needed a place to rest. He ached as real as wounds on his body for the right to rest, in a place where his people could exist as themselves. Not much to ask of the spirits around them, but it felt like an impossible goal from the aching feet on which he stood. The only thing he was allowed to think about was the next step.

With the steady forward beat of his people's march, The Traveler felt the clawing wound of the clouds he carried inside him reach around his heart, anxiety the blade of its knife. What future did they have? What sort of people would they be without the island they called home? Would they know the gentle side of the sea? How to catch a fish? The satisfaction of the juice of the fresh fruit on their tongues? Without giant turtles? All the little things that didn't seem to carry with it much weight on their own made up home. It was these things that connected them to land and let them know it loved them back.

Even if they survived, without these things would they know the same songs and why they sang them? Would they understand the stories they told? Someday, when his people no longer had a use for the words for these things, would they understand him? The Traveler wondered if he would be another thing lost.

He wondered if it was just enough to make it to another day.

The footprints of The Traveler were stained maroon with ash and blood as he felt another wave of grief roll over him. He mourned for the death of the future that could never be. For the hole inside him of things he could never replace. He never let it cross his face as he marched, for fear of the clouds, but he ached for the things he didn't know and never could. His stomach lurched as he felt the weight and responsibility of the things he did know. Sometimes the dreams of those no longer with them were heavy as the tent packs he carried on his battered back.

He came to the top of a mountain and listened to it sing a song older than anything else. Red earth and yellow stone formed the gentle slopes and sudden cliffs. Gentle cedar green as far as the eyes could see. From his place on high he could see a great rattlesnake. He watched it slide free of its old skin in the valleys below, slow and careful. A white haint battered and bruised was left behind while the snake's new scales shone like the rocks from the bottom of a river. It flexed in the sun, the same as always, if bigger.

There had been a period of quiet, if not peace. In the cold north, they learned how unprepared they had been for the land away from their homes. But they had found shelter with Five Sisters. For a while, the clouds had not been able to find them. They could, for a while, rest. He didn't feel that burning slag clogging up his throat with every breath. The footprints he brought didn't blacken the snow and moss.

These people they met, in their infinite kindness, introduced them to the land they walked. They used new words to describe the relationship they built but the emotions were familiar. A mother that cared, the responsibility to your relations, that care and work you put into these relationships would be returned. They were taught which plants carried good medicine, what the animals were saying, and how to survive the harsh cold they could expect on the mountains. The Traveler became The Listener and he had found the control he had thought he lost beneath the waves that night long ago.

Time had passed and soon it had been years since The Listener's exile from the Land of Giant Turtles. He had lost count of exactly how many. Enough that he remembered emotions outside of grief. Elders had passed, new life was born, and the burden of the weight he carried grew as he learned the hollowness he carried with him a little more intimately.

But The Listener knew this was not their home either. That ashen soot still clung to his body like a reminder.

Eventually the clouds had found them. And when they had found him again, the bodies he saw with them were more fresh, more familiar. Sometimes they wore the faces of those he held dear in an attempt to lead him out of the safety of his friends and family. They used their words and voices to call out from the dark, twisting the sounds in ways they were never meant to carry.

When he became The Traveler again, he was not unprepared. They carried with them the seeds for something more, both the ones they carried with them, and the ones that they were gifted by the Five Sisters. What they did with them was up to them.

By night's end he would be The Traveler no more, one way or another.

He was tired of being tired. He was tired of aching feet and no place to sit. His muscles burned with every stride as they slowly climbed those old mountains and he took the next step. Back to where he heard those mountains sing. Where he saw the snake shed its skin. As he came to the mountain top he could see the stars, the same ones his people had sailed under, the same ones some small part of him hoped somewhere out there they still were.

These mountains would be their new home because they would make it so. They would be the ones who carried his ancestors and the generations of ancestors before them. Their songs, struggles, and joys would live on because he would make it so. They would not conquer these mountains, but build new relations. They built and found new ways to care. They would make mistakes. They would learn. They would find new songs to sing. And different berries to eat. And that they could fish in rivers. As long as they survived, they would still be, if a bit more than before.

And they would celebrate that. They lit a sacred fire. They made plans about what the future held for them. They danced and ate together and as they did the ash that had clung to their skin was shed like that of a great serpent. *Anigilohi, Anisahoni, Aniwaya, Anigotegewi, Aniawi, Anitsisqua, Aniwodi.* These were the names those seven canoes took, shedding ash as they sprouted fur, hoof, and feather. They became wolves, deer, and pumas. They became the ravens, bears, and the twirling winds themselves.

They danced with bells and rattles for those that were still with them. They sang for those that had moved on and passed. They told stories about people that could not be there with them in the hope that would keep them alive. The new panther told stories about his old lover and listened to others talk about the others that might still be out there under the same stars.

The celebration was high and even as the clouds gnashed and cursed and bit from the edges of their shadows, the clouds could not reach them. As long as the seven clans of his nation in all their varied forms could tell their stories about where they had come from and how they got there. As long as they carried with them the lessons and relationships that mattered, the land of giant turtles would still be with them in the oldest mountains. They would be themselves, if a little more.

AS THE GODS DEMAND

NIGHTEYES DAYSPRING

Author's Note: There are multiple versions of the negative confessions known to Egyptologists. I have used two short excerpts from Chapter 125 of the Book of the Dead as found in Ancient Egyptian Literature: The New Kingdom *by Miriam Lichtheim, copyright 1976, 2006 in this story to provide authenticity to the writing. Also, thank you to the anonymous author(s) of the story* Setne Khamwas and Naneferkaptah *whose work has survived since the time of the Ptolemies and provided inspiration for this work.*

Nehi, lector priest of the Temple of Anubis in Saka, unrolled the scroll carefully. It had seen better days; the edges of the papyrus had frayed, the ink had faded, but the hieroglyphics were still clear and legible. The story it told was a strange tale about a vision and a form of prophecy that allowed two seers to look into the future, speaking in paired voices. The vision spoke of something distant yet near, and the shaping of destiny, but it was missing a crucial bit. The scroll didn't say how to gain the power, just how it could be used.

The jackal sighed and shook his head. There was no great truth to be found in this account, at least not for him. The cheetahs described therein had powers to see far more than the simple divinations he could do, and the paired technique was unknown to him. He rolled the scroll back up and regarded it for a few minutes. While the technique was lost, the account should not be discarded, and he made a note to himself to have one of the temple's scribes copy the account onto fresh papyrus. It would not be good to see wisdom like this unpreserved, even if he could not use it.

He scratched behind his ears, and considered what he could do. He needed answers, but there was nothing he could find to help him in the temple's collection of scrolls. He needed guidance and without that he was powerless to help Idu. He had already poured water into a bowl and tried to see what signs Anubis would send to him, but nothing had come. His mind was too clouded to see. The only way to truly find out what he needed to do lay inside the thing that scared him the most.

Standing, he stretched, replaced the scroll in its cubby, then stepped out of the small room. He walked down the hallway, passing storerooms with fine wine and incense inside. Next there was a treasury that held jewels and clothing to adorn the statue of Anubis. All the tools to worship the god were here, carefully secured in the inner part of the temple. Only the high priest and his lector priests were allowed in here, and Nehi was lucky to have achieved such a high rank at such a young age.

He paused before the double doors that provided entrance to the inner sanctuary. The other nearby shrines were currently empty since no statues of other gods were visiting this temple, but the Shrine of Anubis was still occupied. Since it was dark out, Anubis was supposed to be sleeping, and he was not to be disturbed until the morning. Only on special nights when devotees would entertain the god would the shrine be unsealed after sundown. Tonight however, it had been violated after it was sealed for the day, and the clay seal lay broken on the ground outside of the shrine. Nehi had shattered the clay himself.

He pushed the doors open and entered, quietly. Inside an oil lamp burned, and before the statue of Anubis sat another jackal, Idu, deep in prayer. He was as motionless as the statue, head bowed, body held in supplication to Anubis. His muzzle was pointed down, and his tail was still. In the weak light from the sole oil lamp, the details of Idu's tawny face fur and darker shoulders were obscured. Nehi knew Idu's fur was lighter in tone than his own and had traced the transitions of the cream fur along his stomach many a night. He loved Idu with all his heart, maybe more than even Anubis. Was that why the god would not answer him and send him a sign?

Nehi shut the door carefully and approached the shrine. The life-sized statue of Anubis stood there clothed in fine cloth, holding an ostrich feather in front of him to symbolize his service to the truth in Ma'at's name. It was his job to weigh the heart of the deceased and render the judgement of Ma'at in the Hall of the Two Truths. Behind Anubis, Ma'at's wings were drawn on the wall, to symbolize Anubis's connection to judgement and truth.

Carefully, Nehi sat down next to Idu and bowed his head to join him in contemplation. Idu stirred and looked over at him.

"Did you find anything?" the other lector priest whispered.

"Nothing. I cannot see anything in the water and looking over the texts in the library offers no clues."

Both their eyes turned to the statue of Anubis and the scroll sitting in front of the god, waiting. It looked so innocuous, yet it was anything but. It had all the answers Nehi needed, however, he knew better than to read it.

"It shouldn't be here," said Idu.

"I know, but how did it get here? It was buried over a hundred years ago, and yet here it is."

"It looks like someone went and found it, then realized their mistake. I found it with the offerings, sitting on top of a sack of barley in the storeroom. I didn't realize what it is," said Idu with a shiver, ears going back.

"It's okay," said Nehi, reaching out. "You only read the first spell."

"Thoth did not want the book to be shared by those who were not trusted with it. His vengeance on those who steal his secrets is well known."

Nehi leaned forward to nuzzle his love and embraced him. "I know the story, and yet here it is, in our temple. We will take care of it for Thoth. In the morning, I can send a messenger to the governor asking if he knows of a magician who can read signs. It is possible one of the priests in one of the other temples in town would know what to do with it."

Idu shivered against him. "Is that wise? Whoever stole it obviously left it with us to reinter it. I do not think it a coincidence that it arrived after the high priestess went to Luxor."

Nehi frowned and let go of the other jackal. "It might not be, but what can we do?"

"We put it back in the tomb of Naneferkaptah. The legend says the scroll was returned there by Setne after he had taken it. That is where Thoth wants it to be. If this story is true, the tomb is somewhere in the necropolis of Men-nefer, but the tomb is said to be lost."

He considered. "Are you sure it's the Book of Thoth and not just a book of spells?"

Idu drooped his muzzle to look at his paws. "I understand the songs of the birds now. If the story is correct, the next spell tells you how to see the gods themselves. I refuse to read further."

Nehi got up and walked over to the scroll. "I'm going to read the first spell."

Idu stood up in shock, moving to block Nehi from approaching the statue of Anubis. "Why would you do that?"

"Out fates are twined. I will not let you suffer on your own, and if this truly is the Book of Thoth, it will give me the power to understand all the beasts of the world too. Let Thoth's rage be directed at us both."

Idu wrung his paws. "Nehi, this is a serious matter. He will not be kind to us."

Nehi looked at the statue of Anubis, carved in black stone. "It is a matter of the gravest severity and tempts death, but have we not served the Master of Secrets, the Foremost of the Westerners, faithfully? I do not think he would let Thoth destroy us and scatter our kas."

Idu inhaled sharply at the suggestion. Neither of them wanted to lose their ka, and have their spiritual selves be destroyed. There would be no afterlife for them then. "It is foolish to assume we know what the gods want. I do not wish to see us both buried in our tomb so soon. The Lord of Divine Words will be angry at us both then."

"It is indeed foolish to assume we know what they want, but let us suffer together as we have served together," said Nehi, pushing past Idu. He picked up the scroll. "If our names are to be forgotten, and our hearts eaten by Ammit, then let us together cease to be."

Idu let out of nervous bark as Nehi unrolled the scroll, but he did not stop him. Nehi began to read, and when he reached the end of the first spell, he stopped and rolled the scroll back up. "It is done," he said softly. "We face this together."

"Do you too understand the speech of the simpler beasts?" asked Idu.

Nehi walked over to the entrance to the inner sanctuary and opened the door. He tilted his ears and listened. From there he could hear distant insects coming from the courtyard. They were calling out in the warm summer night, and there was now knowledge and meaning to their calls that had not been there before. He swiveled his ears more and listened, and he heard a distant bull in the temple stables, calling out to complain about pulling a plow through a field all day. He now understood the words of all the animals, not just the ones who walked on two legs and built houses of mudbrick.

"Yes," he whispered, turning back to Idu. He curled his tail tight against himself. "I understand what they say now."

"The next spell in the book lets you perceive the gods themselves."

Nehi shuddered and reached out to embrace Idu. "Let us not tempt Thoth any further and return the scroll as soon as we can."

"Do you think his temple in Men-nefer will know where the tomb is?"

"They might. I will go to the docks in the morning and see if I can find a ship sailing north, so I can send a message to Sadah asking that she come at once. She would be the best person for this, and I trust no one else with a secret like this."

Idu considered. "You know, she would be the perfect person to talk to. Her knowledge of religious law is above all others. Tomorrow we will go together after we do our morning recitations. Let us seal up the shrine for the night and leave Anubis to his rest."

The wind howled as Nehi walked through the hypostyle hall of the temple among the tall pillars, a sandstorm angrily whirling outside the building. He was searching for Idu, but he couldn't locate the other jackal. None of the scribes or laborers who maintained the temple were present either. The hall was devoid of people, and the large stone columns offered no clues to where they had all gone. During the day there was always someone about. Instead, he was alone, and a sandstorm had engulfed the temple.

He hurried to the core of the building, passing through the entrance at the back of the hall into the inner portion of the temple. He was hoping to find Idu in the inner sanctuary, but he was not there either. Instead, the shrine was deserted and the incense unlit. The statue of Anubis was missing, and a fine layer of sand had settled on the floor.

He took a deep breath and turned to see if the barque shrine—the wooden boat that was used to carry the god when he left the temple—was still there. When not in use, it sat in front of the doors to the inner sanctuary. That space was empty now.

Had the porters come and taken the statue to transport it somewhere? Was there a festival he'd forgotten about? Surely, Idu would have come and found him if there was a reason to take the statue somewhere. And where was everyone, anyway? Even if the god had left the shrine, perhaps to visit one of his other temples or to travel the land, taking his lector priests with him, someone would be behind maintaining the temple and guarding its storerooms.

Desperate, he called out. "Idu! Idu, where are you?"

There was no response, only the sound of wind from the storm. It growled louder and louder, and as he looked, he could see sand from the hypostyle hall blowing into the inner parts of the temple.

Confused and alone, Nehi reentered the hall with its grand columns. Even though he had just been here, the sand was starting to pile up, and he had to stumble his way through it toward the colonnaded courtyard at the front of the temple.

"Idu!" he called out again, growing desperate. Where was everyone? Why had they left without telling him?

The courtyard was filled with a fine sand that he easily sank into. The storm here blew against him, and he had to fold his ears back as the wind pelted his exposed chest fur and tore at his pleated kilt. But that wasn't what drew his attention.

Standing before the pylon at the temple entrance was a lone figure holding a khopesh. It stood silently, and Nehi wondered who dared brave such a maelstrom when he realized this strange traveler stood not in the storm, but inside a pocket of calm air. They were the source of the storm.

Nehi gulped against the wind, and the figure turned to fix its gaze upon him. A long beak was upon its face, and the eyes burned with rage.

"Thoth," said Nehi, stumbling back, ears pinned against his skull. He could feel the rage, and his tail tucked tightly behind him.

The god raised the khopesh, pointed the blade at the jackal, and screamed a challenge at Nehi that stabbed right at his heart.

Nahi awoke with a wordless yell, his heart jumping erratically. His paw pads burned from the sand that was not there, and his tongue was dry. He could still taste the sand in his muzzle. Idu stirred next to him but did not wake. Instead, he whined like a puppy as something troubled his sleep.

The night was quiet, and a bit of moonlight had intruded into the room. Nehi got up and walked over to the wall to adjust the reed mat that covered the high set window. He didn't remember leaving it open, but maybe Idu had gotten up to adjust it.

He caught a glimpse of the crescent moon, and he paused for a moment. Something was touching him, almost as if someone was raking claws through his fur, trying to grasp hold of him.

He spun around and stepped back trying to find whatever it was. Confused and shaken, he went to adjust the reed, and the moment he stepped back into the feeble moonlight, he could feel the sensation again.

With a loud yelp he backed up away from the window and sat down on the far side of his small room, away from the moon. It wasn't someone trying to touch him, it was the moon trying to grasp him.

Idu stirred with a groan. "What's wrong?" he asked groggily.

"He knows we have the book," said Nehi shakily.

"Who knows?"

"Thoth. I saw him in my dreams."

Idu scrunched up his muzzle and got up from the bed. "Perhaps it was just a nightmare."

"No, it's the moonlight. Thoth is using his powers to seek us out."

Idu's ears went back, and he walked over to the window and gingerly stuck a paw into the shaft of moonlight. With a yelp he pulled it back, hackles shooting up. "By the gods!"

"We can't wait for Sadah to come. We need to take the book to her immediately."

"If we bar the window," offered Idu, "we might be able to keep Thoth at bay."

Nehi whined, tail between his legs. "No, the window was closed. Thoth's power will only grow as the moon heads towards full. His magic is always more powerful then."

"We have less than a tenday to get to Men-nefer then," said Idu, pacing. "We can go to the docks before dawn and ask every ship there if anyone plans to sail north. Who though will take care of the shrine in our absence?"

"I will instruct the scribes to leave it sealed. Anubis will understand. When we return, we will see that he is taken care of."

Idu frowned. "The high priestess won't like it. Rai trusted us to conduct all the rituals in her absence."

"If we don't get this scroll back to the tomb of Naneferkaptah by the full moon, Rai will need to find herself two new lector priests."

They left the temple just as the light of day was touching the distant horizon and walked down through the empty streets. Even the farmers weren't up at this hour, but they'd both barely slept the rest of the night. Nehi had woken one of the scribes before they departed and given him detailed instructions, but the cheetah was plainly confused why they were leaving.

"Did a messenger from Rai come in the night?" he asked.

"Of a sort, yes," said Nehi. He opted not to give the man the truth. Rai would be very confused and upset to find her temple untended if she returned before them, but they would explain it all to Rai, if they survived this. She'd understand the urgency of the matter and the need to be discreet. And if they didn't make it back, well, she'd just have to train someone new. Some of the scribes were quite promising candidates for the job. Rai would be able to make do.

In the predawn light, they were barely silhouettes in the darkness, silently treading through the darkened streets of Saka. They wore only simple collars and kilts. Idu carried a basket on his shoulder with loaves of bread along with dates, apricots, and figs, while Nehi carried a bag containing brushes and spare kilts. Nehi also had a jar of wine on his shoulder, their payment for the voyage to Mennefer.

Nehi and Idu asked all the boats if they were heading downriver, but only the last boat, captained by a portly baboon, was heading in that direction.

"Awake early," yawned the captain, regarding them.

"We have urgent temple business in Men-nefer," said Nehi. "It is important we reach the city as soon as possible. We bring a jug of the finest wine from the temple stores to pay our way."

The baboon looked over the jackals. "Is the wine from the temple of Anubis?"

"Indeed, made for the god himself," said Nehi.

The baboon scratched behind an ear. "We're carrying obsidian, ivory, and spices from the south. I don't have anything in the way of accommodations for passengers outside of the papyrus shade in the aftercastle. You can stay there while the crew works."

"That will be fine," replied Idu. "Do we have a deal?'

"Indeed," said the baboon. "My crew will appreciate the wine greatly tonight. Come, climb on board. We sail when the sun touches the sky."

Nehi and Idu boarded the ship and the baboon walked them to the back of the boat past the cargo loaded in the middle. In the back there was indeed a shade built over a frame of wood, and the captain bid them to stay there while he roused his crew and made sure each was ready for the day's sailing.

As they stood there, they heard the animals of the land and the birds of the sky calling to each other, starting to welcome the coming of the day. Where once the calls were meaningless to them, now they understood everything, and it made them both nervous. They grasped paws and tried not to focus on the words.

The journey from the seventeenth nome of upper Egypt to Men-nefer, in the first nome of lower Egypt, was stressful and trying. There was no privacy on the boat, and the baboon quickly figured out the two jackals were a couple. The crew were thankful to see that priests were on board, saying the gods would favor this journey, and neither Nehi or Idu had the heart to tell them there was at least one god that wished them ill. With how tight the boat was, they didn't want to discuss the book. Any conversation above a whisper could be overheard, and they had no interest in drawing attention to the sack with the book in it, tucked out of the way under the shade.

One of the sailors, a lioness, let them borrow her copy of Hounds and Jackals, and they played the game over and over till they were bored. Rarely did the jackals win either, no matter who played as them.

Beyond that, the trip passed slowly, and too often the crew let the current carry them downriver instead of rowing to pick up the pace. The jackals had nothing to offer them to make the captain order the crew to the oars, so they waited, and gave quiet reassurance to each other even though their plight grew more and more dire.

Each night, they went to the front of the boat and slept there with the oarsmen and oarswomen up front. The captain offered them the opportunity to sleep in back where he rested, but they chose the front where more people were. And each night, the moon grew a little fuller, and they felt Thoth's rage against them more keenly as they curled up together. Being with the crew stilled Thoth's talons, but as they lay there listening to the insects speak to one another in the darkness, they felt their anxiety grow.

While Thoth chose not to attack them while they were awake, they dreamed the same dream. They were trapped together in a tomb of stone each night. Endless corridors with a thousand images of Anubis passing judgement were painted on the walls. They ran as fast as they could from a beast of fang and fur that screamed mindlessly for their flesh. They ran with their paws entwined, afraid to let each other go. Always they were one step ahead of it. Always there was another turn and split in the passageway, and they were able to keep ahead of the nameless creature that sought them. And yet each night it felt closer, and each night its cries grew more ravenous.

In the morning they whispered a few words about the trial of the night before and they knew their dreams were the same. They would then fall into silence and anxiety, trying not to pick the fur off their tails. Thoth was putting them on trial, and each day that passed his magic grew in strength and their shared dream grew longer. All they could do was hope the ship made the journey quickly, before the moon reached full.

On the morning of the eighth day, as they sat under the shade, both exhausted from the journey and the trials of their dreams, Idu finally reached the end of his patience.

"What happens if we just let the monster catch us tonight?" he whispered to Nehi, after the sun was up and the boat back out into the channel. His frayed nerves had finally worn down his sense of caution.

Nehi frowned. "I don't know. It could be like being thrown to Ammit. Our kas might perish, and we would be lost."

Idu sighed. "Surely a dream can't be deadly."

"We should have our own dreams, but ours are the same right now. Thoth is making known his demands. The book must be returned." They glanced back to where the baboon was calling out orders to his crew, hand on the tiller. "He says we should reach Mennefer tomorrow."

"I know, but does Thoth not realize we will do for him what we do for Anubis?"

"One would hope, but the gods are fickle. They each have their own goals."

Idu grumbled and tugged on his ears. "I need to feel the warm, calm winds of Shu within myself again."

"Soon, my love, we will return to the temple and recite the daily devotions, and worship our lord like he deserves. When our duties are done, I will bathe your paws and serve you wine as my beloved."

Idu lowered his muzzle, embarrassed. "As I will do for you also."

"We are in this together," said Nehi.

"I know, my love," replied Idu, and they touched the side of their muzzles together so they could feel each other's warmth.

That night, their dreams were unsettled with images of endless sand and swirling water, but they were not chased. The dream had changed, and neither knew what it meant. They slept better that night than they had in a tenday, and they were the last to wake that morning. The oarsmen had gotten up with the faintest hint of light, wanting to make Men-nefer by that afternoon and be discharged from the boat to enjoy their wages in the taverns by the docks.

Idu and Nehi felt their spirits lifting. The moon would be full tomorrow, but with Sadah's help, the ordeal would be over. It was still early morning when they saw the first distant pyramid on the west bank of the Nile.

Nehi and Idu came to the railing then and watched the pyramid come into view upon the valley rim, and slowly fade away as the boat moved on. They still needed to pass the pyramids of Dahshur, and then the boat would reach Men-nefer, the ancient capital of the kingdom. The tomb of Naneferkaptah was somewhere here, perhaps in Giza, north of Men-nefer, or one of the other necropolises that were built in this area.

"Where do you think the tomb exactly is?" asked Nehi, after the first pyramids faded from view.

Idu shrugged. "I don't know. We've been burying our dead here for two thousand years up on the plateau. The tomb could be anywhere. With luck, Anubis will give us a sign, and we can be done with this."

Two hours later, as the sun was beginning to reach late afternoon, the outskirts of Men-nefer came into view. Both lector priests breathed a sigh of relief, but something caught their attention.

"What is that?" whispered Nehi, swiveling his ears.

"It's a bird, calling out about something in the river," said Idu.

"Captain, there's a whirlpool ahead!" someone in the front of the boat called out.

The baboon strained to see from the back of the boat, adjusting the tiller. "What! I've never seen one near here."

One of the sailors came running toward the back of the boat. "It's straight ahead!"

"Everyone row!" yelled the baboon, pulling the tiller to one side. The boat shifted to the right as all the sailors grabbed an oar. Idu looked around and spotted one that sat next to the cargo unclaimed.

"Come on," he said, moving down the deck to pick up the oar.

"I don't see another—" The boat jerked suddenly to the left as it was caught in the pull of the whirlpool.

"Damn sandbars!" cursed the captain as the boat was yanked violently by the whirlpool. Nahi tried to grab the edge of the boat as he was thrown against it, but his paw pads slipped across it, and he went over the side into the river.

"Nehi," screamed Idu, but Nehi could not hear him as he was sucked under, caught in the whirlpool. Panicked, he tried to swim toward the surface, but the water pulled him down.

"No!" he screamed in a burst of bubbles, fighting to reach the surface. If they couldn't find his body, he wasn't going to be buried with Idu. Would he be able to find Idu in Aaru? Could he even make the journey through the afterlife without preparation?

Yet as he struggled against the current, he could feel talons around his chest, dragging him down. Thoth might let one of them live, but it would not be Nehi. He had tempted fate by reading the scroll willingly, and as he sank, he realized that mistake. Nehi had promised they'd do this together, but now Idu would be on his own.

Yet as he felt the life fading within himself, something scaly bumped him and pushed him. Feebly he pushed against it and it bumped him again, not down like the current was pushing him, but up.

His strength was gone now, but suddenly he broke the surface. He gasped for air, spitting out water, only to realize he was being carried on top of a crocodile. Was this Ammit herself, he thought? Had she adopted a feral appearance to take him now, while he was still living?

Apparently not, since the creature pushed him toward a sandbar. Feebly he was able to climb through the shallows and reach it before the crocodile sank back into the water. He spat more water out of his muzzle, then turned back toward the boat. It was now in two parts and sinking into the river. The crew seemed to be swimming away, and on the stern stood the captain, hand still on the tiller. The baboon's eyes were full of panic, but his gaze was fixed on Idu.

Idu had lifted his hands up, and the jackal was intoning words. It was not a prayer to Anubis or the other gods, but directions to the simpler animals of the world. The crocodile surfaced, and Idu stepped onto its back carefully, thanking it for this as he did.

The baboon jumped into the water and started swimming away from the boat as the whirlpool pulled it apart. Idu rode the crocodile to the sandbar, and then gingerly got off, only getting his paws wet. "Nehi, you're safe!" he exclaimed.

Nehi was soaking wet and shaking from the experience. His heart raced from excitement and fear at what had just happened. "You saved me," he murmured.

"Yes, I..." Idu paused, and looked at the sinking ship. "I asked for help," he said, turning back to the other jackal and leaning down to offer Nehi one of his paws. In the other paw he had the bag.

Nehi took it and was pulled up. One of his footpaws was twisted, but it didn't seem to be broken. "You could have let Thoth take me."

Idu's ears went down. "He caused this?"

Nehi nodded. "I think so. Already the whirlpool seems to be disappearing."

Idu turned. The rapid that had taken the ship was vanishing. The other jackal took a deep breath. "We promised to return the book together. Thoth will have to take us both at once, or let us serve him."

Nehi lowered his ears. "We should make for the temple quickly and find Sadah."

The sudden sinking was drawing attention, for other people were coming. A reed boat was approaching them, a jackal fisherwoman pushing it through the water. The baboon and crew seemed to have swum in the opposite direction and some were already on the shore.

"Yes, let's hurry, and hopefully no one saw too much," said Idu, before he called out to the approaching jackal. "Could you give us a lift?"

The woman on the boat nodded as she worked her way toward them.

"Quick, give me the bag," whispered Nehi, "and jump in the water when she approaches. I know the baboon saw what you did, but she might not have. You need to be completely wet if we're to get to shore and escape this."

"Good thinking," said Idu, with a whisper, handing over the bag. He then clambered into the water, in front of the boat. "Thank you so much," he called out to the fisherwoman.

She poled over. "Aye," she said when she got nearby. "Just as the sun rises, I am here to help. It is strange to see a sudden sinking like that. Here, let me pull up and you can climb on. I can get you both over to the bank in one trip."

"Thank you," said Idu. "The sooner we're off the river, the better."

Once on the shore, they disappeared into the streets of Men-nefer soaking wet, heading straight to the temple of Thoth. Many people were hurrying toward the docks because of the commotion the sudden whirlpool had caused, so they were able to quickly slip away, tails between their legs. They didn't wait for the baboon or any of his crew to ask them about what had happened.

At the temple there was a stir that two soaking wet lector priests of Anubis had come from Saka, and word spread quickly through the complex. Once Sadah heard they were there, she came and took charge of them.

"I know these two well. Please, let me see to them," she told her head priest, who bowed and let her take them to her quarters to be dried off and cleaned up. She bandaged Nehi's twisted paw, and only when they were all alone in her quarters and the cheetah had poured wine for all three of them to sit back and enjoy, did they finally open up to the purpose of their visit.

"You are lucky to have escaped the sinking so easily. It is a curious sight to see something like that," she remarked.

"It is unnatural," replied Nehi.

The cheetah tilted her head and lifted her cup. "Possibly. I did not receive word you would be coming."

"We made the trip unexpectedly," said Idu. "We have business to attend to here."

"Ah. Do you need an audience with the high priest? Or is there a matter of religious law in the seventeenth nome that requires divine guidance?"

"We need guidance, but the issue is one best handled with discretion," said Nehi. "I trust no one with this but you."

Sadah took a sip of her wine and lashed her tail. "Intriguing. So, it is a religious dispute."

"Of a kind," said Nehi, pulling out scroll from the bag he was carrying, and set it down on the table in front of them. "This was left as a donation recently with the barley for our Temple's granary. We need to return it to its home."

The cheetah reached for the scroll. "What's so special about this?"

"It's the Book of Thoth," said Idu.

She took a sharp breath and drew back. Her tail grew suddenly still. "Are you sure?"

"The first spell gives you the ability to understand the speech of the birds and the simpler beasts," said Idu. "It was quite helpful today in rescuing Nehi."

"What do you mean?" she asked, eyes narrowing to slits.

"When the boat was caught in a whirlpool, I asked a crocodile to carry him to safety, and it did. I then rode that crocodile over to the sandbar."

She inhaled sharply. "So he did find it."

Idu's ears perked. "Who found it?"

"A few months ago, a lion came to the Temple of Thoth asking questions about the book. I thought him a fool myself, but he seems to have found the scroll."

"Where is this lion?" asked Nehi.

"I have no idea. It surprises me though that he would part so easily with it."

"The scroll is cursed," said Nehi. "The whirlpool was no accident. Thoth seeks it back. We must return it to the tomb of Naneferkaptah at once, before the moon reaches full."

"That is not so easy. I cannot tell you where the tomb is exactly. It is said that Setne, one of the many sons of Ramses II, took the Book of Thoth from the tomb of Naneferkaptah over a hundred years ago. He returned it after Naneferkaptah haunted him, and Setne had the tomb sealed up. Since then, it has been lost. It is rumored to be somewhere in one the necropolises that surrounds the city."

"If this lion can find it, it cannot be hidden anymore. Have there been any reported tomb robberies in the last month or two?" asked Idu.

"I can ask, but the type of power a scroll like this gives is something a sorcerer would seek out. It's possible he already knew some magic and could have covered his tracks well. The necropolises are not guarded like the Valley of the Kings is. The pharaohs of old built their tombs over quite a vast area."

"The moon is full tomorrow, and already Thoth has tried to kill me once, and haunts our dreams," replied Nehi.

"Can we just give it to you?' asked Idu.

She laughed. "Knowledge like that is not for us mortals. I'd suggest burning the scroll, but that wouldn't mollify Thoth." Sadah stood up. "Let me see what I can do. Please, make yourselves comfortable, and I will make some discreet inquiries."

"Thank you," said Nehi, as he sat back and sighed. Sadah left the room, and Idu and Nehi exchanged glances.

"I hope she can find something out," remarked Idu. "We have very little time left."

Nehi's ears went back and he picked at the tip of his tail with a claw. "Me too. May Thoth be merciful with us."

It wasn't until the next afternoon that Sadah had anything useful to go on, and even then, what she learned was not particularly detailed. There had been a strange tomb robbery noted a distance from the city, out in the desert. Great piles of sand had been shifted suddenly and shepherds passing through the area had noticed it. This, combined with the strange sorcerer seen riding the crocodile the day before, had the city of Men-nefer abuzz with rumors and speculation. At least one account said that Anubis himself was visiting the city along with Ammit, and those who had attempted to deceive the gods would be swiftly punished.

"Colorful," was all Idu could offer, as they walked through the city toward its outskirts in the afternoon sun. The heat of the day kept many inside their mudbrick homes and workshops, and the streets were quiet. The city's craftspeople worked in the shade if they could; there was only so much panting you could do to stay cool.

Nehi chuckled. "You would think tan fur would not be mistaken for black."

"It's in the ears," purred Sadah. "Had you been a cat, they'd have thought you were Bastet herself come to visit with the mortals."

Nehi shook his head. "This entire situation is far too fanciful and wrong for me to understand it anymore."

"We'll fix it," said Sadah, a shovel over her shoulder. "We need to find a broken stele of basalt in the western necropolis. The scribe I talked to said the tomb is marked by that."

"What if the tomb is buried again?" asked Idu.

"We dig," said Nehi, "like desperate tomb robbers."

Idu barked, amused. "And here we've been dedicating ourselves to protecting tombs and seeing people are taken care of correctly so they can make their journey through the afterlife. Now we're attempting to break into a tomb."

"Consider it a form of restoration," replied Sadah. "We restore the book to its rightful place, and if Thoth wants it to stay hidden, he'll make sure the tomb is buried. We'll pray to both Anubis and Thoth when we're done to erase that cursed place from the eyes of mortals forever."

With the full moon being that very night, they hurried out into the desert. While they had a general sense of where the tomb was supposed to be, nothing was obvious when they reached the vicinity. Old mastabas dotted the desert and nearby cliffs had tombs cut into them, but nothing looked to be recently disturbed, and the broken stele could not be located. They searched, moving as quickly as they could with Nehi favoring one footpaw, but the sun sank lower and lower, heralding the coming of night.

A few hours in, they stopped to drink from their water skins and catch their bearings.

"There's nothing here," said Idu. "What did they say to look for again?"

"A curious pile of sand and a broken stele of basalt. You would think dark stone would show up in a sandy landscape like this," said Sadah.

Nehi shaded his eyes and looked out over the desert. There were more mastabas in the distance, but nothing was obviously disturbed. "The sands could have already shifted." He pointed off toward the horizon where clouds were piling up to the north. "It looks like a storm is blowing in too. Something like that could have easily buried the tomb entrance."

Sadah glanced to the north and the growing clouds, before scanning the area more. "You mean like a sandstorm?"

"Yeah, a sandstorm would do it," said Nehi, still squinting into the distance. "Are you sure it's within sight of this incomplete pyramid?"

"That's what I was told," she said.

While Nehi looked around, Idu had fixed his gaze on the northern horizon, and his ears were back. "That's not just any storm out there. That is a sandstorm, and it's quickly moving this way."

Sadah and Nehi's attention were drawn back to the north. Already the clouds seemed to be advancing toward them with surprising speed.

"We need to find the entrance quickly," Nehi said, starting to panic. He hurried off.

"We should seek shelter," suggested Sadah.

Idu squinted at the coming maelstrom as lightning flashed in it. "This is no natural storm. It's Thoth's doing."

Nehi had climbed onto a small outcropping of stone twenty feet away, trying to get a better vantage point. "If it's Thoth's doing, we have to be close," he called out, scanning the horizon.

"Regardless, we need shelter," said Sadah. "There's no way we'll find the stele once that hits."

The wind was picking up and the sand started to blow, even though the storm was still distant. Idu walked toward the storm and paused as it whipped dust around him. He turned and found himself sinking into the ground. "Give me a minute. It seems the sand here is very fine," he called out, having to pick up his footpaws.

Sadah was going to join Nehi on the outcropping of rock, but she noticed Idu was struggling. "You okay over there?" the cheetah asked.

Idu was trying to move, but he found it increasingly difficult. His footpaws were quickly sinking into the sand. "No, I'm not."

Sadah scrambled over, quickly trying to reach Idu. "Give me your paw, Idu," she said, wading through the fine sand toward him, and then having to back up.

The more the jackal moved, the faster he sank, and he was quickly up to his waist. Sand from the maelstrom was stinging his face. "It's another one of Thoth's traps!" He barked in alarm as he desperately tried to climb back on top of the sand.

"Idu!" Nehi screamed in panic, having had to climb down from the outcropping. "Fight it!" he said, rushing past Sadah, trying to grasp Idu as he flailed around.

"Nehi," he groaned as the sand continued to pull him down. Their digits touched, but they couldn't get a grasp on each other. "Go on…"

"No, I can't lose you," the jackal cried out, but the wind ripped his words away as he fumbled to hold onto his love.

"Our kas will meet again," Idu sobbed, as his paw slipped from Nehi's, and he sank up to his shoulders.

"No!" Nehi growled. "I didn't ask for this. Neither of us did." His own footpaws were almost buried up to his knees as he struggled to reach Idu.

Sadah grabbed him and started yanking Nehi back. "If you keep trying to grab him, you'll be joining him!" He fought her, but when Idu's muzzle vanished below the sand, he let her pull him to safety.

"If we locate the tomb quickly, he might be okay." Sadah offered.

"The tomb could be anywhere," he growled. "There's only one thing left to do," Nehi said, reaching into the bag and pulled out the Book of Thoth.

"What are you doing?"

"Asking the gods directly," he snarled, and unrolled the scroll to the second spell and started to read. The wind that whipped at him took on an ominous hiss.

"Nehi…" said Sadah.

He shook his head and kept reading, and when he reached the end of the spell, he looked up. Even though the storm had engulfed them, he could still see the sun in the west, or he could have. The sun wasn't there anymore. Instead, Ra sat on his solar barque, guiding it through the sky. On top of his head was the sun disk, along with a cobra wrapped protectively around it.

Nehi took a deep breath. He could see the gods now, which meant he could speak to them. He dropped the scroll and knelt down.

"Foremost of the Westerners, Master of Secrets, the Dog Who Swallowed Millions, I call to you now! I have served you faithfully and kept your sanctuary clean. I have lit the incense and worshiped you, and tended to the tombs and temples under your protection. I have collected the dues of your fields and stored the grain to feed your priests and scribes. As appointed by Pharaoh, ruler of the two lands, I have served you as is your due," he called out.

Sadah realized what he was doing and knelt down next to Nehi.

"Foremost of the Westerners," Nehi said.

"Master of Secrets," Sadah added.

"The Dog Who Swallowed Millions, we call to you now!" they chanted together.

The sandstorm that was bearing down on them parted, and a figure of a jackal stood among the dunes.

"Foremost of the Westerners, Master of Secrets, the Dog Who Swallowed Millions, we call to you now!" they intoned.

Out of the dunes he came, striding forward with fur as black as night that swallowed the light of day. He carried an ankh in one hand. He raised the other and the sand that had swallowed Idu gave him up, and suddenly Idu was on the ground gasping. The storm that had attempted to engulf them abated.

"Master," said Nehi, bowing low.

Sadah also bowed. She had not seen him at first, but suddenly he was there, having revealed himself to the other mortals.

"Rise, my priest. Why have you risked the wrath of Thoth," spoke Anubis.

"I seek only to return what is his."

"And yet you read from my scroll willingly," said a voice from behind.

The ibis was there also, his eyes smoldering with rage.

"Please your holiness, let us give this back to you," said Nehi, bowing again.

"My lord," said Sadah, also bowing.

"I'd have thought better of you, Sadah, getting caught up with these two," said Thoth. "Tomb robbers they seek to be now."

"We seek only to restore what is yours," she said.

Idu had gotten back to a seating position and had managed to get his senses back. "We do not wish to keep this knowledge; we wish only to give it back to you."

"How can I know you speak truth without having Anubis weigh your hearts?" asked Thoth.

"We are willing to be judged and speak the negative confessions," said Idu, bowing low.

"Yes, we are. You may judge us, and if we are worthy, we shall go to Aaru and live in the field of reeds. If we are unworthy, you may summon Ammit," bowed Nehi.

"I also will submit to judgement if that is your wish, my lord," said Sadah, bowing low.

Anubis looked at the priests and then back to Thoth. "You could have taken the book on the boat and not done this with my priests," he said. "You knew they journeyed north to place your book where they thought you wanted it to be."

"Lessons, my friend. Lessons. I have asked Ptah to allow me to enact divine judgement on any who have stolen my knowledge, and he granted it to me. These two jackals are thieves."

"Sadah is your priest, and you may punish her as you see fit, but you have no right to my priests if I deem them not ready to go to Aaru," said Anubis. "They have come to give back what is yours."

"And yet they have a bit of knowledge they should not," said the ibis. "Knowledge given cannot be taken away except by forgetfulness. You will weigh their hearts, and I will record if they are pure of heart," he said. A reed pen along with a papyrus appeared in Thoth's hands.

Anubis was silent for a moment, considering. "They have not prepared for this test."

The ibis lowered his beak. "I ask you to weigh their hearts now, for the knowledge Nehi and Idu have obtained is not for mortals to know. As the Master of Secrets, you must protect this knowledge."

Anubis's ears flicked and he nodded. "As you wish." He swept his hands and suddenly they were no longer in the desert. Instead, they were all standing in the Hall of the Two Truths, before the scales for weighing the hearts of the dead. In his hand Anubis now held the feather of Ma'at, and behind Thoth another was present, silent, and hungry.

The goddess Ammit stood there beyond the light of the room, lurking in the shadows, waiting to be fed. Only her mouth was clearly visible, and it was agape just enough to show all the teeth in her large, crocodilian snout.

"I will weigh Sadah's heart first," said Anubis.

"Very well," said Thoth.

The black jackal walked over to the cheetah, and she tried not to tremble before him. "I will need to reach inside of you. When I remove it, you will feel lifeless. Do you understand?" asked Anubis.

She nodded, tail twitching with nervousness, ears back. "Yes, my lord."

Anubis reached toward her chest and then through it as if it was not a solid thing, and his paw closed around her heart. With a tug, he pulled, and her heart was removed. She staggered, and her tail fell still. Her ears drooped, and yet her chest showed no wound. When Anubis pulled his hand out, the heart beat with life, awaiting its judgement.

The black jackal walked over and placed the feather of Ma'at on one side of the scale and then the heart on the other. He knelt to adjust the scales as Thoth wrote her name down.

In the meantime, Sadah began to whisper to herself the negative confessions. "I have not done crimes against people. I have not mistreated cattle. I have not sinned in the Place of Truth. I have not known what should not be known..."

Carefully Idu slid next to Nehi and whispered into his ear. "We can't do the negative confessions. We know what should not be known."

Nehi, who had been watching, turned to whisper back. "I know. They both know this."

They all waited for Sadah to finish, and Anubis stepped back from adjusting the scales. The feather was heavier than the cheetah's heart!

"Sadah has committed no crimes against the gods," intoned Anubis, picking up her heart. "I return her first life to her so that she may continue to live, and when she dies, I will weigh her heart again so that she may pass on to Aaru and dwell in the field of reeds."

"So be it," said Thoth, making a note on the papyrus. "She is pure."

Anubis walked back and reached back inside of her chest, repeating an ancient word of power, and she jumped suddenly, all of her fur shooting up. He pulled back his hand and the heart was gone. Then he looked at Nehi and Idu. "Nehi?" he asked.

The jackal bowed his head. "Yes, my lord."

Anubis walked over and repeated the motion he'd done on Sadah and pulled Nehi's beating heart from his chest. Nehi felt his body go cold and all the blood in his body froze. Then he watched as Anubis walked over and placed the heart on the scale. He knelt and adjusted the scales.

Nehi started on the confessions. "I have not done crimes against people. I have not mistreated cattle. I have not sinned in the Place of Truth." He paused. "I have not known what should not be known."

The scales tilted as his heart betrayed him and sank. *This is it*, thought Nehi.

"Nehi is not worthy of Aaru," said Thoth. "Ammit shall eat his ka, and he shall pass into nothing."

There was a murmur of satisfaction from the shadows, but Anubis stood up from the scales. "Take the knowledge back, Thoth, and let him repeat the confession."

Thoth seethed. "Why should I?"

"They are my priests, and they were serving me. I judge their actions as extraordinary, but necessary. You may note that down."

The two gods stared at each other, eyes locked. No one moved. Finally, after what seemed like an eternity, Thoth shook his head and relented. With a scowl, he stalked over and touched the heart. He said something magical and pulled back. "Very well. Repeat the confession," ordered Thoth to Nehi. He then marked the irregularity down on the paper, as Anubis rebalanced the scale.

"I have not known what should not be known." The scales remained balanced, and Nehi's voice caught in his chest.

"Go on," said Thoth.

Nehi took as deep a breath as his now lifeless body could. "I have not done any harm. I did not begin a day by exacting more than my due..." The scales stayed balanced until he finished all of the negative confessions.

Anubis stepped back from the scales. The feather remained heavier than his heart.

"Nehi has committed no crimes against the gods," said Anubis, turning to Thoth.

"So it is noted," said Thoth with just a hint of remorse. "Return his heart, and weigh Idu's."

Anubis walked back to Nehi and returned his heart. Nehi gasped as his life was returned. Anubis then went to Idu and took his heart. This time though, before he set the heart upon the scale, Thoth took the knowledge back, and they went through the ritual with Idu reciting the negative confessions.

Anubis stepped back and the scales stayed balanced.

"Idu has committed no crimes against the gods," said Anubis, taking the heart back. "I will return him and Nehi to life, so that they may live, and we will judge them again when they die. If worthy, they shall go to Aaru. Are you satisfied, Thoth?"

The ibis was quiet for a bit. "You have the scroll?" he asked the two mortal jackals.

"I did, but I dropped it when I went to call to Anubis," said Nehi. The jackal blinked and the scroll was suddenly in his hand again.

"Give me the scroll, and the matter will be concluded."

Nehi held it out and Thoth reached over to take it. Nehi felt claws against his chest, but they released as Thoth hefted the scroll from his paw and stepped back. The ibis said nothing, and just regarded the mortal carefully.

"Very well," said Anubis. "It is done. We will go now," and with that, Nehi, Idu, and Sadah were no longer in the Hall of the Two Truths.

They were lying in the desert under the full moon alone, their bodies drained. Idu and Sadah groaned as Nehi slowly sat up. The moon was full, and in the distance, insects buzzed, but Nehi could not tell what they were saying.

"It's over," he said, "but oh gods do I have a splitting headache."

Idu sat up and felt around for the bag he was carrying, He opened it to check. "The scroll is gone."

"I feel like I've died," said Sadah.

"I think we all feel that way," said Nehi, brushing sand out of his fur.

Idu crawled over to his love and hugged him. "Thank you," he whispered.

"You're welcome," Nehi replied, rubbing his muzzle against Idu's muzzle. Their bodies were warm in the cool night air. Judgement had been rendered against them and they had survived. "As I said, we'd do this together," he whispered.

Idu's ears just lowered, and he held Nehi for a long time, until Sadah finally got them to separate so they could all journey back to Men-nefer.

THE VIXEN WITH THE CROOKED MUZZLE

CASTERWAY

A long, long time ago, before the realm was hammered into one piece, there were many small, disparate kingdoms. What was once one, kept together by the Firstpup of the Heavens, was left splintered when the barbarians from the west sacked their way into his capital and left it in rubble.

However, there were beasts who stood against the torrent of chaos. Smaller dukes and margraves rose up from the ashes, and fearing the wrath of the Heavens, called themselves Hegemons instead of usurping the divine lineage of old. I presume you have heard many times of the exploits of the Cultured One of the Valleys, who wandered around the realms looking for shelter from his half-brothers, and who spent his reign repaying those who had rendered him help? You would also have heard of the twin lords of the Estuary, who overcame their barbarous nature to wrestle with each other for All Under Heaven? And who could forget the Dignified One of the Great River, who overcame the senseless pursuit of pleasure, donned a crown of his own and asked how much the ritual-vessels weighed?

More than anything you have heard about how vixens become the ruin of dogfoxes. After all, they were but accessories to beasts who had the right birth.

They were but servants of fathers. They were but accessories to husbands. They were but rearers of sons.

Like all servants shame would be heaped on them before their lord was tainted with a single drop of it.

"That is incredibly unfair!" I heard you say, and you would be correct. Thus, I shall present to you a different type of fable.

This tale I am to tell you is about a vixen, deprived of beauty by the Heavens, but through her wisdom and dedication managed to forestall her country's ruin, brought about by her fool of a husband. Good kings do not allow themselves to be called the Regrettable, after all... but I digress. Here is the tale.

There lived a vixen in a village, who had a crooked muzzle, malformed in the womb. Of course, beasts laughed at her, since back then only beauty mattered to vixens. Of course, *our* vixen was different, as you are to see, but Crookedmuzzle they called her. Since the histories do not recall the names of beasts who were not kings or scholars, hers was forgotten as well. Thus, this is what we are to label her as well. I doubt she would mind.

It did not take long for her fellow village-foxes to realise something was not right with Crookedmuzzle. When her name was called she often took too long to respond, and her smiles were far and few between. She talked little, and never looked others in the eye when she did.

As she grew up her sullenness did not abate, but manifested in other ways. Unlike most vixens, or dogfoxes, for that matter, she did not manage to form friendships, but always kept to herself. However, she obeyed her parents in every command and avoided causing them distress. Nobody dared to be a bad kit who brought dishonour to their family back then, but she appeared to take this dishonour much more seriously than her peers.

Her village was like any other, I assume, considering its name was also not recorded. But we can utilise our imaginations. There should be a river flowing to the side, and channels to give fields of rice and millet receive their water, and in doing so fill the bellies of the little commune. There might have been walls to deter bandits and wild beasts, or inns to house weary travellers, but the only thing we knew for sure is that by its roads mulberry bushes grew. Some of them were sweet, and others sour, but as long as they're not rotten all foxes would savour every single one they can stuff into their mouth.

One fateful morning she set off to harvest said berries, as that was what her parents had told her to do. That day, the king was on one of his many progresses and passed through the village, and all the foxes, young and old, came over to see him. All but our Crookedmuzzle, of course.

When the king saw her, he found her disinterest in him puzzling. So after she was no longer busy he summoned her to him and spoke to her. "When We were travelling all manner of foxes would drop what they do and come to see Us, for it is a rare and fortunate occurrence, and it is not often for common eyes to gaze upon their king. Why, on the other paw, would you not stop gathering your berries?"

To which the vixen replied, "It was the will of my parents that I pluck berries from bushes, and not waste my time fixing my eyes on uncommon sights."

The king nodded, but turned his head and said to his ministers, "This is indeed a wonderful vixen, but alas, her snout is bent."

The vixen did not budge. "My greatest obligation is to obey my parents and do what I am bidden. There is no evil this disfigurement could cause, so why dwell on this thing which my parents had given to me?"

The king clapped his paws and exclaimed. "You are indeed a virtuous vixen!" He then attempted to bring her into his palace, but Crookedmuzzle shook her head and refused.

"I am glad that I am able to serve closer to you, Your Highness, but if I were to leave for your court without the approval of my parents I would be eloping with you, and such behaviour would be punished by your law. How would you love me then?"

The king dipped his head in shame as the vixen continued to speak. "I am a pure and simple vixen, so if things are not done according to the rites, I would rather die than follow you."

As a result the king sent her back home, with two attendants carrying fifty taels of gold each. Her father was surprised by the news, and tried to persuade her to bathe and get better clothes, but the vixen was reluctant to do so. She replied thusly, "If I were to see the King and I change my appearance, how would he recognise me? I must meet him the way he met me."

In the meantime, the king returned to his palace. If you go to where it once stood, you would see little more than common houses, but to the southwest of the city lay a massive construct, the work of no fewer than five kings and thousands of workers. In front of it were the kingdom's most prestigious metalworkers, who found patronage through royal favour. If you walk through its outer gates there was a massive stone square, enough to fit all the realm's notables as the king makes his sacrifices of flesh and fruit to the Heavens and the spirits that resided within. And after you walk through the inner set of doors you would find buildings within buildings, gilded with gold and bronze and painted red and white, housing ministers, eunuchs and concubines as they danced as one to a royal tune.

As he rested in his luxurious quarters, the king told all his consorts that he had found a vixen with much virtue, and that he would add her amongst their number. Thus they all put on their best clothes, their ceremonial dresses of silk, and waited for the vixen.

When she came her appearance was much more shabby, and the king's consorts could not suppress their laughter. Feeling ashamed, the king told them to stop their chuckles. "She is merely without grooming. If she were to do so, she would be prettier by hundreds of times!"

The vixen shook her head as her ears folded. "The difference would not only be hundreds of times, but hundreds of thousands."

"Why do you say this?" asked the king.

"You should know that foxes should be judged by their habits," answered the vixen. "Have you forgotten the tales of the previous Firstpups? The first ones decorated themselves with nothing more than benevolence and righteousness, and they never cut down forests to build new palaces, nor did they repair old ones. Their consorts were clothed like other vixens, and their feasts were far and few between. Thousands of seasons have passed, and they are still praised by all foxes under Heaven."

"But if you look at the last Firstpups, those who see their lines end in ruin, they are of ill will and poisonous hearts. Their laws were harsh, and they built palaces with high walls and deep pools filled with wine. All their vixens amused themselves with pearls and silk and jade, never satisfied until they outdid each other. Is it any surprise that after their states fell and their body rotted, their reigns and lives are little more than jokes?"

The vixen bowed once more. "Your Highness, it can thus be seen that a fixation on one's body instead of one's obligations would cost much more than a hundred times!"

All the king's vixens were ashamed at what they had heard, but the king took the revelation well, and set Crookedmuzzle up as his queen. Immediately after the wedding he declared his new edicts – the court size was limited, palace food and music had their expenditures cut, and the king's concubines was also brought into line after he sold their luxuries off. His kingdom's workers fixed all the roads, and there was no city that did not fear the armies of the Gulf. The Regrettable king also formed an alliance with The Prominent of the Mountains, attacking the three remnants of the Valleys and crowning each other Emperors - a sign of things to come, perhaps. The condition of the Gulf had been elevated above the clouds, and Crookedmuzzle obviously deserved her credit.

The chronicles said she died a peaceful death, and all joy turned into sorrow as her king suddenly became like a headless gnat. Without her, who could lift him up when he was down, and who could humble him when he was proud? Within the span of two years his kingdom had almost been extinguished by that Kingdom of the

Sands, and his head was carried off by his own subjects. While in spite of (or perhaps because of) that the realm was recovered it was all downhill from there. The king's son would do as his father did, and marry a vixen with a mind far superior to his... but that would be another tale.

Joy and sorrow are two serpents biting each other's tails – they spring from one another and cannot be separated. She was perhaps too old to wed when the king found her, likely because of her features, but wed she did, and she became the envy of all the common folk.

But who said marrying a mighty king was always a blessing? It was likely she did not serve him in bed as much as in court. After all, a good king or prince must wed for the state. The Regrettable of the Gulf did not get an alliance, but he did receive an advisor. We know he had more than enough vixens for sensations of the flesh.

Perhaps she would be better off spending her whole life with her paw pledged to no fox, her only pleasure being the berries she harvested. But we can be sure that she would never have admitted that. She did her duty and saw her kingdom raised high due to her efforts. Queen or otherwise, an advisor could do no more with a king of such a temperament. Maybe her final illness could have been caused by his negligence of both her person and his state, but it simply would not befit us to speculate.

And thus our tale draws to a close. What moral would you have liked to hear? A king must marry well even if it means marrying down? Behind a great dogfox there is always a vixen? Never let go of your duty and good things will happen? Speak the truth, especially to those who hold power above you?

It matters little. You have looked into the mirror that is the past – what lessons you learn and what actions you are to take are things you can spot on your own.

HEKA

FAOLAN

Every step was pure excruciating agony. His heart was pounding in his chest, and his hands wouldn't stop shaking. He tried not to clutch the linen hanging from his hips, fearing that he would dirty it. "You can do this. You can do this. You have trained for this. You will be fine," he muttered to himself under his breath as he watched his hooves walked up the dirt road towards the most important building in the land. As he looked up, he once again laid eyes on the magnificent white stone that made up the royal palace. This building hosted pharaoh Sekhen, the most powerful person in the entire world. He lived there with his family, his most important officials, and all the servants that took care of their every need. Tekem hoped to join their ranks that day.

Tekem was a young zebra trained in the art of dance. He had honed his skills for years in the hopes of one day creating a better life for himself. He was in the middle of a dance class when a messenger arrived, proclaiming that the pharaoh was looking for new talented court dancers and would be holding auditions the next week. This was his chance. He would impress the court with his skills and earn himself a place in the palace. His parents had worked hard to be able to pay for these lessons, and the mere thought of failing and disappointing them weighed heavily on his soul. He could not fail.

Failure also meant that he would follow in his parents' footsteps and become a crafter. His father supported the family by running the shop and crafting sculptures of the gods out of stone, while

Tekem's mother crafted jewelry out of stone and bone. She occasionally managed to get her hands on some semi-precious stones through trading, but these occasions were rather rare. His family wasn't rich, but they had a comfortable life.

Thinking of his family had drawn his thoughts away for long enough that he was startled by the loudness of his hooves touching the stone that formed the long staircase up to the palace doors. He swallowed hard and climbed the steps. It felt like ages before he finally reached the palace doors, where he was stopped by two enormous guards, a crocodile and a rhinoceros.

"Halt! What is your business here, boy?" the rhino boomed, his hand moving to a heavy bronze mace the side of a small child. The crocodile sized him up but didn't seem alarmed. A slender zebra like Tekem hardly posed a threat, so the man's khopesh hung idly at his side.

"Good day to you. I have come to audition for the role of royal dancer," he said, forcing a smile on his face despite the guard's intimidating glare.

The rhino turned to his fellow guard, who nodded. "You may leave any weapons at the door," the reptilian spoke calmly.

"I have none on me, sir," the boy answered.

"Then may Hathor guide your feet today."

He beamed at this show of support and bowed his head politely. "Thank you, sir. May Sobek guide your arm if needed."

The guards took hold of heavy rings attached to the metal doors and pulled hard. Tekem stood in awe at the sight of those glorious doors opening for him. There were detailed depictions of the royal family and the gods all over the gleaming bronze. He cleared his throat and entered the royal palace. A change of sound drew his attention to his hooves while he walked. The ground inside was made of mud bricks, something only the wealthy could afford. He smiled and swayed his hips to the rhythm of his own hooves, until he passed under a sandstone arch and reached a spacious courtyard filled with numerous trees and plants to create a beautiful display of greenery inside the palace walls. Some servants could be seen tending to the plants and flowers. They paid him no mind. He walked up to a second set of doors, guarded by two spear-wielding jackals.

"Excuse me? Could you please tell me where I have to go for the dance auditions?" he asked.

They looked at him and nodded. "Do you see that cat standing near the doors to your right? He will take you where you need to go," one of them said.

The zebra turned his head and spotted a grey cat standing near a wooden door. "Thank you," he said, bowing his head, before walking around the garden and to the cat dressed in an official's robe.

The man saw him coming and smiled. "Are you here for the auditions?"

"Yes, please. I would love to show my skills to the pharaoh," Tekem said, bowing his head. He still felt nervous but was so in awe by the beauty around him that he almost forgot what he was there for.

"Follow me, please. Others have already gathered, so I think we can start soon."

It was no surprise that there were others. It was foolish to think that he would be the only one to go for the opportunity to change his life for the better. He followed the cat, past animal stalls containing horses and camels, and many doors the rooms behind which he could not even guess at. The cat opened one of the doors and let the zebra in. There were indeed others inside the room already. Tekem could see a fennec, two gazelles, and a hippopotamus, among others. There seemed to be entire groups of dancers in the room. The fennec seemed to be meditating, a shiny blade in his lap, while the gazelles, they looked like twin sisters, were limbering up. The hippo looked about as nervous as Tekem felt, so he walked up to her.

"Hey. I'm Tekem. You're here for the dance audition too?" he asked. Of course she was, but it felt like an easy question to shift the sands.

She gasped and looked up, shocked out of her daydream. "Oh, eh, yes! Yes, I am! I'm Heba. What kind of dancing do you do?"

"It has no name yet, but my teacher has trained me to move very gracefully and fluently. What do you do?"

"I'm trained in striding dances," she smiled. "Are you sure you wish to display an unknown dance for the royal family?"

"What better way to get their attention, right?"

"You may have a point there. May the best dancer win." She giggled.

Tekem felt a lot less nervous after talking to Heba, even though many of the dance groups around him looked quite intimidating. He felt his chances of becoming a royal dancer slipping away from him, but he was not yet ready to give up. He needed to take this chance to improve the lives of his family. He'd forever curse himself if he did not at least try.

He had just limbered up when the dancers were all called to the throne room. They were made to wait in a room right next to it and were led inside one by one. The zebra would have loved to watch all the others perform, but that was a privilege reserved for the royal family. He was called in as one of the last, right before Heba.

"Good luck! May Hathor guide your feet!" she said.

"May Hathor guide you as well, friend." He smiled.

He was led inside by the cat official and made to wait right in the middle of the enormous room. Numerous sandstone pillars depicting the epic tales of the gods held up a ceiling higher than the tallest trees. Long curtains of the deepest blue hung down just short of where he would be able to reach them. The splendor in the room was incredible. Everywhere he looked was something wonderful to see. He looked across the room and noticed the pharaoh was looking directly at him, as were his queen and his daughter. The pharaoh was a cat of the purest obsidian, which was a trait the princess shared. His queen's fur, however, was a most brilliant white. Her stunningly blue eyes seemed to look straight into his soul. The weight of that gaze nearly caused him to stumble, but he played it off by kneeling and bowing his head.

"What is your name?" the black-furred Sekhen asked. He sounded bored and the way he was sitting reflected this. Apparently, the act before him had failed to entertain the Pharaoh.

He swallowed hard and cleared his throat. "My name is Tekem, my Pharaoh."

"And what have you come to show us today?"

"A new style of dancing my teacher picked up in the far East, my Pharaoh."

"A new style, you say. How intriguing. What is your wish today, boy?"

"To be good enough to be chosen by you, my Pharaoh, so that I can improve the lives of my family."

"A noble goal. May Hathor guide you."

The zebra lowered his head in appreciation of those words. He slowly stood back up and looked at the musicians. He nodded at them, after which they started playing. The percussionists started with drums, followed by the sistrum, flutes, oboe, and the lute. Tekem closed his eyes for a moment to ground himself, before swaying his hips and letting the music guide him. He made sure to move through the room and to get closer to the royal family as well, to make sure they could see his fluid movements clearly. He spun about and smiled as he danced. It wasn't long before he was completely lost in the music. The music eventually died down, and the zebra ended his dance with a sensual pose on the floor.

The princess clapped her paws together, a bright smile on her dark face. The queen looked pleased as well. Unfortunately, Sekhen did not seem to match their enthusiasm. He raised his paw and shook his head. "Thank you for your nice performance, young zebra, but it is not what I am looking for. Sadiki will show you out."

The man who led him to the room started walking up to him when a tall bronze-scaled cobra in white robes slithered onto the floor. "My Pharaoh, if I may?"

The black cat nodded and leaned back in his throne. "What is it, Seb?"

"If it would please you, I would like to take this boy in as my apprentice.

"Your apprentice? Why would you do that, Seb? You already have one. Did you see something in this one?"

"Yes, My Pharaoh. I detected clear signs of magical aptitude during his performance. It would surely please the gods to have one such as him under my wing."

Sekhen rubbed his chin while he pondered this, and ended up nodding. "Very well. He is yours. That is, if he agrees." The snake and cat turned their eyes on Tekem.

It wasn't the outcome he had hoped for, but priests were revered throughout the land. To be able to dance in the name of the gods was a huge honour, and it would certainly improve the lives of his family as well. He had no reason to say no, even though the cobra was quite intimidating as he towered over him.

"It would be a great honour to study under you," he said as he bowed politely to the priest.

"It has been decided then. Take good care of him, Seb. He is your responsibility now," the pharaoh said before waving his paw.

The priest bowed to the cat before turning around and leaving the room. Tekem hesitated for a moment, looking at the royal family in confusion. Princess Leila pointed at the priest and nodded her head towards him. "Go," she mouthed. He knelt before running out of the room, after his new mentor, one question on repeat in his mind:

"Magic?"

He was sent home to gather his things, since he'd be living with the snake priest and his other apprentice from that moment on. His parents were thrilled for him, though, understandably, very surprised. Nobody in his family had ever shown any magical ability beyond the average person's, which made him curious as to what the priest had seen in him. Tekem couldn't help feeling like one of the legendary heroes from the legends of old. He chuckled to himself at the foolish thought, even though it was an entertaining thing to fantasize about.

The sun was close to setting when the zebra made his way back to the palace, where Seb was already waiting for him. "Come," he said before turning around and slithering away through a door opposite the one the dancer had last entered. "Tekem, right?"

"Yes, sir, that's right." He rolled his shoulders to adjust the weight of the bag on his back.

"Good. You must be wondering why I'm taking you in as my apprentice, correct?"

"Yes, sir. You said something about seeing magic in me?"

"Yes, though it was more sensing than seeing."

"What was it that you sensed?"

"Natural affinity. There are numerous dancers who dedicate their performances to the gods, telling their stories with their bodies. There are, however, only a handful of dancers who truly reach them. When you dance, you radiate magical energy. I do not yet know what form this will take when you are trained, but my curiosity and the gods demand that I find out. I have seen you in my dreams." He led the boy through a series of corridors, not stopping anywhere long enough for the zebra to properly take note of his surroundings.

"In your dreams? Are you also a seer?" Tekem asked as he hurried after the cobra.

"Not a very skilled one, I'm afraid. The gods saw fit to show me you while I was in the land of dreams. I will find out exactly what your talents are, but it will take time. Do you know which god we worship in particular in this palace, Tekem?"

"Bastet or Amun, sir?"

"A logical thought, considering the royal family are cats, and Amun is the king of gods, but no. We worship all gods, of course, but we put more emphasis on the worship of Heka."

"Heka? The god of magic and medicine? I thought he wasn't worshipped. At least not in temples."

"Not traditionally, no, but Pharaoh Sekhen is a firm believer in the importance of magic in our society. He ordered the architects and builders to design and construct a temple inside the palace dedicated to the primordial god. All magic originated with him, so this was a logical decision."

He stopped in front of a pair of tall doors. "This is the temple area of the palace. You are prohibited from entering the sanctuary unless I tell you otherwise. In here, you will be trained." The priest opened the doors, revealing a wide, open space with several wooden doors and one set of bronze ones. There were about a dozen people walking around, cleaning the temple, or carrying things. "The bronze doors lead to the sanctuary. Your sleeping quarters are behind the wooden ones over there." He pointed to one of the doors along the wall to the right. "You will share the space with Nenet. She can answer any questions you might have about the day-to-day life of an apprentice and the chores you will be tasked with. Nenet!"

Someone in the room moved and a dark-furred lioness came into view. She quickly made her way over to them. "You called for me, high priest?" she asked after bowing her head.

The newest apprentice looked her over, his eyes lingering on her wide hips. She was wearing a simple cotton wraparound gown and a simple lapis lazuli necklace. Her outfit wasn't remarkable in the least, but Tekem thought she looked beautiful.

"I did. Meet Tekem. He is to be my latest apprentice, so teach him all you know and assist him when needed," he said before turning to the zebra. "Despite having the same status as you in name, Nenet has years of experience on you, so pay close attention to her. You have not undergone any further religious education apart from the basics, correct?"

Tekem bowed his head in respect. "I have learned several dances designed to appease and honour the gods as well, high priest. Aside from that, I admit I know little beyond the basics."

The snake nodded. "As expected. Nenet, show him to your room. You will sleep in the same space from today forward. You will spend the rest of the day showing him around and explaining what will be expected of him in the time to come."

"As you wish, High Priest," she said, bowing her head again. There was a note of enthusiasm in her voice.

"Good. I will see the two of you later," Seb said as he turned and slithered through the bronze doors.

As soon as the heavy doors closed behind his long tail, Nenet jumped up with a squeal and wrapped her arms around Tekem. "Welcome! I'm Nenet! I am so happy you're here! These days can be awfully boring when I have to spend them on my own!"

The young dancer was overwhelmed by this wave of joy and found himself laughing. He moved his arms around her as well and blushed every so slightly at this close contact. He'd never been this close with a girl before, and he found that he quite liked it. He held her for as long as she allowed it, which was surprisingly long. Eventually, though, she let go of him and stepped back.

"Whoops! Sorry about that. It's been a long time since I last hugged someone. I guess I missed it more than I thought," she chuckled.

"No, no, it's okay! I didn't mind it at all! Uhm…you can do it again if you want to." He surprised himself with those words as he was usually more reserved than this. The hug did feel nice.

She smiled and shook her head. "Maybe later. Right now, I would like to show you where you will be staying. Walk with me," she said before turning on her heel and walking to the wooden door furthest away from them. Behind it was a small frugal room with two mats of woven reed on the floor, each with a small wooden chest next to them, as well as a wooden headrest. "We don't sleep as comfortably as the royal family does, but it's not that bad. The room stays pretty cool somehow, so it's better than what most people have to endure." She sat down on one of the mats and looked up at Tekem. "This one is mine. The other one is yours. You can store your belongings in the chest."

He put his bag in the chest and sat down on his mat, facing Nenet. "So…when did you became an apprentice here?"

"Three years ago. I come from a line of seers, so it was only natural for me to receive my training here. The Pharaoh puts a great deal of his resources into the realm of the gods and the unseen. His majesty wishes to get a firmer grasp on it, I believe. Some things are beyond his control though."

"Have you ever had a vision before?"

"I have! I foresaw that you would be joining this room today!"

He stared at her. "Really?"

She shrugged. "Well, kind of. I foresaw that someone would be joining me soon. My visions are still rather vague, I'm afraid. Seb thinks more clarity and depth will come with age and experience. I hope he is right."

"That's still impressive. I was brought here because he sensed magic inside of me somehow, but I don't even know what he is talking about or what kind of power this is. I just danced."

The lioness smiled and looked him over. "The high priest is never wrong. He'll figure out what it is he sensed sooner or later. Heka will guide him to the answer."

He smiled at her and nodded. The two spent the rest of the evening talking about life as an apprentice and all the chores that came with it. Tekem's head was positively buzzing from all that had happened that day and the information Nenet had relayed to him. While the lioness had already gone off to the land of dreams, Tekem found it hard to catch sleep that night. He found himself staring up at the ceiling, into the darkness of the pitch-black room for what seemed like an eternity. Thoughts surfaced and disappeared like fish in a murky lake, with one thought popping up more than any other. What would the morning bring?

Tekem did not have the luxury of waiting until the next morning, as he woke up to the sound of Seb's voice and the sensation of scales rubbing against his furry body. He stirred and opened his eyes to see the high priest hanging over him. The boy gasped and pulled his legs up, his mind needing a few seconds to realize that he was in his new room, instead of in his old home with his parents next to him.

"Ah, you're finally awake. Good. Come with me, Tekem. It is time for your initiation," the cobra said as he rose to his full height and moved his tail off the zebra's leg. He left the room without uttering another word.

Tekem couldn't recall the last time he was woken up so abruptly, and he looked over to Nenet, wanting to know what she thought of this. Unfortunately, the dark lioness was fast asleep, a small stream of droll flowing down her cheek. Tekem chuckled softly at this and got up. He put on his loincloth and turned to look at the lioness once more before leaving the room.

Seb was waiting on the other side of the room. "Hurry up."

The young man ran over to the cobra, who opened the door. "Inside."

The room behind the door contained a large pool sunken into the ground. The water was clearer than any Tekem had ever seen before. Surrounding the pool was a plethora of plants the boy had never seen before. The room was a man-made oasis. The high priest pulled off his robe and slithered into the water. "You must always cleanse yourself before entering the temple. Not doing so would risk the purity of the shrine. Get into the water and wash yourself."

Tekem took off his loincloth and walked into the water. It almost felt like a shame to dirty this beautiful water with the dust from his fur and hooves, but he would not disobey his teacher. He took great care to wash all the dirt out of his fur. He swore his white had never been brighter. This was the most luxurious bath he had ever been in, and he'd have loved to stay in the warm water forever. Unfortunately, his teacher had different plans.

"Tekem, wake up," he said as he was towering over the boy again, his arms folded. He was wearing his robe again.

He must've dozed off, because he hadn't noticed the snake getting out and moving up to him at all. He shook his head to clear it and got out of the pool. A nearby jackal handed him a towel.

"Oh eh, thank you."

The jackal bowed before he walked away. The zebra dried himself as best he could before donning his loincloth again. He walked up to the tall cobra and bowed his head. "I am ready."

"I hope so too," he answered. He slithered back through the door and made his way to the bronze doors, apprentice in tow. "You are allowed entry tonight, but only tonight, unless I tell you otherwise. Understood?"

"Understood, high priest."

The man nodded and opened the doors, revealing a spacious room with a large black stone statue of Heka in the middle. The only light inside the room came from a large hole in the roof, through which the light of the full moon shone directly onto the statue. "Tekem, this is Heka, the most revered, while at the same time most hidden, god of our time."

"How can a god be revered and hidden at the same time exactly?"

"Magic is prevalent in daily life all over Egypt, child. Even if most citizens are not aware of it, their actions strengthen Heka."

Tekem nodded at the explanation, trusting the priest's word.

"Tonight, we will perform an initiation ritual to strengthen your bond with Heka. As a future priest, it is important to stay in all the gods' good graces, but since Heka is the one considered most important by the pharaoh, we will focus on him today. I trust that you have worshipped before? Hathor, I assume? Goddess of fertility, beauty, music, and dance, among others?"

"Yes, that's right. My family are proud worshippers of Hathor."

"Excellent. From now on, though, I would like you to focus on Heka. This does not mean that you must neglect Hathor and the others. Understood?"

"Understood."

"Good, now, get on your knees and close your eyes, boy."

Tekem thought this an odd request, but he was in no position to question the highest authority in the temple. He lowered himself onto his knees, placed his hands on his thighs, and closed his eyes.

He could hear the high priest moving about him. Things were being moved, and a sudden sweet scent entered his nostrils. He recognized the mixed scent of resin, saffron, cinnamon, myrrh, and honey as Kyphi. He deeply inhaled the familiar scent and let it calm him. The scent reminded him of home, and of festivals during cool spring nights, during which he would dance in honour of the gods and to entertain the festival goers. A smile crept over his face as he was filled with the warm memories of his past.

He was brought back to the present by the feeling of Seb's cool scaled hands on his shoulders. "Deep breaths. Deeper each time, until you have reached a comfortable limit." He led by example, which the fresh apprentice followed. Tekem felt himself sinking into a trance. The world around him fell away bit by bit, until only the incense and Seb's hands and voice remained.

"Heka, god of magic and medicine, personification of magic itself. One who witnessed and allowed the creation of life. Heka, I, your humble servant, have brought you new blood. Speak your name, child."

He felt a presence joining them in the void. The air around him felt heavy, but not unpleasant. He felt watched. "Tekem."

"Heka, do you accept Tekem as your servant? He will devote his life to your teachings and will worship you every day. In return, we humbly ask that you reveal your new servant's hidden talent. Show us how he may best serve you."

Tekem could see a streak of blue light resembling a shooting star flowing towards him from the darkness. It circled his body a few times, before settling in his stomach. He gasped and lost the ability to breathe for a few long seconds. He could feel the light spreading through his body, flowing out from his stomach into the very tips of his fingers. He felt warm and powerful, as if he could take on the very world and emerge victorious.

"Thank you," he whispered.

"Thank you, Lord Heka. This gift will not be wasted." The cobra patted his charge's shoulders. "Deep breaths again, a little shorter each time, until you're breathing normally," he whispered.

Tekem did as instructed and felt the heaviness subside, the pressure dissipating as he was brought back to the present.

"Open your eyes."

The zebra carefully opened them, squinting at the bright moonlight, which had shifted from the statue to him. "I feel different," he said softly.

"Shhh... Tomorrow. Eat," Seb said as he held up a bit of bread.

It was frustrating to not be able to discuss what he had experienced, but he trusted the priest and took the bread. He took a bite and felt more grounded immediately. His knees were starting to hurt from having been in contact with the sandstone floor this whole time.

"We will leave the incense burning until it goes out by itself. I want you to go back to bed and meditate on what you experienced tonight. Tomorrow, we will talk."

Tekem nodded and put the rest of the bread in his muzzle. He got up and left the room after bowing to both Heka and the high priest. He found Nenet right where he'd left her and smiled at her peaceful face. The zebra lay down as carefully as possible, hoping the lioness wouldn't wake up from his moving around. The bed felt much softer than before, and he was carried off to the land of dreams before he had a chance to ponder the ritual and the presence he had felt.

Tekem woke up to a loud scream next to him, and he turned to find Nenet sitting straight up in her bed. She was staring at the wall. It was hard to make out any details in the dark room. "Nenet?" he asked softly.

"Black cat. Dark cloud. The Nile. Field of Reeds..."

"Nenet?"

"Black cat. Dark cloud. The Nile. Field of Reeds..."

The zebra moved over to her and gently laid her back down. "Come on... Time to sleep," he whispered as he pet her for a moment.

The dark lioness fell back asleep almost immediately, after which Tekem returned to his bed. He frowned and thought about her words before drifting off, forgetting them again.

"I would like you to dance for me."

Tekem stared at the black cat in front of him. The was wearing a white dress of the finest cotton and her neck was decorated with a necklace made of the highest quality lapis lazuli. His cheeks flushed pink at the unrivaled beauty of princess Leila. Her gold eyes never strayed from his while she waited for his answer.

"I-I'm sorry, princess. The high priest ordered me to sweep the temple floor," he spoke softly, bowing his head out of respect. Was he even in a position to refuse her? She was royalty after all.

"And now I order you to come with me and dance for me. Drop the broom, Tekem," she said firmly, but with a mischievous smile on her face.

She remembered his name! His heart fluttered with joy at the realization that his performance had been memorable enough to leave an impression on the princess. Seb was nowhere in sight, and Nenet had been sent off to the market to get more incense and talismans from the vendors. Tekem was on his own.

He decided to take the path of least resistance. He could always apologize to his mentor later, which was easier than trying to get Leila to back off. Besides, wasn't becoming a royal dancer his original goal?

"As you wish, princess," he said, kneeling to place the broom on the floor.

"Wonderful! Follow me!" she said before walking away. She looked over her shoulder to see if he would follow.

The young priest-to-be followed behind her, his eyes drawn to the swaying of her hips as she walked. She was smaller than him, but of average height for a female cat. The black coat covering her subtle hourglass figure shone like polished obsidian, so much so that it seemed to reject the sun's rays.

"Tekem?"

His eyes shot up and met hers. "Oh, eh, sorry, princess!"

"For what? I was asking how your night was. The first night at a new place is usually the worst, right?"

"Oh! Well, I had a pretty good night, princess. There's no need to worry about me," he smiled.

She giggled. "It is a princess' duty to worry about her subjects, Tekem," she spoke. The girl led him through a couple of corridors, before entering through a door at the far end. They stepped into a large room dominated by a big wooden bed. It looked so comfortable that Tekem couldn't help but desire to lie down in it. The room was decorated with various musical instruments, pillows, drapes, and wooden furniture. One of the desks along the walls was loaded with jewelry, and even had a large thin slab of reflective obsidian resting on it. The zebra walked over to it check out his own reflection. He'd never seen it this clearly before.

"This is my room. I hope it is big enough for you to dance in."

He looked around and nodded. "There is more than enough space, princess. However, I don't see any musicians."

"I will accompany you on the benet," Leila said as she walked to the far corner of the room, where a beautiful bow harp made of wood and decorated with gold and precious stones was waiting for her. She picked it up and carried it over to the space the zebra was supposed to dance in. The princess knelt down and placed the instrument in front of her. She ran her slender fingers over the strings and plucked them to test their sound.

"I trust that this won't be a problem?"

The dancer shook his head. "Of course not, princess. I am deeply honoured that you would play for one such as me."

She smiled at those words. "Prove it. Show me how well you dance to my music."

She started playing a melody that was well-known among every walk of life in Egypt. It was a song Tekem had danced to numerous times, so his body moved of its own accord, his hips swaying, his body twisting, and his arms waving as he moved to the rhythm of Leila's harp. He closed his eyes and allowed himself to get lost in the music, his body taking over. It was like he was in a trance again, the feeling similar to when he was introduced to Heka by the snake priest.

The song picked up, so the dancer naturally followed suit. He twirled and weaved his way through the dance, letting the sweet melody guide him along. His eyes were open, but his mind was far away. His body new exactly what to do. Leila was an expert musician, never missing a beat or playing a false note.

Eventually, the song ended, and the zebra slowed down to a final elegant pose. Before the vibrations of the final note vanished from the room, Leila clapped in delight. "That was wonderful, Tekem! It's a shame my father failed to recognize your talent. I would have tried to convince him if Seb hadn't snatched you away."

Tekem blushed brightly at this wonderful compliment, and he rubbed the back of his head. "You honour me with your words, princess. I am not sure I am worthy of them."

"Nonsense! Also, call me Leila, Tekem."

"I shouldn't, princess. It wouldn't be appropriate."

"Perhaps I don't want you to be appropriate." She smirked while looking him over.

Tekem stammered and clenched his hands into fists at his sides, not knowing what to do with them. He grew even more red in the face and in his ears. He was saved by someone knocking on the door.

The black cat pouted and sighed, rolling her eyes. "Enter!"

The door swung open, revealing the high priest. "Ah! There you are, Tekem. I thought I asked you to sweep the temple floors. Imagine my surprise when I find the task half-done." His eyes moved over the princess sitting behind the benet. "Though, if the princess required your services, I can't fault you for that. However, it is time you come with me, boy. It is time for your training."

The zebra looked from Seb to Leila and back again.

The princess waved him off, sounding annoyed. "Fine. Go then. I will ask you to dance for me again some other time."

Tekem bowed deeply in her direction before quickly walking out of the room, following the cobra.

"You mustn't let her distract you, Tekem," Seb chided him as he slithered through the hall with his arms behind his back. "Distractions are detrimental to your progress. You do want to become a successful priest, don't you?"

No, I want to become a successful dancer. "Of course."

They met pharaoh Sekhen as they turned the corner, and bowed deeply. The cat spared them a look and nodded. "Good afternoon," he nodded.

"May the gods guide your steps," the priest and his apprentice said in unison, as Tekem had been instructed. They would keep their heads low until Sekhen was out of sight, before moving on.

"Focus on your duties and your training, boy. That way, you will truly become useful to the royal family. You will make your family proud."

He felt a clear sting of resentment in his heart at those words. His parents were already very proud of him. They always have been. Him becoming a successful priest or a mediocre one would not change their feeling towards him one bit. Seb didn't know that, of course. He didn't know his family. Tekem decided then and there that he would dance for the princess whenever she wanted him to. He had felt great while dancing to her music, better than when he was sweeping temple floors.

They arrived at the temple before long, and the high priest turned to face the zebra. "Today, I'm going to teach you a divination ritual also known as scrying. Nenet, coming from a family of seers, already mastered it. I wish to know if you have the same affinity as her." He let his charge to a small wooden altar that hadn't been there before. On it rested a stone bowl filled with water.

"Water divination has existed for many generations and will likely continue to do so for many more. It is one of the most common methods to deciphering what the gods may have in store for us mortals. Watch closely."

Seb closed his eyes and took deep breaths, breathing slower after each exhale, just like during Tekem's initiation. The snake opened his black eyes and peered at the water. "In order to scry, one needs to have a calm mind. It is important to know that you have no control over the speed at which possible messages appear before you. You may see them in the water or in your mind. Perhaps you hear a sound that nobody else can hear. It depends on the person," he spoke softly while staring unblinkingly at the water.

This ritual seemed a little vague to Tekem, and he frowned. "Am I supposed to just stare at the water?"

"Yes...and no... One must look beyond the water."

This only confused the fresh apprentice even more, and his frown grew deeper. He tried to copy his teacher and focus on the water as well when a flicker of light distracted him. He looked up to see nothing out of the ordinary. He looked back at the water to see another flash of colour somewhere in the corner of his eye. Blue? He tried to follow it, but it would vanish as soon as he tried to focus on it. This happened several times.

"I keep seeing the colour blue."

"Blue? Where do you see it?"

"The corner of my eye, but...wait... It's around you as well," he said as he took a good look at his teacher. Blue whisps were radiating from the snake. "It's...coming from you?"

The priest looked a tad confused. "Are you saying that the blue you see is coming from me? How interesting. I have heard of this before. I believe what you say may be the traces of certain types of magic, or it could be that you see people's auras. What do you see when you look at me now?" The priest took a few deep breaths.

Tekem focused on him and squinted as if that would help him see better. "The blue...is fading. There are no other colours, except..." He trailed off, moving a little closer to look at the priest's amulet. It was a rather common amulet used for protection, but the material was gold, instead of stone or bronze. "Green?"

"It has been imbued by protective magic. If what I remember is correct, different types of magic leave behind traces visible as different colours. Your training will be to learn the differences between these types and to map the corresponding colours. What we do here may be of great use by later generations, Tekem. Do not take this lightly."

"I won't. Shall we get to work?" he asked, eager to get started.

The cobra chuckled in approval. "Let's get some food in your first. Magic takes a toll on our energy levels. Follow me."

The next few months kept Tekem occupied with his priest training, his temple duties, and regular dance sessions with the princess. He was allowed to visit his family from time to time, as long as it didn't get in the way of the aforementioned tasks. His parents were very proud of his progress and happy with his contributions. Their shop had flourished into one of the most popular jewelry stalls in the market. His father had a higher demand for statuettes as well. His mother had gifted him a necklace of lapis lazuli and bronze for his birthday, which he was allowed to celebrate with his family. Nenet was invited too, and they had a wonderful time together.

Everything seemed to be going right in his life, and there were no reasons to suspect that would change, until the princess' dance requests suddenly stopped.

"I'm sorry, Tekem, but the princess is currently indisposed. I'm afraid she cannot come to the door right now," Leila's personal servant girl, Hasina, a gazelle, told him. She looked worried, but couldn't do more for him at the moment. "I'm sorry," she repeated before closing the door. This had been the third day in a row he hadn't seen the princess. Was she okay?

The zebra sighed and looked up at the sandstone ceiling. What was he supposed to do with his time now? He already trained with

Seb, who was currently out, and his duties were all done too. He figured he'd go for a dip in the pool. After all, one of a priest's most sacred duties is to keep a high standard of hygiene. It was the perfect excuse to soak in the water for hours.

He went into the bath chamber and dropped his loincloth before stepping into the water with a relaxed sigh.

"Hello, Tekem," a familiar, friendly voice said.

The zebra looked around and spotted Nenet in the water off to the side. She was hanging onto the ledge and rested her head on her arms. She looked him over and smiled. "Finally escaped that old snake?"

He gasped. "You can't talk about him like that!" He lowered himself into the water and slowly swam over to her.

"Relax, he isn't here to hear it. There isn't even a servant around right now. See?" she asked as she drew a circle in the air with her finger. "It's just us."

Tekem looked around to see she was right and nodded. He turned away and washed his upper body and arms, as well as his face. "Have you heard anything about the princess? It seems she is not feeling well."

"Not yet. Why? Are you sad because of your...sessions with her?" she asked, a subtle sting of jealousy in her voice.

"I was looking forward to dancing again, but I'm more worried for her health. I hope it is nothing serious."

"If it is, I am sure Seb will be summoned, who will then ask for us to accompany him. If he hasn't been alerted yet, I am sure the princess is fine."

"I guess you're right."

"I usually am."

Her voice was suddenly very close, and he startled upon feeling her paws on his back. The lioness stroked up and down, following the lines of his defined dancer body. "Your body is so hard," she spoke softly.

"Nenet? What are you doing?" he asked, caught off guard by her physical closeness. They hadn't done this before. It felt nice to have her touch him. Her paw pads were softly and squishy, and the subtle sensation of her claw tips trailing through his fur sent shivers down his spine.

"Helping you wash your back, dummy. What does it look like I'm doing?" He could hear the smile in her voice and knew exactly what look she would be giving him, were they facing each other. Her paws slowly moved down to cup his rear.

Tekem gasped and turned around. "Nenet, I don't think we sh-"

She shut him up by covering his lips with hers. The lioness pressed herself against him and placed her paws on his chest and shoulder. Tekem's thoughts of protesting evaporated like puddle in the desert sun, and he gave in to temptation. He had eyed her since he'd first laid eyes on her, but had not made any moves out of respect for both her and his priestly duties. At that moment, there was no doubt in his mind that Nenet felt the same way about him, and was just as curious.

The young zebra moved his arms around her, resting one paw on her hip and the other on the back of her head, when they were rudely interrupted.

"What is the meaning of this?!"

The two parted as if touched by a branding iron, blushing furiously, and turned away from each other. Tekem licked his lips, the lingering memory of Nenet still on them. Seb was standing in the doorway, looking furious.

"How dare you! This is a place of purification! I will have none of this here!"

Tekem looked down. He bowed his head and prayed that Seb would go easy on the two of them.

The bronze cobra huffed and folded his arms. "We will talk about this later. Right now, I need you two to come with me. The princess is in need of our help. Dry yourselves and meet me in the princess' room," he said, before turning around and slithering out of the room.

The two apprentices hurried out of the water, and exchanged a few guilty looks between them while they dried themselves to the best of their abilities given their limited time. They got dressed and hurried over to Leila's room.

Nenet knocked on the door, which was opened by Hasina. "Please, come in. The high priest needs you," the gazelle said softly as she stepped out of the way, head bowed.

The two walked into the room familiar to Tekem by then. The huge difference was that it was now crowded by several priests who fetched all manner of items and necessities for Seb to work his magic. The cobra hung above the princess, who was lying in her bed, looking absolutely dreadful. Her coat had lost its shine, and her eyes stared weakly out of her gaunt face. Her gold eyes, now closer to a dull ochre, moved to look at the apprentices.

"T-Tekem…" Her voice was barely stronger than a whisper. Her paw reached out for him.

"You must not speak, princess. Conserve your strength," Seb spoke while he waved incense around above her in an attempt to cleanse the room of evil spirits.

Tekem hurried over to Leila's side and knelt down before taking her paw in his. "I am here, princess. You will be all right. Seb will heal you," he said, hoping his confidence in his mentor's abilities would give her some strength.

Nenet moved to the other side of the bed and looked at the black cat, before looking at Seb. "What do you require of us, high priest?" she asked, betraying no emotion.

"We must find out what spirits or demons haunt her, Nenet. Only after identifying the problem can we work on remedying it." He lifted his head to speak to the other priests in the room, many of which merely assisted in mundane things. "I need you all to form a crescent around the bed and invoke Sekhmet, Thoth, Isis, and Heka," he commanded. "Nenet, I need you to keep a cool cloth on the princess' head. She's burning up. Tekem, dance. Focus on your energy."

Tekem looked confused and looked at the snake. "You…want me to dance?"

"Yes. Invoke Heka with your movements and use your gift to identify the problem. Let the gods guide you to the answer."

Pharaoh Sekhen and Queen Nakia burst into the room. "What is the meaning of this? Why wasn't I informed immediately? Seb! I had to find out from a priest I came across!" The man was furious. However, his quickly turned to fear upon seeing his daughter in her current state. "Leila, my desert flower! What is wrong?" He stepped closer to her, but his wife held him back.

"Careful, my love. What she has could be contagious. Let the priests do their work and let's not get in their way. Come," she said as she pulled her husband towards the door.

The man freed himself and ran over to the bed, where he bumped Tekem aside and took his daughter's paw in his. "Leila, please stay with me. I cannot lose you!"

The boy quickly stood and stepped away.

"Sekhen! You are in the way!" Nakia argued.

"Silence, woman! What kind of father would I be if I left my precious daughter to fend for herself! The power of the gods flows through me, and thus it shall flow through her to aid her!"

Nakia growled out of frustration and stuck to the side of the room, arms folded.

Sekhen looked at Seb and nodded. "Do everything in your power to save her, Seb. I will be forever indebted to you."

The high priest nodded and looked at Tekem again. "Dance." He looked at three other priests and pointed them to some instruments in the room. "Play! Now!"

Tekem closed his eyes and started swaying his hips before the first notes of a well-known melody reached his ears. His body flowed and twisted while he danced in place, not daring to use his legs too much. It was too crowded for a dynamic performance. He focused on the music and the way his body felt while sinking deeper into the darkness behind his eyes. He felt what he would describe as a soft breeze part the striped fur of his body. His feet were planted firmly on the ground, and energy flowed upwards through his hooves.

Flashes of light dashed before his eyes like fireflies. He could smell the incense still, but as if it were coming from behind a closed door. He felt a presence with him. It felt bigger than the entire palace combined. Tekem took deep breaths and tilted his face upwards. He lifted his arms up high. Please, h*elp me. Grant me the power to help my friend. I, Tekem, your humble servant, beg you for just a sliver of your power to save her life.*"

The breeze circled him and entered him through his nose. It flowed through his entire body, from the tip of his ears down to the very tips of his hooves, before exiting through his mouth. He opened his eyes and gasped upon looking at the princess. She was covered in an energy darker than any he had ever seen. It was such a dark shade of red that it almost seemed black.

"What do you see, boy?" Seb asked while placing precious stones on Leila's head, chest, and stomach. Carnelian and Topaz, Tekem knew.

"A dark energy. Dark red. Almost black," he said. "It has enveloped all of her."

Nenet gasped as she changed the wet cloth on the black cat's forehead, almost dropping it. "My dream, Tekem! The black cat, the dark cloud, the Nile, the Field of Reeds! She is dying!"

The snake growled and looked down at the princess. "Someone has cursed our beloved princess! This is not a disease sent by the gods or spirits at all!"

"What?! A curse?! Who would do such an awful thing to my little Leila?!" the pharaoh demanded.

"We are about to find out," Seb said as he rolled his shoulders and moved his hands together, fingers spread out, above Leila's chest. He closed his eyes and took deep breaths. "By the power of the gods instilled in me, I call upon Heka, almighty primordial god. Heka, who made creation possible, who lent the other gods his strength, who has lent me his strength since my birth, whose very name is synonymous for all the magic we use every day, lend us your strength again this day. Save this innocent girl from the terrible curse that she has been afflicted with. Take this curse and send it back to where it came from. May the curse giver be struck by their own maliciousness and feel the wrath of the gods, for this person has harmed one of their own. Take this evil energy and return it. Return it! Return it!"

Tekem witnessed the dark energy slowly flowing upwards. The princess groaned and whimpered as it left her body. It accumulated into a dark spiraling cloud that hung menacingly over the gathered crowd. Leila's eyes fell shut, and her breathing slowed into a more relaxed pace.

"It's working! The energy is leaving!" Tekem said.

"Follow it!" Seb ordered.

"Oh, my darling, desert flower! You will be all right! Thank you, Seb, thank you! Thank the gods for their help!" Sekhen turned around to look at his queen. "Nakia! Did you hear that?" he asked before looking confused. The white queen was nowhere to be seen. "Nakia? Where is my queen?!" he demanded.

Tekem hurried outside along with a few other priests. The group of priests scattered to find the queen, while the high priest's apprentice followed the cloud of dark energy at a light trot. It was difficult to keep track of it at times, as the energy wasn't hindered by physical boundaries. He'd had a few people calling out to him, but he had no time to waste. He had been given an important mission, and he would not fail. He needed to find the person responsible for hurting his friend.

He found himself being led to the throne room, where only a single person was currently standing in the middle of the room. The dark energy was circling her, closing in.

"You?"

Queen Nakia turned to look at him and gave him a haughty look. "How dare you speak to me. Kneel before your queen, boy!"

Tekem immediately dropped to his knees and lowered his head. "Forgive me, My Queen." This couldn't be. Why would Leila's own mother curse her in such a way? Could Seb have done something wrong?

More priests trickled in, but the quickly made way for Sekhen and Seb. They took in the scene, the pharaoh's gaze hardening. "Nakia, what have you done?"

"What are you talking about? How is our daughter?" she asked, feigning innocence.

"Tekem, where did the curse go?" Seb asked, his voice loud enough to echo through the open space.

The zebra swallowed once before pointing at the white cat in front of him. "It is entering the queen, high priest," he spoke softly.

"Our daughter is doing much better, now that your curse has been lifted, you wretched woman! How dare you! I should have you executed for this! She is your own flesh and blood!"

Nakia let out a cold laugh that bounced off the sandstone walls. "Oh, I know all about how you feel about your own flesh and blood, Sekhen! I have seen the way you look at her! Noticed the way you touch her! Don't insult me by thinking I don't know about your nightly visits!"

The pharaoh stammered and pointed his finger at her. "How dare you! Guards! Arrest her!"

Nakia simply laughed before she started coughing. She fought desperately for air, but her efforts were in vain. She fell down to the ground and flailed like a fish on dry land. Her eyes were turning red.

"What is happening?!" the pharaoh demanded.

"The curse has been returned to the sender," Seb explained calmly while watching the queen writhe on the floor in agony. "The gods will not help her."

Sekhen nodded and watched his wife as she seemed to collapse in on herself. Her fur looked dryer than cotton, her body turned feeble and emaciated, and her eyes nearly fell from their sockets.

"S-Sekhen..." she wheezed. "Curse...you..." Nakia stretched a skeletal paw towards the black pharaoh, before she let out her final breath.

"May the gods bar her from the afterlife," the pharaoh growled before stomping out of the room. "Clean it up! Burn her!" He slammed the door behind him as he left.

Tekem was still on his knees, looking at the sad heap of fur and bones and was his former queen. Seb helped him up and held him for a moment. "You did well, Tekem. Let's go," he said, guiding his student out of the throne room and back to Leila, who Nenet was tending to. The princess already looked much better, but she was sound asleep.

"She is resting," the dark lioness said as the two walked closer to towards the bed. Most of the other priests had already left. Hasina was moving around, cleaning and putting things away.

Seb checked the princess one more time and nodded. "She will be fine with some rest. Tekem, are there any leftovers of the curse?"

Tekem squinted and shook his head. "No, there is only a faint green glow of healing magic," he said.

"Excellent. Nenet, Tekem, you can go. Bathe yourselves and take the rest of the day off. You have earned it.

The two apprentices bowed and left the room. He hated leaving the princess along after all that had just happened, but there was nothing more he could do for her. "Poor Leila... It was her own mother who cursed her," he spoke softly as he walked to the bathing room with the lioness.

"A firm reminder that unhappy families exist in all walks of life," she replied after walking in silence for a few seconds. "What happened to her?"

He squeezed his eyes shut and shook his head to keep the image from taking hold in his brain. "She died after Seb reflected the curse." He opened the door to the baths and undressed before letting himself fall into the water.

He sank to the bottom, where he would have liked to stay for a bit. It was silent underwater, serene in a sense of its own. He had to come back up for air, though, and Nenet was waiting there for him. She moved her arms around him and nuzzled his neck. "It is over now, Tekem. The princess is safe, the queen will be mourned in one way or another, and life will go on the way it always does."

He looked at her and moved his arms around her, holding her close. "Seeing her like that frightened me."

"Who? The princess?"

"Yes, but the queen as well. You should be glad you didn't see it. It would haunt your dreams for sure," he said. He let out a sigh. "I wouldn't be surprised if that happened to me tonight."

"Would you like to sleep with me tonight? You know, like against me?" Nenet asked as she nuzzled him again.

Tekem smiled at the thought and nodded before squeezing her tightly. "I would love that."

A FORTUNE IN RUINS

FOPFOX

The job was never easy, no sir, but in such troubled times as these, one had few options when it came to matters of fortune. Kumar, my favorite of all the gods, save for all the others when I have need of them; disliked nothing more than a man who ignored opportunities and would curse those who performed such a disgrace to always wear a hole into their money purse.

Such things as the end of the world meant nothing to him, save for what you could grab in the chaos.

"Here!" I said proudly to my recently obtained apprentice, a short fox whose fur matched the dry summer dirt in the plains. "You can rest here!"

I pointed towards an obelisk jutting out from the ground, casting a shadow across the sun-baked land. It had four sides to it, the top of each had a different god carved into it.

"This is what I like to call the Peace Tower, though it is certainly not a tower nor was it made in honor of peace, at least not willingly!" I said. My apprentice panted as he made a bee-line to the shade, leading our packhorse along with him. "Look, you can see the Hill Folk's Sun God on that side, see the lion? And right next to it, a jackal like me, that's the Stone Piler's god of the dead and he should normally be painted deathly white!"

"The Stone Piler's and the Hill Folk, if any of them are still around, hate each other. Why would they build this, Mithon?"

"Mithon the Shrewd," I corrected. "I'd like the Gods above to know my full name at all times, wouldn't want them mixing me up with another Mithon!"

Abd sighed, "Why would they build this, Mithon the Shrewd?"

"Ah, you see, it was the conclusion of another one of their endless wars over who ruled what part of our land! A great hobby of both of them, though they never thought to invite us to take part in the game," I stepped up to the base of the obelisk and tested the first foothold in the bricks for stability. It was still good. "Never seemed very fair to me but I supposed that was kind of their point. Easier for them to just use their sword to take what they want. Be glad you were born after that."

"But now we got the Sea Folk," my apprentice took a blanket from the saddle and rolled it onto the shaded ground. "And they're far worse!"

"Indeed, murderers and looters the whole lot of them! If rumors are true, they don't even show their foes the mercy of slavery! Or hells, I've even heard they drag captives back to toil in their kingdom deep beneath the ocean! But!" I exclaimed as I began climbing the obelisk. "If it weren't for them, we wouldn't be here today facing fame and fortune!"

"I still think pickpocketing is easier!"

"You're a grown fox now, Abd, you're too old to play childish games like that!" I leaped from my foothold and grabbed onto the snout of the jackal god.

"Deepest apologies, my lord, I do not recall your name nor what favors you prefer. Please, if you desire anything, send me a messenger and I will repay you," I whispered to the jackal. He may not be my people's god, but now was not the time to make enemies!

"I was living it up quite well until you came along!"

"Yes!" I grunted, swinging my leg up along the god's snout and pulling myself atop it on my belly. "Be glad it was me who grabbed your wrist and not the King's guard! You're too old to be given a light labor sentence and a slap on the wrist, next time you're caught it will be the death of you."

Sitting on my rear, I scooted to the end of the jackal head and let my legs dangle over his nose. I closed my eyes and adjusted my seat until I found the right spot atop the snout. I had done this job enough times that I swear my butt was wearing a groove into the old god's muzzle.

Opening my eyes, I was greeted by clear skies and the distant, dusty horizon. Smoke was trailing up in the distance beyond an endless plain of abandoned farms and burnt homesteads.

I opened up my hip-bag and pulled out the wax tablet I used last time and a fresh one. I held the old one up against the horizon, the same view I had sketched many times with perfect accuracy, if I do say so myself. My life depended on it, after all.

"Excellent!" I exclaimed, grinning wildly. I pinched my claws together in front of the tablet and measured out the distance between the smoke on the drawing and where it was now. "The source of the smoke has moved, it is now a half-day's march south of where it once was!"

"So what?" Abd called out.

I put the used tablet down and began scratching into the fresh one with my claws, "So? That means the Sea Folk have moved onto another place to raid and left behind their old site!"

"And?"

"Kumar bless him," I hissed lowly. My strict love of Kumar and his virtues made me almost snap at the lad for not catching on, especially since I had already explained my profession to him. Dagun, Father of the Gods, with his paternal wisdom won over my mind. It is far better to encourage an apprentice to ask questions than to berate them and make them fear searching for knowledge.

"Lad, we're going to go to where they used to be and comb it for treasures the Sea Folk left behind!" I continued scratching out the horizon. "The Sea Folk move through locations like lightning, grabbing all the loot they can as quickly as they can before moving on. They always, always miss more subtle hiding spots."

"Are they stupid or something?" Abd asked. "They destroyed the Hill Folk army without so much as blinking, wouldn't they have all the time in the world to loot?"

"They are not stupid!" I barked, scratching off the final details of today's observance and shoving it back into my bag. I carefully slid down the side of the snout and grabbed hold of the top foothold. "For whatever reason, their tactic is to raid and move onto the next place as soon as possible. If we understood their tongue, perhaps they could explain but…"

"Some people think they are demons."

"No, they're not," I sighed, crawling down the side of the pillar. "They are strange beings, the likes of which you've never seen before, but I believe they possess a soul just like us."

"Why do you think that?"

I landed on the dirt and brushed the dust away from my tunic, "I once was trapped, hiding in a cabinet, inside a house that we thought they had abandoned. A whole day without food or water before they left. During that time, I saw them laugh and sing, tell jokes, all sorts of behavior you and I would do. Of course, I also witnessed them beheading captives, so they also possess cruelty, much like us."

"We?" the fox asked. He was holding out a slice of flatbread with crumbly cheese.

"Ah, yes," I rubbed my chin. "My former master, the one who taught me all about this trade. He left me for dead and took my cut."

"What!?"

"Let me be clear, there will be no rescue party if you're caught or trapped. The same goes for me. Do not attempt to save me from the Sea Folk, for I won't save you from them."

"That seems wrong."

"No, it is a mercy. No sense in losing two lives to the Sea Folk," I grabbed the bread from the fox and took a bite. The bread was soft and warm, heated up in the saddlebags under the noon sun. The cheese was heavily salted, just the way I liked it. "Let's go!"

By the time we neared the old raiding ground, the sun had begun to set. Abd had grown tired on the journey and I allowed him to sit atop our horse while I guided it, much like a child would.

This mercy did not stop Abd from complaining and raising objections, trying my patience quite a bit.

"How is this safer than pickpocketing, again?" Abd asked as I was trying to goad the stubborn horse to climb the last steps up a hill.

"Pickpocketing is a crime, scavenging in ruined towns and estates is not. Our King has made it very clear he is not going to prosecute any folk like us who are brave enough to take the risk," I clicked my tongue at the horse and pulled on the reins. "Besides, most of the estates were run by Stone Pilers and Hill Folk nobles, and their masters are far, far away now. They stole from us for years, now it's time to take it back."

"I think I see it!" Abd called out, raising his neck up and pointing past me.

Miraculously, the horse finally budged and I was able to see what Abd was talking about as I rounded the peak of the hill.

A stone road ran along the ruins of a wall that had been thick enough to guard one of the great River King cities. From our height, I could see beyond the rubble a grove of olive trees and grapevines plucked dry and several adobe buildings including one large estate house in the center, all in various degrees of burnt.

A grin wrapped itself around my muzzle. "We are going to be rich."

"This is the Sadiki Vineyard, isn't it?" Abd asked.

I had a hunch...no, perhaps a desperate plea that my next target was the Sadiki's. They were among the most wealthy of the Stone Pilers who came to occupy our land, owning the largest grove of wine grapes and olives in the region. So paranoid were they of the locals turning on them, they commissioned a stone wall to protect themselves.

So untouchable, they thought themselves, that they holed up and refused to leave when word of the Sea Folk arriving came when the rest of us poor souls fled to the nearest King's city for protection.

And now where were they? Their groves no longer bore fruit, their walls were breached, and their army of slave workers were gone.

"What a treat for your first day on the job!" I laughed and guided the horse down the hill. Perhaps the dumb beast had picked up on my joy, because it picked up the pace and no longer resisted my commands. "Maybe you'll retire young, hm?"

"You think they might still be there?"

"The Sadikis?" I asked and responded before Abd could confirm. "No, they would have had the torches out by now and their tavern would be open for travelers. The Sadikis are too arrogant to let something like a raid stop them from keeping a pretense of success up."

"I meant the Sea Folk."

"They're long gone," I motioned towards the breach. "Notice the lack of any heavy foot traffic? The summer dust and eastern sand has covered it up, they're far away from here."

Abd swung down from the horse and began walking at the horse's side with a slight skip to his step. He may be a grown man, but the child in him had not been fully extinguished by age.

That would change.

It changed for me when I almost died of thirst in that cabinet.

We tied the horse to a palm tree next to an outcropping of rocks jutting out from the earth near the wall. Hopefully that would be enough to hide the horse should someone stop by. Though there was no legal authority here, some folk didn't take kindly to us taking our fair share.

"Alright," I handed Abd a shiny bronze dagger, similar to my own.

"Am I supposed to stab someone with this?"

"There's that pickpocket brain of yours again!" I lightly rapped Abd atop his head with my knuckles. "No, apprentice, this is for opening up chests and locks. You'll find that a good bronze dagger is better than a key sometimes!"

"But if I had to..."

"Don't attack a member of the Sea Folk!" I growled. "Their necks are like tree-trunks, you're not going to kill one and even if you do, his friends will kill you!"

"But what if one attacks me?"

"Use it on yourself," I said bitterly. "It will be a mercy, trust me."

That was the first time I smelled fear on Abd. Good, the lad needed to know this was a serious job, not just a serious payout. He had been contemptuous and mocking of everything until this point, even when I coerced him into joining me in exchange for not turning him into the guards.

This was not a game and he knew this now.

"If you want to back out," I swished my tail. "There's a cavern an hour north of here, you can hide out there until morning and make your way back to the city."

"I'm not afraid of anything," Abd lied, poorly I might add. The lad would have gotten chewed up a month longer as a pickpocket.

Still, I entertained his childish notion.

"Good."

We stepped over the shattered stone bricks of the breach in the wall and hopped down onto the soft dirt of the estate. Aside from the groves, there were also a few date palms and imported ferns planted in the ground. The Sadikis were intent on not only running the most profitable plantation in the region but also the most extravagant.

"Gods!" Abd covered his black nose with the sleeve of his shirt. "What is that smell!?"

I sniffed, catching a whiff of bodies decomposing. I had grown used to it, it was part of the job after all. This was normally a strength but in this case my apprentice's intolerant nose alerted me to a particularly strong source just behind us.

"Ah ha!" I unsheathed my dagger and knelt down. Pulling a brick away, I revealed a left paw covered in flies enjoying their banquet. I swept the flies away and found a copper ring wrapped around his finger.

Chopping away at the bone, I quickly freed the ring from the confines of death's paralysis and tossed it towards my apprentice.

"First one's yours! Never forget your first treasure, keep it safe! Kumar wills it!"

Abd grimaced and washed off the flesh from the ring in a narrow irrigation canal, "One of the Sadikis?"

"I think they'd consider copper to be a bit too poor for them to wear on their fingers," I tried to lift more bricks but the ones atop the poor soul's body were too heavy. I was only able to get a glimpse of his rotten, naked shoulder and chest. Most definitely was not a Sadiki or one of their tavern patrons. "My guess is that this fellow was a slave overseer, one given special privilege to boss the other slaves around. Probably was given the ring as a sign of favor, but not favorable enough that they need to break out the precious metals."

"And now it's mine," Abd grinned and fitted it on his middle finger

"That's the spirit!"

"So where to now?"

I scanned the area and was feeling awfully generous, so I pointed over at the manor house, standing two-stories proud, "Why don't you cut your teeth on the house and I'll take a look in the farm buildings?"

Abd's fur puffed up at the back of his neck, "Are you serious!?"

"Yes, go nuts, I'll catch up with you!"

The fox practically leaped towards the manor house while I casually strolled over to what appeared to be a storage building.

Though I was being generous, I had an ulterior motive. Amateurs often believe that the only jewels are in the landlord's home, but you can uncover surprising finds in the least likely places.

Scandalous relationships with the stable-master or a favored slave, whom the lord saw fit to reward with some precious jewelry or perfumes from the River Kings. Paranoid nobles hiding their family jewels beneath the floorboards of the chicken coop.

Every site I scavenge has a story waiting to be uncovered, usually with a fine reward.

The lock on the door had already been smashed open, so I slowly pulled it to the side.

Chains glistened from the rays of the setting sun. Straw was scattered on the floor and the smell of waste caught my nose.

Slave quarters.

I grimaced and headed on in as the door squeaked shut behind me, leaving only a crack of light entering. As mentioned, sometimes grim places like these hold rich stories, so they're always worth looking into. However it did not make them any less unpleasant.

The first stall, for lack of a better word, that I went into, I found nothing more than broken chains buried in the straw.

Disappointed, I went over to the next. While there were also broken links in the straw, something more round and fine rubbed against my pads.

"Ah hah!" I pulled out a gold ring dotted with rubies. I placed my palm against the adobe wall and looked down at the broken chains. "I'm sorry, my friend, you probably earned this ring either through stealing from their coffers or stealing Lady Sadiki's heart, but I must take it with me. Hopefully your story will be reward enough for you, wherever you are."

I pocketed the ring in my bag and stood up. My grin faded as a cold sensation crept down my spine.

I looked around the room. Every single chain was smashed open.

On the far end, there was even a punishment room, a small hole they'd toss a disobedient slave into. The bars on that were also broken.

The Sea Folk were not liberators of slaves, not in the slightest. They killed without discrimination to class and privilege. This was not fitting the typical operation of one of their raids.

Which meant...

"Oh no..." I whispered and quickly dashed to the door.

On my last step before reaching the door, I heard heavy footsteps off in the distance. I halted, held my breath, and slowly took one more step, creeping up towards the crack in the door and peering through it.

Those pale titans, all too familiar to me, were walking in the front entrance of the plantation. Their wedge-like snouts and black eyes expressed no emotions I could understand, though their guttural language gave some hints into their soul. Thick tails with fins ran out from beneath their bronze chest-pieces and skirts, trailing against the dirt.

Scaleless fish was what they looked like, but the lakes and rivers back home housed nothing like them, feral or otherwise.

And they were heading straight for the manor. Ten of them.

I had made a fatal mistake. I assumed the smoke on the horizon two days ago had been from a Sea Folk raid. What else could it have been?

No, the slaves revolted and cast off their chains.

Curiosity had me wondering how they tore down the wall and why, when they could have just battered down the gate, but I had no time to ruminate on such things.

It was time for me to leave. Every soul for himself!

I continued to watch as the Sea Folk all filed into the manor. They grew increasingly rowdy and boisterous as they raised their weapons and chests of loot.

There was no yelps from Abd or call for alarm from the Sea Folk. I waited for it, but it never came.

Abd was hiding.

Good for him! He might just get out of here in one piece, but it wouldn't be of my doing! I told him the rules!

Smoke began to sift through the chimney of the manor. I could hear wine being poured and more cheers from the barbarians.

They were settling in.

A good time for me to leave, sorry Abd, but I told you the rules!

I found myself still in the slave quarters when night had fallen and my thought process had not changed. I was still so busy apologizing to Abd for my promise to leave him behind that I hadn't yet had time to keep it.

Kumar, what is wrong with me?

The Sea Folk had grown quiet and the glistening of the fire in the windows had grown dim. They were not all asleep but no doubt all were partially drunk.

A perfect time to leave.

But instead I found myself grabbing a stick from the ground, just outside the door, and kneeling on the straw matted ground. I made a bundle of kindling and planted the stick tall atop it.

"Sekh," I whispered, rapidly rubbing the stick between my palms, "bring me your blessing."

I sped up the motions, my joints were already starting to ache.

"I offer you a copper ring," I promised her the lad's ring now, there was no turning back, I had to fulfill it. Sekh was quick to anger. "Please, I beg of you, lend me your blessing."

Smoke drifted up from the straw and I tossed the stick aside and blew gently.

Please, Sekh...please...

Tiny flames erupted from the burnt straw and I stood up, blowing kisses into the air.

I would kiss your idol if I could and if it pleased you, beautiful Sekh!

Sneaking out of the quarters, I kept low and quietly ran across the plantation towards the manor. Reaching the adobe walls just before the room with the brazier, I sat on the dirt, out of sight of the Sea Folk and perked my ears up.

Sekh truly blessed me this day, for the slave quarters suddenly burst into flames and a piece of the roof fell into it with a deafening crash.

That punched the drink out of the Sea Folk. They bellowed and stormed out of the manor's front entrance in a panic.

One, two, three, four, five, six, seven, eight, nine...

I waited as they rushed towards the burning building, grabbing buckets to fill from the canal.

One's still there.

Carefully, I lifted myself up and peered into the window. There was, indeed, one of them sitting on a stool, wedge-shaped head resting on a table.

Gods, they even have gills!

I figured he was out for the count and swung over the windowsill, landing softly on the floorboards.

Aside from the table, there were also numerous cushions lying around the floor. A room for food, drink, and socialization. The Sadikis sure had it all...

But what caught my eye was a wooden cabinet across the room in a dark corner. Pressing my nose against the floor, I could smell a familiar fox had been in this room. The scent had been dulled by spilled wine, but he was still here.

Slowly, I tip-toed across the room, carefully avoiding any floorboards that dared to begin to squeak.

My greed did cause me to stop and lift a silver candlestick from the corner of the table and stuff it into my bag though. I was still running a business, after all.

After that momentary lapse of judgment and having seen the Sea Folk had not stirred from his slumber, I continued creeping until I reached the cabinet and pressed my ear against it.

I could hear someone breathing lightly.

I scratched my claw lightly against the wood grain, hopefully in a way that Abd would recognize were my claws.

Please don't stab me.

Abd was paralyzed when I uncovered him, shocked beyond words that I came to his rescue. His green eyes darted across my shoulder and I turned.

Grumbling, the behemoth on the stool stirred from his sleep and lurched his neck around until his cold, black eyes met mine.

I didn't even think. My dagger was in the air before I knew it and slammed straight into the Sea Folk's neck. The monster silently fell backward, screaming breathlessly into the air.

"We need to go," I whispered.

Without waiting for Abd to reply, I threw him and his bag full of treasures across my shoulder and ran out into the night.

The fire was too loud for the Sea Folk to realize what had happened. I could hear the one I had attacked knocking furniture over in a vain attempt to alert them, but if they had ever noticed, me and Abd were clear over the rubble and fleeing north into the night with our horse.

"Alright," I dropped the torch on the cavern floor and let the light dance along the jagged walls. "Let's see what we got."

My loot was quite disappointing, as expected. Nothing more than the ring and the candlestick.

I expected something similar from Abd but my expectations were dashed in quite a pleasant manner. The fox's bag had been stuffed with coins, sapphires, and rubies.

"By Kumar!" I exclaimed and ran my claws through his loot. "You found all of this!?"

The fox nodded silently. He had been quiet ever since we reunited.

I suppose the slaves took freedom as a priority rather than looting. No wonder the manor had such a haul.

"Mithon," Abd's voice was raw. The fox was on the verge of tears, I could hear it, "why did you come back?"

"You foolish pickpocket!" I rapped him on the head. "After praying to Kumar, I realized that I would have to pay his priests a far greater sacrifice to make up for the fortune earned at the expense of an innocent! Far greater than the cut I would have to give to you!"

I grabbed a handful of rubies and shoved them in Abd's face.

"Speaking of which, I'm increasing my cut just this one time! If you have any moral decency, you will understand why!"

Abd smiled, "All about profit, huh?"

"Damn right it is!"

"I think you prayed to Dagun instead and he appealed to your kindness!"

"How dare you!" I grabbed another sapphire. "Make another mockery of me and I'll increase the cut!"

"First you spare me the guards and now this! You're a good jackal, Mithon!"

I threw a tiny sapphire at his forehead and he caught it in his paw.

"See?" Abd laughed. "Now you're increasing my cut!"

"Curse you!" I grabbed two more jewels to make up for it. "Curse you and go to sleep already! And use my full name, damn you!"

Abd curled up in his bedroll and yawned, "Okay, goodnight, Mithon the Kind!"

Tossing another gem at the back of his head, I cursed and rolled myself up in my own bag. I didn't bother to fetch the gem.

"I'm taking your copper ring, by the way!" I snapped.

"That's fine!" Abd laughed. "The jewels you gave me just now are worth more, Mithon the Kind!"

What an impudent fox! To accuse me of being disloyal to Kumar and his virtues!

But ah, he is still young yet, and there is plenty of time to teach him the way things are.

I just have to keep him alive first to teach him.

CLASSICAL

THE MOUSE FROM MYKONOS

HUSKYTEER

"Friends! We present to you tonight a comedy, a story of young love, trickery and deception, heartbreak and suspense, to honour the goddess Aphrodite at her festival! Meet the strict father, his handsome son, the stranger from a faraway land who upsets their ordered household, and me, Philikon, the wily slave! Cry and laugh with us, at our tale of... *The Mouse from Mykonos!*"

I bow, wave, and run from the stage into the wings. There I pull my mask off and pant. I'm not in the opening scene, so I get a chance to catch my breath and get my thoughts together.

Tonight is the night. The festival, the play, and then drinking and dancing and celebration. My chance, my final chance, to make a move on Leptos, the marbled polecat who plays the son of the family. Who's in love with a poor mouse, but his father disapproves. There's disguise and misunderstanding and mistaken identity galore, so it's lucky they have me to sort everything out and make sure everyone ends up with the right person.

Comedy is *complicated.*

Leptos is onstage now. He's telling his father, played by Ptolemas the lion, that he's going to marry his girlfriend whether or not she's low-born and unworthy of their family. It's not a huge role—Ptolemas and I carry the weight of the play—but Leptos fills it with passion. He's deadly serious, and that makes it funnier for the audience, who laugh more the more he protests the depth of his love.

I've heard his speech time and time again in rehearsal, but tonight it feels real. I imagine it's about me. Right now, his beautiful dappled coat is rubbed with yellow powder and his fluffy tail, as long again as the lithe body, is bound except for a tuft at the tip, turning him from polecat to a young lion. At the party he will be himself again.

"Akkis! Akkis? Hey, fox!"

I forget, sometimes, that my name isn't actually Philikon.

"Ptolemas." Lion mask over lion face, the features exaggerated, the mane a straggle of straw mixed with his own auburn locks. He's hoarse and panting from roaring at his stage son.

"Lot of energy out there," he says. When he sits next to me, his body is hot from working hard, and his scent is strong. I cock an ear. There are chuckles from the audience, shouted advice and yells of disapproval. The serious worship is over and they're out to have fun.

That's Big Ears, the Mouse from Mykonos himself, striding up the parodos. He's actually a rat, but he plays the part well, exaggerating his small stature, his confident walk and his enormous lies. His ego is almost that big off-stage, too.

I've been living and working with these people for weeks—years, in the case of Ptolemas; we've played opposite each other countless times—but I still get tangled in the threads of real names and character names, species and stage species.

Leptos, though. Leptos is…Leptos. The Slender One. Slinky, spotted, moves like liquid.

Ptolemas's heavy paw lands on my shoulder. It's my turn again.

On my way to the stage I nod to the statue of Aphrodite, the deer goddess, and to smiling Thalia, the comic muse, whose hedgehog prickles remind us that comedy can be barbed. This is it: my one big scene with Leptos.

SCENE: THE STREET

PHILIKON: Young master, why do you growl like an angry dog, when you are a lion?

THE SON: My mane is not yet grown and I cannot defeat my father.

PHILIKON: The 'mane' thing is, you're still on your 'feat'! You are young. There will be other girls for you to love.

THE SON: Not for me. I love this one, heart and soul.

PHILIKON: And other parts as well, I'll be bound.

THE SON: I must look after her. After all, it is not her fault that I speared her with my dart.

PHILIKON: You... did?

THE SON: My aim was true. And now, she grows fairer each day.

PHILIKON: She... does? [ASIDE] By the gods! I didn't think he had it in him. And now she has it in her.

THE SON: My love is great, Philikon, and growing greater. It waxes in secret, in the dark. It is become so large, I fear it will consume us both!

PHILIKON: All right, my lord, that's enough. If I wanted to see a picture like that, I'd go to the public toilets. But... *you* are a *lion!* And *she*...is a *mouse!*

THE SON: Love knows no boundaries, Philikon. Perhaps it is the work of the gods.

PHILIKON: Indeed. They do enjoy watching us for their sport, or so I've heard.

PHILIKON looks out at the audience, suspiciously.

THE SON: But the gods hold no sway over my father. And so I turn to you, Philikon, for help.

PHILIKON: Young master, if I were a household god, would I spend so much time washing dishes and sweeping floors?

THE SON: O Philikon, please, I beseech you! In our home you are more powerful than Zeus the bull, wiser than Athene the owl, and know more about love than Eros the rabbit!

Pause

Philikon?

Pause

Philikon? You will speak with my father?

PHILIKON: Er, yes, young master, of course! Go to your girl and bring her here. I will help you face your father. The old man never has been able to resist my tongue.

THE SON: I... didn't know that. I did not wish to know that. Thank you, Philikon! Always have you helped me, ever since I was a cub stealing honey cakes. You will be richly rewarded!

PHILIKON: And now your goal is something even sweeter than a honey cake, and more forbidden. And probably just as bad for you.

THE SON: I love her, Philikon. And nothing shall get in the way of our love!

Exit.

PHILIKON: Cubs! They fall in love as easily as they fall out of bed! But I can turn the old man around. I will receive my reward, and then I shall buy my freedom! Also wine. Lots of wine.

Exit.

"You were great," I tell Leptos the second I get off the stage. His fur is bristling.

"What made you dry up?" he snaps back at me, and I feel my tail lose its confident perk. He's tense, I tell myself. We all are. Keyed up for the performance.

"I was thinking of something else." I grab the water jug and drink deeply to hide my hurt and embarrassment.

"Well, don't think! Keep your mind on the play. Stupid though it is."

Big Ears joins us. He's the most recognised of the cast, with the longest history. It's his name that's pulled in tonight's crowd.

"You'd rather be doing the old stuff, is that it? All fart jokes and strap-on willies, and it ends with one of the gods swooping in from above to fix everything? Cheap laughs, Leptos."

"Says the man dressed as a girl."

In a long white dress, Big Ears is beautiful and perfect. You believe in him as a woman and as a mouse. He never hams it up with swaying feminine hips or little rodent twitches, because he knows the secret of comedy is to play it as seriously as tragedy, if not more so. .

"Don't speak to your betrothed like that!" says Big Ears. He gives the polecat a peck on the cheek and I burn with envy. Leptos looks stunned, as if a chorus of frogs had started talking to him. That's the thing about Big Ears: he can, and does, stay in character when he's not performing, and it works for him. The rest of us don't have the balls.

Out there, Ptolemas is delivering his soliloquy. There's a rumble of laughter from the audience; our play isn't the kind of funny that has you holding your sides and howling, more a steady flow of chuckles and groans. Light stuff, after the blood-soaked tragedy the other company put on earlier. Get everyone in the mood for a celebration afterwards.

Speaking of which...

"Looking forward to the party?" I ask Leptos.

"Oh yeah!" He gives a sinuous little wriggle of excitement. It's adorable. "All those people wanting to touch an actor. And more, if you know what I mean."

Which isn't quite the reaction I wanted.

Big Ears flaps his paw to shush us. He's waiting for his cue. Leptos shuffles closer to me and lowers his voice so the rat's famous ears won't pick it up.

"Hey. At the party. Do you think you can grab a jug and a couple of wine cups, put them aside?" He's mumbling into my ear, and I thrill at the intimacy of it. My tail starts to twitch, then swing from side to side, as he delivers his request. He wants me! He wants *me!*

"Some bread and oil, and some of those little snacky things, olives and dates?" the polecat continues.

"Of course, Leptos!" I say, too loudly, and clasp the marbled paw between my two. He springs away with a significant glance at Big

Ears, who's throwing on his costume for the next scene: when he goes to the father disguised as an old woman, pretending to be the Mouse's mother to convince him she is of noble birth after all.

There's a burble of laughter from the audience—not the good kind, when a line comes off just right, but the other sort.

Something's gone wrong on the stage.

SCENE: THE HOUSE

PHILIKON: Did you call me, o master?

THE FATHER: Er, no, I... er... About time! As you can see, the hem of my robe has become caught in the door.

PHILIKON: [ASIDE] Silly old fool! He shouldn't be allowed out by himself! [To THE FATHER, as he frees him] There we go! Naughty, naughty door! It shall be punished!

PHILIKON kicks the door. The set wobbles. The actors watch it anxiously.

THE MOUSE enters.

THE MOUSE: Ah, most noble father of the house of Leon! I have come to... what is your slave doing here?

THE FATHER: He was assisting me with an, er, intimate matter.

THE MOUSE: I shall not enquire further.

THE FATHER: He was just leaving, weren't you, Philikon?

PHILIKON: Of course, master. You're welcome, by the way!

Exit.

THE MOUSE: Anyway. I have come to assure you that my daughter is a fine match for your son. As you can see, I am of noble birth, and most richly attired.

THE FATHER: I do see. If I may say so, madam, your beauty exceeds that of your lovely offspring.

THE MOUSE: You are too kind!

THE FATHER: Could I tempt you to dine with me this evening? To discuss the future of our children, of course.

THE MOUSE: Of course!

THE FATHER: Then you will?

THE MOUSE: Oh! I meant… well, all right, you sweet thing! Tee-hee!

Exit.

THE FATHER: Goodbye! Hurry back! Philikon, Philikon! Philikon, I have seen a vision!

Philikon enters.

PHILIKON: Really, master? [ASIDE] Is the old man losing it at last?

THE FATHER: A vision of loveliness. Such a sweet creature, a beauty. Her looks have only increased with her age.

PHILIKON: [ASIDE] Help! He thinks the lady is her own mother - well, that was the plan. But this was not part of the plan at all! The old master and the young master are in love with the same woman.

THE FATHER: We shall meet tonight to discuss our children!

PHILIKON: Your... ? By the gods, he's a fast worker! First the son and now the father! That's not only forward, it should be impossible! The dirty beast! Whatever am I to do now?

THE SON enters.

THE SON: Ah, Father! So you have met my beloved's noble mother! Do you see now that we can be together?

THE FATHER: Oh yes! I can see the lady mouse is of the noblest stock!

THE SON: So do I have your blessing to marry her?

THE FATHER: On one condition.

THE SON: Oh, anything, darling Father whom I adore! Just ask!

THE FATHER: You won't mind if I marry her mother.

THE SON: ... Not that.

PHILIKON: If I might interrupt?
THE SON: Please do. Please, please, please do!

If you're educated, you'll know how the play ends. If you're not, go see it! Suffice to say that good old cunning Philikon sorts it all out. Everything neatly wrapped up, with happy endings for all. Now to make that happen in real life. No comic misunderstandings. No cunning deceptions. No reversals. Just lovely, luscious Leptos for me.

I change out of Philikon's slave garb and brush my fur where it's matted and clumped from the sweat of hard acting and all the running in and out of the last scene. When I pop my own clothes over my head it takes me a few minutes to adjust the folds—just because I'm hoping to have my tunic ripped carelessly off doesn't mean I don't want it to look nice—and by the time I'm ready, I can hear the party already in full swing.

Some of the crowd don't give me a second glance now I've changed my clothes. Some nudge each other and whisper and giggle. And some...

"I thought you were really good." The lynx leans in. "Really, really good."

"Thank you. Glad you enjoyed the play."

We manoeuvre. I want to get past, grab some food—I'm always too nervous to eat before a performance—and find Leptos, but the lynx sidles around so my back's to the wall and I can't escape.

"Can you... " There's wine on his breath and his paw finds my tunic, holding it where it opens over my chest. Like a supplicant making a request, but slipped a little.

"Can you introduce me to Leptos?" he asks. *No chance, mate. He's mine*, I think, even as I bristle over the fact that he's using me to get to the bigger star. I didn't want a fan. But I did.

I glance over the crowd at hedgehog Thalia, up on her column. She's smiling. Ha ha, comic muse. Very funny.

"Sure. Find me later, okay? I have to go and do…actor things. Um. Exercises. For my muscles. After all the acting. You know." And, just to make the lie more awkward, I flex my nonexistent biceps.

The lynx nods understandingly and lets me go. He seems happy to have been trusted with this secret of the mysterious, magical thing that is theatre.

Ptolemas, his leonine head towering above most of the revellers, is getting his share of attention. I can hear his rumbling laugh and I know he's telling stories about the theatre life, although I can't make out the words. He has fans who remember when he used to play romantic leads years ago, as well as admirers of his comedy chops. Me, I've gone from playing a young, skinny slave to playing a middle-aged, chunky slave.

Big Ears is standing on a table, swaying like a dancer. Unmixed wine goes a long way with a little guy like a rat. He's got hold of a loaf of bread and is holding it in front of his groin, waggling it about. As I watch, he lifts the back of his tunic and holds his nose.

Looks like people do still appreciate willies and fart jokes after all.

I'm scanning for Leptos and spot him watching Big Ears clown around. Fine, let him stay there while I prepare.

I take figs, ripe and juicy and suggestive, and grapes, because you can pop grapes into another's mouth. Olives because I know the polecat likes things salty. Honey because I want him to think I'm sweet.

Ptolemas glances across at me and his ears raise in surprise. "Performance took a lot out of you, did it?" he rumbles. "Or are you bulking up for your next role?"

"Just peckish," I reply, tucking a loaf of bread under my arm. We're not well-paid, and the feast is always a good way to catch up on a few meals. But this time I'm out for seduction, not a full belly. So I mix water with the wine before making off with the terracotta jug, because I don't want us to get too hammered before the final performance of the evening.

"Thanks for rescuing me in the mother scene," he adds.

"No problem." It's not like the lion to be fazed by a little thing like snagging his tunic, but improvising through these mishaps is part of acting. Keep going when it goes wrong, fool the audience into thinking it's all part of the play.

I choose a spot on the grass, below Thalia on her column, and lay everything out so it looks pretty. The wine jug, I notice, is decorated with satyrs engaging in some surprising and gymnastic, but definitely possible, acts of love. Maybe we'll start at the spout side and work our way round to the handle…

Later, later. For now, how should I arrange myself? Reclined full length on the grass? No, that's too forward. Sitting pensively with my chin in my paw and my tail curled round my toes? Surprised mid-bite, a fig held before my lips?

Leptos arrives while I'm still deciding on a pose, so I'm standing awkwardly among the good things. But I don't mind. He's here, slim body taut like a bowstring, tail free of its binding and gorgeously fluffy.

"Ah, Akkis, thank you! You're a star."

I grin. He's my star. And soon we'll be starring in our own private show. Like a true hero, I've overcome all obstacles to win my goal.

The lynx sways up to us. No, no, no!

"I thought you were really good," he says to Leptos.

Even though I'm thoroughly enraged he's shown up to spoil the moment, I manage to find a little extra annoyance that he's tried the same line on both of us.

"This is a private party," Leptos tells him.

"Oh, I won't bother you for long. I just wanted…"

He sways towards the polecat. Leptos gives him a little push away. His splayed paw leans on the pillar to get his balance. It wobbles.

We all look up as the head of Thalia, with its marble spines, teeters, rocks on its base with a scraping sound, and finally falls.

It's the god, my god, my Muse, swooping down from above to fix everything!

I push Leptos out of the way, to the ground. Thalia shatters beside us. I'm straddling the polecat, who's rubbing the back of his head where it hit the earth.

"Are you all right?" I ask. Leptos lifts a paw...

...and Big Ears takes it in both pink hands, shouldering me aside as if I don't exist. Leptos smiles bravely up into rodent eyes that are round and soft with concern. Scattered around the rat are parcels of cheese and spiced meat he's dropped in his worry. His contributions to the picnic Leptos had me prepare... for him and for Big Ears.

I back away, brushing dirt from my tunic.

From the deeps of my misery, I feel a heavy paw on my shoulder. It takes effort, but I drag my head up and look into Ptolemas's golden eyes.

"Let's get you a drink," he says, and he leads me through the excited crowd.

PTOLEMAS: There it is. Love is for golden youth, not for grumpy old men and their cunning slaves. Not for the ugly ones.

AKKIS: You're not ug–

PTOLEMAS: At least, that's the way it is on stage. Boy falls in love with girl, never with boy. To think of sex when you're old is dirty and contemptible.

AKKIS: Don't rub it in.

Pause

Oh, come on. That was a good line!

PTOLEMAS: For a comedy.

AKKIS: And what is this?

PTOLEMAS: I don't know. Not a tragedy, I hope. Or a satyr play. Perhaps it's real life?

AKKIS: It'll never catch on.

PTOLEMAS: On stage, love comes as swiftly as a lightning bolt, and stays forever. But off the stage, is it so smooth?

AKKIS: Your speech is certainly smooth, friend.

PTOLEMAS: I swear to Thalia, it is unrehearsed. And I know not if the audience I hope to please will laugh or cry.

AKKIS: Or perhaps throw rotten fruit?

PTOLEMAS: Akkis, Akkis. What I'm trying to say - I know you've had your foxy eyes on Leptos ever since the cast for *Mouse* was picked.

AKKIS: I...

PTOLEMAS: Don't try to deny it! I've acted with you for years and you never dry up on stage like that. Only love could be the cause.

AKKIS: You dried too!

Pause.

Oh.

PTOLEMAS: Yes.

AKKIS: Me?

PTOLEMAS: Yes.

AKKIS: Love?

PTOLEMAS: It doesn't come so quickly in real life, does it? But maybe it can start with…

AKKIS: … a drink?

PTOLEMAS: Play a slave and be treated as one. Play a lover and people think that you are loveable, and that they love you. I know because that was me, before I played grumpy old men. Then they realise it's all masks and string wigs.

AKKIS: And when the masks come off?

PTOLEMAS: Let's find out, shall we?

THE SATRAP'S MARK

THOMAS "FAUX" STEELE

"Chin up, Pantea. You've barely touched your gheymeh nesar." The elder Persian leopard topped off her clay water cup while glancing at her daughter from across the hornbeam table. Nearby, their servant Niloufar—a lynx in an ankle-length linen robe—busied herself packing a lunch of dimpled sangak and hard cheese. "You should finish your stew. You'll need your strength for the day ahead."

"You say that every morning, Mother." Pantea managed another bite of the repast, brilliant yellow and slightly peppery, before shoving her plate away. Her tail flicked back and forth behind her, poking through a narrow slit in the chair's backrest. Frowning, she noticed that the hackles along the nape of her mother's neck were standing erect. "What's got your coat so puffed out? You're not worried, are you?"

"You're set to be challenged today." Farva nervously drummed her manicured claws on the edge of the table, near several deep scratches in the otherwise-unmarred surface. Broad shoulders, accentuated by sharply-trimmed fur, rose, then fell as she chose her words carefully. "Need I remind you of the importance of this occasion? It is not every day that a young leopard is challenged to see if she's worthy of joining the ranks of the Athanatoi."

"I still haven't been told what this 'challenge' is." Pantea rolled her eyes as she glanced at an idol of the god Haoma, set in a place of honor beside the family hearth. He was the god of the harvest, granting strength to those whose labors fed the mighty Persian Empire and bestowing vitality upon those who ruled it. "Can't the Satrap just tell you?"

"It wouldn't be much of a challenge then, now would it?" Farva turned just enough to showcase the twisting scar running like a flowering tree branch along her bare shoulders. Devoid of fur, it served as a reminder of how she'd earned her place as an Arashshara, one of the nobles that supervised the provincial city of Hamadan. "The Satrap has spoken to your tutors and observed you closely. He will know what challenge to present you with, just as he knew what challenge to present to me when I came of age."

"Will I be marked by a scar like yours?" Pantea knew that every Anhā of noble birth earned their Mark during the challenge, though it came in many forms. "I'd prefer simple fur-paint, if it's all the same."

"Only the Inner Temple knows where and how you'll be marked. We leave that secret to the gods alone." Farva smiled softly. "Once you are marked, the Satrap shall dictate your assignment. This is the way of the King of Kings."

"Such is the way." Niloufar added. Though she was not from the imperial heartland of Mhedia, the lynx was ceaseless in her devotion to the Empire's traditions. Once a domestic slave, she had been freed by the arrival of troops under Farva's command many years ago. "The sundial has passed eight marks, mirza. You should cleanse your spirit before you leave."

"Let us all pray together for good fortune. May the light of Ahura Mazda shine on us all." Farva rose from her seat, extending her paw out with her index finger pointing downward. At her gesture, Niloufar removed a pair of prayer-rugs woven of rich cashmere from a chiseled alcove beneath the shrine. Each bore a pattern of leopard spots surrounded by delicate fronds of sacred saffron.

Pantea took a singular step onto the rug before her mother reprimanded her with a piercing glare. Releasing a grunt of annoyance through her teeth, the teenage leopard turned and joined her mother at the washing basin near the front door. Crisp, cool water flowed across a bed of weathered sandstone stone in a steady stream through a miniature qanat—an underground aqueduct. "See? I didn't *completely* forget this time."

"You must do better. A future Athanatoi must strictly honor these traditions," Niloufar admonished. "They are the adhesive that holds the Anhā together. Though we are diverse in religion and culture, we are united in our reverence for the gods of the Empire."

Farva bent over to wash her daughter's feet with a sweet-smelling elixir of ambergris blended with myrrh and catnip. Their pupils dilated in tandem as the divine vapors diffused upward. "We are a cadet branch of the royal family. This means that the Anhā will look to you for leadership. Their piercing gaze will soon lie heavy upon your brow."

"So, I'm not allowed to slip up?" Pantea groaned as her mother began to groom her like a young cub while the lynx finished the task of washing her feet. Her least favorite of the rites involved her mother stroking her barbed tongue through her cheek ruffs to smooth out any errand tufts of fur. "I'm not imbued with sacred wisdom just because I was born with the right spots."

"You know that's not what I meant," Farva replied. Stepping out of the washing basin, she dried her fur by walking across a bed of stones heated by a pipe running from the hearth. "By virtue of your birth, you've inherited a certain privilege. There is no escape from the position our heritage places us in, and it is our duty to use it to further the public good."

"Shirin is allowed to do what she wants when she's not at the training arena." Ears folding flat against her skull, Pantea's cheeks burned as she dried off before padding over to the hearth. Perching cross-legged on the prayer rug, she used her muscular tail to tilt herself forward until she reached the reverent thirty-degree angle. "Can't I have a little fun in the morning for once?"

"If Shirin ate a bowl of poisonous grapes, would you enjoy them also?" Farva poured a large measure of plum wine into a fine silver cup before placing it on an offering dish before the idol. "Sagaris are commoners—ones of high status, perhaps—but commoners all the same. They live by different rules."

Biting her tongue, Pantea bowed her head. As the youngest, it was her obligation to offer the sacred invocation. "Ahura Mazda, Lord of the Inner Temple. We pray for you to protect the Anhā. May the rivers flow uninterrupted into our fields and may our wheat grow tall. Aid us to sit present with one another, mindful of our purpose. In a world where many beasts are hungry, we give thanks for our full bellies. Remind us of the necessity of good thoughts, good words, and good deeds. Lord of the Inner Temple, hear us now."

"Good." A slight smile peeked at the edge of Farva's muzzle. "I sense that Shirin is here to escort you to the Pasargadae. The Satrap will see you once you arrive. I want no misbehavior from either of you on the way. Am I clear, young leopard?"

Pantea nodded as her gorgeous caracal bodyguard stepped into the hall. Richly oiled leather armor dyed yellow with iron oxide from Hormuz adorned Shirin's chest and shoulders. Her lower body was covered by a tunic fastened neatly at her knees, patterned with a design that resembled blooming water lilies.

"Clear as a sacred pool, Mother," Pantea said.

"Good morning, Arashshara. Good morning Pantea." After a polite bow, Shirin took the basket from Niloufar, her oilcloth cloak fluttering over well-muscled shoulders. Peeking inside a leather bag tucked into the lunch basket, the caracal grinned before popping a hunk of wild boar jerky into her muzzle. "Let's get moving, before the heat of the day sets in. Don't forget your blade...though I doubt you'll need it."

"I keep one on me at all times," Pantea replied with a wink. A flirtatious flash of her inner thigh revealed a sheathed dagger bound taut against her fur. Its leather scabbard was adorned with fine engraving depicting hunters chasing a fallow deer. "But I'll also take my sword, since you insist."

Pantea grabbed a sayf alsharqa, the short sword with a curved blade that nearly every Athanatoi carried. Wielded by an army ten-thousand strong, there was no enemy from the Balkan Peninsula to the Indus River that could stand against the mighty saber. The leopard's dexterous fingers secured it around her waist with a length of hemp cord.

"Listen, you two: I mean it this time. If I hear from the City Guard that you've broken the Satrap's peace again with your ruffian behavior, so help me, I'll tan your hides raw like you're both toddlers still in catch-cloths. Speaking of which, do you remember the time—"

"Okay, bye! Love you, Mother!" Pantea ducked out the door before her mother could once again embarrass her in front of Shirin. The young leopard had an inkling her mother had picked up on the simmering attraction and gave a coupling her tacit approval, albeit replete with playful ribbing. Slamming the hunk of beech behind her, Pantea turned to the bemused caracal. "So, straight to the Pasargadae?

"I dunno, what do you think?" Shirin said with a sly smile, glancing at the mud-tile rooftops of Hamadan peeking out beyond the walls of the interior courtyard. Sentries in sun-faded leather armor patrolled along the parapets, while a cook slow-roasted several ducks on a rotisserie for the evening feast. "We could, you know...take the *scenic route.*"

"B-but–" Pantea's eyes went wide. "What if my mother finds out?"

"There won't be many eyes on the ancient road. I'm sure we'll pass unnoticed." Shirin winked, her ear tufts perking up as she subtly brushed her paw along the leopard's flank. "What do you say?"

"I suppose if you're leading the way." Pantea relented, taking Shirin's paw. The caracal gave her palm a tender squeeze as they passed through the front gate. "Do you have our route planned out?"

"I was thinking we could stop at the market first and get a picnic lunch," she said, licking her lips with anticipation. "I heard Bijan has put barbequed fallow deer back on the menu. He'll sell out quickly, so we need to use the shortcut to get there in time."

"Do we have to? The abandoned temple gives me the creeps every time we pass by it." Pantea followed Shirin down a deserted thoroughfare half-overtaken by ferns and sedges. Invasive bullfrogs croaked from the stagnant drainage ditches that ran on their side, each choked to a standstill by fast-growing water weeds. "I feel...watched."

"It's just stone and mortar. There's nothing to be afraid of," Shirin said, pressing confidently ahead. She occasionally used the wicked edge of her shamshir to clear bits of intrusive brush from their path. Formed in the style of one of the Anhā supplicating themselves, an ancient structure of sandstone peeked out from an overgrown clearing off to their right. "See?"

"Are...are those beacons lit?" An expression of alarm raced across the leopard's muzzle as she noticed the temple's 'eyes' glowing bright with scarlet fire. Paw darting toward the leather-wrapped hilt of her weapon, Pantea scanned nervously through the foliage around them. "You're seeing that too, right?"

"It's probably just a few miscreants. Wanna scope it out?" Throwing the full force of her body behind a swing of her shamshir, Shirin slashed through a gnarled tree to clear the descent. The caracal cracked her neck, the outline of her bulging muscles visible beneath her sandy fur. "I doubt it'll be too dangerous. You trained with one of the Syaf, right?"

"Perhaps the best," Pantea replied. She drew her sayf alsharqa, the oiled blade sliding free from the sheath like a whispered threat. It gleamed bright as polished silver in the dappled patches of sunlight that broke through the heavy clouds above them. "My mother said Syaf Hafez commanded caravans across the South that stretched so far along the horizon the sun would rise and set before you could see their end. Protected by his blade, not a single shekel weight of cargo was lost to bandits."

"Would you ever want to go and see the South for yourself?" Shirin asked. Pantea knew that only a few traders seeking goods for the royal court ventured into the golden sands that separated the Empire from the rich ivory and salt of Nubia. "I've heard that out past the end of the rivers, twinkling stars glow bright over an endless sky."

"If you came with me," Pantea replied. "I'd love to see those stars with you."

By the time the leopard snapped out of a particularly steamy daydream, the pair had reached the barren floodplain that blocked direct access to the temple. Changing seasons had already brought with them a steady flow of water, sweeping across what had once been a bridge—but what was now more of an artfully arranged heap of stones—running through the center of the tributary. "I'm starting to have second thoughts about this, Shirin."

"How about a kiss if you make it to the other side?" Shirin used her natural agility to dance across the slick rocks, her feet landing with the elegance of falling raindrops. She lingered on each for but a moment, using her extended foot to propel herself forward. Pirouetting on the other bank, the caracal gave a bow worthy of a traveling performer. "Just wade across if you can't manage the rocks. I have a fishing rod in my bag to haul you out if you slip!" she jested.

"Hm...I'll take that deal." Pantea took a deep breath, gathering her courage before she hurled herself forward like a charging stallion. Less sprightly than the caracal, she used the copper-tipped claws on her feet to find purchase in the crevasses between river stones. Powerful calves held her fast against the raging stream as she took her first arduous step forward against the full strength of the current. "What I'd give to have your acrobatics right about now!"

"I wouldn't mind having strength like yours!" Shirin shouted, cupping her paws around her muzzle. A bullfrog's piercing mating call cleanly sliced her next sentence in half. "—love you! It's not that far!"

Pantea lacked the spare brainpower to reflect on this newfound advancement in their tacit courtship. Gritting her teeth, the leopard barely managed another step. Her thighs burned as she turned herself sideways to minimize drag. While an adept swimmer, she was almost certain the water would sweep her far downstream before she could paddle to the other bank. "Do you...happen to have that fishing rod handy? I could use it right about now!"

"You're a leopard. Is this the best you've got?" Shirin clapped her paws with the sharp intonation of a Syaf demanding she repeat a drill. Fire glowed in her amber eyes, a smoky warmth that radiated outward from her inner pupils. The caracal wasn't giving up on her. "Faster! Would a self-respecting Athanatoi yield to this turgid trickle?"

Shivering from being immersed up to her bust in snowmelt water, Pantea dragged herself slowly to the muddy shore. The last few strides required her to punch her crampon-like claws firmly into the slick riverbed to hold herself fast. Just as her strength began to fail, a warm paw clamped around her wrist. Shirin tugged Pantea upward as though the leopard was Reynosa, the half-drowned god whom the locals once worshiped.

Pantea rolled onto her back, every muscle in her body flexing as though she were afflicted by lockjaw. Grabbing her by the scruff of her neck, Shirin dragged her over to a lonely patch of sunlight against the trunk of a date palm. "Mm… world-class suggestion about the river crossing," the leopard gasped.

"Maybe spend a little more time on the field of branchless trees at the training grounds, huh? Leaping between poles does wonders for your agility." Shirin stripped off the larger pieces of Pantea's armor, leaving her in a pair of ankle-length long underwear. "Going across a river takes far less effort than plowing through it."

"Thank you." Pantea sighed with pleasure as the beating sun fell upon her soaked garments. She was grateful for the warmth, water droplets on her cheeks gleaming like uncut diamonds before evaporating into the parched air. "I'll have to remember that…for next time."

"Just breathe easy. I don't want you to strain yourself." Shirin tilted the spout of a wineskin into her muzzle. Bold and sharp, the unaged tangerine wine blended with water and fortifying herbs quenched the leopard's raging thirst. "Better?"

"Yeah. I should be good to move in a few minutes," Pantea replied, watching as Shirin downed the remainder in a single gulp.

"Aren't you the brave one?" Brushing aside the mop of water-soaked headfur on Pantea's forehead, Shirin leaned in close. Hot breath tousled the leopard's cheek ruffs, remnants of richly spiced jerky blending with alcoholic vapors to form an intoxicating perfume. "Even if you're not yet an Athanatoi, I think you're already up there with the best of them."

Pantea's skin prickled as warmth surged through her fingertips. She raised her head and was instantly reassured by Shirin's tender gaze. A bolt of lightning shot through the leopard's heart as she tensed up with anticipation. "Gods above, I love you, Shirin," she confessed. "Do you...share my feelings?"

"Of course, ahmaq," Shirin replied with a chuckle. Suspended in the air between them was a spark of the divine. Somehow familiar yet entirely unknown, Shirin's lips brushed against hers. Like the curved blade of her shamshir, a smile crept at the edge of the caracal's jet-black lips. "I love you too, Pantea."

Pantea flushed beneath her fur, paws trembling as they curled around tough iris stems. Any wound to her ego sustained by the river crossing was immediately healed by sharing her first kiss with Shirin. Breathing deeply, she grasped the caracal's cheeks as they rose with lips entwined.

In the distance, an ominous thunderclap reverberated through the clearing as the sky flashed white as purified salt. The sun fully retreated beneath watersmooth-silver clouds while shade overtook them. "Mm...as much as I'd like this to last forever, we should find shelter," Shirin said. "Your mother would kill me if I let her daughter get struck by lightning."

"Wait just a moment." Pantea narrowed her eyes as she scanned through the brush. She couldn't quite shake the pernicious feeling of being watched. "Do you see anything? I swore I just caught a glimpse of a goldcloak."

"No, damn it! We don't have time to see if we're being followed!" Shirin shouted while gathering up Pantea's armor. As the heavens opened, their fur was violently pounded by pea-sized hail. Drawing her waterproof cloak over their heads like an old woman's shawl, Shirin escorted Pantea across the open field while lightning bolts danced across the sky. Their feet had barely touched the cold stone of the temple floor before the hail shifted into a torrential downpour.

"Looks like we won't be going anywhere soon," Pantea said. The leopard inspected a cracked torch mounted haphazardly in a rusted iron sconce while suiting up. Constant background noise assaulted her ears, a mixture of rainfall and the scurrying and scratching of uncountable creatures that had made their homes in the temple's walls. "Do you still have your spark stones? I think there's still a little pitch left on this one."

"Of course. How could I forget them?" Ruffling around in an oil-cloth case held fast against her thigh by a length of sun-dried oryx intestine, Shirin pulled out a pair of handheld flints. "Here, give me that. I have a little kinnikinnick left if you'd like to pack my pipe."

"I'd rather wait for when we have something to celebrate," Pantea replied. "Let's partake once I earn my Mark, yeah?"

"Mm, fair enough." Flames sparkled in Shirin's eyes as the pitch caught fire. Holding the blazing torch aloft, she threw flickering light onto stone walls covered with intricate drawings, each chiseled by the paw of an expert artisan. Wind-thrashed patches of gold leaf adorned the cloaks of animal-headed figures. "What do you think these are?"

"I think they're pictographs...probably recounting some kind of myth," Pantea muttered. She was instinctively drawn to a figure of a leopard, standing alone, head raised in a gesture of ecstasy as he grasped a crimson phial. A trace of distinctive Tyrian purple remained around his shoulder pauldrons. She had only seen the color once before—in the inner halls of the Pasargadae. "Perhaps something involving the old gods?"

"It is a myth the Satrap has kept hidden from you." A lynx stepped out from the shadows, the hooded cloak around his shoulders perfectly still in the dead air. Dyed rich crimson, a pattern of dried roses adorned the fringe of the silk garment. "Though it is really less of a *myth* and more of an...instructive text."

Treating the torch like a fire-club, Shirin angled it downward as she drew up to her full height. Baring her fangs, the Sagaris interposed herself between Pantea and the stranger while a resonant growl danced in her throat. "Let your name be known. You come bearing an unfamiliar scent."

"I am Hashmed. My people once ruled the same city that you now claim as your own." Slowly coming closer, he pitter-pattered his claws on the stone wall like butcher-cracked bones falling into a rubbish pit. He exposed the sharp edge of his ribs for an instant as he turned to admire the morphemes. With his hooded face concealed, Pantea caught only the reflection of the firelight in his hazel eyes. "You look too young to have seen these lands before the conquest. Am I correct?"

"I was born after," Pantea said. Her paw darted down to grip the handle of her sayf alsharqa, only to touch empty air. Eyes widening with alarm, she cursed herself for not checking for its presence earlier. It was probably a fair distance down the stream by now. "But I was whelped on the soil upon which we stand. I am no stranger to this land."

"You are no stranger, and yet you are no friend. Would a faithful compatriot forget the gods that were once honored here?" Hashmed's voice was imbued with strange magnetism. Pantea and Shirin found themselves unconsciously matching his strides as he headed toward the depths of the temple. "I can teach you their ways...and bestow upon you the power that comes with their favor. Surely an Athanatoi of your status would desire such a bounty. All I ask for is a little something in exchange."

"What power?" Shirin asked. "There is no force greater than Ahura Mazda."

"I speak of course of an older and more potent force...that of *blood magic*." Pantea's muzzle was suddenly stuffed full of cotton as her tongue turned leaden against her teeth. It was the darkest and most savage of practices, one that the Satrap had almost entirely stamped out. "You've heard of it, haven't you?"

"The Satrap wisely guards the secrets of that dark art," Shirin said, storm clouds rising in her eyes. "One should not deprive Anhā of their lives in the pursuit of temporal power. Above all else, it corrupts the soul. The Satrap forbade its practice outside of the deepest sanctum of the Inner Temple for good reason."

Sloping almost imperceptibly downward, they soon approached the underground heart of the temple. An enormous crystal mounted in the ceiling cast feeble light upon root-studded walls. Carved from a single tree so enormous its shade would darken the White Tower of the Pasargadae, an altar stretched off into pitch black at the other end of the room.

"What if I told you that 'Immortal' could be more than a title?" Hashmed said with a silken tongue. The lynx practically purred with each syllable. "With blood magic, you can have power that even Ahura Mazda cannot bestow...that of eternal life."

"What exactly is the cost to live forever?" Pantea asked skeptically.

"Nothing of great importance." The lynx threw his hood back. His cheeks were dyed with crushed lapis lazuli, while carmine pigment shifted the fur around his eyes to resemble the hue of freshly spilled blood. "The cost is minor compared to the value of such knowledge. It is a sounder investment than taking stake in a trading caravan."

Pantea and Shirin shared a hesitant glance. "Could you be more specific?" Shirin asked. "No investment ought to be made without first doing one's due diligence."

"Let me offer my hospitality first." Drawing an enormous clay jar from beneath the altar, Hashmed filled three bronze tankards with golden liquid. "The fennec foxes of the South call this tarikh alkhumur. It's a curious drink made from dates that have cured in the sun for thirty days and thirty nights. I find the flavor to be like drinking the spirit of honey wine."

Pantea accepted the tankard, the metal cool against her paw pads. Vapors wafted upward to sting her nostrils, leaving a sickly-sweet odor lingering in her sinuses. It was far more potent than the unaged wine or small beer she usually consumed. "You drink first, stranger."

"Ha—fair enough, young leopard." Tilting his muzzle sideways, the lynx's throat bulged and receded while he took a gulp. He wiped his muzzle off with his shirt sleeve before shamelessly belching. "See? Perfectly safe, although I should warn you that the spirit of the desert sun burns all the way down."

"How is it, Shirin?" Pantea nervously drummed her paws against the side of the tankard while she observed the caracal cautiously sip. "You okay?"

"Yeah. It's quite strong." Shirin's muzzle twisted as she clenched her paws and exhaled through gritted teeth. Parting her lips, she washed the liquor down with a long quaff of water. "Far more potent than anything available at the bazaar in Hamadan, that's for sure."

"Maybe a little too strong..." Moments after taking a sip, Pantea was suddenly overcome with a wave of nausea. She staggered forward, claws scratching the altar as she fell to her knees. Bile scorched her throat as she emptied the contents of her stomach onto the floor. "Something's wrong!"

"A little henbane. Don't worry, it's not fatal," Hashmed said with a mocking grin, his eyes bulging out of their sockets as he fought the herb's sedating effects. Shirin collapsed face-first onto the ground, tankard clattering with a metallic *brrring*. The caracal's quivering paw reached for her shamshir, only to go limp just as it wrapped around the grip. "That part where you die comes next."

Pantea toppled forward, cheek resting against the cool stone. The world turned dark, echoing footsteps ringing for a moment in her ears as Hashmed approached with a binding cord in his paws. And then, there was nothing at all.

"Fuck," Pantea muttered as she came to. A length of moist hemp cord bound the leopard's paws firmly behind her back. Lifting her head caused her vision to gray out around the edges. "In the name of the

Satrap, I command you to answer! Who *really* are you!?" she yelled into the crushing darkness around her.

"I told you already. Do you think I fed you lies, young leopard?" A torch blazed to life, illuminating the cramped chamber. The red-cloaked figure bearing the light crawled forward, rich silver bangles on his wrists subtly glinting. Apple flesh loudly crunched as he tore a chunk out of a luscious red fruit. "I am Hashmed Fallingstar. It's obvious to you what the sacrifice is now, isn't it?"

Pantea snarled, impotently thrashing about. The unyielding rope held her fast, binding her to a wooden stake secured in the stone with a corroded brass pin. She struggled against the rising claustrophobia in her core, the ceiling just a few inches above the tip of her ears. "I never should have trusted you!"

"Obviously," Hashmed replied, rolling his eyes. "I must admit that I hadn't expected you two to be quite so naïve. Still...if you hadn't accepted my hospitality, I would have had to employ less civilized means to bring you down here. Perhaps it was for the best then, hm?"

"Die in a pit, grandson of a stinking jackal!" Shirin shouted as she regained consciousness. Keeling over from the henbane had chipped one of her incisors, leaving her grimace jagged and uneven. Gathering her strength, she hawked a chunk of blood-tinged phlegm at the lynx, missing his muzzle by the width of a wheat stalk. "Give me my shamshir back and I'll show you just how naïve I am!"

Rolling his eyes and snorting, Hashmed crawled to the opposite side of the room, his tail sweeping across the ground as if hunting for something. While Pantea continued to fight her bonds, he fastidiously examined the wall by scraping his claws across the mortar. After a few minutes of searching, his whiskers twitched with delight as he found a small lever concealed near the ceiling. "Do you know what this temple was used for?"

"Sacrifice. Anhā sacrifice." Pantea instinctually arched her back in anger, pupils dilating to let in more light. "That's what these stakes are for, aren't they?"

"You're absolutely correct." Flicking the lever downward, Hashmed opened the sluice gate. A stone aqueduct brought frigid water from the river down into the temple, nearly sweeping the lynx onto his side as it rushed in. Grunting with effort, he locked his claws into ragged grooves worn by those beyond memory to keep himself rooted. "I think there's time for a little history lesson before you breathe your last."

Pantea scanned across the ceiling, recognizing the outline of one of the old gods—Reynosa—carved into the stone. Trident firmly grasped in one hand, he gazed at fields of condemned Anhā staked along the banks of the Tigris River. "Good transpires for those who do righteous deeds for their own sake, not for the search of reward. Those who do evil for search of foul reward shall have divine justice brought down on them with three-fold intensity," the leopard snarled.

"Please, do not cite your imported faith to me. I do not fear Ahura Mazda's justice," Hashmed replied. "I have power even your highest priests lack."

"And yet here you are." Cool water rolled across Pantea's calves as a low-pitched grinding heralded the descent of a stone staircase from the ceiling. A small water wheel mounted above the sluice gate transferred power to a rotating shaft, each revolution lowering the steps a bit further. "Hiding in ruins and sacrificing teenagers to your petty god speaks volumes to your true power."

"Save your breath." Once the grinding stopped, Hashmed dragged himself onto the first step, only inches above the swirling torrent. "The ancient blood sages knew of a sacred alchemy that granted everlasting life so long as the proper sacrifices were made. It was the highest and most beautiful work of blood magic. Then, your Satrap came and ruined everything!"

"He knows the difference between necessary violence and self-indulgent brutality," Pantea snarled, the drowning post's splinters digging into her bare knuckles. Vision finally adjusted to the dim light, she was overcome with horror as she realized the true extent of what had transpired in this place. Judging from the pictographs adorning the walls, thousands of Anhā were drowned in this very chamber. "I'm glad he put an end to it. So many lives snuffed out, and for what?"

"I see now that you'll never understand." Hashmed laughed bitterly. "There is no afterlife for creatures like us. The gods care little for their mortal creations. All we can do is take a scrap of their power for ourselves while we still draw breath."

"It's not too late to stop this!" Pantea could barely feel her fingers as the water rolled across her biceps. Fur puffed out along the crest of her spine as Shirin violently yowled while fighting to break free. "The Satrap is merciful. He will spare your life if you repent."

"A mortal life is no life at all." Hashmed mockingly flicked his tongue over his lips. Contempt dripped from his burning eyes like rubber sap from scored bark. "Nothing will replace what was lost when the Satrap slew the blood sages, but your deaths will start to set things right. I advise you not to fight the water; just relax and take a deep breath. I'll be going now...it always turns my stomach to watch."

As the pair thrashed about in the water, Hashmed ducked through the archway at the top of the stairwell. He left them alone in the pitch-black chamber, the raging torrent swirling all around them like the raw fury of Ardvi Sura Anahita. Pantea struggled to avoid giving into the panic rising in her chest.

"Think! That's always been your strong suit!" Shirin shouted. "Is there something Hashmed might have overlooked while tying us up?"

"Can...can you reach my dagger?" Pantea asked in a moment of sudden clarity. "I think it's still bound to my inner thigh."

"Working on it!" Shirin grunted. In better circumstances, the leopard might have enjoyed the feeling of her Sagaris' paw pads stroking so close to her intimate areas. Right now, it only served to spike her almost overwhelming sense of dread as the caracal hunted for the scabbard. "Something in the scabbard is jammed. I can't pry the dagger out, so I'm going to have to cut it free!"

Searing pain shot through Pantea's thigh as one of Shirin's claws tore through her flesh while severing the cord. A moment later, the caracal used the blade to saw through Pantea's bindings. Once Shirin broke through, Pantea had to cling tightly to the drowning post to avoid being swept away. "I'm free. Now pass me the dagger and I'll return the favor!"

"Right," Shirin grunted, panting with exertion.

There was no time for Shirin to try and maneuver the knife to pass it safely beneath the water—not that Pantea could see anything through the silt. Accidentally cutting her palm on the wicked-sharp edge, the leopard freed Shirin as the freezing liquid touched the bottom of their muzzles.

"Got it. Now let's get out of here!" Shirin shouted. "You go first; I'm right behind you!"

"Thanks! Though, if I had to choose to drown with anyone…I'd choose you," Pantea gasped while struggling onto the staircase. She rolled onto her back as water trickled from her undercoat, chest rising and falling like the pumping of a bellows.

"Let's save the talk of a romantic death for after we escape, eh?" Shirin threw herself upward just as her foot claws lost traction. "Shit!"

Grunting as the current gripped her thighs, Shirin's paws fought for purchase on the slick stone. It took every ounce of muscle the Sagaris possessed just to tread water. The rough-hewn ceiling pressed against her back as the water level crested. A moment after her air pocket was extinguished, the leopard seized Shirin's wrist and tugged her from the white-headed torrent.

"Let me pull *you* from a watery grave this time around!" Pantea shouted.

The caracal collapsed onto Pantea's chest with a soft sigh. Amid the struggle, the sunlike warmth of her Sagaris' body was like fresh-baked bread to a starving man. Soothed by the sensation of Shirin's thundering heart, Pantea allowed her heavy eyelids to droop—just for a moment.

"As much as I'd like to stay like this, we should move," Shirin remarked, tenderly brushing a paw through the leopard's headfur. She began discarding her waterlogged armor, leaving only her chest plate in place. "We're not out of danger yet."

"There's no one I'd rather face the danger with." Pantea climbed to her feet, applying pressure to her bleeding paw. Though the cut was deep, she hadn't severed any tendons. "You take point. I'm not the most able fighter in my condition."

"Don't undersell yourself. An Athanatoi isn't out of the fight until their burial shroud is pinned in place." Unsheathing her claws, Shirin kept a few paces in front of the leopard. Tremors shot through her shoulders as every muscle in her body fought desperately to generate warmth. "We're in this together, right?"

"By Ahura Mazda we are," Pantea replied.

Halting at the top of the stairwell, Shirin blinked as a water droplet fell gracefully from the ceiling onto her brow. Like a capful of twinkling starlight, it streaked downward through her fur before coming to rest on the tip of her pink-black nose. "If we get out of this...maybe I can take you out for that barbequed fallow deer?" the caracal asked hesitantly.

"I'd like that...I'd like that quite a lot, actually." Pantea reached forward to affectionately caress her Sagaris' shoulder. Her trembling fingers stroked through soggy fur as her cheeks suddenly felt sunbaked. "It's a date."

"You...you weren't supposed to survive that!" Hashmed shouted, leaping out from the shadows. "You were *supposed to die!*"

Shirin barely registered the dull glint of Hashmed's weathered dagger before it pierced the meat of her shoulder. Screeching with a mixture of rage and pain, she grappled Hashmed to the ground and began cuffing his muzzle. The dagger slid out of her thrashing flesh, skittering across the floor before coming to rest at Pantea's feet.

"Now I have to get my paws dirty!" Hashed growled, fighting to put Shirin in a chokehold. "You're going to regret this, cur!"

"A little help, please!" Shirin shouted, delivering a sharp elbow to the lynx's groin. Hashmed let out an agonized screech, doubling down on his assault as he tore at her flesh wounds like a vicious oxpecker. Blood gushed through her fur as she returned the favor, claws slashing Hashmed's chest like a five-tipped sword. "Ya gazma! May the gods take your soul!"

"On it!" Before Pantea could sink her claws into the lynx's shoulder, his heel slammed backward into the center of her chest. Ribs creaked ominously as she staggered backward. Gasping for air, she was left doubled-over as Hashmed cinched his forearm around Shirin's throat.

In that instant, all the leopard's pain vanished, transmuted into the anûsiya of an Immortal. Consumed by soul-shearing wrath, she leveraged her righteous fury to force her body beyond its limits. She leapt on top of the lynx's back and began brusquely hacking at him like a training dummy. Shrieking with enough force to shatter glass, Pantea barely felt his retaliatory blows, each landing as though it were a padded sword in the training arena. "Don't you...fucking...touch...my girlfriend!"

Squirming out from beneath Hashmed's weakened grip, Shirin went on the offensive. Blinded from the blood trickling from superficial wounds on her forehead, she brutally slashed at the lynx with her natural weapons as he managed to get a bloodsoaked paw around Pantea's throat. The distinctive thudding of leather armor from somewhere down the hallway signaled the approach of others, though it was impossible to tell if they were friend or foe. "Let go of my girlfriend!" Shirin screamed.

Hashmed groaned as Shirin's index claw caught an artery in his neck. Flopping backward to smash Pantea against the hard stone floor, he rose alone as the leopard sprawled out from exhaustion. Too weary to stand for more than a few moments, he reached the opposite wall and collapsed. The crimson hue of his cloak intensified as he futilely applied pressure to his wound.

"This is at an end," Shirin growled. "Let me help you. I'd prefer you live long enough to supply the Satrap with information."

"You will never...defeat us. We will have...your blood." Hashmed gasped, light fading from his eyes like a falling star dipping beneath the horizon. His paw fell to his side, revealing a deep lightning-bolt gash across his throat. It was far too large for even spell-impregnated dressings to seal. "The Satrap....*will fall.*"

As Shirin scanned the corridor for her pack, Hashmed gasped and went limp. Placing a finger against the side of the lynx's neck, she sighed and shook her head. "Damn it. He's gone."

"Pantea...Shirin! Are you alright?" The pair gazed upward as flicking torchlight fell upon their slitted pupils. A golden jackal with a cloak the color of dried hay looked them over, bearing the leopard's head sigil of the Satrap's Guard on his pauldron. Pantea realized he must have been the goldcloak she'd caught a glimpse of outside the temple. "Thank the gods, you're safe."

"Forgive my transgression, Commander Esmaeili," Shirin bowed. "I did not mean to place Pantea in danger."

"There is nothing to forgive." Escorted by two more golden jackals, the Satrap—a great leopard clad in armor of the finest bronze—stood clear and bright as the moon on a cloudless night. He seemed to radiate mystical power, his golden eyes subtly glowing like the gills of a jack-o'-lantern mushroom. "Commander Esmaeili alerted me as soon as you disappeared into the Temple of Reynosa. Fortunately, it seems our intervention was not needed."

"I was...unable to interrogate him before he passed," Shirin said, glancing at the leopard beside her. "I was too focused on protecting Pantea."

"You fought valiantly," the Satrap said, voice layered with fatherly warmth. "Let Commander Esmaeili tend to some of your wounds while I speak to your Immortal. It appears that she has earned her Mark."

"Yes, Satrap," Shirin replied, slumping against the wall. "That sounds...wonderful."

"I must seal your Mark while the cut is fresh." Towering over the teenage leopard, the Satrap had to squat down to brush his enameled claws across Pantea's forearm. They came to rest on the wicked gash on her paw. "Earned in triumph, the scar from this wound shall mark you as one of the Athanatoi. Though this is not the challenge I prepared, it was a worthy test of your mettle."

"Thank you...Satrap." Pantea struggled to remain upright. "I'm ready."

The Satrap drew a dagger lightly across his forearm. Murmuring a rich and melodic incantation in Farsi, he mixed his blood with a sacred blend of herbs and the ground leaves of the hemorrhage plant. The leopard spread it across Pantea's laceration until it was completely covered with a sienna-brown paste. "Rise, blood of my blood and servant of the King of Kings. You fought valiantly against a foe I thought long vanquished. In doing so, you earned for yourself the status of an Immortal. Wear your Mark with pride, Pantea Zaman Immortalem."

Pantea basked in the glow of triumph as a rush of endorphins surged through her mind. Her eyes widened as the Satrap stripped the poultice away to reveal a gleaming scar across her palm. It was a Mark exactly like the one her mother bore. "T-thank you."

"If you would excuse my impertinence...who was he, really, Satrap?" Shirin—now covered in linen bandages—stood up and coughed. She threw her arm around Pantea for support as her left knee gave way. "He tried to kill Pantea. I need to know if she's still in danger."

Readily bearing her weight, the leopard sighed as Shirin's warm body pressed close against her side. "If you're comfortable sharing your wisdom, Satrap," Pantea respectfully added.

"A great civilization existed here before the Empire. They were practitioners of a twisted form of blood magic. By drawing vitality from those they sacrificed to the gods, they believed they could bestow upon themselves unnaturally long lives." The Satrap shook his head. "Though I have researched blood magic, whether such advanced techniques were real or merely superstition, I cannot say...but this lynx obviously believed in the myths."

"So, using our blood—" Pantea gulped nervously.

"He hoped that he would have enough power for a spell of substantial strength. Fortunately, he picked a capable Immortal and

Sagaris. Many others in your place would have drowned in that chamber." The Satrap gazed at the swirling waters, now even with the top step of the stairwell. "I will have this temple sealed once Commander Esmaeili oversees a full search of its corridors."

"Let us leave our marks, then." Picking Hashmed's dagger up from the floor, Shirin roughly scratched their names into a patch of wall that had been worn smooth by the touch of thousands of worshippers. Once she was satisfied that the engraving would endure the ravages of time, she sheathed the blade and presented it to her Immortal as a war trophy. "There. Now a part of our triumph here will endure."

"As it should. Still...this is no place for you two to linger." The leopard's face brightened as he gave Shirin an approving nod. "You defended her well, Sagaris. I sense much fire in your heart."

"I was only doing my duty," Shirin said, turning to meet Pantea's eyes. The caracal traced over every detail of her delicate emerald-green irises for what seemed an eternity. Suddenly, Pantea felt like stripping off her waterlogged armor as her skin once again prickled with heat. "You have my word that I will give a full report to Commander Esmaeili once I escort Pantea home, Satrap."

"I will look over the cuneiform once it is prepared. Did this lynx say whether he conspired with others?" The Satrap shared a concerned look with one of his captains, a tall golden jackal with henna-dyed fur on his wrists.

"Unfortunately not, Satrap. If there is a conspiracy afoot, he made no mention of it. I—" Shirin grunted as she suddenly keeled over. Only Pantea's quick reaction prevented her from plunging onto the hard stone. Though she was freezing and exhausted, the Immortal somehow found strength enough to bear the caracal's weight. "I need to help with the search."

"You need to rest," the Satrap said, applying a potent healing spell to the wound on Shirin's shoulder as he met her gaze with stern eyes. "Let me take it from here. There's nothing more for you to do but see Bahram, my Master Healer. I don't have strength enough left to mend all your wounds," he said, taking the arm of his captain for support.

"Satrap, I—" Shirin grunted.

The leopard turned to Pantea with the look of a parent telling their cub to eat their ab-doogh khiar on a hot summer day. "Please, escort Shirin there at once. I'll have one of my goldcloaks meet you there to offer you his sword until Shirin's injuries have fully mended."

"Thank you, Satrap. I think I can manage that." Pantea lowered her head with an exhausted sigh. "Will there still be an official ceremony?

"Yes. In a few weeks' time, a clay tablet from Persepolis will arrive bearing your commission. From there, you will travel south. Word has reached my ear of darkness stirring somewhere beneath the desert sands. Perhaps it is related to what transpired here today."

"May I take Shirin with me?" Pantea asked, trying to conceal her excitement as Commander Esmaeili returned with Shirin's battered pack. The Satrap tucked something inside before slinging it over the caracal's back. "Please?"

"I will recall her from the court guard. You will need one skilled in arms to escort you through such treacherous lands." The Satrap held a small gold phial beneath the tip of Shirin's muzzle. After taking a deep whiff of the vigor salts, the caracal groaned as she managed to stand under her own power. "Now, get going, while you still have strength. Do look after her, young Immortal. You two make for a fine partnership.."

"Thank you, Satrap. I am ever your servant." Blushing beneath her cheek ruffs as she slung Shirin's arm over her shoulder, Pantea helped the caracal limp to the end of the hallway and into the warmth of the late afternoon sun. They collapsed together, back-to-back, against a date palm tree. "So...a journey to the South together, huh?"

"Gaze at the stars while holding paws?" Shirin cocked an eyebrow as she examined her pack. Nestled at the top was a large beeswax pouch embossed with the Satrap's seal, completely stuffed with still warm barbequed fallow deer. She cocked an eyebrow before cracking it open. "I guess this counts as our date, right? I just wonder how he knew."

"He is the Satrap, after all. His wisdom is legend. And just for the record...I think it counts." Leaning in close, Pantea's lips caressed the cheek of her Sagaris as her heart filled with the purest love of youth. Rich spice blossomed across her tongue as she popped a hunk of meat into her muzzle. "I can't think of another way I'd rather have earned the Satrap's Mark than fighting alongside you."

"The pleasure is all mine, my Immortal." Shirin leaned in close, and once more, Pantea's lips met hers under the warm sun of the Persian Empire.

A PERFECTLY NORMAL DAY

KAYODÉ LYCAON

The sun is rising from the swelling ocean into a blue horizon streaked with wispy clouds, and a warm, salty wind ruffles though my ear tufts. Before me, the city of Portus Agrillae Rubrae sprawls out from red hills, gently sloping towards a stone-walled harbor; A sea of red tiles glowing in the sunrise.

It's going to be a beautiful day.

I imagine myself master of the world—Primus Marti the Wise. It would be easier if I wasn't six flights of stairs up a building halfway up Ibex Hill. Being able to see the Arena so far in the distance isn't exactly prime real estate. Not that anyone would make a caracal master of anything—we aren't native to this land.

While it's not prime real estate, this neighborhood is respectable. The temple of Ithou, the eight-horned oracle of waters, is at the top of the hill, next to the second largest of the city's five mountain aqueducts. The prestige of having an important temple in the district inspired the local magistrate to tile the streets and ensure all the buildings have bases of stone. The upper wooden floors may creak and sway in the wind, but they don't crack and pop like some places I've lived.

I hear a click of claws behind me and I swivel an ear. Long strides step carefully from support beam to support beam to avoid the wood creaking. With a little more care, the footsteps would be completely silent.

"Hey Kobi," I say without turning my head.

The painted wolf sits down beside me and leans back on his paws. He kicks his legs back and forth like he's on the side of a pool, fidgeting. My best friend and roommate is fifteen years older than me and comes off about fifteen years less mature.

"Whatcha up to?" he asks.

"Enjoying the sun. Having delusions of grandeur." I smile and look at him. "The usual."

"Sounds about right. Yup, yup," Kobi chirps. "The people's man, Marti Short-tail. Promise all the stars in the sky; take them for yourself."

"I'll split them with you, 80/20?"

"So generous." He places something hard against my neck, right where my spine meets my skull. "Better deal than yesterday. Yup?"

"Well," I drawl, trying to hide the shudder going down my back. "I suppose I could be a bit more generous to a friend, given the incentives."

"Smart kitty." He scoots back to kneel slightly behind me. "Comb your back? You missed some spots."

I smile. "Thanks."

Kobi gently runs a comb through my fur—each stroke economical and precise. "You're buying dinner. Yup?"

"South dock plaza?" I offer. It's almost all the way across the city from here but there's an otter who sells crispy fish with black pepper.

He doesn't answer right away and I can feel the painted wolf tilting his head. "Bit far. I'll be working near the Arena."

"You're a good runner and it won't be busy that late."

"Okay," he says quietly. "Dinner at the plaza. You can invite Lia to dinner, yup?"

My ears freeze for a moment before I force them to relax. I turn and look over my shoulder to smile at Kobi. "Sure. I'll ask her as soon as you're off to work."

The tiger used to be our roommate and I'm on good terms with her but she found Kobi to be a bit too eccentric. Which is kind of sad because my friend has a bit of a crush on her. Probably for the best—never mix roommates and romance.

"Do you have any plans?" Kobi asks.

"Not really." I don't have a steady job. Most of the time I wander around. I know where every bathhouse and theatre is in the city, but I usually stay clear of the nicer districts. "Maybe I'll go to Domus Libri for lunch and a bath."

He finishes combing my fur and nuzzles me. "Sounds delightful. Stay safe today. Yup?"

"Yup," I reply, mimicking him.

After Kobi leaves, I hop down to our small apartment. It's not much more than a place to sleep and keep a few things but it is plastered and painted a wonderful sky blue. Kobi tried adding some green vines a few weeks ago but he isn't an artist.

We don't have a bed, just a mat and soft bedding for the floor. Right now they are hung up to air out on heavy lines running just below the ceiling.

The shelves don't have much clutter, just my shrine to Ithou and some overpriced figurines Kobi bought at the Arena. I think they are tacky, but Kobi pays the rent and he can spend his money however he likes.

We're not rich, but neither are we destitute. When I have money, I buy things that will last. When I don't, I go without. When times are lean, the market to the east has good deals—good bread, decent oil, and fresh hummus. When times are good, we dine on the plazas. Times aren't great right now but we can afford it once in a while.

I dig through my chest and check a hidden compartment. Coins clink as I count them. Not a lot, but definitely enough if I'm careful. I place a few in a pouch and then look at my shrine. Kobi asking to have dinner with Lia is unexpected. Definitely a day to check omens.

I collect a dozen wooden dice of various colors. Then I touch a paw pad to the chest of the bronze-plated ibex with eight horns fanning out from the back of her head. She isn't one of the great gods but she has been good to me.

"Guide me true," I pray and roll the dice in the sunlight coming through the window.

The dice start ominous, but become strangely specific: expect trouble, stay away from home, dress nice, and bathe this afternoon. My tail flicks. Time for a trip to the temple.

I listen to the omens and pull out a knee-length sleeveless green silk tunic with silver embroidery. It is one of the nicest things I own and by far the most expensive. The generous pleating hides tiny pockets on the inside and the arm holes are a bit longer than is currently fashionable.

From a hidden panel in the side of my chest, I withdraw four slender knives, balanced for throwing. I tuck them neatly away so they won't be visible. Then I wrap a narrow leather and gold belt around my waist. Enough to be fancy, not enough to be distinctive. A proper outfit for any modestly wealthy merchant.

I settle a hooded cloak of the same fabric on my shoulders, lace up my sandals, and step out the door with a smile. Trouble better be prepared for me.

I walk lazily through the narrow streets lined with tall, utilitarian apartments. The lower floors are bare gray stone and wooden upper floors are pink-tinged whitewash with brown painted window frames. A few open doors show more brightly painted rooms like mine. I pass three more buildings until the tiled side streets connect to the cobblestone main road.

On Ibex Hill, the houses and shops along the main road are brightly painted and folks of all kind can be found. Most of them are herbivores, but there are a few felines. I'm not the only one with ear tufts.

At the top of the hill, tiny shops make a ring around the sheer stone walls of the temple. People of every species, a few from other lands, pray before the murals of cresting waves. The Oracle of Waters is the only temple of Ithou outside of the mountains and Portus Agrillae Rubrae is the only city to which her waters flow. There is never a shortage of worshipers.

There are many petitioners are waiting ahead of me but my silk tunic allows me to wade through the crowd and enter under the leaping dolphins of the west gate.

Inside the walls, the Oracle of Waters towers over the courtyard. Geysers of water, rendered in stone, hold up the roof of horn-gray tiles. Green, rusted bronze heads of the eight-horned Oracle adorn the corners of the roof.

The murmur of conversation is surprisingly quiet inside the walls. No one wants to draw attention to themselves, lest one of the younger acolytes turn them away. Refusing to leave invites being cursed with bad omens. Then the other petitioners start throwing rocks.

I confidently step towards the moated waiting area for those better dressed than I could ever afford. The ibex and hare who guard the bridge wear the green robes of senior acolytes. The hare's ears straighten and she looks sternly in my direction.

For the wealthy, one traditionally brings a clay token marked with the specific service requested. They are usually purchased and signed in advance. I reach inside my tunic and pull out a stamped iron token and a small copper coin.

I bow and hold both out to the hare—token on top, coin hidden underneath.

"I am willing to wait for Caius if he will be available soon," I say in a low voice. Asking for someone specific isn't unusual, the coin is.

The hare makes no effacing gesture and takes my petition with a curt nod. She must feel the coin but does not react to it. Bribes are common and, while considered poor taste, they are still discreetly accepted as long as no one is looking.

I wait outside the moat, keeping my ears relaxed and tail still. A few minutes later, a young brown bear emerges, wearing a closely-wrapped red robe that only covers his right shoulder. He gestures, inviting me to follow him through the temple's bronze-plated doors.

Inside, water gurgles and splashes from fountains on either side of the main hall. Behind a large altar and through a hallway is a walled garden filled with pomegranate trees. Small, colorful alcoves line the walls. I'm taken to a white one with dark blue curtains where an ancient ibex with a broken left horn sits on a soft pillow.

Caius smiles and offers me a plain cup of cold water fresh from the aqueduct alongside the temple. His patchy fur is gray and a purple robe covers both his shoulders. My token lays on the short table between us.

"Good morning, Most Honorable Caius," I say with a brief bow.

"Good morning," he replies warmly with a deep voice worthy of his wisdom and age. "What troubles you so early this day?"

I smile and take a swallow of water before repeating the omens I've read and lay out my plans for the day. After he rubs his chin in consideration, I ask my first question.

"Should I invite Lia as Kobi asked?"

Caius' ears flick and he chuckles—almost a laugh. "Do you truly need me to read the omens for that?"

I smile and shrug with open paws. "I'm not sure where to start. If there's trouble, I'd rather not get her involved."

"Ah. I still do not believe we should trouble Ithou for this."

"Perhaps not, but I could use your advice."

"Kobi and Lai are your friends."

I nod.

"And you're worried it will be awkward."

Now I feel sheepish and look away. "That's probably part of it."

"Take an old man's wisdom." Caius smiles and takes a sip of wine from a gem-encrusted and gold-plated goblet. "She's perfectly capable of hearing your omens and making that decision for herself. Trust her to make the right decision."

I fold my ears down. "I'll do that."

"Now, did you have any other questions?" He frowns. "I would not think you'd waste my time on relationship issues."

"What kind of trouble should I expect?"

"Ah!" Caius sets his goblet down and rubs his hands together with a grin. "Now that is a question for Ithou."

He rolls a great number of dice and pulls painted tiles from a basket. For a minute, he slides tiles around until they are arraigned in five columns.

"Hmph." He runs a finger down the first column. "Help the lame debtor." He looks up. "Anyone you know?"

"No." My tail flicks then I give him a lopsided smile. "At least, not yet."

Caius smiles. "You do have a way of meeting people." He moves his finger to the left and reads the next two. "When the coin calls, does the fox hear it? Well, that's cryptic. Hmm. Do not turn down a friend for a coin." He looks up. "Always good advice."

I grin. "Says a man who has never needed a coin."

"Ha!" He smirks. "A fine point young caracal. But scoring points on your elders rarely profits." Then he frowns. "Oh dear." He looks up. "Are iron and yellow the colors of nightmares?"

"Nightmares?"

"Literally translated—which is not the same as accurately translated—the tiles say dreams of sorrow. I don't have time to go over the specifics and nuances to justify my reading of it. This is more art than logic."

I fold my ears back at his gentle admonishment. Then he snorts and my ears perk up.

"And beware the thief in the night." Caius sits up and shakes his head as he slides the tiles into their basket. "Just how many ways can you get yourself into trouble?"

"Always trying to find one more," I say with a lopsided smile. Then I pass him my empty cup. "Can you tell me anything more about the nightmares?"

"Not without doing another reading," he says cooly. "Which is guaranteed to give you more questions than answers."

"Sorry." I wince and bow my head. "I've already asked once and I shouldn't have asked again."

He nods and then gives me a warm smile. "Apology accepted, my tufty-eared son. Don't worry about it. You always bring me interesting omens." He slides my iron token towards me. "Let me know how they turn out."

The North Hill district west of the temple is somewhat less well off. The buildings are low and made of clay bricks. The side streets are dirt, compacted by thousands of feet over many years. In a few places on the backs of hills the buildings are so short you can see the vast green farms in the lowlands before the sharply rising Vetiti Mountains.

Out of habit, I keep my ears swiveling constantly, taking in the mood of the crowd as I walk down the only tiled road. I'm always looking for an opportunity to earn an honest coin or two. Unfortunately I'm too well dressed for that today and that rankles a bit.

I decided long ago that hanging around a roommate with a steady job was better than being hungry and a thief. To do my part, I would take care of the domestic work and take the occasional odd job. Kobi is generous and kind. I try not to take advantage of him.

It's not that I don't want to work or that people don't want to work with me. I'm honest and have a good reputation. But I do favors, I don't take orders. There's nothing I hate more than living on someone else's terms.

The sun is getting brighter as I finally reach the market where Lia works. This one is enclosed, with bright green walls. Wood stalls line the inside with a small, open-roofed courtyard in the middle.

There aren't enough people for it to be crowded yet and I peruse the two dozen stalls. My weakness for plums gets the best of me. I stop and pick through the selection, limiting myself to one perfect specimen. They aren't ripe enough to be sweet and soft, but I've always preferred a plum with a drier, crunchy flesh—less messy with sharp teeth.

I'm munching happily when I walk past a clothing merchant's booth. Out of the corner of my eye, I can see a tiger haggling with a short, fat marmot. I catch the marmot's disparagement of the fabric's quality and Lia's sharp, but humorous, retort about the buyer's honor. She's always been great at putting on a show—deftly separating a customer and their coin while leaving them feeling they got the better of the bargain.

I bite off the last bits of plum and step out of the market to a nearby public latrine to wash my muzzle and paws. Then I carefully work my way back in around the growing crowd. Lia's customer has left and she looks positively smug. Until I walk up.

"Good mor—" Her smile turns into a scowl and her tail lashes. "What are you up to?"

"Enjoying a fine day." I give her a completely innocent smile. "And running an errand."

She crosses her arms. "You buying?"

I look at the selection of cloth. The light blue wool is lovely—and more than I can afford right now. "Just want to pass a message."

"I have customers," she asserts. "Ask me after I'm done working."

"I'm having dinner at the south dock plaza. If you're not busy, Kobi wanted me to invite you."

She narrows her eyes. "Why?"

"Kobi didn't tell me, but the omens are ominous." I shrug and give her a lob-sided smile. "Hope you're up to letting a sad, love-struck puppy down gently. He's probably going to propose."

Lia sighs. "Fine. I'll go after I close up."

"Thanks. You're a dear," I say and turn to leave, but I get interrupted.

"Marti?"

I flick my ears and turn around to see Caelia—Lia's boss—standing next to her. The middle-aged squirrel looks uneasy. From the way she's leaning on her cane, her foot must hurt. My ears perk up as I hear Caius whisper in my ear. *Help the lame debtor.*

"Yes, ma'am?" I say wondering who she is in debt to.

"Do you have a moment?"

"Of course." I step behind the display, to the back of the stall.

Caelia doesn't waste any time and starts whispering. "I'm two days late on my tribute. Business has been slow this month."

Fuck. I hate this district. They have a Praetor instead of a proper elected magistrate and the current bastard loves to bleed his clients dry. If it wasn't for someone Lia cares about, I'd run.

I fold my ears back instead of flattening them, but I can't stop my tail from curling. "Do you have the money?"

"Yes, but this is the second time I'm late." She points nervously at her foot. "I can't walk far and I don't want to send Lia."

I grimace. "Probably for the best. I can deliver it, but only if you have the full amount."

"I do." She nods emphatically and pulls out a small box.

I motion for her to sit down on a stool, while I use a clay tablet and a stylus to count the coins and double check her sales. Thank the gods, it's all there. I promise everything will be alright and tuck the coins in a pouch. We can work out a deal later—perhaps something in blue.

To the south, the tiled street quickly gives way to a cobbled road lined with large concrete villas with high painted walls. I hesitate at a lavender villa. Its purple door displays Tatius's white phoenix. After the last Praetor mysteriously died three years ago, this district had gone from bad to worse. Well, omens said there would be trouble. I flick the hanging bell with a claw.

A tall pale red fox opens the door and narrows his eyes. Wonderful, of course it's Felix. Why did it have to be that bastard's sniveling serpent of a man.

"I don't know you," the fox says.

I smile thinly and hold up a pouch. "I have Caelia's payment."

"I'll take that," Felix says, ears aggressively forward, grasping out with his paw.

Like hell. I almost pull a knife when I remember the omens. *When the coin calls, does the fox hear it?*

I pull out a copper coin instead and hold it up with two fingers. "You may not know me, but I know you, Felix. I can smell your sticky paws from here." I pause and look him in the eye. "And it tires me to see a fig fall so far from the tree."

The fox huffs and crosses his arms. "The Praetor isn't here."

"I'll wait."

The fox yanks the coin out of my paw and points towards the garden in the middle of the villa. As he closes the door, I hear him whisper a curse under his breath. "Fucking cats."

The fox hears.

Instead of settling on a bench for a long wait, I stretch and slowly work through through my exercises. Focusing on something helps keep my mind clear. Out of the corner of my eye, I see Felix looking at me oddly. He doesn't seem one to spend time at a gymnasium and wouldn't be familiar with the latest fads among those pretending to be rich. That or my apparent lack of concern confuses him. But I knew this month's passphrase and he can't kick me out without a good justification.

When the sun reaches its height, the Praetor returns and I move to sit calmly on a bench before the back door has fully opened. Felix whispers and a small, short lynx comes into the garden. I bow and wait for the lynx to speak.

"Why isn't Caelia here herself," he asks reasonably.

"She has hurt her foot and can't walk," I reply. "I'm here to deliver her payment."

The lynx scowls and raises his voice. "This is the second time! Tell me why I shouldn't have her hanged in the plaza!"

His tantrum goes on for several minutes. At one point he throws a pot in my direction and I flinch. Tatius isn't above beating the messenger as an appetizer to his rage.

"Tell me why!"

"Sir," I say evenly, keeping my ears respectfully to the side. "Caelia has always settled her debts and been honest with you, even if she hasn't been as prompt as she should be."

The Praetor fumes silently but waves for me to continue.

"This is out of character for her and I will impress on her not to be late. You have been more patient with her than she deserves."

"You're right on that," he grates but breathes out slowly. "Do that. I will not be patient a third time."

"By your leave, I will attend to it immediately."

"Wait a moment," he says and then walks away.

I stay standing for a few minutes before he returns with Felix.

"Has she paid you?"

"After a fashion. We have agreed on a trade," I lie—kind of—she hasn't agreed to it yet but I know she will. "I would not ask for her coin given the circumstances."

"And that would be?"

"A new tunic, nothing fancy."

He nods and grunts. "You have impressed me cat. I may have need of you later." He waves at the fox. "Give Felix your name and where you can be found." He hands me a silver coin. "You will find I settled *my* debts promptly."

"Yes, sir."

I don't go back to Caelia. Instead I head towards the Swan Aquifer district and its tall stone and concrete buildings. I meander down several tiled side streets decorated with poorly-hidden, anatomically-correct graffiti. I amuse myself by guessing the species of each phallic work of art.

Just after mid-day, the streets of the city empty out and most of the shops close; even the clay pits to the east of the city shut down. Those who are sensible and not poor are eating and napping, looking forward to an early afternoon bath. Next to the white and orange Swan temple, I walk through an archway of red brick into Domus Libri. It's a thermae, much more than a simple bathhouse. I show my membership token to the mouse at the door.

Just inside, the smell of grilled meat and warm herbs fill my nostrils. I pay at the counter and leave my cloak and tunic in the dressing room.

At the center of the thermae is a broad atrium bordered with pink walls adorned with murals of athletes. The garden it surrounds is covered in soft grass, with comfortable cushions on low platforms scattered throughout. To one side, there is an open grill with a pair of lynx cooking and serving the other patrons on ceramic plates. I walk up and clean my paws in the wash basin, then accept a plate of spiced lamb and carrots.

A brown weasel waves me over as I look to find a seat.

"Marti! Wonderful seeing you here," Albus says, waving a bone towards an empty cushion. "Lounge with me?"

I smile and stretch out lazily, picking up a carrot with my claws. "Been a month. Has business been good?"

"Good enough for spring."

A dormouse in a yellow tunic passes by. He refills Albus's drink and hands me watered wine in a blue clay cup painted with nude dancing hares.

I lie back and sip the cool, refreshing wine. I like this place. There is art and whimsy everywhere. The patrons are very fit and no one is getting drunk. You have to take care of yourself to get in here. You do need to watch yourself on poetry night though—it can get quite lively—makes debate night look positively sedate.

"You busy?" Albus asks casually, but the weasel's eyes are watching me closely.

"Need something delivered?" I look up at him. It wouldn't be the first time. A discreet, trustworthy courier can be hard to find in large cities. Besides, we go back a fair bit. Reliable customers are even harder to find.

"Nothing large."

But possibly troublesome, I add mentally.

"Sure." I smile. Then I see a painted wolf walking in with little more than a red cloth loosely around his waist. My ears flick. What's Kobi doing here? I make a quick decision. "Ah. I have a bit of a prior... engagement. Would tomorrow work?"

"It is rather urgent." He frowns. "I can pay extra."

"Well..." I rub my chin and turn my head to look at Kobi. *Do not turn down a friend for a coin.* This is going to look bad. "How soon?"

"This evening?"

"I'll do my best," I say while keeping my eyes on the painted wolf.

Albus's relief is audible. "Thank you."

"No problem." I take a sip and look back to give Albus a sheepish smile. "I deeply apologize."

The weasel finally turns and sees Kobi. "Oh."

"I hope you understand."

"He's cute," the weasel comments, but I can see him reevaluating me.

"A friend did me a favor," I say with a grimace and a shrug. "Kind of stuck between obligations."

His eyebrow raises but then he gives me a small smile. "I think I can wait an hour or two."

I lean in to whisper and wink, "better make it three. I'll meet you at your place."

"Have fun," the weasel says matter of factly, raising his cup.

I touch my cup to his. "To business."

Albus snorts.

I set my plate next to other used plates on a counter and make my way over to Kobi. The painted wolf's ear turns deliberately towards me, but it's the only sign he gives that he notices me. I walk up to him and place a paw on his arm.

"Hey."

"You're here, yup." Kobi grins and I smell fish and peppercorns.

Albus is looking the other way, so I wave towards the baths without any exaggerated flirting.

"What are you doing here?" I ask quietly, keeping my tone and smile light. "I thought we were doing dinner. Almost had to turn down a job."

Kobi reaches over to tickle my ear tufts. "Later, yup?"

I flick an ear and swat at him playfully. "Paws off the ears. You haven't even bought me dinner yet."

"Touchy, touchy caracal." He all but sticks his tongue out at me.

"If you want any touchy, touchy, you'll leave my ears alone," I chuckle.

A short, tawny fox walking past us smiles and Kobi stops playing with my ears. The painted wolf's ears are perked up and his posture relaxed, but I can see the care in how he places his feet. Something has him nervous.

"You got time?" I ask.

"Plenty, yup."

We step through a red arch into the dressing room and hang up our wraps before moving into the hot bath. A ring of pale yellow tiles surround a giant circular pool. Skylights, covered with sheer fabric, illuminate the room.

Kobi eases into the pool. There is underwater seating along the edge but he heads towards the deeper center, where a large red stone flower stands on a wide green base. Water bubbles up from the flower's center and flows down across the five petals. An otter floats between two petals, letting the cascade of scalding water flow over his stomach.

Kobi and I stand halfway between the fountain and the edge. The water is up to my shoulders, but only to Kobi's chest. The painted wolf crouches and waves his arms back and forth in the water to keep his balance, so he doesn't tower over me.

The steady flow of water fills the room with the sound of spring rain on a lake. It's just loud enough to fill the gaps between conversations. No one is likely to overhear us.

"What's so important it's got you looking for me?"

"Change of plans, Marti. Are you busy tonight?" Kobi asks with surprising seriousness.

"Just a quick run for Albus," I say in guarded tones. It takes more than a little effort to keep my ears from perking straight up. "Shouldn't take me past sundown."

"Camilla has a job for us."

"Oh." I look down at my paws. Then I snap my head up to look Kobi in the eyes. "You knew." It's a statement, not a question.

"Knew it might." Kobi grins. "If not, dinner would be nice, yup?"

That's why he asked me to invite Lia. The fur on my neck prickles. Lia does not like surprises—through telling her is going to be entertaining.

"Lia is going to kill me. Well, least I wore my good tunic," I snort, "—thanks be to Ithou."

"Good omens?" He asks, stepping around me.

"Strange, but accurate so far." I turn my head to follow him. "What are you doing?"

"Rubbing your shoulders," he says as he starts kneading the muscles in my neck.

I lean back into his strong fingers and sigh. The day isn't even half over.

"You're tense, kitty." I can hear his tongue sticking out in concentration.

"You try getting omens about nightmares and then have a visit with Praetor Tatius."

He's quiet for a moment before he rests his muzzle on top of my head.

"Tell me later, yup?"

"I will."

I close my eyes, letting the heat seep into me and the bubbling water drown out my thoughts. Despite Kobi's jokes, his muzzle resting on my head is far from condescending. His presence is like a thick, warm blanket on a cold winter's day.

"I really do love you," I whisper some time later. "You're the best friend in the world."

"Love you too. Yup, yup," he says cheerfully.

My ears flick but I choose to smile while I quietly purr. Kobi's idiosyncrasies could really grate on you and ruin a beautiful moment if you let them. You have to look past them and feel his earnestness.

After a while, people start leaving the hot bath. It's not heard, so much as felt. The room seems larger and less cozy than it was.

"Should we wash off?" I ask quietly.

"Okay!" Kobi hugs me for a little bit too long—and yet not long enough.

Back through the dressing room and to right is the washing room. It's still warmer than outside but after soaking in the heat of the bath, its chilly.

We pick the right-most of the three long arch-ceilinged corridors separated by half walls of white stone. Each corridor has its own stream of water flowing slowly down a narrow, chest-height channel. There are wooden benches against the walls and ladles hanging from hooks between them.

Several bare-chested female otters in very short orange waist wraps offer us combs, cloths, and jars of oil in exchange for a coin. A private booth and more personal attention are available for few more. Kobi hands over a single coin with an appreciative smile.

The room echoes with conversation. People mingle and talk as they ladle cold water over their fur and then comb it smooth with oil, before wiping the excess away. There is always someone willing to help you wash hard to reach fur on your back. Washing rooms are a great place to meet new friends—or friendly enemies. Arguments and roaming paws are frowned on in public, so you never need to worry about someone's intentions.

My ears swivel and my eyes scan the room, searching for Albus. I don't see him. Kobi's paw on my shoulder nearly startles me.

We stop at a bench and set our things down. Kobi always starts by pouring water over his head. I don't understand it. The water, fresh from a city aqueduct, is positively frigid. I start with my legs.

Kobi's fur, like most painted wolves, is short and thin. I have thicker fur that takes twice as long to clean. I don't talk much and Kobi doesn't press me—I have a lot on my mind. Possible strange nightmares? And now a mission from Camilla? Enough to make a less confident caracal positively anxious.

Soon enough, we're both clean and we head to the steam rooms. They are more private than the bathing and washing rooms. The heat from the fires under the baths flow up the chimneys between the booths to heat them.

We find an empty booth and close the thin, translucent curtain. Before long, we're both panting as our fur dries.

"What's this job?"

"The patricians have decided Praetor Tatius needs a warning," Kobi says quietly.

"Huh. Just a warning?"

"Yup, yup."

"Good. About damn time. Why does she suddenly care now?"

"Not paying his share, yup."

"Greedy bastard. With the way he's been squeezing his 'clients', that doesn't surprise me."

"Yup."

"Since we're sending a message, can we loot the place?"

"Nope, nope." He folds his ears back and shakes his head. "Just his lockbox. Camilla wants the records. We take the rest as our pay."

I sigh and lean back. "Well, I can live with that. What happens if we get caught?"

"Boss lady says no witnesses."

"Including the Praetor?"

"Yup, yup."

"Great. Let's not get caught." I close my eyes. If we get caught, Camilla is going to deny everything. *Beware the thief in the night? Who's the thief? Me? Lia?*

"Yup, yup. Haven't yet."

My errand for Albus doesn't take long. I deliver his message to the Oracle of Waters and stop at a small local plaza on the way to Lia. The shadows are getting long—it's half an hour before sunset. I stop by a shrew under a red canopy and buy two rolls—heavy with sage, thyme, and olives. On the far side of the market an old boar is selling fried chicken pieces. I pick up three livers heavily battered with chickpea.

When I arrive, Lia is tidying up the store—folding fabrics and clothes to put them away. The tiger looks up.

"We're clos—" she stops suddenly and sighs. "Marti."

"Don't worry, I brought dinner," I say cheerfully.

She raises an eyebrow. "Thanks? Where's Kobi? Weren't we going to the plaza?"

"Turns out he's working late."

"You're joking," she says and places her paws on her hips.

"Unfortunately not." I roll my eyes in exasperation and walk up to hand the food over. "He'll join us later."

Lia accepts the food and sits on a table to eat, tail flicking. "This isn't like him," she mutters around a mouthful of roll. "So where are we going?"

"The Praetor's house."

"What?"

I fold my ears back. "We're actually meeting Kobi there."

"Are you serious?" She starts swearing, "Damn the seven fucking hells! Dinner my tail. I'm going to hang him by his toes."

My ears betray my amusement as they perk up. She really is cute when she's pissed off. Sadly she stops after a few words—she's beautifully and artistically profane in three languages when properly provoked.

"Give me the details," Lia says and then bites into her second roll.

I summarize what Kobi told me and watch her expression—it turns sour but not angry.

"You can wait outside for this one, if you want." I say placatingly.

"No. You need someone who knows what they are doing behind you." She states. Then she pokes a finger into my chest. "And you need a change of clothes."

Hours later, thousands of tiny stars twinkle in the clear night sky as we walk down the narrow dirt side streets of North Hill. We talk softly and walk slowly, like two old friends catching up.

Back at the shop, I traded my green silk tunic and cloak for dark red linen ones. There wasn't time to alter the tunic to hold my thin throwing knives, but that was only a minor problem. My belt has loops I can slip the blades of the knifes into. As long as I keep the borrowed cloak around me, no one should be able to see them sticking out.

Both of us have iron knuckledusters on strong leather cords around our necks. I would have liked a gladius or a pugio but both are heavy and difficult to hide. Hopefully, I won't need to use any weapons.

The alleys are eerily quiet as we step behind houses. When we get close to the villas, we run into guards—two mice in armor and wearing swords. They pointedly look away as we walk past.

We find Kobi hiding two villas down. The painted wolf is dirty, with soot covering his whiter patches. His scent is nearly impossible to distinguish from the reek of smoke.

"Everyone is sleeping," He whispers and gives me a knife made of wood and bone with the hilt wrapped in leather.

I look at it and feel its weight in my paw. It's fragile and close to useless as a weapon, but not all weapons are meant to kill. The official seal stained into the blade makes its message clear.

"Ready?" I ask everyone.

Lia nods. "Let's go."

Lia and I hurry across a road and down a narrow alley to the back of the Praetor's villa. The guards are missing but the servant's door is barred or lashed from the inside—not unexpected. Lia laces her paws together and I step onto them.

She uses her enormous strength to throw me to the roof. I land softly on all fours but something rattles and cracks under me. A tile slips out from under one of my feet and I land on my belly.

"Oof," I grunt and hold my bruised nose. That hurt.

To my surprise, the tile does not smash to the ground. Lia must have caught it.

I look over the peak of the roof into the courtyard below. The central garden is empty but there is a faint yellow flicker of a lamp below me. It casts long shadows into the garden as its holder walks past the columns holding up the overhanging roof.

I focus my ears forward and hear claws clicking on the tile of the floor—not a cat or an herbivore. I slip the leather cord over my head, settle the knuckleduster on my right paw. The steps sounds like just one person. Long stride. Tall? A cough. Long muzzle, wider than a mouse or shrew. Fox?

Lia hisses softly and I reply with a single bird-like chirp, followed a few seconds later with another one. There is only one person up and walking around.

The shadows shift and I slide to the inside slope of the roof. The person holding the lamp is behind a column. I drop to the ground, using the edge of the roof to slow my fall. I land on my feet with barely a scuff. I risk a peek around the corner. It's a fox—a very familiar fox—Felix. What's he doing here at night? Fuck. *Beware the thief in the night.*

A quick glance around confirms no one else is near by. Felix's back is facing me and I'm in his shadow. The cloak slides easily off my shoulders. There is no way I can get back to the roof on my own—I'm committed.

I crouch and pull my right fist back. With a single step, I slide out from behind the column. With my left paw in front of me, I leap into motion. In three steps I'm behind Felix. I grab his neck and swing to hit him behind his right ear. Iron cracks against bone and the base of the knuckleduster thumps into my palm.

The fox drops to the ground, senseless. His muzzle lands in pool of oil next to broken shards of clay. I stamp a foot on the wick before it can set the oil on fire and bite my tongue as it sizzles against the pads of my foot.

I hurry to the back door and lift the wood bar to let Lia in. The tiger steps in with fluid grace. We tie Felix's paws behind his back and gag him with strips of his shirt.

The villa is a sprawling building, not quite a palace. I pass room after room with Lia carrying Felix close behind me. Behind a red door with a phoenix crest, we find the Praetor's office. Lia ducks in and lays Felix on the floor. I head towards a hallway at the back of the house. It leads to a small courtyard with a fish pond at its center. Around the courtyard are small rooms. I press my back against the wall as I hear heavy breathing and grunting. After a moment, I realize the two people behind the second door to the left are very occupied. I dart past and find the central door on the back wall has a gold seal nailed to it.

I put an ear to the door and hear nothing. I slip a throwing knife into my free paw and use the other to open the door. Wood scrapes across the stone floor and I wince.

Inside, I find Tatius. The lynx snores softly—and thank Ithou he's alone. I ease my throwing knife back into my belt. Then I pull out the bone knife and set it next to his pillow.

The door closes easily and I make my way back to the office off the main courtyard.

In the Praetor's office, Felix is still out and Lia is having difficulty with the lock, swearing in a foreign language. The harsh, guttural syllables would be funny if we weren't risking our necks.

The lock clicks and Lia opens the heavy lid. It's filled with documents, jewelry, bags of coins, and random junk. I take all of the paper while Lia stuffs everything else into a heavy wool blanket and rolls it up. Two thick belts cinched tight keeps things from shifting and making noise.

We hug the walls and walk out, closing the door behind us.

We go our separate ways and meet up behind the market. Kobi arrives last, with a loaf of bread and wet but otherwise clean fur. Lia lets us in and drapes a thick cloth in front of an empty stall to hide our lamp.

Safely concealed, we unroll the blanket. To my disappointment, much of the jewelry is unique and will need to be fenced. The coins though, are gold. Totaled, it's about seven years of Lia's pay for each of us. I should be excited but I feel sick to my stomach.

"We get to keep all of it?" Lia asks.

"Yup, yup." Kobi chirps. "Camilla says yes."

"That's the most we've ever made," Lia says.

"Yeah," I agree. Then I sit up straighter. "Eyes on the job, all. How did it go?"

"Four guards paid off. No complications," Kobi says through a mouthful of bread.

Lia looks at him and sighs. "Don't chew with your muzzle open."

"Sorry," Kobi says, spraying crumbs.

"Gods, you are hopeless." Lia smacks her face with her paw and then looks at me, hiding her smile. "Damn that rusted lock to the seven hells."

"I had some complications. Door was barred. Tripped on the roof and knocked a tile off, nearly gave us away. And I caught Felix walking around."

My stomach twists and the thump of Felix hitting the ground resounds through my ears. Hitting someone hard and accurate enough to knock them out is difficult. Felix's brain had to have rattled against his broken skull. He was breathing when we left but not well. We shouldn't have left him gagged. He'll probably live, but being knocked out that long isn't good. He may be crippled for life.

"Knocked him out with one blow. Just about perfect." I swallow and try not to choke. "He didn't get up."

Lia pats me on the back and then tries not to growl. "No need to shed any tears for that monster."

"Yup. Consider it a public service, yup."

"I guess," I say quietly. "Everything else went well."

"Successful mission," Lia says, leaning back and stretching. "We're getting too old for this."

Kobi frowns. "You're not even thirty yet."

"Too old for this." Lia repeats slowly.

"Leave it," I say softly. "If Camilla calls, we should answer. She's been good to us. Unless you all want to go back."

"No. You're right," Lia says.

"Good deal, yup. We're free, we have food, and we have favors to call on."

"Alright," I say, "let's call it a night."

Lia rolls up the blanket and hands Kobi the papers. We walk out and Kobi and I walk quietly to our apartment.

Once we're back home, Kobi lays out our mats and bedding while I hide the papers in the bottom of my chest. Then we curl up under a large blanket.

Kobi wraps his arms around me and rests his chin on my head. He's asleep almost instantly but I stay awake. I can't stop seeing the flickering yellow light of the lamp as my iron-clad fist swings. Iron and yellow are indeed the colors of nightmares.

I live my life by omens. Today, they were all true and I'm home safe. I'll have nightmares about Felix for a long time, but they should fade. Other nightmares have faded before.

I close my eyes and tell myself tomorrow will be a beautiful day.

THE MERCHANT AND THE MARTYR

CASIMIR LASKI

Kato the mink was not much for prayer. Or, perhaps more accurately, prayer was not much to Kato. And so he let himself drift with the tide of the crowd, feeling the eyes of the gods bearing down upon him. Blank and lidless, they gazed at the mass of long-tailed, furred bodies before them, a dozen marbled forms standing in frozen vigil around the circumference of the temple's central chamber. The twelve Numenarios, chief deities of the burgeoning Tiberian Republic, imports from the Elladene. At their feet, hearth fires burned low, ever-hungry for offerings. But when Kato dared to meet those eyes, expecting solace or condemnation or even simple, unbridled arrogance, this time, he found only cold stone.

To Kato the gods were, in essence, simply another step beyond the earthly rulers who governed his life, and worship, therefore, was a natural, if rather dull, affair. When a merchant like himself desired connections in Istria, he was obliged to invest some of his wealth in the port city's aristocracy—and seeing as commerce was the domain of Parassus, an offering to the god was a logical part of the whole affair. If building rapport with the local magistrate was an obvious step for someone likely to become entangled with the law, was it not likewise sensible to pray to Korastor, father of the gods and patron of justice?

At the end of the day, it all came down to simple economic calculations, a field he was rather well versed in: He had needs, and they had power. As so, in service of time-honored instinct, he turned to those beyond himself.

From her place upon the central dais, the violet-robed form of the Sacreda led the procession, attended by several slender priestesses clad in glistening white. "And so gathered today we beseech you, Korastor and Mayka, heavenly father and mother, and all the Twelve Most High, bestow your blessings upon us, upon the Republic, and upon our consul, Lykeno Aventius Callidenus, that you may guide his paw and illumine his heart." As one the crowd, kines and does, kounavi and kisenos, patrician and plebian, answered in affirmation. Kato remained silent.

Lykeno Callidenus, the general-turned-politician, was proving even more troublesome in his third term as consul of the Republic. "The Wolf," as he was known to follower and foe alike, continued to consolidate power in an ever-smaller number of offices, guiding the waves of plebian discontent that had gripped the city against the aristocratic foundations of the Senate. And with every reform, every transfer of authority to some new office in the clawed grasp of the consul, Kato's own losses and debts mounted.

Once more, the mink reminded himself that the pact he had bound himself to was necessary: for the good of the Republic, as much as his own household. He stifled the ghostly dissenting voice that alternated between whispering doubts and shouting condemnations.

But lurking deeper, like a viper coiled around his heart, was the sting of his wife's recent betrayal: When he closed his eyes, he could still see the foreign kine's claws picking their way through Marenna's tawny coat, the doe looking more at ease on the stranger's arm than she would ever bother to by his own side, within his own home. *Their* home. An otter—and she hadn't even had the decency to attempt subterfuge.

Dwelling on it, Kato would shift from rage to grief to utter despair in the time it took a drunk to sputter out a verse of mangled poetry, but what pained him most was the steady undercurrent of empty indifference. After all, what had become of the bond they once hoped for, all those years ago? A sour marriage now as loveless as it was childless, save for the briefest span in which the gods had finally allowed their union to bear fruit, only to whisk it from them just as swiftly.

Blinking away the memory of Sophia, the mink tried once more to focus on the service. Kounavi of every race, marten and mink, weasel and polecat, joined their voices in ritualized response. Glancing around as he muttered alongside them, Kato noticed a few kisenos—non-kounavi such as otters and prokyons, and even a sand-furred mongoose clad in white robes and a crimson turban. His bitter glance at the nearest otter was followed by a flush of guilt, and gratitude that the look went unnoticed. Owing to his wealth and station, the merchant could have attended the more selective ceremonies, standing shoulder to shoulder with senators and centurions, but the last thing he needed right now was to be reminded of his precarious position.

The Sacreda descended from the dais, and the crowd parted like wheat before the scythe. Approaching the idol of Korastor, father of the Numenarios, god of law and justice, fatherhood and regency, she bowed low, draping her tail over the cool marble. Her attendants knelt beside her. With a flourish the high priestess rose, flicking something into the fire, which roared and leapt in response.

"Korastor, may your light serve as a beacon to the just, and the wrath of your flame a warning to the wicked." From here she moved on to the statue of Mayka, mother goddess, patron of families and children, and genuflected once more. "Mayka, may your love fill the hearts of all does blessed with children, and may your grace protect those most vulnerable."

By the time the procession arrived before the stern form of wise Milosha, Kato's mind had wandered to more pressing matters. He drifted on a tide of worry throughout the rest of the service, the purple Tyrene cloth he had purchased as an offering threatening to tear within his grasp. It was only when a weasel behind him began to prod hesitantly at his chiton that Kato realized the Sacreda had finished the rounds.

Muttering a quick apology, he stepped aside, tracing patterns in the cloth with his claws. It had been purchased for a denarius, a not-insignificant sum, to be cast into one of the twelve hearth fires as a display of piety. And in exchange for their blessing, of course. He had intended to call upon Parassus, swift-footed god of commerce, diplomacy, and crafters, for assistance with his business' current troubles—but as he approached the towering, slender figure, frozen in a marbled form that still somehow conveyed a sense of agile grace, Kato hesitated.

For the task that he and his comrades were undertaking, would it not be more sensible to make an offering to Korastor? If what they planned was truly just, surely the father of the gods would not forsake them?

But as he made for the northern section of the temple, where Korastor and Mayka stood side by side, looming over the mortal masses, a marten couple passed him paw in paw, elegantly dressed, their young son in tow. The mink's eyes turned to the latter statue, wondering if perhaps the goddess might be able to mend what a lowly kine had allowed to break. Or simply heal the wound that had never truly closed. Tongues of fire, fattened by the stream of offerings made by those far more decisive than he, beckoned.

Kato's throat was dry as sand, and tight as a fist. He had a greater obligation, a duty that transcended the needs of any one kine. To do what was right, regardless of the cost. For the good of his nation.

Striding to the statue of Korastor, he murmured a hasty prayer and cast the cloth before him, not even bothering to watch the flames devour it.

Shuffling amidst the throng of pilgrims, Kato trotted down the steps before the temple's vestibule, relishing the sunlight and open air. All around him, Tiber hummed with the bustling energy of the thousands upon thousands who daily strode the city's streets, kounavi and kisenos alike flocking from every corner of the world to share in the rising glory of the maritime Republic. Of the former, the mink spotted a number of his own kind, who per the nation's abstruse codes ranked below martens and above weasels in general social standing; many of the latter, he noticed, appeared to be servants or slaves. The only other kounavi, polecats, were likewise in abundance, their distinctive red coifs marking them even as they mingled with the other races.

There were, of course, plenty of kisenos as well: those distinctive enough from the musteline races to warrant their own grouping in the eyes of the law. The mink spotted otters hawking their latest hauls from the sea beside stout, grey-furred, ring-tailed prokyons, expert crafters whose dexterous paws were ever sought-after. A party of lanky viverrids, clad in exotic robes of lavender and pale yellow, marched alongside a wagon loaded with spices from the east, the roe deer that pulled it taking in the fervor of the markets with the dull, wearied gaze of a lesser beast.

As Kato made his way down the main thoroughfare, merchants bartered and haggled in every language he could think of, the familiar and the alien swirling in discordant symphony: the mink heard the staid tones of his native Tiberian tongue laced with the graceful inflections of Elladian; the gruff, stone-hewn syllables of the northern barbarians clashing with the liquid lilting of the Levant; all of it underscored by the chittering of polecats. Pausing beside a fruit stand, Kato bought an apple for a half-eram, tossing the slender copper coin to a golden-furred mongoose whose rose-colored eyes did all the talking necessary. In the shadowed alley behind the stall, a pair of feral foxes yikkered over scraps.

Where the street opened even wider into a square adorned with fountains, a pair of magistrates and a small contingent of legionaries worked to snare passersby with generous enlistment bonuses. As Kato strode by, his ears caught mention of Khemmet, the breadbasket of the eastern Mediterranean and clear object of the current consul's envy. The rewards of two years' service, he had to admit, were reasonably tempting to a kine of lesser station. Though with any luck, and the gods' blessings, the Wolf would not live to wage this latest war.

The mink was halfway across the square, and nearly to the Forum, when he spotted his first street preacher of the day: a mongoose doe, clad in a rough grey tunic, her golden fur blazing in the sunlight. A Jakastrian, Kato figured, or perhaps an adherent of one of the Chashemite sects—these days, new prophets were cropping up like weeds after a spring rain, and always with the grandest claims of understanding.

It occurred to the mink that, strange as it might seem, his own line of work had revealed the greatest of truths. The philosophers of the Elladian city-states could engage in endless debate between the rigid code of the Stoics and the carefree indulgence of the Apathetes; priests might pronounce the will of the gods while the initiates of the mystery cults claimed to have divined the secrets of the universe, but Kato knew better. As it turned out, the world operated according to two fixed principles.

The first was that everything had a price. From the oceans of grain that fed the Republic to the vessels that daily plied the Mediterranean to deliver it, and from the innumerable slaves who passed through the markets of Tiber, destined for domestic servitude or the brutality of the mines, to the very hours of a citizen's life given freely in paid labor, Kato had long ago learned that the question of cost was never *if*, but *how much*.

The second principle was that said prices depended on the circumstances. Typically, in the capital, a loaf of bread would go for a single copper eram, but any number of complications could shift the price: Following a bountiful harvest, a half-eram might suffice; should safe passage be threatened on the roads or sea-lanes, or tariffs be levied, the price might double, or triple. Kato had heard that during the three-month-long siege of Sikelia, the cost of a single loaf within the walled city had risen to nearly a denarius—a full day's wage for a common free laborer.

Likewise, wages themselves were never fixed: A kine might earn far less than that during a surfeit of cheap labor, or significantly more if his particular skills came into demand. A soldier's life might be weighed alongside ten thousand of his comrades against the security of a trade route, or the bounty of a fertile borderland; a thief branded and condemned to slavery, fattening his new master's coffers in the mines of Iberia or Pannonia in exchange for the simple reward of survival.

And perhaps, in very certain circumstances, the liberty of a nation might be purchased for the life of a single kine. But that, as with all things, depended very much on factors well beyond Kato's command. The task of a merchant was far less about exerting control, and far more about divining the countless currents that flowed invisibly through daily life, then navigating them as best you could, all the while praying they would not dash your fortune upon some unseen shoreline.

The preacher's voice, rising over the crowd, cut his thoughts short. "The gods of Tiber and Elladios, of Khemmet and Saarenia demand tribute in exchange for their blessings, and you bow before them as a servant before a capricious master. But the true God, our Heavenly Father, has already given us more than we could ever hope for: redemption, through the death of His Son, Yesha Kyrie, offered as ransom for our sins."

Struck by an unnamable spark of curiosity, Kato settled against a trickling fountain to listen while he finished his apple.

"The philosophers speak of the true source beyond the gods, the eternal Logos, as a force uncaring and alien—but I tell you that this very Logos was incarnate in mortal flesh as a lowly kine, to suffer and die so that we might be exalted. Now, through Yesha Kyrie, history has been fulfilled, and our fallen nature redeemed. The Kingdom of God is at hand, and all have been called to join…"

Her voice blended into the din as Kato continued down the street, tossing the apple core aside. He'd heard plenty of mention of the Kyrienites, especially in recent years—adherents of some Levantine prophet martyred a few decades back—but never bothered to learn more.

Before him towered the splendor of the Forum of Kaius Aurelius, first consul of the Republic, deposer of the last king of Tiber. Several vigiles, kines of the city watch, milled about in the shadow of its colonnade, their woad-dyed tunics showing sky blue beneath maille coats. Feathered plumes of crimson sprouted from the leather galia atop their heads, bristling in the light breeze. Most were minks, like himself. Further from the Forum's steps, a large crowd of ordinary citizens had assembled, and though they remained conspicuously quiet, the mass of bodies—mainly weasels—simmered with resentment.

Pointedly ignoring them, Kato strode forth, receiving little more than a glance from the nearest guard: sessions of the Senate were theoretically open to all free kounavi, though entry could be denied at their discretion.

From the interior of the Forum's arcade, Kato's ears caught echoes of formless speech, punctuated by pauses and jeering, shouts and applause. A few figures clad in chitons or togas stood aside, conversing in whispers beneath carvings of decade-old victories or long-dead senators. Most paid him no mind, though one young marten shot the mink a glance laced with suspicion.

As the din steadily grew louder, the powerful voice of the consul cut through the others, the words themselves still indecipherable. Kato halted a moment, breathed out deeply, and then stepped into the vaulted semicircular chamber. Beneath the central dome, rays of sunlight bathed the Republic's ruling elite in the light of high noon, leaving the observers on the periphery in the shadow of twilight. Within a ring of exquisitely carved pillars, the floor dropped away in three tiers, each ringed with a row of high-backed wooden chairs, before rising again to form a dais, upon which rested the consular throne.

Its current master, Lykeno Aventius Callidenus, towered just before it, the marten's toga fringed with golden borders, his rich brown coat burnished where the sun graced it. The golden laurels signifying his rank, resting between his tufted ears, glinted with its fire. In his paws he gripped the Aurelian Rod, chief symbol of his office, said to have been forged from an artifact of the long-vanished Ancient Ones. By his side lingered two other figures, each clad in the crimson-bordered togas of senators, while a similar figure stood at the foot of the dais. Kato knew one of the former to be Senator Talinus, stalwart defender of the consul, and his brother by marriage.

"Still debating Quintus' new proposal," a familiar voice beside him said. Kato turned to see a fellow mink, only slightly older than himself, clad in senatorial garb.

"Senator Iustares," he replied with a slight bow. The other mink scoffed.

"Come now Kato, no need to go all formal on me."

Kato gave a meek shrug. "It seemed appropriate, *here* of all places, Felix."

"Good to see you too, friend," Felix murmured stiltedly through a smirk. He began to walk, gesturing for the mink to follow, nodding to another senator as they passed. "So, how have things been?"

"Well," Kato deliberated for a moment. Like himself, Felix was party to the conspiracy—the one who had brought the merchant into it, in fact—but this was no place for candid conversation. His eyes wandered to a nearby pair of stoats: members of the Kirkassian Guard, foreign mercenaries from the steppes of eastern Epirus, summoned by Lykeno after an assassination attempt several years prior. With no ties to domestic politics, they swore unfettered loyalty to the consul, and had caused quite a commotion among the ranks of the Senate.

Felix shot Kato a questioning look. "As I was saying, they've been at it for *hours*, on raising new legions in times of emergency without senatorial consent. We were *supposed* to be debating the new tariffs on Parthian imports, but the Lexivitates were... *insistent.*" He sighed knowingly. "As they *always* are."

The mink snapped a finger, and moments later a slave appeared beside him, head bowed. "A glass of wine," he said sternly, "and one for my friend as well."

Kato raised a paw. "I'm fine, thank you."

His companion shrugged, then sent the servant scurrying with a wave. "Tell me, how familiar are you with the Kyrienites?"

"As a matter of fact, I just spotted one of their preachers on the way here."

Felix arched a brow, and, without looking, accepted a glass from the slave. "Well, there's been a bit of a stir among the ranks of the Fourth Legion. An officer, a young marten, was taken by the new faith, and now refuses to swear to Voyokan, or any of the gods save his own." The senator sniffed delicately at the violet contents of his glass, then downed a mouthful. "Ah, now, er—this convert happens to be the second son of some smaller patrician, and rather popular among his kines, though his superiors were *livid*. Patricians themselves, mostly—and from more vaunted stock than our poor convert's. So they tried to have him hanged for sedition, but the officer's father appealed to friends in the Senate."

He took another sip, deeper this time, grimacing. "And, seeing how Lykeno has been courting the masses, among whom this new faith is proving... *disconcertingly* popular, the consul has agreed to preside over the trial—here, in the Forum." Felix held his empty glass out, waiting until a slave collected it. He shot a surreptitious glance at the nearest figures, several paces away, and leaned in ever so slightly. "I take it you see the opportunity this affords." His gaze settled back upon the consul. "Were you able to arrange everything?"

"Yes, I spoke with the last of them yesterday. They will back us." Kato ran his claws through the fur atop his head, then picked at his wrist. "Or, at the very least, not interfere."

At that, Felix relaxed, letting his eyes linger for a moment on the speakers before turning. "Good. I'll inform the others." He reached out to clasp Kato's paw. "The gods are with us, Kato. The high priest himself took the signs at sunset: a flight of six vultures, westbound, followed by the call of an owl." Kato wasn't particularly familiar with the various practices of divination, but he knew enough of augury to recognize the fortune implied by the former sign, and the presage of death in the latter.

The senator strode to the balustrade, resting his elbows upon it, letting his tail swish over the mosaiced tiles with a longer sigh. Joining him, Kato recognized the figure standing opposite from Lykeno as Korvo Petronius, the black-furred patrician, head of one of the oldest and most esteemed families in Tiber. Known as "the Raven," as much for his shrewdness as the color of his coat, he led the Princeps, the aristocratic party opposed to Lykeno's series of populist reforms. The Lexivitates, the consul's own party, numbered few among the old blood of the Senate, but enjoyed significant popularity with the plebian masses, holding sway over the Common Assemblies.

"The Raven and the Wolf," Felix chuckled, waving a languid paw toward the speakers. "You know, when I stand here and listen to them prattle, I can't help but be reminded of the theater. You have the audience, the stage, the actors," he paused, his gaze going distant, "and every kine playing his part." The senator stared another moment before asking, "Do you go to the theater often, Kato?"

The younger mink cleared his throat. "No, Felix, I don't."

"You should. Aside from the obvious leisure value, it can prove most instructional. One I have always loved, ever since my father took me to see it performed in Neapolis as a youth, was *The Tyrant of Makketon*. Though of course, Aesophocles played rather fast and loose with the history." The mink's eyes remained fixed on the speaker, his face hardening, lip curling to reveal a hint of fang. "In the end, the great poet presents us with an alternative to the past, in which Thestor, after uniting the Elladene within the grasp of his bloodied claws, is slain by a group of noble princes from the other cities. And thus by a single act of murderous subterfuge is liberty preserved for generations."

Only then did some of the tension pass from Felix's countenance. "A fascinating play. I would... *very much* like to see it again sometime." The senator's focus drifted gently to his friend. "You seem distracted, dear Kato. It is a matter of business?"

"Business? Oh, no," Kato shook his head, gaze slinking across the floor. "Well, *yes*, but," he paused to take in a deep breath. "To be truthful, it's a rather personal matter. My wife, you see—"

Felix flashed a row of needle-like teeth, then tilted his head back to laugh. "Ah, I know how it can get—my first wife, Serrana, I swear she must have been a fury plucked straight from Mirod."

Kato forced a wan smile, but it quickly died on his lips. "It's not like that. We've just... grown distant. I fear I haven't been there for her."

"Well, you could always take her to a play." The older mink's lips curled into a self-satisfied grin. "Something delicate, of course—perhaps one of Daristanes' comedies. Stories of *violence*, and *politics*, are... not for the weak hearts of does." On the dais, the consul had finished speaking. "Indeed, there is no room for doubt within these halls, friend." With that Felix turned, and began striding away, then raised his voice. "I trust I will see you at the gala this weekend." He didn't wait for an answer.

Kato turned, watching as the consul ceded the floor to Korvo, who despite his age could deliver a rather rousing speech. But the words held little interest to the merchant. He had heard them a dozen times before: thunderous appeals to liberty and natural law, warnings of the dangers of unchecked power and the ignorance of the masses, pleas for the sacred traditions of the Republic to be upheld. In the end, the esteemed Raven of the Senate was like any other kine; his currency lay in speech as well as coin, and he would use both to purchase what he sought.

As the consul ascended from the floor, the light catching his golden laurel crown, several stoats materialized from the shadows, clad in matching burnished armor and regal crimson cloaks, plumes of white feathers dancing atop their helmets. Surrounded by his Kirkassian mercenary guards, Lykeno waved off several attempts to approach and strode casually into a side chamber. Kato watched him go, wondering who exactly the vultures the augur had seen were meant for.

The mink hurried down the steps as the distant sky roiled with angry clouds. Outside the Forum, the placid crowd from earlier had begun to churn and chant, though Kato couldn't make out the words. The autumn chill had done nothing to douse their anger. The vigiles looked to one another with unease, clawed fingers flexing over the hilts of their blades.

Kato had hoped to fit in another appointment that afternoon; surely these rabble would not do him harm *here*, of all places. But as his sandals slapped over the cobblestone steps, a stranger's paw stopped him. It was one of the vigiles. "Careful, sir." He nodded to the mob, whose chants were rising and falling like the swell of the ocean. "Might want to wait for us to disperse them."

As Kato surveyed the crowd, looking for a path that would keep him free of the unruliest plebians, a cold rain swept over the city in a gentle patter. He wiped the water from the fur of his forehead, shook himself for good measure, and pressed forward.

The mink reached the bottom of the steps, hunching his shoulders and scurrying through the growing downpour. He had made it nearly halfway across the square when a shout reached his ears through the din of the crowd. Kato turned to see a clawed finger stretching towards him, soon joined by another. Heads craned, and even through the falling rain he could see eyes narrowing in hatred, fangs baring at the chance for retribution. He quickened his pace, only to find more kines cutting him off.

Kato slipped on the rain-slicked stones, struggling to his feet as the mass of bodies pressed closer. The mink raised his paws plaintively, but the shouts cut through the steady drumming of the storm. His ears caught something like, "One of them!" alongside a mention of the Raven.

A stone sailed from the mob, bouncing harmlessly against his chest. Kato whirled, seeking an exit, when another cracked against his skull. The sharp spike of pain sent him careening to the plaza with a splash. Through blurring vision, a shadow loomed. The weasel raised a paw, and Kato shielded his face—but the moment stretched, and no further blows came. Peering from behind his trembling paws, the mink spotted a new figure, clad in a grey tunic.

"...good will this do?" It was a doe's voice, oddly familiar, collected even as she castigated the crowd. "I see good, faithful kines among you, and yet how easily do you fall to savagery? You should be ashamed!" Kato blinked through the dull, throbbing pain, watching as the strange doe scanned the mob with her gaze before settling it upon his prone form, sprawled on the watery cobblestones. When she knelt before him, he recognized her as the preacher, the mongoose he had seen earlier that morning.

"Kaius! Help me with him." After a moment the doe craned her neck. "I know you are still here." Even when simmering with anger, her voice still held a peculiar tenderness to it. "Come on, let's get you up." Another pair of paws wrapped around him, and Kato was hoisted to his feet, only to slump against the doe's shoulder. Though the mink's vision had not yet fully cleared, he could see the kines of the mob slowly backing off, the rage and resentment in their faces now diluted with guilt. Somewhere behind him, the cry of an officer cut through the steady drum of rainfall.

"Don't worry," the doe said, patting the paw he had draped over her shoulder. "We'll get you somewhere safe." And so Kato let the two strangers lead him into a narrow alleyway, the exhaustion of the prior few days and the strain of this latest hour easing him gently into unconsciousness.

Kato awoke to a dull throbbing in the back of his head. Probing with his fingers only made it worse, and so he sat up and looked around. It appeared to be an insula, one of communal apartments that housed most of the city's underclass—though, seeing as how the merchant had never actually been inside one, he could not be certain. Pale daylight trickled in from a row of curtained windows, while a flickering candle sat atop a small table.

"Just stay put. Nadrine will be back shortly." Kato jumped at the voice, then spotted a figure sitting a few paces away, fingers toying idly with a wood knife.

Kato stared at the stranger as memories of the assault returned to him. "You... ah" He winced at another wave of pain. "Weren't you one of them? In the crowd?"

The other kine turned away. "I suppose you couldn't've been hit too hard, then." His lip curled up in a rueful smirk. Kato merely growled before laying back down. "You know," the weasel went on, "that was pretty stupid, showing yourself like that. What did you expect?"

"To not be attacked by a bunch of rabble in broad daylight?"

"Well, it *was* raining." Now it was Kato's turn to grin. "Still, a supporter of the Princeps should know better." Seeing the surprise in Kato's face, he added, "One of the others marked you for one."

"I'm no politician."

The weasel shrugged. "Ah, so it's not *you*, it's just your *friends* who fight tooth and claw against everything Lykeno does for us. And let me guess: It's *your* coin that lines their pockets?"

Kato scoffed. "And why shouldn't we oppose him?" He lay back, rolled his eyes. "I don't know how you people fail to see he's just using you. Nothing but a petty tyrant—"

"Watch your tongue, merchant!" The weasel thrust his knife towards Kato, eyes narrowed and burning. "We *finally* get someone who listens to us, and you lot can't have *that*, now, can you?" He huffed out a breath, then settled back into the chair. "Besides, even if he *is* just using us, we still get something in return. Isn't that how everything in the world works?" He ticked off points on his clawed fingers. "Raising plebians to the Senate? Increasing our wages? Bread for the poor? Appointing magistrates who actually recognize our rights?" He leaned in further. "*Abolishing the Nexum?*" A vengeful grin crept across his face. "Hmm... but you and your friends probably opposed that, too. After all, debt slavery is good for business, so long as it's not *you* being sold off. Or your parents. Or your *children.*"

Plunging the knife into the wooden table, the weasel rose. "And what does it matter—we're just *rabble*, right?" He sneered, then stalked out of the room.

"You'll have to forgive him," the mongoose said, having slipped in through the curtained entryway without Kato's noticing. "But the words he speaks are not empty." She walked over and began examining his wound. "I pray that God may stay his temper." The doe chuckled at the look that flashed across her ward's face. "My name is Nadrine, by the way."

"Kato. Kato Aminarus."

"Well," she smiled, "it isn't often we entertain guests with a proper family name." Kato waited in silence while she prepared a salve, then raised his head and gently applied it. "Yarrow. It should reduce the pain, and prevent inflammation. Though fortunately, the wound is minor."

"Th—thank you." Kato winced slightly at her touch, then breathed out as a delicate numbness drowned out the pain. "You're a preacher, aren't you? A Kyrienite?"

"Yes, I am a disciple of Yesha Kyrie." She stretched the last term to three almost-musical syllables.

Kato shifted in the bed. "You must be rather fond of the consul as well, I take it?"

Nadrine's lips tightened. "Lykeno is a kine, and like all of us there is good and bad in him. But he has done much for Tiber's poor—has spoken for them when few else would. I admit, I do worry where that may lead, knowing that the hearts of even the greatest are tainted by the mark of sin. But such is the way of the world."

Kato looked up and met her gaze. "Then… why are you helping me? Even back in the plaza, why did you step out in front of that mob? Why risk yourself like that for a stranger?"

She cocked her head. "Why would I *not*?"

"Because... I'm not one of your people, by blood or by faith. And from what I can tell, your own kind have reason to hate me."

"But you *are* one of my people: We are all children of the same God."

"Tell me, then," Kato asked, "what do you expect to receive, from this god?"

Nadrine blinked a few times. "What do you mean?"

The mink sat further upright. "Everyone else has something to offer: honor and remembrance, some secret wisdom, blessings or favor, in this life or the next. Even the Apathetes' godless creed promises freedom to pursue pleasure. So, what is it that your god offers to the faithful?"

"God has already given us more than we could ever hope for: redemption, through the death of His Son, offered to ransom our sins. And beyond that, hope, in the Kyrie's resurrection, triumphing over death itself. What you do with these gifts remains your choice." The doe turned away, and began washing her paws in a low-standing basin.

Kato watched a moment before rising from the bed, stretching his sore limbs. "You aren't going to try to preach to me?"

"Words carry power, but actions matter more." She clasped his paw, patting it gently, as if he were a mere kit. "I take Yesha Himself as an example: 'Show me how a kine lives, and I will tell you of his soul.'" The doe stepped back with a smile. "Now go in peace, Kato... and if you find it in your heart to do so in service to God and love for one another, then so much the better." She led him to the entryway. "You should be fine, but if anything troubles you, our door is always open. I do hope to see you again, Kato Aminarus."

Outside, the rains had ceased. Amidst the faded stones of the street, puddles shimmered with newfound sunlight. Kato turned back and studied the doe, feeling a strange longing within his heart—not of the flesh, but of something deeper, something he could not quite manage to hook his claws into. In the end, he settled on a simple, "Thank you," mustered the sincerest smile he could, and went on his way.

Kato's domus lay in the upscale neighborhoods of Avelline Hill, encircled by a ring of greenery that muted the sounds of the city even at midday. Now, as he strode the streets in the peaceful quiet of dusk, he could allow himself to forget, even for a moment, the troubles of his life. Autumn leaves danced atop pools of water left by the passing rains, the scent of their decay evoking cozy childhood memories. Candles flickered like benevolent spirits from a window here, a doorway there. In the distance, a lantern of one of the city watch bobbed through the twilight shadows.

Arriving home, a slender, older weasel flashed a gentle smile and beckoned him in. "Welcome back, master." He stepped aside, then closed the door behind them. "Would you like something to drink?"

Kato waved with a shake of the head. "No, thank you, Denno. Er... is my wife still awake?"

"She's in the foyer, master." The slave shrugged knowingly, lingering in a shadowed alcove.

The mink sighed. "That will be all, Denno."

"Yes, master. Good night."

Kato dragged a paw across his face, slapping his tail on the cool tile beneath his feet. Then, mustering a weak smile, he sauntered into the next room. The hearth smoldered at its center, casting low shadows in all directions, hinting at the form lounging on a couch made of bronze and lined with cloth.

"Out late, dear?" The voice echoed from the darkness. "You missed supper." A moment later, the tawny form of his wife sat up, eyes twinkling with firelight. He could not make out her expression.

"It was a rather busy day, all things considered." There was no point in mentioning the details. He approached the hearth, but when she did not make room for him on the couch, Kato chose a wooden chair, a gift from Marenna's father. "You know how senators can be."

Marenna gave a soft snort, setting aside a sheaf of parchment. "Speaking of senators, I spoke to Laira, Lucius' wife—you remember them, from the Seikenalia last spring?" She stretched her jaws to yawn, teeth glinting in the light. "Well, Laira said her husband was willing to revisit the terms of your deal—apparently this year's harvest has..."

The doe's voice faded from Kato's awareness as he gazed into the dying flames, watching the last of them flicker and dance atop glowing embers.

"...the import contract is sitting in your study. This should at least partially cover last months' debts." She rose, the draping folds of her loose-fitting stole shimmering in the half-light. "Oh, and don't forget, the Selenius' gala is three days from now, and we truly do *need* their cooperation—I've already ordered the gifts, but please do try to at least *pretend* you want to be there." She flashed a smile, one that might've passed for coy when they had first met. Now, it seemed almost rueful.

"Marenna," Kato began. His wife halted, then turned back to him. Between his obligations to the conspiracy and their more mundane financial woes, the gods had left so little time for *them*. "I'm sorry I've been so busy lately, it's just—" Kato's claws fumbled with empty air. "When we've got more time... I could take you to the theater?"

She cocked her head. "Since when were you interested in theater, Kato?"

His shoulders slumped. "It doesn't have to be that. You could... read some of that poetry to me, or—or we could read it together. Or perhaps I could have a special meal prepared?"

She shot him a lingering look; her mouth tightened, while her eyes held a hint of sadness.

"It's been a long day, Kato. I am tired." She turned around once more. Her formal, "Good night," echoed from the hallway.

Kato exhaled deeply, leaning against the cold stone wall, dragging his claws slowly through his fur. Wishing he could hold Marenna like that, wondering who else might enjoy the luxury when he wasn't around. As his wife, it was her duty to preside over the household while he saw to external affairs, which, married to a merchant, gave her all the more chances for the trysts that were typically the domain of kines.

Shaking off his dour thoughts, Kato rose and shuffled over to the lararium, the small household shrine that adorned every proper domus in the Republic. Kneeling before the paw-sized statues and trinkets of the gods, he muttered a quick prayer, his mind straying to the strange god whose teachings had spared him injury, and perhaps even death.

But, like his wife, Kato, too, was tired. Hastily concluding his nightly prayer, the mink retired to his chambers—separate from Marenna's, as was custom—for yet another night of solitude.

Over the next two days, as Kato struggled to balance his ordinary duties with his remaining obligations to the conspiracy, his thoughts continued to return to Nadrine: not only what she had said, but how she carried herself, the sense of inner peace that burned like a star amidst the shadows of strife and poverty.

His mind still lingered on her words as he and Marenna strode up the tiled walkway to the domus of Markus Selenius, several slaves in tow bearing food and gifts. To either side, blooms of rose and violet, lily and iris grew alongside flowers imported from the fringes of the Republic, petals of every color collectively trumpeting the senator's wealth and reach. The colonnade, adorned with facsimiles of Avedo and Milshoa, twin deities of invention and wisdom, beckoned onlookers to humble themselves.

The party was greeted at the door by a prokyon servant, dressed far too well to be a slave, paws clasped in warm greeting. "I welcome you to Domus Selenius," he said with a slight flick of his ringed tail. "Your gifts are most appreciated. Please, deposit them with the slaves in the foyer and feel free to acquaint yourselves with the other guests." Mirne, one of Kato's own slaves, followed the prokyon as the mink and his wife stepped into the atrium, where laurel wreaths hung from marble pillars, and more candles than most families could afford to light in a year bathed the gathering in glowing warmth.

"Ah, Kato, I'm glad you made it," Felix said, stepping over from one of the tables where various appetizers had been arranged. "And Marenna, so good to see you." The other mink clasped his wife's paws, then kissed both of her cheeks. "You remember Iulia, no?" He gestured to his own wife, who was still by the table. She turned at the sound of her name, brushing crumbs from her mouth before gliding over with an embarrassed smile.

"Yes, we met at the Meridias' Seikenalia," Marenna replied. "How are the kits?"

As the two does went on, Felix gently guided Kato to an abandoned stretch of the banquet table, snatching another morsel from an ornate silver tray. Kato's gaze drifted over rows of thin-sliced veal and cabbage drizzled with vinegar, blocks of more types of cheese than he had ever consumed stacked alongside bowls of dried apricots and pears. He selected a legume as his friend's claws hovered over the seafood.

"Several of our compatriots are here tonight, dear Kato," Felix said, absentmindedly eying a cube of salted mullet, daubed with a pale orange sauce. "Mmm, you've *got* to try this. Anyway, I believe they are in the senator's study. Let's not keep them waiting."

The other mink led the way, past a massive mosaic depicting the founding of the city: The legendary king Tiberios, accompanied by his chosen companions, had been guided by the gods to camp atop the long-buried ruins of a citadel of the Ancient Ones. Kato's eyes lingered on the scene, knowing that while most of the patricians claimed descent from one or another of the figures before him, he could never count his own ancestors among such illustrious company. For the others, the failure of their plans might mean disgrace or diminishment of status; he stood to lose *everything*.

Felix cleared his throat. "Right though here." He swept his paw towards a heavy oaken door, ushering Kato inside before closing it securely behind them. Within, crowded around a table and illumined by flickering candlelight, stood the chief conspirators. The Raven himself, Korvo Petronius, loomed at the head of the table, locking eyes with the merchant. The elder senator ran his claws through the black fur of his chin in careful, steady strokes, then nodded to himself. Several other senators, and one kine clad in the garb of the city watch, waited in silence. Sipping faintly from his wine, Korvo set his chalice down on the table.

"If anyone has doubts about the righteousness of our cause, know that the augurs have taken the signs, and foreseen our triumph." The patrician turned to meet the eyes of his co-conspirators, holding each one's gaze long enough to impress upon them his commitment, and receive a show of theirs in turn. "The gods themselves have seen fit to assure us." Kato struggled not to shy away.

"But time is short," the black-furred kine continued. "Lykeno's tyrannical aspirations can no longer be denied. He has eroded the foundations of our divinely ordained republic. He thinks to cast down those of nobler blood in favor of his plebian sycophants; already he has raised more senators from the lower classes than the prior three consuls put together. He wages war after war, knowing that the ceaseless stream of slaves and plunder will keep his legions, both abroad and at home, contented and complacent—and yet he refuses to preserve our culture in the face of this new influx of foreign rabble. Even our very gods come under threat from alien prophets who proselytize on our streets, their ranks growing by the day. My compatriots, there can be no doubt: Tiber is in crisis, and without decisive action, our beloved Republic will die."

Kato held his breath, shooting furtive glances at the others. Most tried to remain somber and dignified; some nodded along angrily, while Felix's face was pinched with a look of nervous tension. In many respects, the words were rather reminiscent of Korvo's remarks in the Forum a few days prior, albeit with the tact and decorum stripped away.

"I trust you've all heard about the trial of this convert officer, to begin a few days from now. The consul and his allies, naturally, hope to balance the support of the military and the Kyrienites." Several of the listeners growled or bared their fangs, and the Raven nodded at their frustration, raising a finger. "*But*, but… should something manage to drive a wedge between them and the faithful plebians, who have merely been led astray by his demagoguery." He turned his paws upwards, giving a deceptively innocent smile.

"So… we need to make sure this officer is convicted?" one of the others asked.

"That would only solve *one* problem. Varrus?" Korvo gestured to another marten, who stepped forward and cleared his throat.

"I'm afraid we must now speak bluntly. The consul… must be killed before the trial concludes. The verdict is of little import. What matters is that the Kyrienites be implicated—the rest of Lykeno's plebian supporters will turn on the foreigners even before his blood is cold."

Kato drew in a sharp breath, steadying himself against the table. Felix, at his side, shot him a perplexed glance, but fortunately, none of the others seemed to notice.

"Lykeno's death removes the primary danger from above," Korvo added, "as blaming the Kyrienites does to that from below. We will be free to move against the subversives, and we will do so harnessing the anger of Lyekno's own blind following." He clasped his paws with a rueful smile. "Slay two birds with one stone."

It was then that Kato dared to speak up, trying to couch his rising unease in pragmatic concern. "Surely there will be questions as to the ringleaders, will there not? How do you plan to account for that?"

"Ah, nothing too strenuous or complicated, of course," Varrus replied. "We'll have the watch root out a few prominent figures for us to drag before a magistrate when the dust settles. To whet the bloodlust of the masses mourning their beloved consul." He flicked his ears with a shrug. "And as to confessions… *anyone* will admit to a crime with the proper persuasion."

Kato watched the ease with which it was said, and accepted by those around him; even *he* had to admit that the senator's plan made sense. After all, were they not weighing the survival of a nation against a few dozen, a few hundred lives? And yet the words churned in his stomach, tearing at his heart: *The Kyrienites must be implicated...*

"But that raises the question," Felix said, standing tall and meeting the senior senator's gaze. "How will we do it? How will..." his eyes darted to the door, then back to the kines who would damn the room to painful deaths should any reveal the conspiracy. "How and where will Lykeno be killed?"

A stretch of silence was followed by several voices clamoring for prominence: "What about those stoats of his?" "As he rides through the city!" "I don't see how we could—"

"It must be in the Forum," Korvo thundered. He repeated it once the room had quieted. "On the Senate floor, no less. We must have control over the scene, and it must be somewhere he is not surrounded by his Kirkassian mercenaries. There is no alternative." He cleared his throat, then nodded. "Captain Lucius?"

At this, a new figure stepped forth: a stocky marten dressed in a blue tunic. "Several of the officers are with us. I'll make sure the right ones have their kines in place when the time comes."

"And we have a contact on the other side," Korvo added.

Felix looked up suddenly. "You mean the Princeps?"

"...Yes."

A flutter of murmuring spread throughout the room: "They know?" "What if we've been sold out?" "How could we trust any of them?"

Korvo waited for the noise to seep away. "Varrus and I made the decision, just as we withheld informing you of the intended date until tonight. It was a necessary one, and rest assured, we were careful."

"Now," Varrus added, "we will return to the gathering, enjoy the festivities that Markus and his household have so graciously provided, and say nothing of this until the trial begins. And may the gods strike down any who falters in his courage, and confine him to the blackest pits of Mirod."

The others nodded as one. With a creaking groan, the heavy oaken doors were pushed open, and the conspirators dispersed, trickling back among the oblivious attendants in ones and twos. Of course, Senator Selenius himself was well aware of their intentions, but his mirthful countenance belied no hint of the murder and treachery planned within his walls.

The middle-aged marten, his rich, brown fur streaked with hints of grey, rotund stature discernable beneath his loose toga, clutched a torch as his guests gathered before the central banquet table. While Kato and his comrades plotted in the study, the servants and slaves had prepared and delivered the true courses of tonight's meal: lamb chops topped with currant and splashed with wine adorned silver platters; fresh peaches and azeroles sat in bowls beside smaller dishes of dried cherries and apricots. Sea bass from the distant Atlantik, roasted and seasoned with garum, lay alongside slender sausages and loaves of rosemary bread, while sweetcakes of honey and cinnamon waited for those whose appetites had not been fully sated. And, of course, around it all, spirits of every conceivable potency flowed freely.

Kato had seen his fair share of such extravagant culinary displays, and even hosted a few himself, and yet, for the first time, his gut soured at the sheer *waste*. He remembered the impoverished forms lingering in the alleyways and tenement housing on his journey back, after Nadrine had aided him—*him*, whom the preacher with so little had risked so much to save from her own kin.

Markus hefted his burning torch, throwing shadows across the richly patterned tile of the atrium. "As we gather here tonight among friends old and new, let us not forget the blessings that the gods have so graciously provided for us. Tonight especially we honor you, Zhetava, to whom the autumn is so dear, as you leave your mark upon the forests and fields. We pray that your bountiful harvest may allow us to endure the winter, drawing near, and that come spring we may gather together once more in the joy of your fertile warmth."

"This we pray," the crowd echoed in unison.

Markus laughed. "And with that said and done," he added, tossing the torch into a large brazier, upon which a slaughtered lamb rested for sacrifice, "I believe we can commence with the feast!" He raised his paws to the acclaim of the gathering, who descended upon tables that could have fed for weeks a hundredfold their number of plebians.

It was only then that, with a jolt of icy fear, Kato noticed the marten standing at Markus' side: Talinus, husband to the consul's sister, and his greatest champion in the Senate. If *he* was present, had their conspiracy been discovered? Kato dared a glance at Felix, but the other mink was busy murmuring to his wife, who giggled softly.

"Aren't you going to eat, dear?" Marenna whispered into his ear, a sly smile dancing on her lips. He stirred, took her proffered arm in his paw, and strode up to the nearest table. "As I said, at least *try* to pretend you want to be here." Willing his blood to cool, Kato looked across the room, but Talinus had already vanished into the crowd.

As with most festive gatherings in Tiber, the guests did not share a table, but dispersed throughout the expansive grounds to feast and drink, chatter and associate in whatever ways they or the wine coursing through their veins saw fit. Marenna's arm was quick to slip from his languid grasp, though with all that was running through his mind, Kato hardly noticed her drift away. After loading his platter with a modest portion of veal garnished with lemon slices and adorned with a creamy white sauce, he scoured his surroundings for a hint of solitude, and found it in a cushioned chair sitting between a pair of potted ferns.

Spearing the meat with a bronze fork, Kato savored the first delectable bite—only for the words of the preacher's companion to sprinkle ashes on his tongue. Had mere bread really meant that much to so many of the city's inhabitants? Of course, the mink had always kept a close eye on the price of common goods, but to him these were merely numbers on parchment: the variables by which his wealth grew and shrank, rather than a matter of daily sustenance. He glanced around, watching in growing disgust as his cohorts ate and drank and laughed with abandon, while servants who could never hope to live half so well scurried about all but unseen, save for when needed.

Hailing one with a raised finger, the mink accepted a fresh glass of wine. Kato was not generally one for drunkenness, but spirits did have a way of easing a kine's troubles, and the gods only knew how his numbered. That the household slaves would replace his empty glass with a fresh one at a mere flick of the wrist did nothing to improve his temperance. And yet, gulp after bitter gulp could not soothe his discomfort.

Sliding further into intoxication, the mink found himself musing: Was this the price of such a life? Had he failed to account for some cost beyond the years of labor and careful planning? Had he paid for extravagance and luxury with some hidden treasure that made its absence known as a gnawing in the soul? His eyes wandered to the corpse of the lamb, still smoldering in the brazier before a likeness of Zhetava, hints of fire flickering in eyes of lifeless black. Drunken revelers milled about beneath the harvest goddess' blank gaze, hearts set, as always, upon base pleasure. On food, wine, sex. On status, wealth, possession. On power.

And Kato... Kato was one of them. He'd been one of them his entire life.

Turning, the mink spotted his wife amongst several other party-goers. His eyes narrowed at the sight of the otter, the very same kine he had seen her with the last time. Tall and lithe in the manner of his kind, clad in a strange fur-trimmed tunic, the stranger laughed, and Marenna draped an arm around his shoulder, her free paw patting at the fur of the otter's chest.

Kato barely stopped himself from snapping the thin stem of his glass. He rose, only to nearly topple back to the chair, then sturdied himself on its wooden armrest and swallowed a bout of nausea. Stalking over to the group, the mink did his best to sound confident.

"Marenna?" His wife turned at the sound of her name, eyes wandering to his form, where they widened. Her claws relaxed their grip on the fur of the otter's arm. The strange kine at least had the decency to look slightly abashed.

Marenna blinked a few times, swaying on her feet. "Yes, husband?"

"I would like to speak with you." Kato struggled to avoid growling the words. "In *private*."

The doe turned back to the others, sweeping her arm around in a grand, if rather uncoordinated, flourish. "Of *course*, dear." She flinched when he seized her paw, but did not resist as he led her to a doorway, out into the cool autumn night. A small brazier laden with incense burned at the corner of the terrace, releasing plumes of spiced smoke.

"Who is he?" Kato hissed.

"A friend, Kato." When he persisted in leering, she continued, "Tristain was a member of some tribal court, up on the Gallican coast. He returned to Tiber with Lykeno after his king swore fealty to the Republic."

"And why are you clinging to him, as if you were his consort? In *public*, no less!"

"I don't see why *you* care," Marenna scoffed. "You hardly even look at me anymore, *husband*." She snarled the last word.

Kato turned, glancing out at the cityscape: Further down the forested hillside lay the modest neighborhoods of the Mercellium, a dark, sprawling expanse dotted with firelight, a warmly colored mirror of the starscape above. Each flickering flame meant a home, and each home a family. He wondered, just for a moment, what a kine down there might have seen when looking back up.

"I admit, I have been rather occupied as of late, but that doesn't grant you—"

"As of *late*?" the doe cut in, drawing his gaze back to her. "I will not pretend that our marriage was founded on infatuation, Kato, but *I* am not the only one with obligations. This last year, you've treated me more like a partner in *business* than a spouse! You think I didn't notice when you snuck out to favor some whore over me?"

The words were a slap across Kato's face. It had only been a few times, and he had thought he'd been discrete—not that males needed to be, in Tiberian society. "Th—that was different," he stammered. "A kine has needs, after all!"

"Oh, but a doe doesn't? Am I but a trinket to sit on one of your shrines, collecting dust?"

Kato drew nearer, taking her paws in his own. She reluctantly conceded to his grip once more. "I did not mean to shun you," he whispered, "but after Sophia, I just... I was afraid. I didn't know what to make of it all. What to make of *us*."

Marenna drew back, steeling her gaze. "You think *you* were the only one to feel the pain of her loss? *I* carried her within me, felt her stirring nightly as I lay in bed! And after all those wasted years of us trying, of me *failing*, I thought I had finally done my duty as a wife, as a *mother*, only for the gods to tear her from my breast the very day she first drew breath!" Sobbing, Marenna collapsed against the railing of the balcony, pressing her paws to her face, tears matting the fur beneath her eyes. "I *needed* you, Kato, and you—you treated me like I was sullied, like I was just... just some livestock that served no further purpose."

"Marenna, please..." He lingered, wishing to embrace her, fearing that she would recoil from his touch. "I am sorry, Marenna. You are right. I," he let out a deep sigh, "I have failed you. You deserve better. If you wish it, I will grant a divorce, including a return of the dowry. My business arrangements with your father can remain, of course."

Her sniffling ceased, and her eyes narrowed, sorrow giving way to rage. "*That* is what you offer me? Shipping me back to my father's estate with his coin in tow?" Marenna staggered upright, only to stumble into him, burying a claw into the fur of his chest. "I don't want to be cut loose, to be... to be set back where I started—I want someone who *wants me*. I want someone who *cares*." Her breath reeked of wine, but her eyes fixed upon him with a startling clarity. "Am I not good enough, Kato?" The tremble in her voice broke his heart.

Kato struggled for breath of his own, his blood stirring at her closeness through the sluggishness of intoxication and the pull of sleep. "I... I don't," He fumbled for words, pulse quickening, as Marenna's claws slowly worked their way across his toga.

"I want to be *loved*, Kato. Is that... is that so much to ask?" Then, much to his surprise, she leaned in even closer, pressed her body to his, and kissed him.

Kato only resisted for a moment before melting into her embrace. Together they fell into the shadows, and as the rest of the city slept below, the embers in the brazier smoldered into ash, cool before the heat of their passion.

When he awoke to dawn streaming in through the windows, Kato's head was wracked by thundering throbs. It took him a moment to recognize that he was in his own bed, alone. He could remember little of the walk home... but he recalled Marenna's breath, as heavy with wine as his own must have been, and her fur, soft within his grasp. Her body, burning against his. The mink stumbled upright as another wave of nausea broke across his skull. Gritting his teeth, he probed through the haze of the prior night, through staggering back home in the early hours of the morning, through the drink and debauchery of the gala, knowing that *something* important lay buried.

Then it fell within his grasp: standing among his co-conspirators in the study, their faces sharpened by the contrast of shadow and candlelight. The senators' words cut through Kato's heart, chilling his blood: *Root out a few prominent figures for us to drag before a magistrate when the dust settles... anyone will admit to a crime with the proper persuasion.*

"Master?" asked a voice from the doorway. The mink turned to see Denno watching him with concern. The weasel's smile was apologetic. "Would you like some willow-bark tea?"

Kato hadn't realized he was still clutching his head. "Yes, Denno. Er, thank you."

As it happened, the ancient cure did serve to ease his headache, and he entered the dining hall to find Marenna already sitting down to breakfast. The doe greeted him casually, as if nothing of note had transpired. Kato waited as the slaves prepared his own meal: fried eggs and a bowl of raisins, accompanied by salted bread rolls and washed down with a glass of fresh milk. Only when he was wiping the crumbs from the fur of his chin did his wife break the silence.

"I don't know if you remember, but I have an arrangement with Camilla this afternoon. I'll be taking Mirne." She rose. "And don't forget, my father is coming into town next week, to discuss the new grain tax. We'll need to have some room prepared."

He watched her start for the vestibule, a strange pit forming in his stomach. "Marenna?" She stopped, turning back to him slowly. But when she met his gaze, his tongue went numb.

"It's a busy day, husband." That she said it so casually, so gently, made it hurt even more. Kato's gaze remained fixed on the entryway long after she had passed through it. But as he sat there, the heartache gave way to guilt, and he recalled once more the fate that awaited Nadrine and her compatriots, should his own succeed. Warning them would be the greatest folly—and yet, the mink found that in the present moment, it was her advice he desired most of all. Perhaps her god would have whatever it was he sought.

Donning a tunic that would hopefully not draw wandering eyes as his regular garb did, the merchant bid farewell to Denno and trotted out into the sunlight.

It had taken Kato some time to find the block where the preacher dwelt. Asking after a 'Nadrine' had yielded nothing, despite the Levantine name being rather conspicuous this far west, and questions about Kyrienites elicited stares as often as assistance, worry and resentment showing in equal measure. It was a trio of otters, unloading fresh-caught fish from a dingy in a small tributary of the city's namesake, who finally pointed the mink in the right direction, sending him on his way with blessings in a foreign tongue.

Kato stepped through the archway of the insula and drew the curtain aside, emerging into the communal kitchen, where the mongoose and several kounavi were busily preparing food. A bready smell reached his nostrils, which caught a sweet hint of olive oil moments later. Nadrine turned as he entered.

"Ahh," she said with a flourish of her tail, "I'm glad to see you weren't scared off by some of our more popular parables." Despite the levity in her voice, the doe's eyes shone pure and innocent. Though they, too, lightened at the confusion on his face.

"I jest—some of the faithful take a rather... *zealous* approach to the Kyrie's pronouncements on wealth and humility." She leaned in with a wink. "But we cannot exclude the wealthy from our charity, now can we, Master Aminarus?"

He waved away the formality. "Please, just Kato."

"Well, Kato," she said, turning back to a row of cast-iron skillets, where a number of cakes of spelt flour sizzled and hissed. "What may I do for you?"

The merchant flexed his fingers, then let them hang by his sides with a sigh. He glanced briefly to the others, a pair of weasels and a fellow mink, who were doing their best to ignore him. "When we first met, you spoke of right and wrong, with a surety I haven't heard or felt since... childhood, I suppose. And not in the way the priests or senators do, of honor and might, of blood and kinship." He looked up, feeling his reluctance ease at the understanding glinting in her eyes. "You spoke of love and compassion, of mercy, and forgiveness..."

The mink began to pace. "You see, there are things I've become involved in, things I've done, things I'm planning to do, that... that feel *wrong*." He huffed out a breath. "Or, at least, I wonder. I tell myself that what I do is right, is *just*... and by the codes I have known all my life, they appear so, but," he trailed off, desperate to ignore the voice in his heart that demanded he warn her.

Nadrine added a splash of olive oil to each of the pans. "So you want to know what is right, and what is wrong."

Kato stared. "Yes, I do. And I want to know how it could be that *your* words feel so different, and yet... ring true, in some way I cannot name."

The mongoose watched him for a moment, then clasped her paws. "I believe that God speaks through our hearts—that even those who have never heard His word may yet behave according to His will, as have many of your own philosophers, throughout the years. But tell me, what do you know of our faith?"

"You're a branch of the Chashemites—or a sect, I suppose. You revere a prophet who was martyred by our magistrates. I know little beyond that."

"Hmm. Well, Yesha was more than a mere prophet—He is the Kyrie, a word we have borrowed from your neighbors in the El-ladene. The title His first disciples used was *'Maschiach,'* 'the re-deemer anointed by God.'"

"That is another thing I could never understand," Kato cut in. "Your one god."

At this, the mongoose chuckled. Taking a spatula, she began to transfer the cakes to platters. "You approach the question from the wrong angle. There is only one God, for all of us: the absolute, tran-scendent, the wellspring from which all is brought into being."

"But that is simply the Logos."

"Indeed it is." Nadrine looked rather pleased. She and the others began to pack almonds and walnuts into the cakes, then drizzle a dollop of honey—which the mink was surprised they could afford—onto each.

"But the Logos is... it's a mere force, as far as I understand it. An ideal, or," he grasped at the air, as if he could pluck the answers from the emptiness before him. "The gods themselves live amongst us, shaping our lives. They are as numerous as the stars, each with their own ways of influencing the world, from lowly household spirits to the Twelve Most High. The Logos is… impersonal. Uncaring. Beyond our ability to comprehend."

"And that," the doe replied calmly, "is where you are wrong, dear Kato." She inclined her head, then gently motioned to the others, who filed out of the room with the cakes. "Tell me, why do you revere these lesser gods, these fragments of the divine spark?"

Kato stared back at her. "Er… their power, naturally. We make sacrifices and honor their majesty, and in return they provide us with blessings."

The mongoose's smile sharpened slightly. "And from where then does this power derive?"

"I'm hardly a philosopher, Nadrine."

Her smile softened. "Well, *your* philosophers, at least some of them, teach that the Logos is the perfection from which all of existence is derived, and through which it, and we, are sustained. I'm curious, though… you speak of the rituals and customs of Tiber, but not of virtue or salvation. What do you know of them, as is taught among your own people?"

Kato turned, scratching at his wrists as he gazed off into the corner. "I couldn't tell you much about the mystery cults—each promises the revelation of some greater truth through initiation. The Stoics claim that the Logos orders all things—that we are but puppets, driven by our weaknesses and desires, each with our appointed station, called to virtuous life: honor, fidelity, temperance, wisdom, and so on." He held out his left paw, away from the right.

"The Apathetes, meanwhile, say that all matter, including ourselves, is simply composed of particles, blind and uncaring—that any pretense of higher calling or virtue rings hollow, and that we should abstain from suffering and give ourselves to worldly pleasures before we cross the Black River, as all mortals must."

"And what do you believe?"

"I…" Kato let out the breath he hadn't realized he was holding. "I don't know. I will admit that the code of the Stoics held a certain appeal to me, especially given my station, but… the more I consider the matter, the more both philosophies seem opposite faces of the same rusted coin. 'All is vanity, so squander your time until death dissolves your spirit into mist.' 'History is but an endless cycle, and we are like unto foxes chained to a wagon, rolling downhill; our freedom is found in choosing either to run alongside the cart, or be dragged by it.' "

He met her gaze once more, to find her golden eyes fixed upon him. When she let the silence linger, he asked, "But what do *you* believe?"

The doe seemed as if she were waiting for him to ask that very question. "I believe that the almighty God loves each and every one of us, His children, in spite of our fallen nature. That Yesha, the Kyrie, was given over to the princes of this world to suffer and die, that death itself be vanquished, and our sins atoned for."

She stepped nearer, taking his paw in hers. "But more importantly, I believe we are called to spread His love to all we encounter. That while the Kingdom of God lies beyond this world, it is our duty to strive to build it here nonetheless."

Kato clung to her paw as if it were all that would prevent him from plunging down a sheer cliff. "But how can you be so certain? All I've seen of the world, all I've *done...* it makes it so hard to believe that anyone truly cares for us. That we can ever rise above the same pointless cycles of greed and violence and hatred. That we could ever be deserving of such love."

"Why, through faith, Kato." Nadrine's eyes softened with a hint of pity. "Perhaps I could show you?"

The mink let himself be led back out into the sunlight, where the trio from earlier were waiting. The patellites they had prepared had been bundled into sacks of cloth. The mongoose took one, and held it out to Kato. "We do what we can, with what we have." She turned one of the cakes over in her paw. "Would you like to come along?"

Kato stared back at the cloth for a moment, then slowly closed his paws around it. It was the least he could do, all things considered. They started in the plaza, surrounded on all sides by cramped insulae, and while the mink thought at first that every kine with an ounce of hunger might clamor for a share, to his surprise, many of the laborers or passersby waved them on with tender smiles. Some even mentioned neighbors with greater needs, or pointed to the sorry forms of paupers lingering in alleyways.

Kato approached one, drawing back slightly when he noticed that the kine was a polecat: thieves and vagrants, a tribe unto their own; kounavi by blood, but not in spirit. The splotchy pelt bristled as Kato's shadow fell over it, and yet the kine's listless eyes did not move. Kato studied the stranger's ragged fur, his gaunt limbs and patchy tail. Was this not a flesh-and-blood person, like himself? And could Kato really condemn another with such ease, knowing all that he had done?

Reaching into his bag, the mink drew out a cake and offered it to the polecat, whose amber eyes widened and focused. His slender claws grasped the patellite, and he brought it to his chest with a hoarse, "Thank you."

The mink moved on, trailing behind Nadrine and her companions as their goods steadily dwindled. Eventually they came to a small park, where a number of children were engaged in a game of calcitrare, kicking a leather ball between them. The kits broke into shouts and cheering at the sight of Nadrine, swarming up to the newcomers and straining with open paws. Kato could not help but laugh; the bags were soon emptied, and just as quickly the children resumed their game.

As the mink watched, his gaze wandered past the edge of the field. There, resting up against the limestone wall, was an older doe, bouncing a young kit in her arms. The sight brought to mind memories of Sophia, and for the first time in nearly a year, he allowed them to surface more fully.

Kato had only been granted one chance to hold her: a frail, sickly thing, too small as she squealed in her mother's arms. He had loved her more than life itself, and after that first dawn she had cried herself to sleep, then slept herself to death. What little sparks of passion might have flourished between the kit's parents had departed with her brevity.

The mink's vision blurred with a sting that threatened tears.

"I suppose I wasn't entirely truthful," Nadrine said casually. Kato looked to her, wiping at his eyes. "When you asked what I hope to receive, for my devotion." The mongoose pointed to the children, joined in carefree laughter, blessed enough to not know what they lacked. "Service carries its own rewards, does it not? You are always welcome to join us, *Master Aminarus*," she added with a grin.

Kato swallowed the lump in his throat, wishing he could match her easy smile. The aching stirred in his breast once more. *Tell her. Warn them.*

"Nadrine..." But what could he say? What horrors would he bring upon himself, upon his family and friends, were he to reveal what was planned? What would befall his household, his *nation*, if they did not act? All that he had worked so hard to achieve would be ground into dust.

And yet, it was said that such was the fate of all mortal achievements, in the end.

With his eyes fixed upon the children at play, instead, he whispered, "I had a daughter, once. My wife and I, we had tried for years... and then the gods took her from us. Why would they do that?"

The doe's eyes softened. "Our sin fills the world with suffering." She laid a paw on his shoulder. "But even God knows what it is to suffer as one of us, now. I have faith that you will see your daughter again, Kato."

But Kato could never hope to be so righteous, to be worthy of such reward. Closing his eyes against the bitterness welling up within his heart, he reached into the pocket of his tunic, withdrawing a small sack.

"For helping me, earlier," he explained. Confusion creasing her brow, the mongoose accepted the bag, eyes widening as she pulled the drawstring.

"Kato, is this...?"

"To help, in whatever way you see fit. I trust it will go to good use."

Her claws stirred through the contents. "I cannot accept—"

"Yes, you can," Kato said, hoping to keep the desperation from his voice. If he could not save all of them, he could at least help in this meager way. "Thirty denarii. I will live without it, I assure you."

Nadrine stared a moment longer, then strode forward and threw her arms around him. The mink tensed, then slowly relaxed into her embrace. The doe stepped back. "This will make a difference for many lives, Kato." Her own eyes were watering now; he could not bear to meet them. "Bless you."

Tucking the coins into a pocket in her robes, the mongoose retrieved a roll of parchment, the sheafs barely longer than her paw. "If you find yourself in need of guidance, do not hesitate to turn to God. Through Him, even the lowliest of us might find peace."

Kato accepted the scroll in a trembling paw, cursing that he still held his tongue. With slow, heavy steps, he left her there, as the children shrieked in excitement and the old doe cooed to her kit. Above, a pair of thrushes flitted through the cloudless sky.

It was all he could do, he told himself once more. Surely, the gods would recognize that.

But the voice in his heart would not tolerate lies. After all, what was a bag of silver weighed against his soul?

The day of the trial dawned crisp and bright. The coming winter hinted at its approach with a thin layer of frost, but this quickly melted as the sun climbed higher into the sky. The proceedings were not set to begin until the third hour of the day, and Kato found himself wishing that the heavens themselves might freeze, if only to delay what was to take place.

The mink arrived in the plaza before the Forum with ample time to spare. The vigiles had been deployed in force, while across from the fountains, a small gathering of disheveled figures had assembled. These remained silent, and it took the merchant a moment to realize that they were praying. He settled down to wait on a stone bench, letting himself be lost in the ceaseless trickle of a nearby fountain.

Kato's ears perked at the thrumming of booted feet. Into the plaza marched a column of soldiers, the Kirkassian Guard moving in lockstep around the consul and his allies. Further behind them trudged the accused, paws bound as he walked between a pair of his comrades: the convert who would swear to the Republic, and its leader, but not its gods. The young officer wore the simple red tunic of a legionary, and marched with the pride of one.

The crowd awaiting their arrival had swelled, and yet few on-lookers dared to raise their voices. The vigiles formed ranks, parting before the consul's delegation, which marched up the steps and into the arched vestibule of the Forum. A number of senators trailed behind the last of the soldiers, among them Korvo and Felix. Kato could imagine the daggers concealed within their togas, could very nearly see them spilling blood onto the storied tile.

Almost as soon as the final figures had vanished inside, the ground beneath Kato's feet trembled as if a heavy wagon had rumbled past. A flight of starlings leapt from the dome of the Forum, scattering across the pale blue sky. Several of the people near him screamed or gasped, but the faint tremor died away without an encore.

Earthquakes were not uncommon in this part of the world, and yet, for one to happen *now* seemed rather portentous. Kato was far from the only one with this thought, as several members of the crowd began to raise their paws plaintively to the heavens. Some, evidently of one faith with the warrior convert, appeared to take heart from this supposed sign. He knew better, offering a silent prayer that the wrath incurred by his compatriots might spare them.

The first hour dragged on with an unsettling mixture of ennui underscored by nervous tension. Had he so desired, Kato could have borne witness to the trial firsthand, though as he would not be allowed on the Senate floor itself, the mink's presence was unnecessary, and he had little interest in seeing the deed be done. He had played his part; the rest was up to his co-conspirators, and the gods.

As Kato waited, his mind wandered to the scriptures Nadrine had entrusted him with. He could not help but read every word as a condemnation, ringing like thunder within his heart. Poverty and humility, compassion for the foe and brotherly love for the stranger; if such were the commandments of her god, how could any kine hope to find salvation? And yet they spoke of a mercy without limit, of a god who cared so much for his creation that he would suffer and die as one of them.

And Kato, in defense of a fortune and power most could only dream of, had resorted to conspiracy and murder, and condoned innocents being set to take the blame of his wrongdoing.

But from the depths of despair, he heard Nadrine's voice, echoed by the scriptures she had given him: *God speaks to us in our hearts. Through Him, even the lowliest of us might find peace.* And yet, how could Kato ever hope to balance the scales?

As the sun was nearing its apex, the mink left the towering majesty of the Forum behind him and headed for the nearest alleyway, praying that he would not be too late.

Neither the preacher nor any of her fellow faithful were in the common areas of the familiar insula. After deliberating between venturing out to locate her himself or asking the locals for help, Kato resolved to wait; he had already received enough hostile stares on his way through the narrow alleyways, and starting a panic *here* of all places would hardly help anyone.

Out on the street, several kines were busy transporting sacks of grain, while others bartered with plebian merchants operating out of the ground level of the packed communal apartments. Kato had been so concerned with Nadrine, but how many of these people had he condemned alongside her? The Senate might only have the prominent Kyrienites arrested, but their disciples would be left to the wrath of their own neighbors.

It was then that he spotted Nadrine striding across the plaza, along with several other faithful. The mink leapt up and ran to her.

"Kato?"

"Nadrine, you have to leave!" He scrambled over and grasped her shoulders, paws trembling. "They will be coming for you, and the others."

The doe's brow creased. "What are you talking about?"

Kato stepped back, forcing himself to take a deep breath. "The consul is to be killed today, by—by a conspiracy of the Senate. During the trial of the convert officer. In all likelihood, it has already been done." He choked down a sob. "I, I... I was a part of them. They intend to blame you, the Kyrienites, to sow discord among the plebians and break Lykeno's bloc." He fell to his knees, clasping at her robe. "I am sorry, I—I knew what they planned, for your people, and said nothing."

The mink glanced up at Nadrine. The doe stood watching him, her golden eyes distant and wounded. Kato looked away. "You need to leave, or hide, and tell your fellow disciples to do the same: preachers, leaders, prominent converts—none will be safe." He closed his eyes against the bitter tears.

A gentle paw caressed the fur of his head. Breath hitching, he looked back up to see Nadrine stooping down to embrace him. "How—how can you not condemn me, after what I have done?" he gasped, voice breaking. "I am a sinner, a wretched sinner..."

"We are *all* sinners, Kato. What matters is that we strive to be better, in spite of our sin." She drew back, raising his chin with a delicate touch, forcing him to stand and meet her gaze. "Know that even when we fail, even when it seems there could not possibly be a bright path through the darkness of this world, that God still loves us, and longs for our reconciliation."

Once more, Kato shied away, shutting his eyes. "What worth could your god possibly see in my soul? What price would weigh itself against my sins?" He bowed deeply under the press of his guilt, but Nadrine leaned forward, planting a tender kiss on the fur of his forehead.

"So long as we draw breath, it is never too late to turn to the proper path." The doe cupped his cheek in her palm. "Kato, when we first met, you told me you believed everything had a price. But what of your daughter? What would you offer, for a chance to see her again?"

The mink's breath caught in his throat. Slowly, he met her gaze once more. "Everything I own, everything I could ever hope to give, would pale before the chance to hold her again."

"And yet, you *do* have something to offer: a life of humility, and service to others. Of compassion for those you do not know, and forgiveness for even those who have done you grievous wrong—gifts God has already given you freely."

Behind them, the general din of the square had died away. When Kato turned, he saw a number of armored figures standing in the midst of the plaza, speaking with several laborers. Kirkassians, accompanied by a troop of vigiles. Gazes turned in their direction, and the kines nearby began to not-so-casually disperse.

"You need to leave," he told the preacher once more. "I can try to distract them."

Nadrine bade him to rise, clasping his paws. "If I am called to bear witness to my faith, I will do so gladly. And should God call me home to Him, I can think of no worthier path. Now go, Kato, in service to God, and love for one another." Letting go of his paws, she stepped out to meet the approaching soldiers. The foreign stoats paid no mind to anyone else as they seized her, though several of the vigiles shot nervous glances at the crowd of onlookers, who had settled like vultures at the scene of a wolf-kill. Kato himself stepped back slightly, limbs trembling, throat raw with guilt and sorrow.

With Nadrine in their midst, the Kirkassians marched across the plaza, the officers of the city watch withdrawing slowly behind them. Several of the ordinary citizens began to jeer, following at a distance. Then a cry rose up, cutting through the tension: "Lykeno is dead! Murdered, by the disciples of the prophet!"

Murmurs rippled through the assembly like wildfire over dead bracken. "Is it true?" "They have long sought to destroy Tiber!"

"Lykeno has always shielded us!" Kato struggled through the press of bodies, listening to protests of innocence and cries for vengeance clash with rampant speculation.

"That's a filthy lie!" Kaius, the weasel who had helped Nadrine bring Kato back, thrust a finger at another kine. The crowd, which before spread unbroken throughout the entire plaza, began to cleave in two. A stone sailed through the air, and a doe cried out in pain. Kato himself was shoved aside as a stranger, a marten, rushed forward with a snarl. The square filled with shouts and growls, and the mink staggered over the rough cobblestones on all fours, choking on dust. He yowled as a foot jarred into his side, then scrambled upright, desperate to escape.

But when he turned back, the vigiles were advancing on the crowd, claws flexing over wooden truncheons. He saw Kaius, struggling to shield a younger kine as the brawl raged around them. The two stood directly in the path of the watch.

Kato strode forward with a wordless shout, and a crack to the skull sent him reeling into darkness.

The first thing he felt upon waking was cold stone splaying the fur of his face. Kato lay there for a moment, steeling himself against a stinging headache. He opened his eyes to nothingness. Panic sparked within his chest, but a moment later he caught the hazy form of the bars before him, and the terror faded into dull dread. Not blind, but imprisoned.

The mink sat upright, pondering his circumstances. Could the conspiracy have failed? But it was word of the assassination that sparked the riot—unless that was itself a lie? Or perhaps he had merely been dragged here at random, in which case he would likely be released soon. A little lighter of coin, but free nonetheless. The only thing to do was wait.

The cell had no window, but was spacious enough to permit the mink to move around. The only adornment was a wooden bucket, which reeked faintly of the prior occupant's leavings. Kato pressed himself into the farthest corner from it and tried to sleep.

He was startled a short time later by the slam of a heavy door, followed by the tread of careful footsteps. Kato sat upright and waited until the figure—clad in the blue tunic of the vigiles—appeared on the other side of the bars. Without a word, the kine set a small bowl of water just inside the cell, then tossed a hunk of stale bread into the mink's lap and departed.

Kato stumbled to his feet, clutching the bread tightly. "Wait!" But the footfalls only continued to recede, and the distant door slammed once more. He slumped back against the wall, then gnawed on the bread. The water was tepid, but welcome.

The first few hours stretched agonizingly, but with no way of seeing the sky, he soon lost track of time. The wooden bowl sat empty as his tongue cried out for water, and his stomach rumbled at the memory of the long-vanished crust. Anxiety was hardly a worthy respite from boredom, and so he slept intermittently, cursing the cold stone that was his new bed.

After what had certainly been at least a day, the guard did not return, and Kato's worry began to fester into something deeper.

Anger simmered in his heart: not only was he a citizen of Tiber, but one of prominence! How dare he be treated as some common rabble? But just as quickly, his passion was doused by the remembrance of how easily he had cast others to the wolves. And now here he sat, with nothing. Was this not what he deserved? His mind wandered once more to the scriptures: *Those who deal in sin shall be repaid in kind.* Muttering the words to himself in the darkness, over and over, Kato let them guide him into sleep.

Though he had no way of being certain, Kato believed he was into his third day in the cell. The stench of his own refuse stung faintly at his nostrils, and the fur of his coat itched fiercely. His throat burned, and his hollow stomach ached; significant movement sent lances of pain through his gut and up into his chest. Not that he had energy for much labor, save to crane his neck and glance longingly at the bars, praying that someone might come for him, if only to toss him another chunk of bread, and whet his tongue with a splash of water.

But the mink knew, in his heart, that he did not deserve such kindness. That this was the reward he had purchased. He only wished he could see Marenna once more—to hold her paw, to feel her embrace, to breathe in her scent as he cradled her head to his breast. To give her the love he should never have withheld. Kato let the tears roll down his face in silent acceptance of his fate, and drifted off once more, unsure if he would wake again.

"Are you all right?" The voice dragged him from the depths of unconsciousness. Squinting, the mink found himself slumped against a cold limestone wall in an unfamiliar section of the city. An icy rain drummed on the streets, the drops stinging where they soaked through his pelt. His eyes crawled up, up to the grim, grey sky, obscured by a stranger's silhouette. "Would you like something to eat?"

Kato's stomach burned at the mere thought of food, but the words would not form on his tongue. He stretched a tentative paw towards the stranger, then froze. Staring back at him was a perfect copy of himself.

"Come," the other Kato said, proffering a paw, "let's get you out of the rain." No sooner did he accept than Kato found himself in his own domus, surrounded by friends old and new, though the mink could not name how he knew most of them. He saw Felix and Iulia, mingling with commoners, and even Kaius was present. The mirror-him stood at the center of the gathering, and by his side, Marenna, clutching a kit to her breast: a newborn, swaddled in white cloth. The sight set the burdens of his heart crumbling to dust.

Suffused in the glow of the love before him, Kato felt a stirring deep within his soul, mighty beyond measure and yet tender as the look in his wife's eyes, ringing with a voice that echoed from the very foundations of the world.

Rise, and follow.

Shifting against the cold stone, Kato found himself back in his cell.

"Kato? Thank the gods, it's you!" Felix's voice pulled him from his daze, and he craned his stiff neck to see his friend grasping the bars.

Felix turned to the guard. "Release him at once!" The cell door swung open with a horrid screech that nevertheless rang like music in Kato's ears, and a moment later, the mink felt his friend's paws grappling for a hold on his trembling, hunger-weak limbs.

"Oh, gods," Felix said. "Come, there's food and drink in the barracks."

Kato remembered little of staggering up the stairs, one arm supported by the senator, the other by a rather irritated guard. After gulping down several glasses of weak wine, the mink was seated at a plain table, with overripe apples, stale bread, and a thin slice of salted pork thrust before him. It was mediocre even by the standards of the city watch, and it was the most delicious meal he'd ever eaten. The thin ray of pale morning light coming through a narrow window was nearly bright enough to blind him.

While he ate, Felix, having brandished his rank to grant the two privacy, explained what had transpired during the course of his imprisonment.

"The consul," his eyes darted around the room, "was killed. Afterwards, the Senate proclaimed Talinus consul."

"Talinus?" Kato nearly choked on the apple. "Was he—"

"Yes," Felix sighed. "With Korvo's approval, Talinus has been granted emergency powers... 'until the crisis passes.' " He leaned back in his chair, dragging a paw over his face. "Tiber has been wracked by riots the last three days, and a number of sectarians have been apprehended." Kato had suspected as much, but to hear confirmation sent a fresh spike of guilt into his heart. But rather than attempt to cast it off, or let it fester, the mink resolved to draw from it the strength to atone.

His friend went on. "The Fourth Legion has been recalled to the city, though the Ninth—under Lenecius—has reportedly begun marching south as well. And a number of senators have fled for the countryside, if not distant provinces, while several of—" with another furtive glance, he lowered his voice—"several of our prominent friends have been found dead. I suppose my being rather unimportant has proven fortunate, for once."

Kato swallowed a bite of bread. "Do... do you wonder if what we did was wrong, Felix?" Seeing the other mink's stare, he waved a paw. "More than just this—what we've been doing our whole lives."

Felix snorted. "Now you sound like one of the converts."

Kato stared at the empty wooden platter before him, a wistful smile creeping across his muzzle. "I suppose I do." Watching his friend's amusement slowly shift into perplexion, the merchant reached across the table, taking the senator's paw. "I... learned a great deal from a stranger, recently, someone far wiser than I expected to find. But they gave me a glimpse of something... *wonderful.* If you ever grow as tired of all this as I have, perhaps I could show you, as well?" His smile soured at the memory of Nadrine, but she would not have wished for him to sulk. After all, there was work to do.

"But first," he added, "I need to see my wife."

The warmth of the sun's rays on his face nearly brought him to tears. Throughout the city, other kounavi hurried by with cloaks drawn tight around tense faces, and despite his joy, Kato could not bring himself to shy from their plight, to ignore it and carry on, as before. Not after what he had done. But neither would he allow himself to sink into despair, or draw about him like a dark cloud the malaise that had kept him listlessly trudging along for far too long. If an ordinary kine like himself could do such evil, then surely good, too, lay within his grasp.

When he and Felix arrived at the familiar façade of his domus, it was Denno who answered the door. The old weasel's face, dour and weary, brightened at the sight of the pair.

"M—master?" he stammered. "It's—it's you!" The slave hurriedly ushered them inside, then directed Kato into the foyer, where Marenna sat, rifling through a sheaf of parchment. Her eyes were red and bleary, the fur beneath them damp.

"...Kato?" She rose slowly, steadying herself against the wall. Shaking off his friend's grip, Kato strode over and wrapped his arms around his wife, pulling her close.

"Thank the gods you're all right." He kissed her forehead, cherishing the way she melted into him.

"*Me?*" Marenna laughed through a sob. "I was so worried! Felix visited, and told us... he told us that the consul had been killed, and there were riots across the city. When you never came home, I thought—I thought..."

Kato stepped back to look her in the eye. "I am here now, love."

"Kato—last night, I dreamt..." Marenna trailed off, her gaze going distant. "I saw you, and somehow I knew you were safe. I saw *us*, together, with so many others, and... and there was a kit. A *new* kit, beautiful and healthy." Her smile widened, tears glinting in her eyes, as she ran her paws over her slender belly. "I don't know *how* I can feel so certain, but... I believe I am with child again."

Kato took her paws in his, drawing her close. "I dreamt it as well." He pulled her head to his breast, savoring her scent, cherishing the press of her over his beating heart. "We have been given this blessing, Marenna. I have much to learn, and much to do, but... we can face tomorrow together." Kissing her once more, he took her paw, then gestured to their surroundings. "When I look upon all that I have, all that *we* have, even with our burdens, I recognize how greatly we have been blessed. And now, it is our turn to do good for others."

The mink turned to see Felix watching him with incredulous eyes. "I must admit, Kato," the senator began, "your newfound certainty… it makes me wonder."

"It is difficult to explain, but I hope to be able to show you. To learn with you." Kato glanced to his wife. "If you are willing, I would like to welcome some guests under our roof, at least for a little while. They will be needing somewhere safe to stay."

Marenna cocked her head. "Are they friends of yours?"

Kato tried to imagine how Kaius would react to seeing him again, and chuckled. "Not quite, though with any luck, that may change." He pulled on a traveler's cloak and headed for the door. "I was hoping you would accompany me, Felix."

"You're leaving already?" the doe blurted out, just as the senator asked "Where are we going?"

"The neighborhoods just east of the Nivallios." Kato stooped to kiss his wife, then patted her paw. "I *will* be back, Marenna. I promise you." She gave a silent nod, lingering in the entryway as he and Felix stepped out into the light of late morning.

The rising sun bathed him in its radiance; a flight of starlings sliced through the air, heading south. Somewhere closer, the melancholic autumn song of a robin floated through the trees. Again the aching in his heart returned, doubts and fears bubbling up beneath the relief of homecomings and reunions: Could he ever hope to tip the scales against the weight of his sins, against the recent bloodshed he had enabled, against the avarice and callous indulgence he had clung to nearly all his life? The mink thought once more of Nadrine, his throat tightening, until he heard her words again, echoing within his breast: *We do what we can, with what we have.*

Perhaps he would simply need to have faith. And so, with a smile on his muzzle and a prayer in his heart, Kato shook the dust from his sandals and headed back into the city.

THE LAMENT OF THE BATAVII

J.S. HAWTHORNE

"Oh, my child," King Juba said as he guided the legionary back to her feet from where she had collapsed. "I'm so sorry." He was a tall horse with sandy tan fur and a shaggy black mane that hinted at distant leonine ancestry, dressed in the purple robes of his station.

"But he was fine," the legionary sobbed into the king's robes, headless of their respective stations. Like the king, she was not Roman, though she had earned the right to the tria nomina—Tulla Aula Agrippina—but they were both loyal to the emperor and to the Empire. That is where their similarities ended. He was tall, handsome, graceful. She was a short and squat mouse, heavily muscled from years in the legions, and covered in dozens of scars from innumerable battles. Her right eye was the blue-grey of a sky dreaming of a storm, and her left eye was missing, as was the top of the same ear. Her hair, a pale blonde just a shade darker than her white fur, was tied up in the complicated side knot common amongst her people.

"He was fine," she repeated, her voice weak. Some part of her brain was screaming at her, telling her she had failed, utterly failed. The rest was overcome with a creeping numbness that threatened to steal the strength from her legs once again.

A dark-honey voice lilted from the darkness, "It was twisted magic, a curse." Aula raised her head and took in, but did not truly see, an Egyptian jackal clad in the raiment of a priestess standing near the entrance to the deeper chambers. Her black fur was painted in gold and silver in the way of her people, and her hair was in long, tight braids to her waist with beads that rattled softly as she moved.

"This is Senhyrus," King Juba told Aula. "She helped tend the princeps while we awaited you."

"I want to see him," Aula said. Before she could be stopped, and ignoring the protestations of king and priestess both, she pushed her way through the guards—praetorian, she noted with disgust, not the Cohors Germanorum, not the princeps' personal bodyguards—and to the room that had once been his bedchambers.

Gaius Julius Caesar, princeps iuventutus, consul designatus, adopted child of Caesar Augustus, heir to the Empire of Rome, the most powerful man in all of the eastern reaches, lay beneath a white-grey shroud in this house perched on the sea cliffs of Lycia, so far from Rome, from his father, from the world that awaited a triumphant return that would never happen.

In honor of his adoptive family, Gaius Caesar's death shroud depicted him, not as an eagle, as he had been in life, but as a rabbit, a true Caesar. The muzzle-embroidery hung oddly over his beak. They had left off the silver circlet, at least, in the shape of a pair of ears wrapped in laurel leaves. The Roman obsession with heritage eluded her, as had the costumes and prosthetics all designed to impress on others that Gaius Caesar, was, by virtue of adoption, lapine, a true Caesar, just as Imperator Caesar Augustus, the Emperor, had become a rabbit by virtue of his adoption by the first Gaius Julius Caesar, never mind that he had been born a wolf to a family of wolves. Gaius Caesar—her Gaius Caesar, to whom she had sworn on her gods and the gods of Rome to protect—had been an eagle, as beautiful and terrible as a sunrise. But it was not Jupiter's children who ruled Rome, but the descendants of Aeneas, who was the son of Venus and took the lapine form of Venus. Aula's people, the Ubii, did not claim descent from the gods, as the Romans and Egyptians did. None of the gods were mice, but each took a form particular to him, her, or theirself, as was their want.

All these thoughts flashed through her mind in an instant, all of her confusion about Roman rules and customs and heritage, all of the invisible walls that separated her from the one to whom she had pledged her sword and her life. For Rome's friendship, her tribe had sworn fealty to the Senate and then to the Emperor. For her devotion, she had sworn fealty to the man who now lay, cold and breathless, under a shroud that hid his true face.

Cold realization ran over her. She would never see him again. Perhaps he might be welcomed into Elysium, forever feted as a true hero, or maybe he would rise, as his grandfather had, on the back of a comet to godhood. Neither of those places were ones that she might follow, her oath be damned. When her allotted time was finished, she might hope to join the wælcyrge, but certainly not Elysium. Certainly the Roman gods would not accept a barbarian such as herself among their kind.

Or perhaps worse. Had she found swifter passage, dared riskier roads, maybe the comfort she had carried with her from Augustus would have been enough to give Gaius Caesar the strength to defeat this curse. Had her failure so stained her soul that her destination was the frozen land of the dishonored and forgotten dead? Would even her gods, then, cast their eyes from her, among the lost and damned?

Once, that thought would have terrified her. Now, kneeling before the shrouded and peaceful dead, it was just one more barb in her mind, slashing and then torn away, to be replaced by a new pain, a new realization of loss. Her imagination conjured for her a thousand lost scenarios and might-have-beens, a thousand different things that she would now never have the opportunity to do. She would have given anything to be the peaceful corpse that lay on the cold stone instead of the regretful and lost survivor.

Time fled, leaving no impression of its passing in Aula's mind. Her knees ached from prolonged contact with the sun-warm marble, but the pain was masked behind the waterfall of her emotions. Tears rolled down her face and dashed against her lorica, shattering to the floor. She was vaguely aware of the movement of the sun and the shadows that that shortened and then lengthened once again.

At some point, she ran out of tears to cry, dammed by the great wall of fear and rage and loss deep within her.

"Child," King Juba was next to her, his hand warm and comforting on her shoulder. "It is time to say goodbye. His body must be prepared to return it to his father." To be cremated, he meant, to have even this illusion of sleep stripped away, before the ashes were sealed in their tomb. Gaius Caesar was as far away from Aula as he could be, and yet this thought, to have him interred where she could not even have the pale comfort of being in his presence, stripped away, very nearly overwhelmed her.

Aula nodded silently, and permitted the king to pull her to her feet. The priestess, Senhyrus, was there, too, and together they guided Aula to her chambers on the far side of the palace. There, King Juba left her in Senhyrus's care.

"He was whole and healthy when I left," said Aula vaguely. Senhyrus half-carried her to her cot. "His injury had been minor. Barely enough to stop the campaign. They sent me to Rome to get messages of comfort from his father."

"Abbadon's treachery," said Senhyrus. "A small thing, a little poison that clung to the consul and drew the attention of a creature. It fed from him, from his hopes and dreams and ambitions. It left him..." She struggled for the word. "Empty inside." Aula gave a small sob, and Senhyrus hugged her. "I am so sorry. We did all we could for him, but he simply never could quite shake the wound. If we could have found a way to remove the poison, to send this creature away, but..."

"I will kill Abbadon," Aula said into Senhyrus's shoulder. "I will rip him limb from limb for this. I will leave his body for the scorpions and the scarabs, and may they choke on him."

"O my daughter," murmured Senhyrus, her voice heavy with grief. She held Aula at arms' length, the jackal's bronze eyes searching the mouse's blue-grey one. "Do not let revenge consume your heart. Abbadon is beyond your power now."

"I will avenge my lord," said Aula, ferocity burning away the despair for an instant. "You said the poison summoned a creature to drain Gaius Caesar's life away. If I cannot revenge myself on Abbadon, I will find and slay this monster."

Senhyrus released Aula, looking discomfited. "None could even tell us what it was. The Romans say it was Parthian, the Parthians say it was Scythean. It was months before we even realized it was in the palace, though surely it had haunted these passages before you had even left for Rome. Only the consul could have told you what it looked like and how it attacked him. All we can say is that it appears gone, now."

"Can it be summoned again?"

Senhyrus frowned, her manner turning from maternal to imperial. "I do not wish to answer that question. This is a dark road you seek, legionary. I would not be the one to guide you along it." Aula started to interrogate the priestess further, a feverish plan forming in the eye of the maelstrom that was her emotions. Senhyrus pressed a finger to her lips. "Rest, Aula. Forget this. The consul's death was a tragedy. Mourn, with us if you wish, alone if you must. Mourn and live.

"Tomorrow, I travel with King Juba back to Mauretania. Return with us. Lord Caesar always spoke well of you; I'm sure his majesty would welcome your presence and treat you as an honored guest in Volubilis."

Aula's cyclopic gaze held Senhyrus for a moment before she nodded her assent. Then she stifled a yawn.

Senhyrus smiled at her. "Rest, then. I shall make the preparations and I will gather you in the morning before we leave." She hesitated for an instant, as though assuring herself that Aula wouldn't do anything foolish, before she left, pulling closed the door to Aula's chamber behind her.

Any tiredness fled from Aula as soon as the door closed, but still she did not move. She sat on her bed, eye half-closed, as the gloam lengthened, and she plotted. When she was finally ready to act, night had fallen completely and the moon hung bright and heavy over the rocky mountain forest outside her window.

In the twilight, she stood and carefully removed and packed each piece of her armor. She treated the items with the utmost care; they represented her rank and station as decanus. Aula was proud to wear the armor of a legionary, proud to be among the Numerus Batavorum, to protect the Emperor and his family.

But she had failed. She had failed in her duties as both legionary and guard. The armor had become a representation of that failure, and she pledged not to put it on again until she had redeemed herself.

Idly, Aula wondered if that made what she was going to do next easier or harder. She bypassed the warm wool and scaly hide clothing of her northern homeland, despite the chill of night approaching, in favor of a knee-length tunic someone had left for her. It was woven in the eastern style and made of itchy wool instead of more fashionable linen, and it took her a moment to get it to hang on her shoulders correctly. One hand went to the knot of her hair, but she couldn't make herself undo that last nod to her homeland.

Aula was still a one-eyed mouse with a barbarian haircut, even if she wore Roman clothing. No one in the palace would take her for anything other than one of the Batavii out of uniform, but, she hoped, she wouldn't be so conspicuous as to be stopped, at least not before she completed her objective.

The gods were with her. Wraith-like, Aula was able to slip through the halls without notice. There was a pall hanging around the palace, Gaius Caesar's death like a specter that muted sound and emotion. Aula was no less affected than anyone else, but she had the presence of mind to use it to her advantage, at least.

A bodyguard—Batavii, thank Thunar—stopped her just outside the hall that led to King Juba's rooms. Once she drew close enough for the guard to see her face in the wan moonlight, he lowered his sword.

"You were sorely missed, sister," the guard told her in a low voice, speaking the tongue of their homeland. "The lord asked of you frequently at the end."

Where were you? she wanted to shout at him. Why didn't you protect him? The maelstrom in her mind answered in a voice that mocked hers: but where was I? Why didn't I?

Her voice was steady, her grip strong as she grasped the Batavii's forearm in solidarity and grief. "Thank you, brother. I wish I had been there to comfort him."

"He took comfort in the knowledge that you had returned to his father," the guard told her, "and that you would return to him. Don't believe that you are responsible for the lord's passing. It was the treachery of Abbadon, not you."

She thanked him for his kind words, and continued to the Imperial wing of the palace. Her luck held, or otherwise no one thought the Imperial chambers required guarding with the consul dead, and she passed by no one other than a group of hired Egyptian mourners.

Inside was cool and dark, unlit even by the light of the moon. Gaius Caesar's shrouded corpse was a pale luminescence in the center of the room, which smelled of salt and herbs, the strange preservatives designed to keep his body fresh for the journey back to Rome. That all of the Empire would cry for him was a cold comfort to Aula. The hole his loss left in her was too big to fill with the wails and prayers of even a thousand empires.

She approached the shroud-covered body. The room was silence given voice. Aula became aware that she was holding her breath. She forced herself to inhale, and then struggled to exhale.

Gaius Caesar was as still and silent as marble and, for the first time, Aula wondered if she had nerve enough. A part of her wanted to pull back the shroud, to reveal Gaius Caesar's true face, but she found that her hands would not obey that command. She twitched the shroud just enough to reveal his left arm, suppressing the revulsion she felt at the odor of early decomposition. Aula couldn't bear to see any more, and she pulled the arm free of the restful pose it had been in. It came easily, rigor mortis long since fading, the flesh cold and lifeless beneath her fingers. Once free of the shroud, she could see the wound easily, a dark, unhealed scar in the midst of the white-speckled red feathers of his forearm.

Aula drew her dagger. She probed the puckered wound with the blade's tip, unsure what she was searching for. Curses were somewhat beyond her experience, but surely, she thought, there had to be some sort of physical talisman, something to connect the curse to the person. She did not want to treat Gaius Caesar's body so shamefully, but she could not admit defeat, and would not permit his death to go unavenged. If grief would not fill the hole in her heart, then revenge would.

The dagger caught on something. With a grimace, Aula fished it out, revealing a sharp sliver of iron coated in a greasy brown ichor. She dropped it into her palm, and the ichor stained her fur. It appeared to her to be a shattered piece of dagger or sword. There was only one thing to do, if she truly wanted to revenge her lord, but it was hard to face that realization. Still. She sheathed her dagger, took a deep breath, and then drove the splinter into the muscle between the bones of her left forearm. It burned as it sank in, vanishing into her flesh and leaving an ugly black wound behind.

The wound still itched the next morning when Aula woke to Senhyrus gently shaking her.

"We are ready to be off," Senhyrus told her. "If you would like to come with us?"

Aula mumbled her assent and begged for a few minutes of Senhyrus and King Juba's indulgence to get her things ready. Senhyrus swept off to inform the king, and Aula struggled from under the blankets. Within a half hour, she had reached the docks and the Grecian style polyreme that the dockmaster assured her was Juba's. She had not found it within her to wear her armor, which was safely stored in her pack with her few meager belongings. Instead, she wore a simple, undyed tunic under a thin cloak, arms and shoulders bare to the golden Mediterranean sun. A wrap of old cloth covered the wound in her forearm. It had not closed overnight but oozed that foul ichor. Already it had stained her bandage. She tugged her cloak over to cover it.

The barge was much fancier than Aula was used to. Her limited interactions with the sea had been largely confined to military transports from one battle to another. A luxury ship like this, more akin to a floating palace than a ship, she thought, was as far beyond her comprehension as the terrestrial palace of Caesar had been when Augustus had invited her to receive gifts and encouragement for Gaius Caesar. Gifts and encouragement that now lay, unopened, in a chest to be returned to Rome with the body of Gaius Caesar.

"Child?" King Juba placed a hand on her shoulder, and Aula started. "You looked a world away."

"Apologies, Majesty," Aula murmured. They walked side-by-side along the gangplank and up to the broad deck. The king was talking to her in his low, reassuring voice, but Aula's thoughts drifted as she watched the crew. They were primarily Mauretanian, with a mix of Egyptians, Greeks, and Romans among them, judging by clothing and hair styles, even a distinctly Brittanic kilt. Aula's eyes were drawn to an unusual figure, a snowy white owl with deep red eyes, wearing a golden Greek chiton and matching cloak. The owl's eyes caught Aula's and the mouse stopped dead in her tracks.

"Child?" asked King Juba. She became aware that her tail was lashing at his ankles. She stepped on it to hold it steady.

"I'm fine, Majesty. If you please, who is that?" She nodded at the owl.

"Who?"

Aula turned in confusion to the king. His brow was creased in worry. She raised her hand to point but, when she looked, the owl had vanished into the crowd on the deck.

"There was an owl," she said. "I swear there was."

"Perhaps one of the crew?"

"She wasn't dressed like crew," Aula murmured. She scanned the crowd, but there were no owls there. "My apologies, Majesty. I... Perhaps I am still unsettled by the lord's death."

"No need to apologize, child," said King Juba. He gave her shoulder a squeeze. "I regret there was insufficient room to find a cabin for you alone, but the berth is still spacious and you will find your cabinmates quite agreeable, if you would like to rest while the ship is made ready to go?"

She bowed deeply. "Thank you, Majesty, but no. I think I would prefer some sunlight. I'll find a place out of the way to sit for a time." They said their goodbyes and Aula headed for the prow.

No one stopped her as she slid ghostlike amidst the crew and passengers, and ultimately found a place to sit, her legs dangling off of the side, hanging above the long oars that were just being lowered into the deceptively placid sea. She laid her head in her hands as she leaned against the railing, her back to the shore. In the far distance, dark green against the golden sea, she could just make a line of islands.

The ship pulled out into the ocean and began the swift route west. They would stop almost every night for the next week at a new city, before they would make open water and longer stretches. In a month's time, when they swapped polyreme for carriage at Tingi, it would be the farthest Aula had ever been from the forests of Germania, across the temperamental Mediterranean, away from everything she had ever known.

A failure running from her shame.

"You have a look about you."

Aula started. She must have dozed off. The deck was nearly empty, the sun high overhead, nothing but wide ocean visible from her vantage point.

And standing at the railing, looking out at the trackless sea, was the strange owl.

"Who are you?" Aula asked. No one had ever snuck up on her before, not that she would admit, and it bothered her that she had fallen asleep as much as it did that this stranger had been able to get this close without waking her.

"It depends who you ask." The gapes of her beak twitched upward in something like a smile. "Around here, they call me Mormo."

There was something about the name that tugged at Aula's memory. "That's Greek, isn't it?"

Mormo nodded. "Though my father was Egyptian, and my mother Trinacrian."

"I've never seen an owl like you before."

"Thank you. Did you know you're bleeding?" Mormo pointed at the bandage around Aula's wrist. It was soaked through with ichor. "A nasty wound, there. Shouldn't you have someone take a look at it?"

"It's fine," Aula snapped with finality. Mormo shrugged. "Why do you care, anyway?"

"Curiosity. I saw you looking at me before, when we were still in dock." She knelt down, fiery red eyes burning into Aula's storm-blue one. "Ah, I see."

The stare was uncomfortable, but Aula couldn't seem to pull away. "See what?"

"Failure," said Mormo with a satisfied smile.

Aula woke with a start and nearly toppled forward into the ocean. She snagged the railing before her momentum could carry her over the side and into the sea. Strong hands grabbed her by the shoulder and hauled her back onto the deck. Looking up, Aula saw Senhyrus's burnished bronze gaze looking down at her.

"Are you alright?"

"I'm fine," said Aula as she scrambled to her feet. The sun was near to the horizon, the ship pointed almost directly at it. Behind her, the deck was alive with sailors making ready to pull into their first port at Rhodus. "I must have fallen asleep."

Senhyrus nodded, but she didn't look entirely convinced. "The sailors say you've been here all day, that you refused food or offers to rest."

Aula's eyebrows drew down as she frowned. "No one's spoken to me all day," she said. "Except for that owl."

"Owl?"

Aula nodded, then hesitated and shook her head. "No, wait, I think that was a dream." She watched the ship glide past the two massive pillars standing guard at the mouth of the harbor; a foot and leg to the knee stood on one pillar, while the other carried the partner of the first but only to the shin. A long arm jutted just above the waves, all that remained of the fabled Colossus.

Senhyrus followed Aula's gaze into the fallen statue. "The Pharaoh offered to rebuild it, you know," she said conversationally. "Ptolemy Euergetes, that is, who ruled when the statue fell, but the city said an oracle had told them it had fallen because it had offended Ra."

"Helius," Aula corrected automatically. Catching the look on Senhyrus's muzzle, she explained. "The Romans call him Helius Hyperion, and I don't think he's the same person as your Ra."

"Does not Helius pull the great wheel of the sun across the sky each day?" Aula nodded. "And so does great Ra. How could they be different? We are not so far from Egypt as to be able to miss a second sun rising."

"In my homeland, I was taught that the sun is Sunna, and the moon her brother, Manni. They race across the sky each day and night, chased by the great wolves, who will one day catch and devour them, ushering the Twilight." She laid her forearms on the railing. "Can it be that a great wolf will one day eat Ra?"

Senhyrus snorted. "Ra's only enemy is the serpent Apophis."

"Then it can't be that Ra is also Sunna. And if he is not her, then why should he be Helius?"

Senhyrus scowled, and Aula changed the subject.

"Will we be staying here in Rhodus long?"

"Only overnight." Senhyrus set a hand on Aula's shoulder. "Come, have dinner with me. There is a taberna near the harbor that I like to visit when I am in the city." There was no easy or polite way to avoid it and, despite feeling not the least bit hungry, Aula found herself trailing Senhyrus as the jackal led the way through Rhodus. The city itself was beautiful, though Aula found her gaze drawn to the remnants of the earthquake, more than a century before, that had destroyed the great Colossus. Stone facades and ancient monuments were cracked or tumbled, unfaded scars from old wounds. It made the skin around her own wound itch.

Aula let herself be shown to a table in the quiet taberna, curling her tail around her waist to avoid being stepped on. She was hardly aware of the food that she ordered, except for a bottle of wine undiluted. A barbarous habit, as far as the Romans were concerned, but it had been ten years since she had had wine at strength instead of watered down, and she felt as though she needed something stronger. She made polite noises as Senhyrus attempted to engage her in conversation, but a one-sided conversation cannot last forever, and they found themselves eating in silence. Aula's food had been prepared very well, but she tasted only ashes.

When it was over, Aula stood and thanked Senhyrus, intending to return to the ship and get some sleep. For whatever reason, she felt exhausted, her day-long slumber notwithstanding.

"Tell me about the owl," Senhyrus said, and Aula stopped in her tracks.

"It was just a dream." Aula didn't know why she felt so defensive about the question, or why her tail lashed the air behind her. She found she couldn't meet the jackal's gaze.

"You said to his Majesty that you had seen an owl when you boarded. I checked, daughter, and there are no owls, no white-feathered people of any kind aboard the ship."

"Why do you call me daughter?" Aula asked, suddenly angry, though she could not say why. "There cannot be more than a year or two difference in our age."

Senhyrus looked taken aback. "I apologize, Aula. It is a habit, I suppose. I joined the priesthood at a young age, as my people are accustomed to such things. I think I began to call everyone child so that they would take me more seriously." She offered Aula a smile and her hand. "Will you forgive me?"

Anger gave way to embarrassment. Aula grasped the jackal's hand briefly, but couldn't find the words to smooth over the moment. Instead she made her goodbyes and fled, haunted by the hurt and confused look on Senhyrus's face.

The owl was waiting for her in the fresh, bright air. Aula scowled.

"They tell me you're not real," Aula said as Mormo fell into step beside her. The two made their way down to the shore and the ship.

"Well, they would know."

"Why does everyone insist that you're not on the ship?"

"Because, girl, they don't trust you. Don't you think they'd have found me if they believed in you? They pity you, sure, the legionary who failed, the messenger who crawled instead of flew. Cursed by Mercury himself, it would seem."

"Mercury isn't my god," Aula growled. She reached for her sword and remembered, too late, that it was safely packed away with her armor, tucked into the hold of the ship.

"Are not Mercury and your Wuodan one and the same? Messenger, healer, god of travelers?"

"Roman propaganda," Aula said, then clapped a hand over her muzzle, her eyes darting around to see if she had been overheard. Mormo smiled wider, and Aula felt the anger returning. "A... mistake. Wuodan has little in common with Mercury, and I am cursed by neither."

"No? Blessed of the gods, are you? Is that why you were late with your tidings of comfort from Caesar? Why you paid back the Emperor's kindness and charity with sloth and delay?"

If she had only returned in time. She closed her eyes and clenched her fists.

"You know that's why Juba and Senhyrus even agreed to take you, right?" Mormo went on, relentless, her voice drilling into Aula's ears. "Pity for the little girl who failed so badly. Pity and the hope that you could be put to pasture somewhere on the edges of the empire, far away from where your bungling could ruin more of Rome's heirs."

"Enough!" Aula shouted. She swung out and hit nothing. When she opened her eyes, the owl was nowhere to be found, but Mormo's haunting laughter followed her all the way down to the ship.

Aula didn't sleep. The glowing coals in the brazier that heated her shared cabin put her in mind of Mormo's red eyes, and every time she closed her eyes to try and sleep, she had the absurd thought that the owl was staring at her, staring and smirking.

She arose with the dawn, and climbed onto the deck in time to watch Sunna or Helius or whoever begin their daily race across the sky. The sailors were already making ready for the trip to the next port, on the isle of Crete. Aula had heard Greeks claim that Crete had been the birthplace of civilization—that was, of course, nonsense, as far as Aula was concerned, as civilization had been taught directly by the gods—and that Crete had flourished for millennia until King Minos had offended Neptune, and the power of Athens had risen.

Aula spent the day avoiding Senhyrus, who seemed determined to be friends. The mouse kept finding dark, out-of-the-way corners to curl up in, her half-missing ear perked for the sound of jackal claws clicking on wood. At the first hint of the priestess, Aula would scurry away to find a new hiding-hole. Easier to avoid by far was King Juba, who made a few attempts to speak with her, but she could always count on some urgent piece of business to drag him away, before she was forced to answer any questions.

Of the white owl, Aula saw not a feather, and by the time they were pulling into port, in the shadow of Mount Cadiston, she was just believing that perhaps she had left Mormo behind on Rhodus.

She chanced standing along the railing to watch the ship dock and get her first look of Crete.

In the bay, just beyond the city, she could see crumbled walls and ancient statues, all covered over in green algae. She asked one of the sailors, who simply shrugged and told her to talk to one of the Cretians if she wanted to know the old city's history. Aula considered the possibility of wandering into the town, but spotted Senhyrus descending the gangplank and changed her mind. Instead, she sat against the railing and watched the hustle and bustle on the dock below. Even that died away after what seemed but a moment. When darkness had fallen, and the docks had emptied, Aula went to her cabin.

It was blessedly empty, the others opting to spend the night in a bed in the city instead of a crowded hammock aboard the ship. Aula doused the coals in the brazier and then, in darkness, sank into a troubled and uneasy sleep.

Her dreams were confused and broken, a cascade of images that made little sense. When she awoke, well before the sun had risen and while all was still and quiet, she remembered only a few, disjointed fragments. Gaius Caesar, dead and moldering, reaching for her from under his burial shadow. Mormo, hunting her on silent wings through an upside-down forest. A great hole in her wrist where she had stabbed herself with the metal splinter. An echoing hole she could fall into forever and never escape.

She awoke to the hammer-beat of her heart and her clothes soaked in sweat. She peeled herself out of them and headed for the dock. A quick dip in the bay might wash away the last remnants of her nightmares. She followed the beach along until she found a secluded cove, hidden from the city by the cracked walls jutting out of the water. Wading out into the frigid water until her feet could barely touch the bottom, she took several deep breaths, then dived below.

Underneath the waves, the bay was like an alien world, far away from the death of Gaius Caesar, from the strange owl, from her bizarre and conflicted thoughts, her nightmares. The icy temperatures were too much to stay submerged for long, but she found she was able to walk along the algae-slick edge of the broken walls to explore. Beautiful mosaics still filled the submerged plazas and streets, depicting people and places and myths she did not recognize. She became so engrossed in the ancient ruins that she lost track of time.

When finally she turned back to shore and the ship, she found herself face-to-face with a stranger. He was much taller and broader than she, a muscular bull with mostly white fur except for large reddish-brown patches along the sides of his ribcage and down to his hips, so dark as to be nearly black. His horns were short and wickedly sharp, and curved forward almost parallel to his muzzle like a crown. He wore his hair in short, messy curls. There was a bucket in his hand.

He took her in with one swift glance, then pointed at her bandaged forearm and said something she didn't understand. She assumed it was Greek.

"Do you speak Latin?" she asked.

The bull made a face and shrugged. "Little," he allowed. "You are Romaios?"

It was her turn to shrug. "Close enough." She kept a wary eye on the bull as she climbed onto the beach. She had not thought to bring a cloth to dry herself, and had to content with pulling on her clothes while still damp. "What's your name?"

"Aethon," he said. "You?"

"Tulla Aula Agrippina," she said, a note of pride in her voice. A nasty voice in the back of her head asked her if she should be so prideful, when she had failed so badly. The tria nomina was an honor, did she truly deserve it?

Aethon snorted. "Roman. Your arm? It bleeds."

She glanced down. The wound had, indeed, reopened from the swimming, and the cloth was once again soaked with the strange ichor.

"Looks bad," Aethon said, his voice carefully neutral. Aula heard him splashing into the water, her ear twitching as it tried to follow him by sound alone. "You need a healer?"

"It's fine. I overexerted myself, it will stop in a moment." Fully dressed, she turned around to watch the bull kneeling in the waves and pouring water down his back with the bucket. "What are these ruins from?"

"Old city," Aethon grunted. He kept pouring the water over himself. "They say, Poseidon cursed it, and the bay reclaimed it. Or else Apollo and a plague." He glanced sidelong at her. "You from the ship? With the Mauretanian King?"

"Yes?"

"You going to leave with them?"

Aula tilted her head in bafflement. "Of course."

"They left."

It took a moment for the import of his words to penetrate, but once she understood, she took off at a run down the beach.

Moments later, her heart pounding in her chest, she skidded to a halt on the docks. The big polyreme was already a stade or more away. Aula shouted at the ship, jumping up and down and waving her arms, drawing the attention of the thin crowd milling at the harbor, but the ship did not slow. She lowered her arms and sat down heavily. All of her possessions were in the neat package she had made, now wending its way to the distant horizon, chased by the morning sun.

A lifetime of service and dedication, and through her own stupidity, she now had nothing except for the clothes on her back and the iron splinter in her arm.

"Failure does seem to follow you, doesn't it?" she heard a mocking voice. She spun to her feet, expecting to see the smirking, fire-eyed Mormo standing behind her, but no owl stood there. Instead, Aethon, looking wholly unconcerned and even a little bored, was strolling down the dock. He had gotten rid of his bucket and put on a simple but well-made chiton that left most of his chest bare. The bull frowned at her as he drew close, then looked past her to the departing ship. He seemed to make up his mind, then grunted at her to follow him.

Aula, completely at a loss, trailed after the bull. He led her all the way to the far end of the dock and a small boat with a single white sail. Aethon hopped in and, without a word, began making ready to cast off. Aula hovered at the dock's edge, wringing her hands as she watched the polyreme pull farther and farther away.

"You want a ride?" Aethon asked, and Aula looked down, startled to see the bull's boat was already gliding away from the dock. She leapt and crashed onto the side deck. Her claws scrabbled furiously at the hull as she began to slide down into the ocean. Without missing a beat, Aethon hauled her aboard. She sat for a moment, shivering, while Aethon manipulated the sail to catch the wind. The ship bucked slightly as it gathered speed, zipping away from the shore and into open water.

"Thank you," Aula managed. Her heart was still pounding, but the shivering slowed and then stopped, and she was able to move into a more comfortable position seated on the side deck.

Aethon shrugged. He spared her a quick glance, his eyes catching her ichor-soaked bandage, then turned to squint out into the ocean. They were catching up to King Juba's ship, but slowly.

"Might be a while," he told her.

She craned her head to watch the ship they were chasing, and nodded. There didn't seem to be anything to say to each other.

They finally caught up in the middle of the afternoon. A line was cast down and Aethon made his boat safe to tow while Aula climbed aboard.

She found King Juba waiting for her.

"O child," he said, grasping her by the shoulders and looking her up and down. "Are you alright? We did not discover you were missing until an hour ago. The Lady Senhyrus was arguing with the captain to turn the ship around."

As politely as she could manage, Aula freed herself from the king's grasp. "I am fine, Majesty," she told him with a deep bow. "It was my own fault. I lost track of the time." Aethon wordlessly joined her, matching her bow. "If it weren't for this kind stranger, I don't know what I would have done."

"Then we owe you our gratitude, master sailor," King Juba said, pulling Aethon out of his bow and squeezing both of his hands. "Thank you for returning our friend to us."

"It was nothing, Majesty," Aethon said, flushing a little bit at the attention. He hesitated for a moment, then asked King Juba a question in Greek. Juba's smile became quizzical, and he answered, and soon the two were engaged in a lively, if unintelligible to Aula, conversation. She offered King Juba another bow and muttered an excuse, then slid away from the two of them, uncomfortably aware of Aethon's gaze following her.

What Aula wanted most was to find her armor and simply hold it in her hands, to remind herself what she was, what she had dedicated her life to. But that impulse brought with it a forceful reminder of her failure and promise that she would not don the armor again until she had avenged Gaius Caesar. What she wanted least was to encounter Senhyrus and be drawn into another conversation, but that was unfair. The priestess had done nothing but be kind to her and concerned about her wellbeing, and Aula had rewarded that kindness with neglect. So, with a heavy heart, Aula strode off to look for the jackal.

Senhyrus found her first and, with a shout, rushed forward to hug Aula. The mouse, flushing, swiftly extricated herself. She then had to explain her entire misadventure once again and by the time she was finished, she was feeling extremely foolish. She found herself wishing she hadn't taken Aethon's offer of a ride.

"I must thank this friend of yours," Senhyrus told her. Aula shrugged uncomfortably.

"He's not a friend. Just a kind person who gave aid when I needed it." Had she really needed it? Had she wanted it? She disliked that she couldn't answer those questions. "I'm sorry, Senhyrus, I-I've had a trying morning. I think I will lay down for a while."

"Of course, Aula." Senhyrus gave her another hug before Aula was able to escape.

The cabin was blissfully empty. Aula took the opportunity to change her bandage. The wound still had not healed, and the skin looked grey and lifeless around it, especially in comparison to the strange color the ichor had dyed her fur. She gave the wound an experimental poke and discovered she had almost no sensation there, just a vague sense of pressure. With a shudder, she wrapped her arm in fresh linen.

Once done, Aula climbed back into her hammock and closed her eyes, swaying in the air with the slow rocking of the ship. It had been several days since she had arrived to find Gaius Caesar beneath his shroud, and she had to admit she was no nearer the creature that had drained his life away from him.

"You've just failed him in life and death, haven't you?"

Her eyes opened and she pulled herself up into a seated position, looking around for Mormo in the darkened cabin. It took her a moment to realize that she herself had spoken, not the phantom owl. With a nervous laugh, she laid back down and settled into the silence.

The next few days passed pleasantly enough for Aula. While she was inclined to avoid Senhyrus and King Juba, she was not able to avoid Aethon so easily. For someone with hooves, he was shockingly silent, and seemed to appear, as if coalescing from mist, whenever she found a lonely spot to brood. He did not attempt to force her into conversation or try to pry, but merely sat or stood nearby, the ancient colossus in miniature.

And over the next few days, Aula found herself not minding it. She told herself that it was futile to attempt to escape him and therefore would just sit in equal silence, but truly she enjoyed the company. By the time the polyreme had pulled out of port in Laconia, threading between the Ionian Sea to the north and the Sea of Siculus to the south, she had given up on avoiding him. A few days later, when the southern tip of Italia came into view, she began to follow Aethon around. No longer worried about tracking her down, the bull took to aiding the sailors with their daily tasks while Aula sat on crates or leaned on the railing, watching the sea roll away underneath them.

She checked her wound every night, when the lights had been dimmed in the cabin and she could steal a few private moments. It still oozed, her flesh around it still strangely numb, but she thought it was, little by little, closing. Her skin even seemed to be regaining some color.

The night before they sailed into Utica, Aula dreamed. She was sailing into Carthage a century before she was born. The city burned, turning the night red, but the ship was empty.

"ʿAzrubaʿal's failure," Mormo told her. Aula couldn't see the owl, but her voice echoed around the ship and the dead sea. "See what comes when a soldier falters? Lucius Caesar was dead before you left Lycia. By the time you had returned, both the Emperor's heirs lay beneath the shroud. What fate, then, suffers the great Empire of Rome? Shall the line of Caesar end? ʿAzrubaʿal saw Carthage burn; shall you see Rome, too, in flames?"

And then abruptly they faced, not Carthage and Africa, but Rome and Italia. It, too, burned, its flames fanned by the music of a cithara.

"The Emperor still lives," Aula said, the fire singing her fur. "The Empire endures."

"The Emperor is old, and frail. Who can take his place when he is gone?"

"Gaius and Lucius had a brother." Aula couldn't take her eyes away from the burning city.

"A child," sneered Mormo. "A monster in the form of a boy. Already his petty tyrannies threaten his standing with the Emperor."

"Then the son of the Empress, Tiberius Claudius..."

Mormo cut her off, "A old coward. He hides, hoping to return to exile. He cannot hold Rome."

"Then Nero Drusus, or Drusus's son…"

"Soldiers, not rulers. And you see what happens when one relies on a *soldier*, don't you?" The owl pointed towards the fallen city of Rome.

In desperation, Aula turned to Mormo. "There must be some way to prevent this fate. Please, I beg you, let me rectify my mistake, let me heal what I have broken."

Mormo waved Aula away. "Can you return the dead from the care of Father Dis and gentle Proserpina? What power have you to repair a broken lineage? There are some failures for which one cannot atone."

Aula woke up screaming.

They spent three days docked in Utica. Aula avoided Senhyrus and King Juba, and even managed to avoid Aethon by ducking into one of the smaller holds. Her petite frame let her scramble past the stored trade goods, the bull was too large to fit inside. He was easy to ignore if she couldn't see him. She emerged only for evening meals, and otherwise ate only sparingly.

On the third day, after a desultory attempt at the rich Carthaginian porridge that had been prepared for supper, Aula made her way back to the hold, ignoring Senhyrus's attempts to entice her to stay. She squeezed into the small nest she had made and discovered, perched atop a heavy amphora of Cretian oil, Mormo. The cruel red eyes were fixed on Aula, the hint of a smile on her beak.

"They talk about you, you know," Mormo said as Aula settled herself in. She glanced over her shoulder towards the entrance, where Aethon's large silhouette was already filling the cramped hallway. There was no reason to ask who the owl meant.

"So?"

"Don't you want to know what they say?"

Aula shrugged. She turned her attention away from Mormo—the owl interested her no more than any of her other friends—and unwrapped her arm. The wound had reopened, she was unsure when, and the strange numbness had spread. Her hand felt stiff and foreign, as though they were attached to someone else's body.

"How did you lose your eye?"

"A blade meant for Gaius Caesar. It found my eye instead," Aula muttered, gently dabbing at the wound to clean it.

"Do you regret it?"

"I would have given my life that my lord would live. What is a single eye?" Her cold blue gaze met the owl's blazing red. "I saved Gaius Caesar that day. That is all that has ever mattered to me."

"Such loyalty is inspiring, and deserves reward. Tell me, did Gaius Caesar reward you?"

"What do you want from me?"

Mormo shrugged. "You're lonely. I thought I would offer you my company. If you would rather return to the others," she gestured towards Aethon's silent shadow. "If they would have you, that is."

Aula snorted. "They refuse to leave me alone, why wouldn't they have me?"

"Because you have rebuffed their every advance, because you have made every effort to make them believe you don't want their company." She leaned forward, resting her arms on her knees. "Because they find you arrogant and snobbish, a barbarian who believes she and she alone grieves for Rome's lost heir." Aula found she could no longer meet Mormo's gaze. "They tire of extending courtesy to you, tire of your behavior and your rudeness. The king wishes nothing more than to return to his palace and wash his hands of Romans and would-be Romans. The priestess regrets every effort she has expended. The fisherman wonders why he should have left behind his home, his life, for someone who has kept him sitting uselessly in an empty hallway."

"I didn't ask them to," Aula said. She was aware of the petulance of her voice. "Let them leave me be, it's what I want."

Mormo gave a small, tinkling laugh that faded into a ringing silence. When Aula gathered enough courage to look up, she found the owl gone, and nothing left to mark her passage.

Sure enough, as the coast of Africa Proconsularis glided past, Aula noticed that Senhyrus's attempts to engage her were becoming more seldom. By their third day after Utica, the priestess said no more than good morning and good evening to her each day. By the sixth day, Aethon gave up waiting for Aula and returned to working with the other sailors. Mormo met her every day, however, in the little nest she had made in the hold. Sometimes they talked—or rather, Mormo reminded Aula of the damage she had caused not just to her liege but to the Empire itself, of how she had systematically pushed away the only three people beyond Gaius Caesar who had shown any inclination to help her. Most of the time, though, they sat in silence, the owl's burning eyes drilling into Aula while the mouse silently reminded herself of her failure.

On the tenth day, with the Mauretanian city of Caesarea hovering on the horizon, Aula jumped into the sea.

She had not meant to, had not planned it. She had helped herself to a small bowl of stew for breakfast and then had started to walk to her nest. The hallway had seemed simply too long, too arduous, for her to manage. It had seemed to her a perfectly natural alternative to turn and climb the railing and then, ignoring the shouts of the sailors, jump.

The water hit her like a knife, soaking into her tunic and her fur as a flood fills the plains. She closed her eye and let the weight of her clothing drag her down. She ignored the dull thud of a second person diving in after her, and she did not contest the muscular arms that grasped her around her middle.

It wasn't until they reached the surface that she opened her eye and saw Aethon holding her head above the water's line as he swam towards the boat.

"You should have left me," she murmured. She felt more than saw the bull shaking his head, but he didn't waste breath responding to her. A line was thrown down, and he carried her back up onto the deck. Her sodden clothes were pulled away from her. She heard a soft murmur of concern when her bandaged arm was revealed, and then someone—Senhyrus—was leading her, shivering, down into one of the cabins. Not the cabin she had been sharing, but a private cabin, not large, but comfortable and with a fire burning in a small camp stove. Senhyrus sat her in front of the fire and carefully wrapped her in the blankets.

"Child," King Juba was there, looking worried. "Please tell us what's wrong."

"The wound," Aethon grunted. He, too, had stripped out of his wet clothes, but seemed unbothered by the cold.

Senhyrus pulled Aula's arm from under the blanket and un-wrapped the bandage. Her stained fur showed plainly against the clammy grey skin, which now reached almost to her wrist. There was a long moment of stunned silence.

"What did you do, Aula?" Senhyrus asked. She did not sound ac-cusatory, merely sad.

With shuddering breaths, Aula explained sneaking into Gaius Caesar's room and discovering the metal shard and what she had done with it. When she finished her story, she sat, tears falling from her eye as she stared into the fire.

"Can you remove it?" King Juba asked into the silence.

Aula had the vaguest sensation of Senhyrus manipulating her arm, but the numbness was very nearly complete. On the other side of the fire, Mormo sat, smiling silently.

"I don't know, Majesty," the priestess said, blunt claws probing at the wound. "It is in deep."

"It is a lamia," said Aethon. The others turned to him. "A creature that feeds on fear and self-hatred. It attaches itself to a person and drives them into solitude, away from those who can recognize it, and then feeds until the despair overwhelms the person." He snorted. "I saw the wound, on Krḗtē, and thought it might be."

"Why didn't you say anything?" asked King Juba.

"I could not be sure," said Aethon. His voice was apologetic. "But she has been speaking to a one who is not there, in the cabin where I could not reach her. That is when I knew."

"We must help her," Senhyrus said. She wrapped an arm around Aula's shoulders. "Is there a way to fight this creature?"

"It reveals itself only to its victim." Aethon knelt on Aula's other side and took her hands in his. "Tulla Aula Agrippina," he said, his voice little more than a rumble. She tore her gaze away from Mormo to look up at him. "Is it here? Now?" She glanced back across the fire at the owl.

With a snarl, Senhyrus snatched a small claw jar from inside of her robes and flung its contents, some bone-white powder, across the room. With a howl of anger, Mormo turned and vanished.

"What was that?" asked King Juba.

Senhyrus calmly stowed the jar back inside of her robes. "A protective charm. It is made from the tusk of a creature from Brittania; hard to obtain, but very potent."

Aula felt as though she was surfacing after being lost beneath the waves for an eternity. She shook her head, which felt honey-slow, and looked up, first at Aethon, then at Senhyrus.

"She is... was... feeding on me? Like she did Gaius Caesar?" she asked. Senhyrus nodded, and Aula leapt up and rushed to the door. She would have flung it open, would have dashed through the ship, heedless of her nudity, to find her sword, to track down the owl and exact her revenge, had King Juba not grabbed her around the middle and held her back.

"Child, please," he pleaded. "Stop, think. You have unleashed something terrible, you cannot fight it alone."

"You cannot defeat it with steel, Aula," Aethon rumbled, and it was this as much as anything else that convinced her to step away from the door. Senhyrus draped the blanket over her still-damp shoulders again.

"Then how?" she demanded, rounding on the bull.

He shook his head sadly. "It is not a creature of this world. It found you because there is a darkness here." He touched her chest over her heart. "And it wishes to devour that darkness, and you with it. No mortal-made weapon will harm it."

"There must be something," Aula said. "I summoned her, I called her! I…" The weight of what she had done crashed down on her. She had defiled her liege, had desecrated his body in her thirst for revenge. "Oh, by all the gods, what have I done?"

Aethon guided her back to the fire. "You did not summon it," he told her. "It was called by the despair in your heart. This," he touched her arm gently, "was a gesture, an invitation, but it likely would have found you without it. You grieve, Aula Agrippina, and that calls to it like a feast."

"I must destroy it," Aula insisted.

"For now, Aula," said Senhyrus, "you must rest and recover."

"And to be no more alone," Aethon added. "It seeks you when you are vulnerable." He took her hand. "Let your friends protect you."

She hesitated, staring up into Aethon's kind brown eyes. Then, finally, she nodded.

She slept on a pallet on the floor of Senhyrus's cabin, next to Aethon. She dreamed again, once more of Rome aflame.

"Will you hide behind them, then?" Mormo asked her. The owl hung upside down from the mast of the polyreme, arms folded across her chest. Aula stared out at the burning city.

"Is it hiding?"

"What would you call a soldier who let others defend them? Tell me, what is the punishment for a legionary who demonstrated cowardice?"

"Is it cowardice to allow a wounded comrade to retreat and be healed?"

"What wound? That pittance in your arm?"

Aula turned her back on the owl. "I failed the princeps."

Sensing a trap, Mormo hesitated. "You did."

"And that is a shame I will have to live with." Mormo was silent behind her. "But I think I understand, a little, what Gaius Caesar felt. He was alone, far from his family, in a country that rejected him. I hope I would have been a comfort to him, had I arrived sooner. But I didn't kill him. You did. You ate away at him until there was nothing left.

"It seems to me that it would be a better honor to his memory to continue on, to fight the darkness that consumed him, rather than let it consume me, too. Don't you think?" Still silence. With a satisfied nod, Aula watched as the polyreme began to pull away from the shore, and Rome began to fall away.

She awoke in Senhyrus's cabin. To her right, the jackal was muttering in her sleep, a mixture of Greek and Egyptian that Aula could not understand. She hoped it was something pleasant. To her left, Aethon's breathing was deep and steady, but if he dreamed, he gave no sign of it.

In the darkness behind the camp stove glowed Mormo's red eyes. Aula gave the owl a sad smile.

"I know who you are," Aula whispered, taking care not to wake either bull or jackal. The red eyes blinked once, but no response came. "You're the knot-maker, Locke. The entangling spider who whispers into the ears of gods and mortals alike."

"They're not lies," came the soft whisper.

"I never said they were," said Aula. "Not all of them. But a truth told the right way can stab like a knife all the same."

"You cannot be free of me."

"But I can choose to listen to them," she pointed at Aethon and Senhyrus, "and not you. Good night, Locke, or Mormo, or whatever you call yourself."

It took them a fortnight to pull into Tingi. Every day, Aula rose and met Mormo on the deck of the ship, but the owl did not speak to her then. She ate breakfast with Senhyrus, and then helped Aethon and the sailors with the daily tasks. The work made it easier to ignore the lamia. Dinner was with Aethon and Senhyrus, and sometimes King Juba as his duties allowed. Afterward, Aula would sit near the bow, and Mormo would whisper into her ear, reminding her of her failure, telling her how easy it would be to let the sea claim her.

Aula did not disagree, and she was tempted to heed the lamia's advice.

When the sun had set, she would find Aethon and sit with him in comfortable silence, or else knock on Senhyrus's door and sleep on the floor of her cabin. From time to time she would repeat to one or the other what Mormo had told her, and listen to their well-reasoned arguments about how Gaius Caesar's fate had not been her doing, how important it was that she continue on, how important she had become to them. She did not always agree, but she was comforted by their words all the same.

At Tingi they disembarked for the final time. They spent the night in handsome apartments belonging to the king and, when they departed in the morning, Aula once again wore her armor. Though none of her companions could see it, the lamia rode the entire trip at Aula's side, whispering in her ear. When Mormo's words became too much, Aula would let Senhyrus pull her into a conversation about the gods, or listen to King Juba wax poetic about the history of his beloved Mauretania, or simply ride in silence with Aethon. When her friends were nearby, Mormo seemed reluctant to speak.

They arrived at the valley of Volubilis, King Juba's capital, a month and a week after Gaius Caesar's death. Aula hesitated before passing through the gates, afraid that the owl would contaminate the beautiful city laid out before her, its architecture a smooth blending of Punic, Roman, and Mauretanian styles and ringed in green oleander bushes. Aula imagined the riot of colors in the coming months when the plants bloomed.

Aula found Aethon standing next to her, staring up at the beautiful arched entrance to the city. The bull seemed fascinated by all that he saw, but when he noticed Aula looking at him, he turned his attention to her.

"Is it still there?" he asked.

Aula glanced sidelong at Mormo. She thought the owl seemed a little gaunter than when she had first spoken to Aula.

"She is," Aula told him. "I think, perhaps, she will always be there. And she still reminds me of my failures." She flexed her left hand. The feeling was slowly coming back to her fingers. "But the wound is healing. However, I am tired of talking about her. What will you do, Aethon? You have come all this way for a stranger."

She was surprised to see a faint pink blush glow through the fur of his muzzle. "It was worth it," he rumbled. "But for me, I do not know. I... would like to stay with you, if it will not be an imposition?"

Aula started to blush herself. "I will probably have to return to Rome before too long."

"I have never seen Rome." He offered her his hand. "Would you be willing to show it to me?"

Aula took the offered hand gladly. "I would be honored."

FIRE AND BRIMSTONE

J.F.R. COATES

The tremor struck the bathhouse without warning, the ground shaking with a tooth-rattling roar. Chips of stone and flecks of paint fell from the walls like a macabre snow. Several patrons screamed. They fled for safety outside before the building collapsed around their heads.

Felix simply sighed, putting his hands around an ornate plate to stop it from falling, waiting for the tremors to stop. A few others joined the jackal, securing the more valuable items until the ground was still once more.

The jackal grinned, baring his teeth. "Glad that didn't happen while we were in the pool." He barked in laughter as he returned the plate to its table, resisting the urge to swipe any of the coins that clinked over the copper dish.

"Minevah's succulent tits, how can you be so jovial about it?" A stoat hissed, wide-eyed, as he snatched his tunic from a slave loitering near the mosaicked wall. Like the others, the mustelid's fur was pristine and shiny, bathed and massaged to perfection through the many rooms of the bathhouse.

Felix scoffed. "You can't be from around here if you're so scared by a tremor like that. It's just the gods reminding us of their presence. Nothing to worry about... that is, so long as you have nothing to hide from them." The jackal tapped his claws to his heart, then, like the stoat, he took his tunic from a small red fox slave.

The stoat eyed Felix, mouth pulled back in a slight sneer to show off his needle-like teeth. "You hardly look local either, jackal."

"My parents were from Petraea. They earned their freedom and bought their citizenship so I could be born here," Felix said, fur bristling as he slipped into his tunic. "Where did you earn yours? Fought against your litter in Brittanium? Don't think I don't hear that accent, weasel."

The stoat barked out in laughter. "I'm a merchant, you fool. Or are you so flea-brained that you think the only way to earn respect is to hit someone with a sword or chew out their throat?"

A hand rested on Felix's shoulder, pulling him away from the gnashing teeth of the provincial citizen. "Leave it be, Fel."

The jackal stepped away from the stoat, but he could not resist the temptation to throw a rude gesture in the merchant's direction. Before the weasel could react, Felix allowed the strong arm of the wolf to guide him away.

Gaius cocked an ear as he ushered Felix outside, both squinting in the light of the late-afternoon sunshine. The stoat did not follow them, still seething while the pair of slaves stood passively by the door to the baths.

Once outside, Felix tapped two fingers to his chest, then to his head, before raising them in deference to the great mountain that overlooked the city. He paid it no more attention, the Drakopiia. It was as much a facet of the city as the forum's great pillar that dominated much of the landscape. The wolf's hands did not move.

"You always let the cute ones rile you up," Gauis said with a snicker. He slapped Felix on the back.

Felix snorted and shook his head. "Cute? I don't know what you think I like, but it is not arrogant little twigs like him."

Gaius made a non-committal noise in the back of his throat. Had Felix not been paying attention, he might have thought it a growl. "Whatever you think about the stoat, it still seems like you need to pay a visit to the brothel."

The jackal suppressed a grimace. He could not stop the shudder that spasmed through his shoulders. He tried not to think about the expense of the brothel. Even the cheapest special would cost more denarii than he owned. Not that Gaius would know that. He struggled to twist his muzzle into a nonchalant smile. "Perhaps another night. Though if you wanted to visit, don't let me stop you."

Gaius flicked his tail. "Tempting, but no. My favourite girl won't be there tonight. I was thinking instead of getting something to eat."

Felix continued to try not to think too hard about how light his pouch of denarii was. At least food was a more noble purpose for his precious coin. Going hungry was far worse than avoiding a night at the brothel, and he was to collect on some debts come morning. It did not take him long to arrive at a decision. "Fine. Food it is."

There was only a short walk between the bathhouse and the market street that ran through the centre of the town. Hundreds of townfolk, citizens and visitors alike, walked the streets, with slaves slipping unnoticed between them all. Everyone kept to the raised edges of the road to give the merchant carts space to trundle from the stalls to the port on the edge of town.

Market Street was wide and open. The cobbled road surface had been worn down by thousands of feet and carts, as well as the dedicated work of the slaves who cleaned up the muck every night. But Felix barely noticed any of that. To him, the market was a plethora of intense scents that tantalised his nose and made his belly growl with the hunger of a citizen far richer than he was.

Because of the port, the market had a wide variety of cuisines to choose from, coming from all corners of the empire's great reach. But Gaius ignored all of that and went directly to his usual stall, the most popular vendor in the entire market. As always, the grey wolf wanted oysters.

Felix didn't overly care for them, but he ignored his nose and followed the wolf through the gauntlet of mouth-watering scents. At least oysters were cheap.

A boisterous otter with a wide smile stood behind the stall, overseeing the sale of the oysters, all packaged in bundles and wrapped in a fig leaf. He chewed on the occasional denarii to check the value of the coin before stowing it beneath the counter with an audible clink of metal on metal. Two genet slaves worked hard behind him, carefully spicing the oysters and bundling them up into their fig leaves.

"One each," Gaius said, gesturing with a finger towards the jackal.

Before Felix could say anything, Gaius grabbed two fresh bundles and slipped a pair of denarii into the otter's grasping hands. Once again, the otter chewed on a coin and, satisfied, tossed them into the waiting bucket between his feet.

Felix closed his hand around the pouch of coins held securely beneath his tunic. His ears burned and blushed red as he hurried after the large wolf, empty-handed.

Gaius held onto the two packages of food, leaving Felix to scamper along after him. The wolf's large stride made it a difficult half-jog for the jackal. They passed a cheap wine bar, a surly black-furred wolf behind the counter, wiping down the tiled work surface with a dirty rag.

"At least let me get the drinks," Felix called out breathlessly.

Gaius didn't stop or turn around. "Sure."

Felix doubled back towards the wine bar. Set into the counter were three large amphorae, each filled with red wine. Based on scent, they were all the same blend, and had a slightly bitter tang to their aroma. Not the best wines the market had to offer, but they were among the cheapest. The jackal gestured for two, and carefully counted out the coins to pass to the wolf.

Like the otter before, the wolf tested the coins with a quick bite and lick, then grunted softly to himself. He dipped a pair of goblets into the middle amphora to fill them with a generous serving of wine. Felix thanked the wolf as he took the goblets before turning the chase after his friend, doing his best not to spill any of the wine.

Gaius found some vacant seats in the nearby square to sit, overlooking the central fountain and pool, fed by an aqueduct that carried water from the main branch beyond the town walls. The hustle and bustle of the marketplace persisted, underscoring the trickle of water falling into the pool.

The grey wolf offered up one of the packages of oysters to the jackal, in turn taking the second goblet of wine. Evening sunlight bathed golden off the underside of clouds that loomed over Drakopiia. Felix averted his eyes from the sacred mountain, keeping his eyes fixed on the slate tile rooves of the town. By his side, Gaius cracked open the oysters and slurped up the contents, showing little grace or decorum.

With a sigh, Felix began to eat as well. If he hadn't started by the time Gaius finished, then the wolf would likely claim some of the uneaten oysters as his own. He had paid for them, after all.

Balancing his goblet of wine between his legs, Felix dug his claws into the shell of the first oyster to pry it open.

The world shook. The cobbled stone of the plaza shrieked in protest, cracking and buckling as forces from below shifted. Water splashed from the pool onto the plaza stones, the mosaic lining the inner edge of the fountain cracking.

Felix swore as most of his wine spilled over his tunic and all but one of his oysters bounced onto the cobbles. The tremors stopped, but the pounding of his heart continued. Laughter spread through the plaza and market as everyone began to pick up what had been dropped or fallen.

But Felix did not move. He stared slack jawed at the holy mountain. A faint wisp of smoke rose from its peak, as though the dragon within had awoken. Quickly, he tapped his fingers twice to his heart, and then to his head.

"You don't have to do that, you know," Gaius grunted. He mimicked Felix's actions, tapping his fingers to his head but missing the heart. "It's all a bit... provincial."

Felix pondered the oyster in his left hand, only partially cracked open. "Twice in one day is unusual. It's a warning, I'm sure."

Gaius snorted. "You're beginning to sound a bit like that stoat. Are you going to eat those?" The wolf pointed to the scattered oysters around Felix's feet.

The jackal thought, for a moment, then shook his head and stood. "No, I don't think I'm hungry after all. You have them."

"Suit yourself." Gaius shrugged and began to retrieve the oysters.

The wolf didn't say goodbye when Felix slowly walked away, shoulders hunched and head bowed in deep thought. It wasn't like Felix to put much stock in the gods beyond the respectful prayers and gestures, but two tremors in one day? That was something to be concerned about. The jackal just wondered why he was the only one thinking about it.

But for some momentary concern while the ground had shook, everyone had returned to their usual routines. Felix tapped his fingers to his heart and head again. Once more for luck wouldn't hurt.

The ground quaked three more times during the night, pitching Felix off his bed as the world growled and snarled like some ferocious beast. Or a vengeful deity rousing from slumber. If the dragon could not sleep, then he was making it everyone's problem.

The night was long, bringing no rest for Felix. Dawn came slowly and gently, a rosy light breaking across the rooftops. A cacophonous noise ruptured the peace; a peal of thunder that cracked open the sky.

Felix clapped his hands to his ears as the ferocious crash echoed over and over again, reverberating through the town like nothing he had ever heard before. From the central forum a bell rang, though it was not the time of day for it.

The jackal groggily staggered to his feet, using the wall for support as he found his balance. His head spun, and his gut felt like someone had punched him several times. It had been a long time since anyone had done that. He did not want to replicate the experience. Though he was convinced his ears bled from the aural assault, his hands tentatively came away from his head clean of crimson.

A gentle patter sounded against the roof. Felix's ears flicked up. It was too early in the year, and far too warm, for hail. But it was not rain he heard. Rain never made the roof and walls groan like that. Fragments of dust sprinkled down onto the floor.

His curiosity piqued, Felix staggered across the small room of his home and pushed open the door. His hand instinctively came up to tap against his heart, but the gesture died before he could complete it. The sacred mountain belched forth a column of midnight-black smoke that writhed as it rose towards the sky. His arm slowly dropped back to his side.

"Drako have mercy."

Several others emerged from their doorway to stare at the billowing cloud pouring from the mountain. Many stared slack-jawed, unable to formulate any response for the awe-inspiring terror. Felix had seen nothing of the sort before. The smoke that poured from the sacred mountain was darker than even the meanest storm cloud.

A sharp pain jabbed Felix in the shoulder, breaking him from his reverie. He winced and rubbed where he had been struck, before looking down to find what had hit him. He crouched to pick up a small white stone, much lighter in weight than he expected, even though it was smaller than the claw on his little finger.

Shielding his eyes with his arm, the jackal squinted and peered up into the shadowed sky. More and more of the pale stones fell, ejected from the column of smoke. This was a sign from Drakopiia, a message from the slumbering god that sent tremors through the town. He was sleeping no longer. But was his rousing a sign of danger?

Felix needed to see Gaius: The wolf would know what to do. Would surely know what this sign meant. More importantly, he would know somewhere to flee to, should that become necessary. Looking up at the column of smoke, Felix couldn't imagine how it wouldn't be. He could easily picture the twisting shape of a dragon stirring within the billowing smoke.

Keeping his arm up to protect his face, Felix hurried through the empty streets. Few were out, instead choosing to stay in their homes in the safety that four walls and a roof could provide. The small ashen stones began to fall with increasing intensity, sharply and painfully bouncing off the jackal as he ran.

The distance to the large villas near the protective walls had never felt so great. His shoulders and arms stung from the repeated impacts, his feet sore from treading on the scattered stones. A deep growl rumbled from below the surface, a near constant grinding of rock against rock. Or it could have been the dragon stirring. Felix simply could not decide which he feared more.

The downpour of stones felt more like a painful, solid rain by the time Felix made it to Gaius's villa. He hammered on the door, struggling to be heard over the patter and crunch of the falling stones.

Gaius pulled open the door and blinked several times, stifling a yawn. He barely seemed to notice the falling stones. "Felix?" He yawned again, not covering his mouth.

Felix could tell Gaius had company, and given the dishevelled state of the wolf's tunic, it was not hard to imagine what type of company that was. His sensitive ears and nose detected at least six others, probably all wolves, as most of Gaius's guests tended to be. The wolf did not stand out of the doorway to give Felix the opportunity to step inside.

"Did you need anything?" the wolf asked.

Felix stammered and stumbled over the words that all wanted to burst from his mouth at once. How could the wolf be so calm when rocks and stones fell from the sky? Wincing in pain as he was struck on the shoulder, he struggled to compose himself. "We should... we should leave, quickly."

"Leave?" The wolf flicked an ear back. Laughter echoed from behind him. "Why would I do that?"

The jackal gaped. He gestured to the sky, then to the smoke spewing from Drakopiia. "The gods have woken. And it doesn't look like they are pleased."

Gaius snorted. He reached forward to brush some of the small stones that clung to Felix's tunic. "Because of a few small stones? Trust me. These stones are bigger and stronger than anything the mountain can throw at us." To emphasise his point, the wolf slapped his hand to the frame of the doorway.

Felix's tail drooped. "I don't think the buildings in my part of town will be so strong."

"Listen, Felix." Gaius hesitated and looked back, towards the howling laughter that erupted once more. The wolf chewed on his lower lip, then sighed. "Listen. You're a good jackal. Really. But all this talk about gods waking. It's all very telling about who you are. It's a bit provincial for me."

"Provincial?" Felix spluttered. "Gaius, I was born here."

The wolf shrugged. "You can't breed the provinces out of someone so quickly."

Felix took a step back. He no longer felt the impacts of the stones. "Is that what you really think of me?"

Gaius's muzzle twitched, then slowly broke into a smile. The wolf spread his arms, beckoning for a hug. "Felix, please. You're a friend to me. You're a good jackal. Don't make something out of this."

Felix snarled. "A good jackal. A good provincial citizen. I'm not a true citizen like you wolves. Not a proper part of the empire." He took another step back. "Stay here if you want. I'm leaving before this gets any worse."

For a moment, the wolf looked about to say something else. Then he simply shrugged and pushed the door closed. He didn't even wait for Felix to leave.

The jackal stared at the door, mouth partially open. He struggled to understand just what he had heard. He had always counted on Gaius as a friend, one of his few true companions in this town, despite the difference in wealth. And blood. But was this really what the wolf thought of him? Just a provincial jackal, barely worthy of living in the heartlands of the empire?

Felix was brought back to reality as a larger chunk of stone struck him on the muzzle. He yelped and jumped back onto the smooth cobbles of the road, already covered in a fine layer of the bizarre rain.

A deep rumble came from the mountain. Felix watched in awe and horror as a fresh burst of smoke exploded from near the obscured peak. Lightning flashed in the upper reaches of the plume, a deafening crack of thunder following a moment later. There was no chance Gaius was right. This was the doing of wrathful gods. The only way to survive was to flee. The question was, to where? He had hoped to convince Gaius to flee to his estate, but that seemed unlikely now.

"You know the gods will see you, no matter how still you stand."

The drawling voice shocked Felix into movement. He spun on the spot, his claws dragging through the fine layer of stones that had gathered on the road surface. His tail drooped as he recognised the stoat from the previous day. The mustelid's fur had a few patches of grey smeared through it.

"What are you doing here?" Felix asked, more forcefully than he intended.

The stoat pulled out a pouch from the inside of his tunic. It clinked as it moved, fat with coins. "Someone owed me money. Figured this might be my last chance to reclaim that debt." He glanced towards the mountain. "Speaking of which, I don't really have time to linger. None of us do."

The stoat pushed past and started to walk away, head bowed and shoulders hunched as he leaned into the abnormal rain. After giving one last look to the villa, Felix turned and hurried after the mustelid. "Where are you going?"

"To the port and then away from here," the stoat replied, not slowing down.

The seed of an idea formed in Felix's mind. It was distasteful, especially given his interactions with the stoat the previous day, but right now he wasn't sure what choices he had. He hurried to catch up with the mustelid. "How much to buy passage on your boat?"

"I don't have time for this," the stoat snapped, still walking forward at his brisk pace.

Felix cursed, his hand scrambling beneath his tunic until he found his pouch of coins. It always felt lighter each time he held it, but he offered it up to the stoat as he hurried to keep pace with the mustelid. "Please, I know it isn't much, but it's all I have. I really need to leave."

"So does everyone else. What makes you different?" The stoat continued his relentless march away from the villas, back towards the centre of town, to the side of the settlement that overlooked the wide bay and the sacred mountain beyond.

"Because you were right." Felix slowed and looked to the mountain, shielding his eyes. Another growl rippled through the ground, preluding a fresh column of thick black smoke spewing from the summit. "Yesterday. About the tremors. The gods were upset about something, and you were the only one taking it seriously. Now look. Gaius still thinks he'll be safe if he stays inside."

This time, the stoat stopped. He turned around and picked up a small stone from the road. "No one will be. I've seen stones like these before. It's pumice, but I've never seen them so small. If larger stones start falling, then I'd feel very unsafe. You don't want to be here when that happens, inside or not. So, if you are coming with me, then don't hold me up. Understood?" The stoat did not reach for the pouch of coins.

Felix glanced warily to the sky. The rain of pumice continued unabated, but there was no sign of the larger stones the stoat warned of. Not yet, anyway.

"This way. I know the quickest path to the port from here." The jackal pushed past the mustelid, taking the lead. He turned down a narrow side alley, cutting away from the main road which led to the forum in the centre of town. The fact that it would take them past his home was an added benefit to the route down the alleys.

Though the close walls gave shelter from the falling pumice, Felix still needed to bring his arm up over his muzzle to shield his nose from the thick air. It was growing difficult to breathe, a bitter, ashen taste sticking on his tongue.

Some of the sharper pumice stones dug into Felix's feet as he hurried down the quiet alley. Echoes of urgent shouts came from beyond the stone buildings as most used the main roads, but there were still a lot of people huddling inside their homes. Felix caught flashes of them as he ran past; a scared face in a window or a door hastily shut to stop the pumice from flowing inside.

Dust and fragments of stone trickled down from the roofs. Felix flicked his tail, worry building up within him. There was no end to the relentless rain of pumice, filling the ruts and grooves within the roads and alley surfaces. The stoat was right. They needed to leave, and soon.

Despite his urgency, Felix paused at a familiar step. He put his hand on the front door to his small home. "I'll only be a moment."

"Are you serious?" the stoat snarled.

Felix expected to return outside and see the stoat had already left, choosing not to delay at all. The jackal did not break his resolve. The mustelid provided an easy way out of town, but there would be others. He would escape the wrath of the gods, no matter what.

The jackal knew exactly what he was searching for and where to find it. In the corner of his bedroom was an intricately carved wooden box, more valuable than all of the coins he carried. But it was not the box itself that he desired. He gently opened it to reveal the jewellery inside, a copper bangle inlaid with jade, two silver rings etched with the symbol of the empire, and a pair of iron ear piercings. He quickly tucked them into the same leather pouch that held his coins, then got up to leave. He yelped as he almost bumped directly into the stoat, who stood over his shoulder.

"Are those worth risking your life for?"

Felix chewed at his lip. "They're all I have left of my parents."

The stoat's harsh expression softened, just a little. He sighed. "Alright. But no more delays now."

Felix nodded, but before he could take even a single step he was almost thrown from his feet as the ground shook beneath him. The floor lurched and crunched as deep cracks splintered up the walls. Flecks of paint mixed with dust and swirled through the air, settling on Felix's fur.

"Minevah's tits, that was the worst of the lot," the stoat hissed, once the rumbling had stopped.

Out of habit, Felix tapped his claws over his heart as he stepped outside, into the maelstrom of ash and pumice, which had thickened considerably in even such a small amount of time. The gesture died before he could tap to his forehead. Lightning almost constantly flashed in the great cloud, which dominated over half the sky. Thunder growled as the dragon within the mountain awoke.

Masonry cracked as several impacts nearby caused Felix to duck. His eyes widened as he watched several chunks of pumice roll from nearby roofs and thud onto the road: heavy pieces of pumice, larger than his fist.

"Merciful gods."

"Don't think they're showing much mercy right now," the stoat said. He nudged Felix in the back. "Just start running if you want to stay alive."

Felix did not need telling twice, but as soon as he put his foot down on the road, he slipped and stumbled. Instead of the sturdy surface of paved stone he expected, he found unstable and loose pumice in a thick, uneven layer. It was slippery, making it difficult to walk, let alone run.

The stoat found his footing more easily on the difficult surface, running ahead with a grace that Felix envied. Though the mustelid could have easily run on and disappeared from sight, he periodically stopped to check back on Felix, waiting at the corner of each alleyway.

Heavier projectiles of pumice and ash continued to fall, clattering into the buildings just above their heads. The air was difficult to breathe, even with Felix burying his nose in the crook of his elbow. His eyes stung, watering in the thick and heavy air.

Market Street was no easier to walk. The buildings were further apart and the road wider, but that allowed for more ash and pumice to accumulate, shifting uncomfortably underfoot. There was no sign of the rutted tracks left behind by a generation of merchant carts. No sign of the road at all, but for the dirty grey blanket that now stretched between the buildings on either side.

Most of the people outside their homes had moved east, towards the city gates and the road leading, as all did, to the empire's capital. Few carried anything but the most basic personal supplies. None were from the southern part of the town, where the majority of the richer villas were. These were the poor, with few wolves amongst them.

Instead of going east, Felix followed the stoat against the crowd. They hurried west, towards the port. Towards the smoking mountain beyond the great walls.

Screams filled the street as stones collapsed. A cloud of dust and ash billowed, not from the mountain, but from a building that overlooked one of the storefront stalls. The oyster vendor, Felix realised with horror. The building simply crumbled, dragged down by the heavy weight of pumice and ash that had settled atop it.

Felix shoved through the crowd, ignoring those who moved towards the collapsed building to search for survivors.

More screams. A fox collapsed nearby, unmoving, blood leaking from between his ears. A crimson-stained block of pumice rolled across the ashen road.

Felix staggered on. He could barely see the other side of the road. His throat itched and he coughed several times into his arm. The stoat, his fur greyed by the constant fall of ash, was little more than a shadow ahead of him.

Another roar from nearby. Felix barely had a moment of warning before a second building collapsed right by him. He yelped and leaped away before he was crushed by falling stonework. Voices yelled in pain and were then silenced. A cloud of dust engulfed the jackal. He squeezed his eyes shut to protect them, blindly stumbling on.

The stoat cried out. Felix squinted to see the mustelid dart to the side, towards the collapsed pile of rubble that had, moments earlier, been someone's home.

Felix hurried after his companion, leaping over a collapsed wall. "I thought you said no more delays."

The stoat ignored him, instead struggling to clear away broken stone. A hand rose from the rubble. Two young foxes tried to free themselves, buried deeply by the collapsed building. Felix's eyes flicked to the iron piercings in their ears. He grabbed hold of the stoat's arm. "They're slaves. We don't have time for this."

Felix didn't see the fist coming. He wheezed and doubled over as the stoat punched him in the stomach, ripping his arm free of the jackal's grip. "Slaves? Like your parents were?"

The jackal grimaced, tears in his eyes as he held his hands over his gut. Though the stoat was slender and small, he packed one hell of a punch in his right hand. He wheezed and sucked in what little air he could, almost choking on the ash and dust.

Tears sprung in his eyes. It was not just a physical pain. He stared at the stoat as he struggled to free the two vulpine slaves, a boy and a girl. Had his parents ever been like they were? Trapped and desperate, needing help to survive. How could he have been so blinded to consider them less than him? That made him no different than Gaius and the wolves in the villa.

"Are you going to help or not?" the stoat snapped.

Felix blinked. He shivered and flicked his tail, then crouched down beside the stoat. Together, they scraped away the broken masonry, ignoring the pumice falling all around them, the ominous clatter of roof tiles collapsing to the ground.

The girl was the first to clamber to freedom, dressed in little more than dirty, torn rags that barely covered her modesty. She said nothing, but neither did she flee, instead dropping to her knees to dig at the rubble, joining in the struggle to free the boy.

They worked through the ground's continued rumbling. Pumice kicked up puffs of ash around them, some pieces so large they knocked roof tiles loose. Felix tried not to think about the boat waiting in the harbour, focusing only on the heavy block of masonry pinning the young fox slave down. He dug his fingers beneath the stone, back straining as he struggled to lift it.

Working together, the three of them lifted the heavy block of masonry just enough for the fox to wriggle free. Barely had he done so before the ground shook again. Felix grabbed hold of the fox and pulled him backwards as the wall collapsed further, covering the ground by their feet with another layer of broken wall.

The stoat took hold of the fox boy's hand before he could run into the gloom. "Was your master still in there?"

The young fox nodded. He kept his mouth firmly closed.

A quick glance to the rubble. "They're dead now. Stay with us. We'll keep you safe."

Felix was not sure how they could manage that, but the pair of slaves crowded close, sheltering in the shadow of the two larger adults. He put his hand gently on the shoulder of the young girl, who stayed next to him.

"We're not far from the port now. Let's hurry," the jackal said. He regretted opening his mouth. Everything tasted bitter, the air thick with smoke and ash.

The two slaves needed no encouragement. They scrambled across the uneven path as quickly as the two adults, the road gradually rising as they approached the highest point of the settlement, before they would quickly descend to the port.

There were fewer shadows moving through the ash cloud now. Those who had chosen to leave had already done so, seeking safety beyond the town walls. A few more buildings crumbled under the ever growing weight of pumice and ash, but none within sight of the road. Muffled screams rung through the thick air.

A bellowing roar sounded from deep within the bowels of the earth. The ground rumbled. Felix looked towards the mountain, barely more than a dark shadow in a world of grey.

"Is it my imagination," Felix spluttered, "or is the ash getting lighter?"

Neither the stoat nor the foxes answered as they crested the hill at the highest point of the town. The walls were barely visible through the gloom. The sound of pumice striking the ground had diminished. Only a light haze of ash continued to fall, but still the mountain growled.

Felix felt like laughing as the haze began to clear. A few small stones still pattered around him, but nothing like the deadly chunks that had fallen even moments earlier. "Have we really gone through the worst of it?"

The stoat paused, rubbing at his forehead, sweeping aside a thick layer of ash and dust that had built up in his fur. He squinted down towards the port, barely visible on the outskirts of town, then back towards the mountain. His eyes widened. "Oh, Minevah's tits."

Felix followed the stoat's gaze. The base of the fearsome column of smoke had collapsed, growing unstable. While the dark cloud still stretched most of the way across the sky, blocking out the sun and obscuring the light, part of it now roared down the slope of the mountain like an avalanche. It moved impossibly fast, searing down the incline and gathering speed, aimed like an arrow at the town.

The jackal did not move. Could not. The sight of the avalanche of smoke locked his feet to the ground. The deathly pall swept down the mountainside, more terrifying in its silence than if it had roared its descent.

Dimly, Felix was aware of the fox tugging on his hand, but he could not tear his eyes away. Not even as the catastrophic landslide neared the town. Too quick. Far too quick to run from.

The ground shook as the landslide approached. It crashed into the outer walls that protected the town, splintering stone and felling one of the watchtowers. But the walls held.

Felix gagged as a blast of noxious hot air buffeted him, singing his fur and forcing him to stumble back from the force of the wind. The air was stifling and harsh, searing the inside of his nose and throat with every desperate breath.

"Come on." The stoat coughed as he tugged at Felix's tunic. "We aren't through the worst yet."

Staring at the mountain, Felix could not imagine anything worse. His mouth was dry, his fur caked with ash. Despite the thick cloud that blotted out the sun, the air remained oppressively hot in the aftermath of the avalanche.

A hand cuffed him across the face. He yelped.

"Felix, move!"

The jackal blinked a few times, his eyes sore and irritated. Then he licked his parched lips and slowly moved his head. Both foxes pulled his arms. The stoat stood a few paces away, looking like he had moulted to his winter coat already.

"Are you coming?" the stoat snapped.

At the insistence of the foxes, Felix forced his legs to start moving. He stumbled and staggered, head spinning, pitching him into a drunken gait, but he managed to walk. The jackal kept his eyes down, forcing himself to look at the cracked and broken remains of the road. If his gaze wandered, it would inevitably be pulled back to the mountain. If death came from the dragon within, he would rather have no warning. The gods were a power greater than anything he could comprehend; if this judgement was to claim him, there was little he could do to prevent such a fate. The only way out was in the nameless mustelid's boat in the harbour. And to get there he just had to put one foot in front of the other.

The ground sloped downhill towards the bay. Grey ash rained down on them, the flakes now hot and burning to the touch, like they had fallen fresh from the bloomery. They stung Felix's exposed arms and head, some trickling down the back of his tunic, making him wince. Though he tried to shield the foxes from the agonising rain, they whimpered in pain as the ash swirled all around them.

The sky darkened further. Away from the mountain, shafts of sunlight burned crimson as they shone through the smoky air, casting an eerie and ominous twilight.

Despite the terror coming from the mountain, the harbour was deserted. No one had come this way, though there were signs of hasty departures everywhere. Ropes lay unspooled across the harbourfront, amphora toppled and cracked, spilling their contents across the stone slabs. Puddles of wine mixed with spilled olives and splintered oyster shells, all resting over a bed of ash and pumice. Several merchant vessels floated in the bay, torn free from the dock.

Great patches of ash danced on the surface of the water, splashing roughly against the docks in the churning, turbulent bay. Just one boat remained tied to the dock, a merchant galley loaded with a dozen barrels and at least two dozen amphora. At first, Felix thought the galley abandoned, but then he saw a mustelid head poke up from beyond the barrel. The weasel scampered to the prow. His fur was streaked with grey, just like everything else around him.

"Bollocks to this, Canduroc," the weasel shouted, throwing down a rope to the stoat. "We weren't sure you'd be coming back."

The stoat easily clambered up the offered rope and leapt into the galley. He pulled the weasel into a tight embrace, slapping the other mustelid on the back a couple of times. "Are we ready to depart?"

The weasel snorted. "We've been ready since the mountain started shaking. Who are the wet-ears?"

"New recruits," the stoat, Canduroc, said. He leaned over the side of the galley to help one of the foxes climb up.

Felix's eyes were drawn beyond the galley. Towards the mountain.

Another great tremor tore through the ground. Waves splashed against Felix's feet, rocking the boat as the whole world pitched to an angle for a moment. When it righted itself, the mountain flared in the growing gloom as a spout of purest fire erupted from the peak. Then the entire summit of the mountain collapsed in another terrifying avalanche of smoke and rock.

Canduroc followed Felix's gaze, the young male fox in his arms. "Minevah's tits."

The stoat practically dropped the fox to the deck. "Get ready to launch, now!" He reached out to take the second fox, lifting her from the port and into the galley.

Felix followed after her. His hands slipped on the rope, and he almost fell into the water before finding his grip. His shoulders burned with the exertion, and the claws of his feet dug into the wooden hull of the galley.

Ropes were cast aside and the galley began to move, cutting through the ash that had settled on the choppy surface. A strong hand gripped Felix's wrist and hauled him up. He landed on the deck, collapsing to his hands and knees. When he looked up, he caught sight of the crew as they worked. They were all mustelids: besides Canduroc himself, there were three weasels, an otter, and two badgers.

The pair of badgers put oars into the water, while the weasels worked on the sails, drawing them out to catch what little wind blew beneath the blanket of ashen smoke. Slowly, gradually, the galley began to drift from the port, towards the wide mouth of the bay. Out past the shadow of the mountain.

Felix dragged himself up to his feet. The side of the mountain roiled in chaos and destruction as the second landslide poured from the fiery summit. Gigantic boulders, each the size of an entire building, bounced through the smoke. The jackal's hands tightened, feeling the grain of the wooden planks rubbing against his skin.

"Gods have mercy."

Just like the first, this second, larger landslide arrowed directly for the town. Screams still echoed from the distant streets. Of those who had chosen to flee, not all had made it out of the gates on the far side of town. His gorge rose in his stomach. The roaring avalanche was almost upon the battered walls.

A hand touched his side. He looked down to see the male fox gently rest his dirty head to his hip. Felix ruffled his hand over the fox's head, his fingers teasing up to rest idly at the iron stud in the child's ear. The fox gasped.

The landslide struck the walls. This time, the defences did not hold. The cloud of smoke and rock pulverised the walls, sweeping over the villas behind them. And it did not stop there.

Felix's knees weakened. "Gaius..."

The wolf was in those villas. He had thought he would be safe. So many of the rich and elite had stayed there, in their villas. Now, the wrath of Drakos seared over them, collapsing masonry and smashing everything in its path. Even from the water, Felix could hear the town crumbling, broken apart by the rage of the mountain.

But there were no screams.

Whatever death came to Gaius and his lupine compatriots, it came quickly. But for the roar of the dragon, it was silent.

It took just a handful of heartbeats for the landslide to sweep over the entire town, coming to a halt against the inside of the far walls. Losing momentum, the charged cloud of ash and rock settled upon the town, blanketing the entire settlement in a thick layer of grey and brown rock and sludge.

Remnants of the landslide collapsed into the bay, swelling over the port. Steam erupted from contact with the tumbling boulders, crashing into the turbulent water where the galley had been docked. Waves rolled into the boat, pushing it further out into the bay, towards the open ocean.

Tears wetted his fur, matting the ash streaked over his face. "Do you think anyone survived?"

Canduroc stood beside the jackal. "If they got out of the gates, maybe. But no one inside the town could have survived that."

Felix's legs buckled beneath him. He fell to his knees, the sight of the ruined town and the mountain that had destroyed it falling behind the hull of the galley. He tensed as someone's hand ran over his head, teasing through his fur, crusted with dried ash. "Everything I had... everyone I knew. They were all there."

"They didn't like you." Canduroc's hand roughly pulled at the jackal's jaw, forcing Felix to look up again. "Not really. You were just some provincial fascination. The wolves never thought you their equal, no matter where you were born."

"So they deserved to die like that?" Felix growled.

The stoat's grip softened. "No. They did not. But the gods did not spare them. You have survived. That has to mean something."

Felix swallowed. His mouth was so dry the act hurt his throat. "It wasn't the gods who saved me. It was you, Canduroc. I owe you my life."

The stoat's nose twitched. "The wolves would have claimed that meant I owned you. That you could pay off that debt with servitude." The mustelid paused, turning to the two foxes. He beckoned them both closer, then pulled a small metallic tool out from his tunic. With a twisting motion, he cut away the iron bolts pierced into the slave-children's ears. He tossed the pieces of iron into the churning sea.

"I will not claim that. All three of you are free to make your own choices, but I can offer you something. Sail with us to Brittanium, far from the heart of the empire. Far from the wolves, free to live however you choose."

The jackal's upper lip began to curl at the thought: escaping the heart of the empire to flee to the provinces. But then he turned and looked back at the smoking ruin of his home. Had the hubris of the wolves really led to this? It was not just the ash that left a bitter taste on his tongue.

"We'll come." The young fox girl spoke first, holding the hand of her vulpine companion.

Felix stared at the mountain and the broken summit. Even now, smoke continued to pour from the sacred peak. The dragon writhed within, but had yet to truly show himself beyond the flashes of fire and lightning that momentarily illuminated the dark clouds.

The jackal's head turned. In the distance, sunlight dappled the watery horizon. It was difficult not to look out there and see a more auspicious future. From within the gloom of Drako's wrath, anything looked brighter.

His home was gone, buried beneath ash. His friends, buried with it. What reason did he have to stay? Reaching into his tunic, Felix pulled out the small pouch of possessions, taking out the ring and bracelet that had belonged to his parents. They were jackals, slaves from the provinces. He belonged out there, far from the heart of the empire, away from the wolves who prided themselves on the purity of their citizenship.

He turned to the stoat and the mustelids behind him, the crew all working together to guide the galley out of the bay, controlling the rocking of the ship as it struggled in the rough water. He closed his fist around the precious memories of his parents.

"I'll do it," the jackal said. "I'll come with you."

…AND THE SANDS OF THE DESERT WASH OVER THE WORDS

PASCAL FARFUL

The racks of scrolls in Seleucia's Academy library stretched as far as Agathocles could see. It surprised him greatly that you could fill this much parchment with philosophy, mathematics and governance. It wasn't the complete sum of all Seleucid knowledge, religious documents were generally stored in the shrines and the temples that concerned them, dealings of which were best left to the priests. But within this small room was great knowledge. If one dared to seek it.

It was Agathocles of Halicarnassus's job to do just that.

This quest for knowledge was not grand. On a given day, the mouse would arrive directly from the basilica in a himation and with his helmet under his arm. His research was performed on the express appointment of the governor himself.

It was a job. Which was important as Agathocles had just lost his last one.

Barely a week ago, he was heir to the governorship of Seleucia. However, when the time came, he was replaced with one deemed more suitable. The only consolation being that his replacement saw fit to keep him as an assistant.

Zeuxis never asked complicated questions. Just ones arduous and varied enough that Agathocles had to make the long walk through the agora to the academy and back every time he asked for something.

One such day, the mouse arrived, dull-eyed and bitter, and entered the room full of scrolls. He searched and scanned the labels on them, until he found what he was looking for. He pulled out a long scroll and placed it on a nearby table, eased it from its case, then unrolled it. He studied it for a moment, made a few notes on some spare parchment, then rolled it back up and placed it back in its case.

It was as the mouse went to return the scroll that his eye was drawn to something placed shoddily at the back of the cabinet. Parts of the library were restricted and Agathocles was only allowed to access those by grace of the governor. He was not to pursue personal interests or rummage on Zeuxis' time, but curiosity drew the better of him.

He looked to his left and right to ensure he wasn't being watched, then reached towards the back wall and pulled out a very old piece of parchment. Judging by how rough and battered it was, it seemed nobody had tried to protect it over the years.

He placed it down on the table and studied it. A map. His eyes widened as he noticed a patch. Like something had been covered up. Agathocles was definitely in violation of the governor's orders, if not also in violation of the academy's too. But he had to know.

He fingered at the patch, until it lifted.

He glanced underneath.

He tensed up.

Could it be?

No...

But if it was...

He placed the patch back down and carefully folded up the parchment. He placed it back at the very rear of the cabinet, then put the other scroll in front of it.

"Ah, Agathocles! You return again." The silver fox smiled. Gods, Agathocles hated looking at him. Zeuxis bore most of the appreciable qualities of a king-to-be. Handsome. Muscular. Headstrong to the point of arrogance.

"Indeed, your honour," the mouse said reluctantly. Faking the loyalty was hard, and Agathocles motivation to try was running low. "The farmland you enquired about. When we go ahead with it, it'll give a large surplus during summer and by winter it's still going to be sufficient to feed the entire population. Even the poorest."

The fox closed his eyes and scoffed. "Thank you, Agathocles. Following your research, I feel that this farmland is excess to the requirements of this city."

The mouse recoiled. "Sir! With all due respect, as it stands we barely have enough food to feed everyone during winter. That surplus would put us in good stead to survive any attack from the east too."

"I don't intend to start wars, Agathocles," Zeuxis grunted. "Perhaps you do?"

The mouse sighed and looked down at his feet. "No… no I don't, my lord."

"Good. At ease. I will have the cancellation orders for you to deliver tomorrow. Along with the plans for the statue."

"S-statue?"

The canine's eyes burned into Agathocles' figure. "Yes, a statue," he said curtly. "Something that shows the lineage of Hellenic greatness. Something to remind the Parthians that Seleucia will never fall."

It would have been more polite if Zeuxis had just spat on him. Cheaper too.

"The Parthians? You said you didn't intend to start wars."

The silver fox waved his paw. "They make noise, but their words have no consequence." Zeuxis grinned. "And I said, 'at ease.'"

Agathocles grunted and stared at his feet. "I see that I was a poor teacher," he whispered to himself.

"What?" the fox called. "If you are such a gifted leader for Seleucia, tell me, why are you stood there while I am sat here?" He grunted.

Agathocles made no comment. He cleared his throat and apologised, then lowered his head and walked out of the basilica and back onto the streets.

He walked back through the agora, past the odeon and into the public baths.

While Zexuis's words still rang in his ears, Agathocles's mind kept racing back to that map.

What it would mean if its promise were true.

Inside the baths, the mouse was quick to find the person he was looking for.

"Kleomenes! There you are." Agathocles walked up to a rat. Dark fur, strong, powerful build. The mouse's eyes were prone to wandering when in Kleomenes's presence. Particularly at the baths.

"Finally, you grace me with your presence. That governor does like to waste your time, doesn't he?" the rat snorted.

"I think he finds pleasure in it." Agathocles muttered, easing out of his robe and hanging it up.

Kleomenes scoffed, guiding the mouse into the hot water with him. "Men have odd pleasures, don't they?"

"He took my honour! The Basilica was to be mine!" Agathocles rumbled. "Until Antiochus changed his will on his deathbed. And all that after I taught his boneheaded offspring everything that he knows! Not that he seems to have remembered a grain of it." The mouse sat down at last on the edge of the pool. "Ought that not satisfy a man like him?"

Kleomenes stared deep into Agathocles's eyes. "But not a man like you or I. Of that I'm sure."

The mouse didn't object. Nor complain. Nor refute.

"I found something while doing one of Zeuxis's jobs," Agathocles said after submerging himself in the water. "Something I don't think I was supposed to find."

"Is there forbidden information?" the rat asked, sitting up on the side of the pool. "I was of the impression from people like yourself that all information was of value for all people? That to be educated is the way of civilization."

"There are those who have mastered the arts of philosophy and diction, who guard information they see as being of dangerous value to those not skilled enough to handle it," Agathocles explained.

Kleomenes snorted and swatted the air with his hand. "Producing hard men is an intense enough task as it is without attempting to master oratory and prose too."

The mouse laughed. "The walls of the baths tell me that you are naturally gifted in that skill. Naturally gifted enough that you might not need to devote all your time to it?"

"Go on then." The rat snorted and sat back with a grin. "This forbidden knowledge, entrust it upon a soldier of fortune and see it be wasted."

The mouse gulped. "I know where The Hanging Gardens are."

"Zeuxis, I have news from Susa."

The silver fox looked up at one of his servants. "Yes, what is it?"

"The alliance we offered has been rejected, Sir," the crocodile explained. "And there are concerns that their desires for allegiance instead fall with Armenia."

Zeuxis scoffed. "We are strong. We can weather any storm. With or without the Parthian king."

301

"It'll be about four days' travel from here," Kleomenes rumbled. "If your theory is right."

"I understand that it is quite the undertaking," Agathocles said slowly. He'd had to explain this multiple times for the rat to believe him. "Though consider the honour it shall bring if we were the ones to find it."

The rat scoffed. "We are not exactly men to whom honour is ascribed. I hope your intent is not to be reinherited by the Seleucid king?"

Agathocles's gaze sharpened. "Finding the Gardens of Nebuchadnezzar will be more than enough to–"

"The king doesn't want the Gardens, Agathocles, he wants..." The rat gulped. "Children."

The pair fell quiet. The idle hubbub of chatter felt distant. Even the water seemed to hush up.

The mouse looked into the water, then around the baths. He stood at last, letting his fur drip upon the floor. "Then I shall forgo the love of the king," he said with defeat. "For the Gods have made it clear they deem another fate for me."

The rat scoffed, but soon felt troubled. "If people know of the Gardens' location, then why have they never been exploited before?" Kleomenes frowned. "If the tales are true, then they are a place of inexhaustible bounty! Limitless harvests! Enough food for all the world. Zeuxis would have all the room for statues he wanted, the Parthians would have no cause to seize fertile riverbanks or rich pastures, and the poor need not starve either for war or for vanity!"

Agathocles shrugged. "I know not. But I do know that the Gods have seen it fit that I learn of those secrets."

"At first it was for the love of the king, and now it's for the duty of the Gods?" Kleomenes scoffed. "When did a man such as you gain divine motivation? Perhaps it is impious, but I do remember fondly the man who was driven by his more carnal interests."

The mouse smiled. "Who is to say that I no longer am?"

"May it never be me," the rat chuckled. "Why, if you are the one chosen by the Gods to find the Gardens, you would have no need to worry about affairs of state. Could you not then ignore distractions such as Zeuxis, the Parthians and the possibility of famine? For if the Gods mean it to be you, then who is a simple man like I to question the will of the Gods?"

The pair dried off, then got dressed, Agathocles in his white himation robe, Kleomenes in a black chiton tunic.

"I have to drop something off at the gymnasium." The rat smiled. "You are always welcome to join me."

Agathocles chuckled. "Always a very tempting offer," he said, leading the other out of the building. "But first I need to retrieve the map from the Academy."

"In that case, I will meet you at sundown, near the shrine of Aphrodite Cepoïs. I have a few prayers to make there."

Agathocles agreed and departed for the academy.

Without the grace of the governor, he needed to be far more sneaky and cunning than before. Children of Sparta were raised and encouraged to thieve and steal, as to be more suitable as soldiers when older. Children of Halicarnassus were given no such incentive.

Agathocles entered the building and kept an eye open for Castor, the librarian. The stoat was sorting through some incoming scrolls in the corner of the building. With that distraction, the mouse was able to enter the restricted area again. He kept to the walls, avoiding sight lines. If he couldn't see the stoat, the stoat couldn't see him... right?

Carefully, yet without looking outwardly mischievous, he moved back across towards the corner of the room where the map was hidden.

Quietly he eased the scrolls out of the rack and down onto the table behind him.

One by one.

Carefully...

There it was.

Then he just had to–

"Agathocles."

The mouse jumped. "Oh, hello Castor."

That was it.

He was done for.

"Do you have any spare parchment?" the stoat asked.

Agathocles blinked. "Oh... of course." The mouse reached for a section of the unused material near the side of the table. He prayed to Zeus that Castor wouldn't notice that secret scrap in the cabinet and simply ask for that instead.

Mercifully, he handed a section of the unused parchment to Castor. He could have sworn the stoat glanced into the cabinet. But, the stoat thanked him and turned away, walking back across the room.

Perhaps he didn't see it.

The mouse didn't think twice. He picked up the hidden parchment and put it in his robe, before replacing the other scrolls. With his heart in his throat, Agathocles left the academy with the map and walked to the shrine.

It was dark by the time the mouse reached the shrine of Aphrodite Cepoïs. Entering it, he'd find Kleomenes deep in prayer.

"It is done." The mouse said at a whisper.

The rat jolted, looked around, then stood. "Magnificent," he said.

"I apologise for interrupting your prayers," Agathocles said.

"You have not," Kleomenes said. He approached Agathocles and stared into his eyes. "My prayer had just been answered." For a moment, the stare held. Then the rat kissed the mouse firmly upon the lips, the latter being taken by surprise, before relaxing into it. Slipping at last from the mouse's muzzle, Kleomenes smiled. "I request one final night with you before we depart."

Agathocles blinked. "You're sure?"

"If we fail and we don't make it home, I want my last night to have been with you."

"Very well. At first dawn, we shall voyage out."

"Should we not hire some horses?" Kleomenes suggested. "We will make it far quicker on horseback and it will be easier to carry our supplies."

Agathocles shook his head. "It would require us to explain our mission. And lead a trail back to Zeuxis. Two men alone in the desert are untraceable."

That morning, the last day dawned. The pair slept little, their bed took an ordeal and the previous day at the baths was suitably squandered.

The echoes of footsteps rung throughout Babylon. If nobody cared to hear them, or those ears were deaf to act, it would never be known.

The pair pooled their resources: the food they had to spare, the water, the clothing, and in Kleomenes case, the weaponry. With a hoplon strapped to the rat's arm, sword in the other hand and their helmets upon their heads, the pair departed at daybreak. Agothocoles carried the maps and the supplies, while Kleomenes was to use his wits and arms to try and keep the pair out of trouble.

They departed through the western exit of the stone wall. This bore a road due south, one used by armies, traders and diplomats alike. It was the route to the city of Dumatha and the Arabian wilderness.

"We follow this road down past the first river to the south. When the path heads east, we go west," Agathocles said. "From there, we're on uncharted territory. We'll have to cross the second river through the water itself, but there's a mark on the map that suggests it's shallow enough to wade across."

The rat nodded and the pair made their way along the road out of Seleucia.

By the evening, the city was out of sight. The rising and falling of the land obscured the city from their gaze. Before them, the stretching road, the river and bridge in the distance. And then... the great beyond.

Trade caravans passed them frequently. From Susa to the east and Damatha to the south. Diplomats from Parthia and Armenia too, though far more of them than normal. Even some of those Romans they'd heard so much about.

Old farms sprang up to the left and the right. These used to sell extra food to travellers. Now their owners barely had enough to feed themselves. The hope of the new farms shone bright in their eyes. Agathocles hadn't the heart to tell them that Zeuxis didn't care.

"Did you tell Zeuxis that you will be gone for a few days?" Kleomenes asked, offhand.

"No. He wouldn't have let me go, or would have gone himself. Demanded to see the map, taken credit for it." Agathocles grunted.

"Such is the joy of stolen knowledge." The rat smirked.

The mouse stayed perfectly silent, staring at the scrap of parchment in his hand.

"It's not stolen," Agathocles said at last.

Kleomenes grinned ear to ear. "Ah yes, I should have expected a vagueness from a politician."

"It was behind a series of scrolls in the library."

"In the publicly accessible section of the library?"

"...In the restricted section of the library."

Kleomenes snorted. "So it is stolen."

The mouse bit his lip. "Perhaps it is."

The rat laughed heartily and the pair kept on walking.

By sunset, they had come across the bridge. A small wooden structure with supports down into the river to hold it up. The waning sunlight and rising moonlight reflected in the water below, as people made their way back into the city to sleep or continued along that path far into the distance.

"Isn't this beautiful?" Agathocles whispered.

"Huh?"

"The water in the lake. The moonlight on the plains. All of it," the mouse continued.

The rat paused and stared. "I suppose so," he grunted.

The mouse rolled his eyes as the two stepped onto the bridge. "Of course. A son of Achilles doesn't care to appreciate the vista of the world, now does he?"

"I can," Kleomenes protested. "Perhaps I'm just not as easy to please?"

"Perhaps."

The bridge creaked underfoot. As if the Gods themselves wished to test whether they truly wanted this that badly. The image of the bridge breaking flashed into Agathocles's mind.

The fall.

Into the water.

The bridge held firm.

They crossed.

"There's a temple over there," Kleomenes said, pointing to the distance. "We can sleep inside."

The mouse nodded and the pair continued up the road. The sun dropped below the horizon and the moon was left alone in the heavens above.

Before long, the two came upon the small temple.

The ruin of the small temple.

The roof was gone and only a handful of pillars were left. The ones in the four corners and a few on one side remained intact. The rest lay broken and crumbling.

"Gods... who would do such a thing?" The rat grumbled.

"There are people who do not believe in the Gods of Mount Olympus," Agathocles grunted. "Perhaps they see it as an affront to their land."

Kleomenes's mouth opened to rebuke, but he fell dumbfounded, looking over the ruins.

Agathocles climbed the steps and stood between the pillars and under where the roof once was. "Perhaps we should sleep here. There's no roof to fall upon us. The power of the Gods may still wrap itself around these pillars and it will keep us above the desert floor."

The rat grunted and nodded, joining him up on the marble.

They lay down upon their blankets, keeping their supplies huddled between them for safety.

The night passed slowly. The sound of horses and camels on the cobbled road rattled around their heads. The desert winds goaded them to approach and suffer the consequences.

Restless, Agathocles rolled over onto his chest. As he did so, he noticed a phrase carved into the marble.

"The great among men reap plentiful harvest, yet thousands are left with crumbs."

The mouse blinked. It was still there when he looked again. He sighed and turned away. He figured it was just graffiti and attempted to forget it.

Daybreak.

The elevation had kept the sand off of their fur and their belongings lay as they'd left them, bundled up between each other.

"We should move quickly," Agathocles said. "It won't be long before Zeuxis discovers I betrayed him and will come seeking us."

"We can outrun any army," Kleomenes assured him.

"But not a horseman."

The rat grunted and nodded. "Your argument is fair. Let us walk."

They gathered their belongings and left the temple, continuing down the road into the sunrise.

"You'll regret wearing a himation before long, my friend." Kleomenes smirked.

"It protects me from the sand and wind a lot more than your chiton will." The mouse grinned.

"But you'll struggle to run in it for sure."

"You anticipate needing to run?"

The rat snorted. "You did live a pretty life in that palace, didn't you? Out here in the plains, anything can come for anyone. Some have said that quick footedness is even more valuable than strength."

When Agathocles gave Kleomenes a puzzled look, the rat laughed loudly and slapped Agathocles on the back with his large hand. "I tried that "scholarly research" you mentioned. I'm beginning to see its appeal!"

The mouse answered the rat by pointing into the distance. "There is the turn to the east. Now, we must head west."

The wind swirled.

A dare.

To enter the abyss.

The pair stared into the plains. The uncharted lands.

They stood silent in revelry at what they were about to do.

The foolishness of it all.

Agathocles took the first step off of the path onto the short grass and hard, dry land.

The earth did not swallow him up.

The winds wafted back, satisfied to let them trespass.

"Onward," Agathocles said at last. "And with haste. They could come for us at any time."

Into the plains they walked. Their progress was slower here. The ground was hard and unforgiving against their feet. The short grass snagged at their sandals and rubbed dry on their ankles, yet refused to cushion their stride. The bumps and undulations made a steady march difficult. There was no rhythm. Only persistence.

As they moved further and further into the wasteland, the grassland became more and more sandy. The signs of civilization dried up like the very earth beneath them. As they crested one rise, Kleomenes stopped to turn back and look at where they had come from, only to see no road at all. In the far distance, something caught the rat's eye.

Was it smoke?

Or was it just the heat?

The rat was wise to the mirage and he disregarded what his eyes foretold.

"We are alone," He uttered.

He turned back to look at the mouse.

"We are alone," Agathocles repeated with a grin. "Perhaps at last, you and I can have what we've been looking for."

Kleomenes sighed, then gave a weak smile. "Perhaps."

The mouse closed the distance and kissed the rat again. "But we must keep moving, lest we become disoriented."

The rat nodded and the pair resumed their strides.

Deep into the beyond.

The dunes.

The sand.

The dry grass.

Alone under the all-seeing eye of the sun.

"Zeuxis seeks you."

The pair jumped.

Kleomenes drew his sword.

Before them, a bedouin. A wolf, wrapped in robes, holding a shield and a scimitar, astride a camel.

All three stood their ground.

"But I do not seek him," Agathocles said firmly. "If you wish to claim a bounty, then let the sands bare our blood."

"I do not," the wolf replied. "Why would I do my coloniser's bidding?"

The body language of the two rodents softened, but the rat remained defensive. "So why do you come?"

The wolf laughed. "Must I explain everything in such detail?" He snorted. "Seleucia burns. His remaining men seek you. Whatever you seek, find it quickly and hope it may grant you asylum."

The two rodents stood firm. "If Seleucia is burning, where will they take me?"

The bedouin laughed again. "Surely you don't think they'd take you?" He snorted. "Your death is their prize, Agathocles." He sheathed his scimitar. "But it is not my prize. No, my prize is the joy of watching Alexander's empire fall." He smirked. "Good luck." He grabbed the reins of his camel and departed at great speed into the desert mist.

The two rats stood alone as all evidence of the bedouin's presence was reduced to the memory and the ringing of his words.

"Do you believe him?" Kleomenes asked.

"I would believe anything that suggested Zeuxis was a fool. Come, we must continue," Agathocles said continuing on up the road, at a run.

The rat followed.

Up on a hill, as night began to fall, they spotted another refuge.

"That farm. It looks abandoned, I think we can sleep there," Agathocles suggested.

"I concur," Kleomenes said. "There might even be food there still."

There was not.

The fields had long gone unplowed. The crops had died and desert plants had grown in their stead. They walked through the overgrown fields, before dropping down hard on the tough ground beside the old farmhouse, letting it be shade from the setting sun.

"Brave is the man who builds a farm out here," the mouse muttered.

"Brave or desperate," Kleomenes agreed.

As Agathocles took shelter, he once again saw a bizarre phrase, this time carved into the damaged building.

"Let infinite feast be bestowed upon mortals, bounty enough to feed all."

"Can... can you see this?" the mouse said, nudging Kleomenes.

The rat leaned over and read the text. "I can. I suppose it's just a prayer for the good of the farm. Does it mean something else to you?"

Agathocles looked away. "No. No it doesn't," he lied.

He didn't know what it all meant. But it meant something. the Gods didn't play games.

After such a walk, the pair succumbed to their slumber quickly.

Too quickly.

"There he is!"

"Forget him! His blood carries a pitiful price! Make them starve to death!"

The mouse shuddered awake to see two bedraggled Greek panthers on horseback amassed before them.

"No!" Agathocles shouted, stumbling to his feet. In his disoriented rage, he hurled himself at the nearest horse. The beast staggered, but stayed upright. Its rider swung with his sword, the blade missing the mouse's flesh but catching on his robe, dragging him face-first down into the dirt.

Kleomenes drew his sword, but was held firm by the bow trained on his temple.

"Zeuxis is slain, thanks to you. Where are your Parthian allies now?" one of the panthers shouted, throwing down a large sack.

The other had picked up their bag of supplies and hurled it onto the back of his horse. "Seleucia's blood is on your hands. Be grateful there is no-one left alive to collect on your head!"

The attackers turned away and fled to the north west, one of them carrying the rodent's pack of supplies through the blade of their sword.

Kleomenes remained still, but his eyes drifted away from the cloud of dust, to the sack, and to Agathocles. Stunned betrayal welled up behind his eyes.

The rat scrambled across the sand to pick up the large sack the panthers had left. As the rat lifted it, the silver fox's severed head tumbled out and began to roll down the bloody dunes. "By Zeus…"

Finally, the mouse rose to his knees, the tattered remains of his robe dangling from his form.

"Agathocles…" Kleomenes began slowly.

"Yes? Are you hurt?" The mouse replied.

The rat took a deep breath. "They said you made a deal with the Parthian king to ensure the demise of Seleucia. Is that true?" Kleomenes asked slowly.

Agathocles growled. "I made no such deal!"

"You stole a scroll from the academy library. You led me out here on our own…" The rat turned to meet the mouse's gaze. "Either you saved me from a death you knew was coming, or… or…"

"Or I knew nothing about it, and Zeuxis was a fool!" the mouse protested.

Kleomenes took another deep breath. "Perhaps. Regardless, we have more problems," the rat said. "Our supplies are gone. Surely, this is our last day on the Gods' land."

Agathocles summoned his strength and managed to stand up again. He reached down into the ruined remains of his robe and pulled out the scrap of parchment with the map on.

Was it really worth it?

To starve to death in the middle of the desert?

They stepped out past the farm and onto the plains.

And as they stared across the hazy horizon, the mouse's heart shuddered to a stop.

He could see it.

No.

Impossible.

He blinked.

It was still there.

Slowly, Agathocles raised his arm outstretched.

"There," he whispered.

Kleomenes turned and followed his arm, eyes resting upon a shape on the horizon.

A stone pyramid.

The Hanging Gardens of Babylon.

"Gods be praised..." Kleomenes whispered. "But we have no water, no food."

"The gardens. They are food, they are water," Agathocles whispered, starting to step towards the shape.

"We won't make it," Kleomenes said firmly.

Agathocles stopped.

He stared at the gardens.

They seemed to stare back at him.

He turned to his lover.

"Then I wish to die on the journey." Agathocles tried to tie parts of his garment back together, determined to carry on.

Kleomenes took a deep breath, looking between his lover and the Hanging Gardens in the distance. "Let us do it together," he said at last.

The mouse stopped fumbling with his ruined robe and stared into the rat's eyes. "You believe me?"

"I do. Under the shadow of the Gardens, how could I do anything, less?" The rat placed his hands over the rat's, guiding them aside and proceeding to rip what was left of the mouse's garment off completely. "Embrace it." He whispered with a smile. "If we fall before the Gods on our quest, allow us to enter the house of Hades as we entered this life."

Side by side, hand in hand, they walked into the dawn, eyes fixed upon the Gardens as they grew slowly but surely bigger before them.

Naked, Agathocles had only Kleomenes' hoplon to protect him from the full brunt of the sun and the sand, but still he walked. What he had lost in equipment he now had in spirit.

The legends of the Gardens.

They were true.

It was all true.

Over a dune, they caught sight of the lake. The one they'd have to cross without the aid of a bridge. Beyond the lake, over the rolling sands, the Gardens of Babylon stood proud on the horizon. They could almost see the green leaves dangling from its stone structure.

"I can't believe it," Kleomenes muttered. "It's... real."

Agathocles nodded. "Come, we'll reach the river by sundown."

The pair walked down the hills of sand and rough grass as the sun set.

They arrived at the river under a purple sky. The moon and the stars sparkled and reflected in the river. As if the very magic of life was blooming in this place. Upon arrival, the pair drank heartily from it.

Finally no longer parched, Kleomenes raised his head. "You said there'd be a crossing."

"Yes," Agathocles replied, staring around. "Normally there is a furrow worn in the bank, where many men have marched across, but such an untouched land begets no such thing."

The pair rose and began to walk the bank of the river. The water flowed calmly, but looks were deceiving. Indeed, how deep is a mystic river?

Their answer was soon discovered.

"There, can you see? The land through the water," Kleomenes called, pointing downstream.

There, the reflecting purple water seemed to thin out, a pale patch of sediment visible through it. "Probably little more than knee-deep. I think we can ford that."

Their arrival confirmed this. "The water is faster here," the rat warned. "But if we are steady, we can cross," he said.

"Indeed, we can also wash here too," Agathocles suggested.

Kleomenes agreed.

The rat undressed and they both eased gently into the water, to bathe and wash. He lay his tunic on the riverbank, the pair together in the buff under the rising moon, the setting sun and the billions of stars. Alone, but welcomed warmly to the lap of the Gods.

The business of cleanliness held their attention only briefly in the middle of the shallow river crossing. Their arms around one another, stood staring longingly into each other's eyes. The water flowed between their knees, warm and soft around their achy bones and once-bedraggled fur. With the grace of the river water, their fur was now soft and wet. Warm and gentle. Affection was gratuitous and encouraged in great amounts by the silent spirits on the whispering wind.

"How is something so beautiful so hidden? So many people walked this land, yet such a treasure remained a mystery?" Kleomenes whispered.

"You are much like the gardens," Agathocles replied. "More beautiful, wonderful and delightful than my dreams could have ever foreseen."

The rat stammered and blushed. "My prayer to Aphrodite Cepoïs didn't go unanswered. If anything I feel guilt for just what she has bestowed upon me."

The mouse smiled, coiling his tail around Kleomenes's own, then easing one of his thighs around the rat's own. Warm fur wrapped around warm fur. Warm skin against warm skin. "Come lay with me and love me," Agathocles requested.

Kleomenes nodded, licking the mouse's tongue. Then, he eased him down into the soft mud of the riverbank.

The pleasures of Aphrodite lasted throughout the night. By morning's light, the pair were ready to travel on.

As they collected themselves, Agathocles' eyes were once again drawn to mysterious text. This time carved into the riverbank just next to where they had bred.

"Of this would the poor and the destitute, behold not a single grain."

Kleomenes didn't bother with his tunic. He had nothing of value in it. He and the mouse walked onwards as bare as they had arrived in the world. This day they would reach the Hanging Gardens of Babylon.

The closer they got, the larger and grander it seemed to get.

There was a strange tingling in the air. That tingling had been there at the river, but now it was stronger. Far stronger.

What had been dry and dusty air soon started to get ever so slightly humid. The sand eased away and the grass, once short and dusty became thicker, taller and softer underfoot. Large trees and vines sprouted around them. Water dripped from them.

They were upon the gardens.

The onward strides they took met a path, formed naturally by gaps between trees and plants. Down the path, the trees eased over them and plants rose up, as if to cradle and hold the pair. Bright, ripe fruits dangled from stems ready to be picked.

"Don't take anything," Kleomenes whispered. "the Gardens are sacred, we must not steal."

Agathocles nodded.

"Why?"

The pair froze.

Without realising it, they had arrived at the foot of the stone gardens.

A marble megalopolis, coated in plants and nature. Teeming, joyous and proud with life.

From a balcony above the entrance stood a figure. Agathocles couldn't tell if they had a species or a gender. Scent was of no use, either. There were so many plants and fruits flooding his senses that he couldn't get a hold of the figure's scent.

He wagered they were a mammal, but perhaps they were more than that. A god.

"Wh-what?" Kleomenes stuttered.

"Why would it be stealing?" the figure asked softly.

"Because... because this land is sacred. You can't just... take from the Gods."

The figure mulled, then smiled. "Do I look like Zeus to you?"

Kleomenes's shoulders dropped. "No... No, you don't."

"Then why would his laws apply here?" the figure asked. "Take what shall sustain you, and not a grain of rice more."

The pair nodded and each picked a fruit from the trees next to them and began to eat.

The taste was new, different and otherworldly. The one fruit satisfied each of them and, while it was appealing to taste more, the thought of doing so felt deeply obscene and vulgar. They had come this far, to fall at the first trial would be pitiful.

The figure appeared before them. The only describable features were the black fur, a majestic gait and focused but unthreatening gaze.

"Do you know the message?" they asked.

The pair blinked and looked at one another.

"What do you mean?" the mouse asked nervously.

"You must know the message," the figure said firmly. "Your travels were long and arduous, but you could not be so blind as to miss it, could you?"

Suddenly, Agathocles remembered.

"The great among men reap plentiful harvest, yet thousands are left with crumbs."

"Let infinite feast be bestowed upon mortals, bounty enough to feed all."

"Of this would the poor and the destitute behold not a single grain," he recited.

The figure smiled. "Very good." They stepped aside, revealing the entrance to the garden. "You may enter."

"And my lover?" the mouse asked.

"Of course."

As the two began to step forth, the figure stopped them. "There is… but one condition to your entry." They said. "Once you enter the gardens, you may never return to the world from which you came."

The two gulped.

"Why is that?" Kleomenes asked.

"Your lover just told you."

" "The great among men reap plentiful harvest, yet thousands are left with crumbs. Let infinite feast be bestowed upon mortals, bounty enough to feed all. Of this would the poor and the destitute behold not a single grain." " Kleomenes repeated. "If Zeuxis found the Gardens… he would have hoarded it…"

"Astute understanding." The figure smiled. "But it is not limited to your slain governor. The gardens can only be found by people who will not abuse its power."

Agathocles gulped. "And you know we wouldn't because…"

"Because your mortal home is burned to ash. Your governor is dead. And your lover will surely be executed alongside yourself by your Seleucian king. If there still is one. And indeed, the Parthians would have no reason to trust a pair of Seleucians talking of the Gardens, would they?"

The two looked at one another. "And what happens if we leave?" Kleomenes asked.

"If you choose to return to Seleucia, your memories of the Garden will be lost forever. As far as you will know, the Gardens will have been a myth. And the map, just the ramblings of a madman."

"You placed the map in the library of the Academy…" Agathocles muttered.

"Why of course. Hoping for someone suitable to find it."

"And you stopped Castor from realising I had stolen it."

"Oh, Castor knew."

"Then why didn't he stop me?"

The figure laughed. "I'm not going to reveal every one of Castor's secrets. The honourable dead get to keep their pride."

Agathocles gulped. He didn't want to think about Castor's death. He cleared his throat, then looked over to Kleomenes. "What do you think?"

The rat took the mouse's hands in his own. "You came here to find the Gardens. You said you wanted to find it to impress the Seleucid king. But you are dead to him now, either because of the siege of Seleucia, or because he believes you caused it." Kleomenes smiled. "We have nothing to lose by entering."

Agathocles nodded and kissed Kleomenes again. "I love you."

"I love you too."

The pair turned to the figure. "We wish to live forever in the Gardens."

The figure smiled and gestured them forth.

They stepped forward, hand in hand, walking through the stone archway and into The Hanging Gardens of Babylon.

At one time, the new Parthian king had wondered the fate of Agathocles and Kleomenes, the two that Zeuxis had insisted in his dying breath had been working in his pocket.

'Perhaps their bodies had been swallowed by the sand,' he thought.

'Perhaps they were still in Seleucia, hiding somewhere among them.'

'Perhaps the late Castor's tale that they were headed for the Gardens of Babylon was true.'

Perhaps.

EULALIUS!

There were wolves in the forest.

None of us had seen a wolf before. Not before the invasion. And now there were two, one brown and one grey, prowling by. I hid among the undergrowth, watching the animals pass. They were young animals, a few years older than me, maybe. They wore light armour, hardened leather over their tunics—a far cry from their full soldier's uniform and cumbersome plate armour. They looked relaxed, conversing in their bright, musical language. Their voices carried through the trees, and the green of the forest floor rustled in their wake. They almost seemed oblivious to their surroundings. A curious way to behave, even for these outsiders. What were they doing? Were they tracking something? They were talking too loudly for that. Or maybe they were scouts? I hoped my scent wouldn't carry. I lifted an ear, trying to judge the wind. I knew their senses were keen, and my herbivore's scent would shine like torchlight.

Then the brown wolf twitched his nose.

He glanced in my direction, a glance that lingered a second, two seconds, too long. But he grunted, looked ahead, and walked on. I didn't even realise I'd held my breath until I let out a sigh.

They must have picked up a hundred animal scents, even on the short walk from their camp. I should have seen that as a lucky break and left them alone.

But then the brown wolf reached over, and held the grey wolf's paw.

Two male animals, holding paws.

That got my muzzle twitching.

I definitely should have ignored them then. Two more sons of bitches who only held contempt for us. At least, I thought they were males. No females were allowed in their ranks. But I had to know. Something about them, about the familiar way they looked at each other, smiled at each other, and yes, held each other's paws... it raised my curiosity.

So I stalked them, deeper into the forest. Though they weren't exactly hard to track. Onward they walked, taking out loud, brushing and trampling through the forest. *Cocky brutes.* My wood-axe was freshly-sharpened, and I clutched it tight. I hoped I wouldn't need it, but it was best to be prepared.

There was a stream cutting through this forest. They reached it, and they followed its course upstream. *I know where you're heading.* Gradually, the river narrowed into a valley, the sides growing steeper though still forested.

Up ahead, the stream widened and formed a deep pool. And beyond that was a rushing waterfall, seven times my height, even factoring in my ears. Sheltered by the trees, it offered an oasis of peace. This was where they were heading. I suppressed a growl. This was my place to relax—our place. And now these animals had found it.

But now I could look at the animals, my thoughts went elsewhere.

Even beneath their tunics, I could see the broadness of their shoulders, the strength and pride of their stance. And when they took off their garments, leaving themselves bare-chested...

I wished—how I wished—I could hone my physique like theirs.

The wolves stood on show—one grey, one a bright reddish-brown, and both definitely male. I looked away without thinking—after all, it is rude to stare at another man. These foreigners and their strange customs. Only when they were at the water's edge did I look again. They looked strong, and fit. Well, they were soldiers. The brown wolf led the way, dipping his paw and stepping in slowly. The grey wolf passed him, striding into the chilly water, his every step splash-splashing as he went. They ducked under the water, neck-deep, sighing deep at the cooling waters. When they stood, their fur hung wet, highlighting every toned muscle. They faced each other, thigh-deep in the cool water in this wooded glade. I saw their hunger grow, like starved pups. Every second they spent apart, their panting wolven breaths grew heavier. They held back, like they were prolonging the hunger. That only made their eventual unison all the more animal. And they were ravenous animals, both of them. Paws pressed into pelts, claws combing through. Heads tilted, muzzles locked together, and their tails flowed and wagged behind.

Happy, excited canines.

I wanted to leave. I needed to leave. And yet, I was transfixed. The brown wolf took the lead, holding the grey wolf tight and engulfing his comrade with muzzle and tongue. And just watching them, I felt... strange. Like I did around my girlfriend. Dry in the muzzle, unable to speak.

You shouldn't even be watching them. They are men!

I lowered my gaze, blocking my view of the wolf lovers. Then, unseen, I slipped away. A whine drifted through the trees, laced with an unmistakable hint of pleasure. A twig snapped under my broad foot and I clutched paw to mouth, freezing, pivoting my ear back to the wolves. For a few seconds, I only heard my heartbeat, rapid, thrumming in my ears. Then, two growls carried through the forest—relaxed, even pleasured. I took that moment to climb the steep bank and escape the forest.

I did not know why the wolves left their camp. Maybe they had no privacy. If they shared quarters with other males, it would make sense why they wanted to escape.

I crossed the rolling meadow, almost in a trance. I couldn't shake the image of those two wolves. I knew in theory that two men could couple. But it was shameful, an affront to nature. The gods had blessed us animals with fertility, and we hares were particularly blessed. We had to take a partner, *a doe for a buck and a buck for a doe,* and we had to raise leverets. Otherwise our clan would fade away, and other animals would take our land and take us for meat. Animals like... those wolves.

But they looked so... natural. So happy together. It wasn't as though every buck desired his fellow male. So why deny them happiness?

It was fast approaching sunset. The coarse grass of the meadow gave way to cultivated fields. As I passed the fields, hares were downing tools and making their horses fast for the night. As I climbed the hill and crossed the moat to my village, one of the guard sentries spoke to me.

"Not sneaking off again, are you, Kelin?"

"Only for a stroll along the ridgeway. I'd have spotted any animals a mile off."

"Aye, just you be careful, lad. You never know when you'll run into those invaders."

Indeed not.

Truth be told, I was dreading the return to my village. I went wandering for a reason. It seemed that every day, their mood in my village grew darker. I had never known the village this quiet, this hushed and subdued. When I greeted other animals, they only seemed to reply out of obligation. It felt like a storm was coming, and every hare and leveret was waiting for that first drop.

I do not remember when the invasion started. I was far too young. But even I saw the growing rot. At first they sent scouts, and even merchants to trade with us. Then they sent soldiers, and they talked of 'co-ruling' and 'the protection of Rome'. They demanded tributes—food, land, resources. Though we duly paid, they demanded more. And the last few moons, as summer turned to autumn, our situation had grown worse. Now, the air hung heavy, like the skies before the rain.

A clash of wooden staffs, the flex of leporine muscle. The scuff of a thousand heavy paw-steps had churned the grassy ring to soil and dust. And Kegyden and I were but the latest to tread this ground. Kegyden was a brute of a hare, five years my senior with twice my strength. Two winters ago, when ambushing a patrol, an enemy had torn the young hare's ear, and he wore the damage with pride, always holding that ear bolt upright. Even during a sparring session.

If I had the choice, I would not have engaged him. But I had to. To be the best, you have to learn from the best, and train with the best. After all, one day I could have faced an enemy as strong as him, or stronger—and there were stronger animals out there.

His hand-paws were as swift as his feet, and every feint and second intention drew a split-second reaction from me. I had to trust my instincts. If I slowed to think, Kegyden would take advantage. Words came to my mind—our Master's words. *Make every move count. Make every move real.* My opponent was skilled, but I was nimble, with quickness on my side. I tried to read his attacks, looking for the moment when his attack or his recovery was just too slow. With both paws at one end of my staff, I warded him off. I thought I saw him hesitate, but he was recalculating, determining how to tackle this new threat. He advanced, I stepped back. Again. And again. I couldn't keep retreating, or my paw would leave the ring, and I would forfeit the match. I had to do something. I was sick of him always besting me. Always stronger than me. Always outsmarting me.

He lunged.

But then... his momentum took him a half-step too far. I swung my staff up, striking the hare across the cheek.

Yes! I landed a hit! I couldn't believe it.

The kick to my chest sent me flying. I landed hard on my scut, slid a little further, and saw Kegyden rushing in, roaring, staff held high.

"Hold!"

Kegyden skidded to a stop, almost ending up above me. His narrow-eyed scowl, and the show of buck-teeth, told of his disdain.

I lay my head on the ground, clutching my chest, satisfied I wasn't about to be pummelled. Clouds of soil-dust swirled in my vision, and when I breathed in they made me cough, which in turn sent a dull pain shooting across my chest. I heard another set of paws approach.

"Kegyden, you are still too hasty. Remember, speed is not everything. Speed will only get you so far. And Kelin, don't let yourself be surprised. When something unexpected happens, take it in your stride, and use it to your advantage. And use your body, too. Your weapon does not move by itself."

My training staff lay a short distance away. Master picked it up.

"Unless you drop it. Right, go join the others."

With a paw still on my chest, I struggled up. I left the ring, avoiding everyone's gaze, and I sat on the ground beside my fellow trainees.

"Now listen, all of you. You will have heard your elders talk about our situation. Your parents, Druid Enfys, maybe even the Chief. So you know the stakes. You are no longer leverets, and this is no longer a game. Sooner or later, every one of you may be called upon to fight. To protect our way of life, and to protect our freedom. Right, on your feet, hands by your sides. Come on, come on, quickly now."

The eight of us scrambled to stand. Master stood tall, a beast of a hare. He breathed in deep, and his battle-cry boomed across our meadow.

"*Eulalius!*"

We answered him as one, returning that cry. And an instant later, we were young hares again, saying our goodbyes to each other, slapping each other's backs, thanking each other for a good fight. I was brushing the earth from my pelt when a hare from my class called my name. I paused, swallowed, and turned to face the doe, trying to keep my whiskers from twitching.

"Siran, hello."

"Listen, tough luck there with that spar. We thought you had him with that strike. A lot of us were rooting for you."

I rubbed my chest and smiled. "You don't have to pretend. We all know who's top of the class."

"Well, *I* was rooting for you. But anyway, we're done for the day. So... how would you like to come over?"

"Um, thanks for the invite. But I have other plans."

She smiled an easy smile. "Not seeing another doe, are you?"

"Oh no, I only have eyes for one doe." (Males, on the other paw...)

"Oh, so you're going for another wander?"

That did make my whiskers twitch. "Why does everyone have a problem with that?"

"Goodness, I don't know. Maybe because of all the soldiers roaming around?"

I flexed a hind paw. "Don't worry. I can make myself scarce before any of them notice me. Mind you, I notice *them.* I saw two of them sneaking into the woods the other day."

"Oh?"

"Yeah, two male wolves, they were. I think they were a couple."

"Well they need to be careful too. If their officers find out, they'll be in real trouble."

"I thought they were fine with males coupling."

"Not in the army. They're meant to be equal animals. And by nature of the act, one has to be dominant and one submissive."

Now there was a mental image. I tried not to let on how that made me feel. "The things you learn when your mother's the Chief."

"It's interesting sometimes, meeting their envoys, learning about their customs."

"Sounds more interesting than my family life. My mum's still asking me to help fix the roof. As if my paws aren't sore enough after training. But I tell you what. As I can't join you tonight, how about I head over after training tomorrow?"

"That's even better. Then you can join us for dinner."

This was both a good and bad thing. On the plus side, it meant dinner with Siran. On the negative side, it meant dinner with the *Chief.* No doubt there would be some high-brow conversation on crop rotation or inter-clan politics. I couldn't hold a conversation about those things. I could never think of enough smart things to say. I could just about wield a spear, and that was it.

In the end, the chance for more time with Siran won out. And at least I would be making an appearance in front of the Chief. So I nodded. "Sounds good to me."

Siran's smile widened, and she leaned in to rub noses with me.

"Excellent. Then I shall see you tomorrow."

"Yeah. See you." I watched the hare bound away, trying not to bite my lip. And yes, I will admit I watched her tail. But somehow... it wasn't the same. It almost felt contrived, like I was expected to like does. Siran was... pretty, most certainly, make no mistake. And the fact she was daughter to Chief Mildthyl gave me extra incentive to stay with her. Fancy that: the Chief's daughter, liking me! Of all the hares she could have chosen... four other males in our class alone. She could have had Kegyden, easily. But she chose me.

I was so confused. Maybe if I went back to the falls—assuming the wolves were there at all—then I could convince myself this was wrong.

That was my excuse, at least, when I left the village ("Don't worry, I'll be careful...") and headed back to the forest.

In the forest, the rush of water was the first sound you heard. It was inescapable, a constant force of nature, rushing by for centuries before I was born, as it will do for countless centuries after my fur becomes grass. You could hear the water, all down the valley. The waters flowed fast, the burn rushing over smooth wet rocks, over natural weirs in this shallow valley. The river itself had carved this valley, through the woods.

I crossed into the woods and trudged up the valley, following the narrow path that snaked alongside the river. My paws sunk into the mud, and I was grateful for my sandals. Cleaning dried mud from paws is always a nightmare, especially when they are furred on top and beneath.

Still, soft paws did lend themselves to certain advantages. Such as sneaking up on unsuspecting wolves.

The wolves had not arrived. So I hid in the forest, behind a fallen tree. This close to the falls, the waters flowed loud, offering me extra cover. I watched the waters, listened to their rush, never slowing, never weakening.

I stayed a good long while: just me, the waters, and the distant call of birds. I started to wonder if they would return. Maybe they had duties back at camp?

The snap of a twig caught my attention, and I ducked lower. The wolves were approaching. Calm as before, absorbed in their conversation. My heart rate had jumped, and I tried to still my breath.

Next to the plunge pool was a pile of rocks, taller even than those wolves. A smattering of words, a smile and a laugh, and they hid behind the rocks. I snuck around. Even if they weren't distracted by each other, the sound of the waterfall would have drowned out my approach. All was fluid: the tawny flow of water; the mist and the spray filling the air; the drip of water from mossy cliffs and ivy-leaves; and the soft growling predators, flowing as one. I perked my long leporine ears, and over the waterfall, I heard them: happy growls, long happy-dog tongues lapping, teeth nipping, hectic huffs of breath; and animals pressing together, male animals. By their paws, the waters ran red, rich with iron. The brown wolf just outsized his grey companion, and his kiss was just that little hungrier, his paws that little more adventurous, seeking the hem of the grey wolf's tunic. The animals stripped, quickly as they could. With clothes and weapons to one side, they embraced once more.

Now or never.

Oh, what am I doing?

I slipped from my hiding place and descended the steep slope, spear in paw. I hoped they would notice me first.

And there it was: a twitch of the ear. A parting of maws. A growl of curiosity. A pair of blue wolf-eyes on me, then a golden pair.

The predators dashed to retrieve their blades. *No, no, no!* I threw my spear to the ground and held up my hands, panting while my heart raced. The wolves had reached their swords and were brandishing them at me. Four piercing lupine eyes locked on me. And Frith above, they looked good—*handsome!* Handsome, good looking, as you would expect from two military carnivores at the peak of physical fitness.

I showed them my empty palms. The wolves spared a moment's glance at each other. I took a step forwards.

I am not afraid. I am not afraid.

Step... by step. I lowered my paws and clasped them together, keeping my ears flattened back. I never broke eye contact. I don't even think I blinked. When I was still a few paces off, I stopped. They were still armed. I was not. I swallowed hard, and began to speak, drawing on the little of their language that I knew.

"*Amātōrēs?*"

The lupines nodded, no hesitation. I took a deep breath, stared at them harder, and tapped my chest.

"*Volō.*"

I let those two syllables hang. Simple, yet clear. 'I want.' The grey wolf looked to his partner. I half-expected the brown wolf to prowl, to circle and size me up. But the brown wolf simply nodded. That was enough. They must have understood. I didn't know how common male-on-male couples were, but I had to imagine they were rare. At least I knew why this couple stole away to this forest, far from the sight and sound of their camp.

Not wanting to feel conscious (feeling conscious about being *over*dressed, who would have thought?), I undressed myself. And there we stood. Naked as newborn cubs. My body chose not to respond. The same could not be said for the wolves. Those bones...

The brown wolf closed the gap. Leading like always. My ears dropped like stones. But the wolf just... chuckled. Low and warm in timbre. I tilted my head. The wolf touched his chest.

"*Lupus.*"

He reached out that massive, fluffy paw, placing it on my chest.

"*Et lepus.*"

I don't remember him guiding me. But he must have, because next thing I knew, he was pressing my back to the sloping, mossy stone.

He loomed over me, pinning me down. But there was no aggression in his body. He was panting, showing teeth and some tongue. Then he lowered his muzzle, lapping his tongue against my muzzle. With that broad, strong, wolf-tongue, I had no choice but to open my maw and lock with him. He knew exactly what I wanted, before I could even express it. He growled low and long, straight into my muzzle, while poising his claw-tipped paw on my chest. His tongue roved, lapping all around my muzzle and teasing my buck-teeth. I tried to press back with my own tongue, and the wolf engulfed me. When he pulled away, two glorious seconds later, a thick strand of drool connected our muzzles. He smiled and panted, stroking my head-fur, teasing one long ear. He licked his lips and locked maws with me again.

Oh yes, I was still terrified. But his tongue was skilled, and I felt the tension ease in my shoulders. I had little time to enjoy it, though, before the brown wolf deepened our embrace. Those paws, eider-soft, held me in place, while firm against me I felt my fellow male.

He overwhelmed me. There is no other way to describe what that brutal beautiful wolf did. And when he howled... I have never known anything so animal.

Licks and puppy-nuzzles eased me back into the world. But there was nothing puppyish about what we did. All the way back through the forest of moss-dappled trees, I was trembling. How could my clan keep such pleasure a secret? Did they know? I wondered if I could ever look at another man again. Of course I had seen naked leporines before: my sparring partners, for example.

O merciful Frith, do not let my thoughts be corrupted!

I pictured some male hares I knew. To my relief, not all of them triggered the same response. Yet some did. Including, to my alarm, Kegyden. Just thinking about his legs... all leporines take pride in their hindquarters. They are our engines, our defence, and at times our weaponry too. I remembered the times I looked, in awe, at the tone and definition in Kegyden's haunches. Before, it was simple envy. But now as I recalled the image, remembered the flex of powerful muscle and the splay of his paws, another sin afflicted me. I had felt him drive against me, though I never let our fights become shows of strength. Because he had me well outmatched in that regard. And with legs like that, I bet he could buck too. How would it feel with that beast at my back?

I imagined that big leporine, wrestling me into submission. I still fought, of course, still gave my all. But some part of me (new, untapped?) welcomed those solid paws gripping me, welcomed that big animal pinning me with his weight, holding me down with purpose. I was no stranger to feeling a hare's arousal, though I always thought it an automatic response. "Bucks and their carrots" and all that. But now, thinking of the *purpose* behind the big hare's pin, I wondered.

No such wonder with those Roman lupines. Everything about that encounter made my fur bristle with pleasure: the touch of those paws—*closer, little bunny*—their strength against me, the power and the confidence with which they moved. I moved too, stumbling on the wet rocks until a pair of sure, firm paws held me tight, strong battle-trained arms wrapping around me, and the wolf, big and insistent, claimed his natural place.

I had never known pleasure that deep. Nor pain, I must add, pain which I felt throughout the night and the following day. But it did not outweigh the glow of pleasure. Of course, I knew the rush and the satisfaction of overcoming my opponent in battle. But such satisfaction now seemed base in comparison, even crude and simple.

Even to spend time with Siran, that somehow seemed lesser. Siran's paws and gentle fur were... nice. But she spent so long preening herself, like a dove. There was no such pretence with those wolves.

All the same, I took up Siran's offer the next day, after training. Her family had always welcomed me. Though I definitely had to be on my best behaviour. Considering who her parents were.

Chief Mildthyl, Ruler of the Hares of the Eastern Lands, was a troubled doe. She put on a brave face, though, trying to show the clan that things were mostly fine. "The sun will shine and the crops will grow, come what may." I liked her. She was always nice to me and the other leverets. Telling us stories, sharing candied nuts with us, even sparring with us before she became Chief. Her job must have been really hard.

"Honey, you're staring into the air again."

Her mate reached across and rubbed her paw. She blinked, shaking her head and her ears.

"Oh, am I? Sorry, I just keep thinking about our situation. Thank you for the food, dear. It would be nice if I could just enjoy it, and not worry about things."

She tucked into her food. But a few seconds later... "It is no use. Every week, these Romans demand more and greater levies. If they must tread our lands, why can we not co-exist? Even five summers ago, it was not like this. And their new commander concerns me. He is a creature of war, make no mistake. I hear he has something of a reputation for putting down rebellions. Is that how they see us? Rebels to be tamed? Well, if you keep kicking the wasps' nest, don't be surprised when they sting."

"And for those heroics, he gets three years on our cold, wet land. Some reward."

"Horses for courses. Maybe their rulers want to take a tougher approach?"

"But they are the ones who invaded! And that's no excuse to prowl around like every animal and wild beast belongs to you. Can you imagine Commander Fulvus behaving that way?"

The Chief sighed. "I agree. And I do miss that bear. But only one thing is constant, and that is change. And as the season changes, we must adapt to our new challenges."

"And our main challenge is feeding ourselves. With the wet summer, our grain reserves are dangerously low. We barely have enough to feed ourselves."

"I have made this point to the commander. Yet he says he has a new centuria to feed."

"That is hardly any of our concern."

"Oh it's our concern alright. He will make it our concern. Besides, we aren't the only animals struggling with their demands. Rhaugr and his clan are furious at sharing their hunt with the Romans. If that fox wastes any more Council time complaining about 'all the prime kill we surrender'... I tell you, those wild dogs. I fear it's only a matter of time before someone makes a mistake, and they bite. And if anyone bites first, it will be them."

Worry was etched onto the Chief's face, a carving upon stone. I did not envy her position. Was this the life that awaited all rulers? Politics, infighting, out-fighting? One day, all of this would be Siran's. Was this the life that awaited her? Us?

The following day's training was difficult. Laps of the meadow, speed drills, and more staff practice. At least my various aches were subsiding.

A commotion by the gates caught everyone's attention. Master called a halt to our drills, and we joined the throngs of hares gathering throughout the village. And when I saw which animals were visiting... I could only stare in shock. There were soldiers in our village. Roman soldiers. A column of them, walking *right through our village*, advancing on our Chief's house. Our elders had negotiated, many seasons ago, that no animal would enter the village walls without invitation. But nobody in the village took up arms. Because there was an exception to that rule: the very animal heading the column.

Seated atop a white horse, with his striped face, tufted ears and cruel blue eyes, his appearance sent a shudder down every herbi-

336

vore's spine. The wild cat they called a lynx. The commander himself.

He brought his horse to a stop, and the soldiers stopped likewise. By the time he had dismounted, Chief Mildthyl had emerged from her home. She and the commandant exchanged flurries of Latin, their language, and though few of us could understand more than the odd word, the snarl of the cat, and the pleading of our Chief, traversed all boundaries. The big hare soon reverted to her native tongue. This earned a glare from the cat. The lynx snarled at her, and the two beasts stood eye to eye.

"*Linguam tuam non loquor. Ubi est tribūtum nostrum?*"

"*Um... Quid?*"

I saw the gnarled whiskers quiver. Saw the feline bare his sharp front teeth. I held my breath. This was the last animal we wanted to enrage. The lynx kept his temper, just about, before repeating his question with extra snarl. The commander had come to take even more of our food.

A few more seconds of silence from the stunned hare. The lynx snarled up at Frith, and snapped his fingers. A canine soldier stepped forward, producing a wooden tablet and a stylus. With a red-furred Celtic weasel to act as translator, our Chief and the commander negotiated. They discussed old treaties, old quotas, and why these quotas had changed. I did not understand. I thought we had paid our due. Had we not? Chief Mildthyl certainly argued so, judging by the little Latin I could glean, and the insistence in the Chief's voice. But the commander was more insistent. At least twice he snarled, "*Non satis!*" Not enough! And, well, what could we do? Not every animal saw us as equal, particularly the carnivores. Lose the patronage of Rome, and there were animals who would pounce. Maybe even Rhaugr would start seeing us as meat?

The prey backed down first. Chief Mildthyl pointed out the food stores, and the lynx turned in that direction, flanked by two soldiers. That could have been the end of the matter. Yet the feline was a creature of battle. And the heat of a battle, like all heat, takes time to dissipate.

"*Ecce*, how difficult was that? *Cunīculī stultī*."

That got a gasp from a few observers, then a few secondary gasps as more hares learned what the commander had said. I couldn't tell if the cat regretted his words. But he gazed around at the gasping, whispering hares. He knew what he had ignited. I stayed my tongue, somehow.

Despite the outward similarities to hares, a rabbit is a feral beast who lives underground, paw-to-maw, with no recourse to weapons or trade. It doesn't matter if you're Caesar. You do *not* call us rabbits. And you *certainly* do not call us 'stupid gutter-bunnies'.

Unfortunately, not everyone stayed calm on our side, either.

"You will pay for that insult!"

Kegyden had broken rank and was storming towards the commander, spear point at the ready. A real spear, not a training weapon.

"Kegyden," said Master, "don't be a fool."

"No! Do not tell me what to do. You can stand around and take these insults like timid kittens. But I for one will not."

Romans stepped up but the commander held them back with a paw-wave, and instead, the wild cat drew his own sword while barely breaking stride. I think he intended to disarm Kegyden, but the hare horribly over-judged his lunge and the commander's blade found flesh. At once there was silence. Kegyden went wide-eyed, impaled on the lynx's blade. His spear clattered to the ground. The lynx twisted his blade clean from the unarmoured hare, and stepped back a few paces, sneering at the foolish cadet. As unfeeling as if he'd slaughtered a wild rabbit. Kegyden stood for a moment, wavering on his paws, stunned like a rabbit caught by a weasel. And when he slumped to the ground, alive but struggling horribly, some of the hares cried out. A healer and our Druid rushed to attend him, while others were advancing on the soldiers. But Chief Mildthyl raised her paw.

"Everyone, stand down."

Some of the hares had acquired weapons, and many brown eyes acquired a murderous glint. The Chief took a deep breath, and called to her people.

"Hares! Stay your weapons!"

Over the ensuing quiet, there were cries of incredulity.

"What?"

"But you saw what happened!"

"Indeed!"

"This is an act of war!"

The atmosphere was thin, tense—a strand of spider-web, laden with rainwater. Every animal was acting on instinct, instincts which fired in wildly different ways. But the Chief held firm.

"I said stay your weapons! There will be no more bloodshed today. Wound one of their number, and they will slaughter us all. Let them take what they want."

The anger shimmered in the air, like the haze on a roasting-hot day. These hares wanted blood. Roman blood, in exchange for the blood of our wounded clan-mate. But no animal dared to fight this organised war machine.

The Romans went about their work with customary efficiency. They spoke little among themselves, and not at all with us. With buckets and sacks, they loaded up a cart with our grain. Some of my clan looked away, or simply left. I stayed, and watched, but I understood why others didn't. This lynx, this predator, was taking food from our mouths.

With the cart laden, the commander mounted his horse, and he left our camp with his detail.

I had to see Kegyden. Master insisted we stay back, but as hares of age, he could not stop us.

Keygden was fading badly. A healer offered him herbs, the taste of which made him scrunch his face. Another hare pressed a thick cloth to his body—a kind and vain gesture, given how quickly the cloth had turned red.

Druid Enfys spoke words to the hare—calm words, sacred words. Kegyden's eyes were turning glassy—*can't look, can't look at his eyes.* Was he listening to those words? Did he believe them?

Chief Mildthyl appeared. She fell to her knees beside the young one, covering her robe in earth and blood.

"My child... I am so sorry."

Kegyden stared at the Chief, with failing sight.

"At least... I tried. What did you do?"

Defiant to the end. That brave, stupid hare.

Events moved quickly that day. We buried Kegyden at the forest edge, along with the spear he used in his stand. To acknowledge his defenceless fight, we gave him no shield. The whole village must have attended his funeral. Even Frith wore a shroud of cloud. A light drizzle filled the air, clinging to the pelts of leporines, both alive and deceased. He looked so peaceful there, that big burly animal, his pelt speckled with rain. I listened to the Druid's words, guiding Kegyden to the next stage in his cycle, to become one with the grass, with this land—our land. "And much too soon," the Wise One noted in a hushed tone.

Chief Mildthyl herself gave the eulogy. I had never seen her so tearful. The Chief soon composed herself, however. If it was for appearance for her village, it still worked to calm twitchy animals. The stronger among us, and those who were meant to be strong, gathered in the Chief's house. As cadets, we attended with our Master. The Chief's paws were trembling as she spoke.

"This... this is intolerable. To slay one of our young, in the one place he should have been safe, and then to take our food from before our eyes. This... horde, they could not have stated their intentions clearer. The days of diplomacy are over. There can be no diplomacy, not while that *cat* stalks our land." A rare lapse in the Chief's composure. Perhaps she had stronger words for their fierce commander. "Well, the stall has been set. Either we starve and suffer under their paws, or we take a chance, and show them they underestimate us hares at their peril."

"My Chief," said an older hare, "are you calling for an attack?"

There were a few seconds of hesitation. All eyes were trained on the Chief, every long ear waiting on her word.

"I am."

If Chief Mildthyl expected dissent, none was forthcoming. A masterful reading of the room.

"Then you have our support. Until the hour we run no more."

"Thank you. I thank every one of you for your support. The risk is great, but so too is the reward. I will need envoys to visit our allied clans. To spread the word about our plans."

Several hares raised their paws, and the Chief chose a number by name.

"Thank you. And for the rest of you, here are my orders: prepare your weapons, eat, and rest well. We attack on the third dawn."

The other cadets and I were given the evening off, to clear our minds and to ready ourselves for battle. Kegyden and I had never been close, but I needed the time.

In the village that night, there was no thrum of conversation. To an animal, we were focused on the task at paw. My appetite was weak, yet I made sure to eat. Somehow, I managed to sleep that night. My mother and sister lay nearby, drifting in and out of sleep. I thought of my village, of the animals in my clan. So many brave animals, tough animals, yet like trees they could be felled. How many of them were sleeping? How many of them *could* sleep?

Over the next two days, the preparations began in earnest. We continued our training, though it took on a new, serious tone—little time for levity. And new and mysterious animals began to visit us. They would march through the village, paying us no heed, escorted by a sentry all the way to the Chief's house. Strange hares in the main, though I did also see a band of stoats with long needle-sharp swords, whose leader wore a long mantle trimmed with rabbit fur. All of our pelts were on the line.

The night before the attack, there was rain, and in the morning, a damp sodden mist covered the meadows, hanging low in the valleys. A world in grey, a world in mourning.

In the eastern hills, pale blue light was rising. The birds began their chorus. Though the sound was familiar, that morning I focused on its meaning. Competition for a mate. Survival of the fittest.

With only thin daylight to see by, I made my preparations. I pulled on my coarse tunic, folding my ears down to pass it over my head. Then, for a moment, I stared at my weaponry. My spear, my first choice of weapon, vital in reaching my opponent before he reached me. My sword, a gift from my parents on my thirteenth birthday. I kept it sharp and clean, though to this point it had only cut wood. Now I needed to wield it in an altogether deadlier way. And my shield, long and oval, resting against the wall.

Hares had gathered in the village centre, and they continued to arrive after me. Our horses were untied, harnessed, and ready for battle. And Chief Mildthyl walked among her troops, rallying them, reminding us what we fought for. The moment Frith appeared from behind the hills, the Chief mounted her horse, and we moved out.

As we left our village, we saw a clan of foxes cresting the hills. Savage dogs dressed in skins, armed to their yellow teeth with jagged and rusting iron. They had been baying for a scrap with the Romans, and now their wish was granted. They gathered near our horse-pasture, and we went to meet them. A big male fox headed the pack. He wore jewellery on his arms and a torc around his neck, and he carried a jagged iron blade, with an arsenal of cruel implements strapped to his belt. His ears were torn and pierced, and his right eye was missing. Yet he wore no patch over the wound, so the whole world could see the deep disfiguring cut on that snarling vulpine face. *Rhaugr.*

Our chiefs greeted one another, and together, we marched on the Roman camp. Other animals joined us: a clan of squirrels, a war-band of stoats, even Brocklebush the solitary badger whose forest home was destroyed by the Romans for timber.

I had glimpsed the Roman camp, watched it take shape over the seasons. From a distance, of course. Guerrilla attacks had weakened the Roman stronghold, though not forced them to abandon camp. All of the clans denied responsibility (except the stoats—*"show your enemy they're your enemy"* was a well-known stoat saying). A wooden scaffold surrounded the half-finished structure, and a cluster of tents surrounded the construction site.

We approached from both sides, down in the valleys and hidden from view. Master had briefed us on our role: as the swiftest animals, we would catch them off guard, dealing the first blows and stealing away before they could regroup. Soften them up for the foxes' jaws and the horses' hooves.

Crouched behind a hill, out of sight, I breathed in, savouring the dew and the rain and the grass. I touched the coarse grass, feeling its bounce and dampness. Good grass for running. But the air would not feel so fresh soon. And soon, an altogether richer liquid would soak this earth. But how much would be their blood, and how much would be ours?

Silence. Even the birds ceased their calls, as if they knew to hold the peace. Then, in the distance, as if up from the very hills, Chief Mildthyl raised that ancient leporine battle-cry.

"Eulalius!"

As horde we answered the cry, and into the fray we ran. We surged ahead of all animals, a flight of hares, armed and perilous. It felt like our cries would echo through the hills and valleys for all of time, never to be forgotten.

We struck quickly, before the enemy realised they were under attack. The horses tore through the tents, bringing havoc wherever they rode. Some hapless Romans were slain before they could even prepare. But the majority quickly gathered weapons and shields and fell into formation.

I joined Rhaugr's mob, and together we stormed the half-finished camp, ransacking wherever we went. To my left, a fox snarled and locked blades with a big armoured reptile. The vulpine almost got the upper paw, before a misjudged thrust gave the reptile an opening to snap jaws on the fox's arm. Crack. *Yowl!*

Sword on my belt, shield over my back, I charged at the reptile with spear-point raised. The blade sliced up through the reptile's throat, and the beast staggered for a moment, until I wrenched my spear free. I reached for the fox's paw and he knocked mine away, signalling for me to move. Without arguing, I left him, and I didn't look back.

There were no soldiers in the next block, so I slowed my step. I entered a stone room—colder, sparsely furnished. I saw the bars, and I realised I was in a prison block. And there was another animal in here—just one. Chained by his neck, squatting low to the ground, tracing the cracks of the floor with a claw. And when I saw which animal it was, my heart sank.

It was the grey wolf.

He looked different. Strong, yes, but it wasn't the strength of a trained warrior. Now, he looked wild, and therefore more dangerous, because you cannot read a wild animal's attack.

He snapped his gaze up at me, his eyes blinking and blue, his paw still. I dropped to his level, and he craned his muzzle forward. *I shouldn't be doing this.*

"*Ubi? Amātor?*"

He lunged at me, barking and thrashing and snapping those teeth, every muscle of that powerful body straining the chains. I was grateful for the chains, and thankful that they did not yield. He re-alised how futile his efforts were, and I watched the fierceness fade from his eyes. He sat on the stones, ears hanging low. Our eyes met again.

He pointed to my spear. Then pointed to his stomach.

I had never seen such fire, such determination, in an animal's stare. Kegyden looked determined when he fought me. This wolf was a hundred times more intense. I didn't understand. With all that intensity, how could an animal wish destruction on himself?

I had to leave. Others would find the prisoner, and they would decide his fate. That suited me. I could not take that responsibility.

All around me, sword clashed with spear. Smoke drifted into the sky and billowed across the meadow, the air thick with charred wood and tannin from the goatskin tents. I moved at pace, as though seeking new enemies to rout. In truth, I was trying to escape. That day, I could fight no more.

I escaped their half-built fortress, following the gully between hills towards a nearby wood. I don't know if anyone saw me. I did not care. Beyond the trees, the battle raged on. I hid from it all, seated by a fallen tree. My ears were already hanging, lower than the wolf's. I held them in my paws, tugging them down, breathing hard.

I had to know where the brown wolf was. I didn't even know his name! He must have escaped, or they would have clapped him in chains too. Not in the same cell as his mate, of course. That would hardly be punishment.

But what could I do?

There was a rustle in the trees. The animal made no effort to conceal itself, and my heart leapt like a leveret when I saw who it was. The brown wolf! But wait. What was that in his paw...?

I never got a clear look before the blow struck my head, shrouding my world in black.

TOMES ENTOMBED WITHIN ME

DOMUS VOCIS

Fragments of the past, present, and future burned with the Great Library on that day.

"Take all you can carry and evacuate!" Caecilius barked on his way outside to the grand entrance hall. "Evacuate, then search for as many buckets you can find!"

The past became scorched as I followed his orders, wrapping my arms around as many scrolls as they could hold. Tears streaked down the fur of my cheeks, due to both panicking disbelief and terror. The Great Library's columned corridors, once peaceful like a quiet cemetery, were filled with the sounds of screams, shouts, and coughing due to a thickening black cloud billowing out. I blinked the tears away as my tired legs carried me past other fleeing bodies into the promenade outside.

We'd done our best to fortify the library from rioting citizens and pillaging looters, guarding the old structure during the city's devolved siege. We'd earlier watched from afar as the Roman and Alexandrian armies clashed in the narrow streets. So much blood stained the ground, it could all be collected and used as crimson ink. The battle nearest to the Royal Harbor itself was most brutal, but it all paled in comparison to Consul Caesar's men setting fire to the docked Alexandrian fleet. No sooner did they catch fire than the ravenous ruin subsequently spread out of control, the flying embers setting light to nearby trees, several thickets, a garden, then finally the Great Library itself.

"Take this, take it!" I handed a feline attendant an arm full of parchments from the affected branch. "There is more to be saved! Guard them with your life!"

"Yes, sir!" The attendant shouted behind me as I bolted inside again.

"Where is Tiberius?" I asked a fleeing hound at the entrance, who in turn gripped a large scroll as if it were made of jewels. "Have you seen Tiberius, Khons?"

"He is assisting with the western wing, Caius!" Khons explained between haggard panting, before scurrying down the steps. "No more dawdling, friend! Go inside once more!"

He did not have to inform me a second time. Without considering the stinging in my eyes, or how much the soot blocked my nostrils, I flew back into the fray.

By Athena and Minerva, by Thoth himself, let us not be too late!

The present turned into a nightmare, as the ongoing fire feasted on another branch. For what felt like hours, licking red-and-yellow tendrils and black smoke reached into the sky, while the barbaric echoes of Roman legionaries could be heard coming from deeper within the Royal Quarter. Civilians too afraid to die for the Pharaoh, whoever held it, either stayed within their homes or helped librarians like me place rescued scrolls into neat, orderly piles.

"Caius!" shouted a familiar feline's voice over crackling reverberations. "Help!"

The smaller scroll went inside a tunic's back pocket. I fled down a short hallway until I discovered the imposing, bronze-furred lion of twenty-eight summers holding two thick tomes under an arm each. His extended claws dug into the leather bindings as one tried falling free.

"Tiberius!" I gasped, promptly rushing to assist him. "Give me one and take the other!"

Together, my friend and I carried two of Greece's epics into the outdoor promenade. I had transported the *Odyssey* whilst Tiberius

Ectorius carried the *Iliad*, each tome transcribed from Greek into Latin by myself and another jackal librarian by the name of Lucius.

"Will you be coming back inside, Tiberius?" I asked the lion.

His feline eyes wandered to the growing crowd of fellow Alexandrians, some helping out the Great Library's staff while others watched. Once or twice did one dare to step forward without the intent to help. Tiberius shook his mane side to side. It made sense for the son of a wealthy merchant not to actively risk his life but use it to protect what had already been saved.

"Very well," I said, motioning to the piles. "Protect each book with your life!"

He roared with a bittersweet smirk, "So long as you protect your own, Caius!"

The future appeared uncertain. Between the might of Gaius Julius Caesar, the deathly rivalry of two ruling pharaohs, a beheaded Roman general, and a treasury of wisdom set ablaze, I still didn't falter in my mission. No toxic smoke, hellfire, or civil war would prevent me from completing my duty as a preserver of knowledge.

My knees trembled at the library's diminished glory. With the help of some fellow staff from the neighboring *Musaeum*, we had managed to quell the flames. Bucket by bucket and pail by pail, amidst the ongoing battles and the siege within the Royal Quarter, the fire trickled down to embers until everyone's fur carried the scent of pungent ash.

As everyone else recuperated at their home, a few others stayed behind. Tiberius joined me in surveying what remained, bringing the unharmed texts into what used to be a storage room, alongside a tragic heap of torched literature and records.

"I have no clue if this is Erastosthenes or Euclid..." I mentioned to Tiberius, showing the distraught lion one of the charred scrolls in my paw. "What blasphemy!"

"Half of Callimachus and Euclid's mechanics are gone forever too," Tiberius mentioned, then stifled his tongue upon glancing over my shoulder. I turned, then stiffened into a respectful bow as we said in unison, "Head Librarian."

Didymus Caecilius did not sleep well the night before. Nobody did. The stoic owl's once-respectful stature had turned into an exhausted hunch in the hours since. His age caught back up to him, his eyelids darkening and feathers a whiter shade. The smell of soot touched him too, even after bathing in the Nile, and a change of clothing.

"Caius Benedictus," he stated.

Years of working under his literal wings allowed the other library staff to pick up on his aloof language. Saying your name but not others meant he wanted to speak with you alone.

"Yes, Head Librarian." Tiberius promptly escaped into the exiting hall, yet not before he gently patted my shoulder, offering a smile.

The moment the tall lion left, Didymus Caecilius relaxed only slightly. Regret still laced across his expression. Weeks earlier, after Pompey Magnus of Rome had arrived on Alexandria's shores, the old owl ordered me and the other librarians not to worry about the ongoing crisis. Whether Queen Cleopatra's face remained on our coins or not, the Great Library still needed to be maintained. So, we refrained from gossip and panicking. At least, until Consul Caesar landed with thousands of men. Yet with hindsight torturing Caecilius in the present, visibly much so as he stared at me in the empty room, I wanted to tell him nobody could have foretold this disaster.

"Head Librarian?" I spoke up nervously, ears still crestfallen. "Are you well?"

"No, I am not," he confessed in emotional breaths of air.

"How could the gods allow this?" I asked, despite knowing the answer.

"The gods did not do this," Caecilius said. "Men did. Men like Julius Caesar did this."

Caecilius went on to explain how only a couple branches of the Great Library sustained severe injury, but hundreds of scrolls and parchments within them did burn. Many more so deteriorated from the harsh smoke and thick soot billowing through the hallways and corridors. So much smoke damage affected surviving papyrus scrolls and entwined texts that merely touching it blackened my paws' white fur.

Our worst loss was the *Pinakes*, written by the legendary librarian Callimachus near the library's creation. A catalogue so vast and detailed I had never found a chance to completely read through it.

"What did survive the flames is barely legible anymore," Caecilius hooted bittersweetly while looking at one of the opened scrolls charred black, cracking like leaves from the north in wintertime. His feathered fingers traced along the ruined ink that used to resemble Koine. "I can still remember the sequence, but age has not been kind to me in remembering every syllable."

Ears folded downward, I made a subtle glance to the scroll's interior.

"Wait..." I murmured softly.

My eyes widened as my vision suddenly thrust itself back ten years into the past. I could still vibrantly remember the excitement making my fur stand on end, being a young scholar of seventeen years who wished to follow in the respected footpaws of Zenodotus, the first librarian of Alexandria. Ever since the days of my youth, Mother and Father had prided in not just my articulation for language and grammar, but for possessing an unnatural memory as well. Unlike most mammal cubs, I did not forget easily. As a matter of fact, I never forgot anything, not my dreams nor what I learned wide awake. My own mental library contained books which never disappeared, never faded, or collected mold.

Mother and Father knew I possessed a wonderful gift and had entrusted my education would be used greatly at Alexandria's Library. A decade later, intaking a single breath, I recalled in vivid detail holding that same scroll currently held by Caecilius.

"This contained the Homeric Hymn to the Greek god Demeter, if this is correct?" I asked aloud.

"It is," the Head Librarian walked over to set the scroll down on a nearby table. He turned around to see me. Blinking once, twice, thrice, then a fourth harder time, the wrinkled owl's demeanor changed. The melancholic stoicism from before found itself replaced by intrigue. "You are the lad who is capable of remembering everything he reads, correct?"

"I am, Head Librarian."

The old owl breathed inward, as if he were preparing for disappointment.

"If that is the case," he requested, "then are you able to tell me the first nine lines? Only the first nine lines of Demeter's Hymn, if you will."

"As you wish, Head Librarian..." I bowed my muzzle, then recited in perfect Koine, " 'I begin to sing of Demeter, the holy goddess with the beautiful hair. And her daughter Persephone too. The one with the delicate ankles, whom Hadês seized. She was given away by Zeus, the loud-thunderer, the one who sees far and wide. Demeter did not take part in this, she of the golden double-axe, she who glories in the harvest. She was having a good time, along with the daughters of Okeanos, who wear their girdles slung low. She was picking flowers: roses, crocuses, and beautiful violets. Up and down the soft meadow. Iris blossoms too she picked, and hyacinth. And the narcissus, which was grown as a lure for the flower-faced girl by Gaia. All according to the plans of Zeus. She was doing a favor for the one who receives many guests.' "

He continued to stare as his beak curved upward. "What of the final ten lines then?"

I required only ten seconds of thought, then inhaled and exhaled as I recited again in Koine, " 'And there they abide at the side of Zeus, who delights in the thunderbolt. Holy they are and revered. Olbios is he whom they, being kind, decide to love among earth-bound mortals. Straightaway they send to such a man, to reside at his hearth, in his great palace, Hadês who gives riches to mortal humans. But come, you goddesses, who have charge of the dêmos of Eleusis, fragrant with incense, and of Paros the island and rocky Antron. Come, O lady resplendent with gifts, Queen Demeter, bringer of hôrai, both you and your daughter, the most beautiful Persephone. Think kindly and grant, in return for this song, a rich means of livelihood that suits the thûmos. And I will keep you in mind throughout the rest of my song...' "

Blinking once, twice, thrice, then a fourth harder time. "My boy, I have a heavenly task for you," he proclaimed, the wrinkled owl's grinning beak almost frightening me.

"Wha-what is my task?" I asked him.

"Your unnatural memory has already saved literatures from the void, but now it must be put to papyrus!" Caecilius stepped forward to grasp my arms, smiling as if he had never smiled before. "My boy, if you do this task for me—for Alexandria, Egypt, the world—people will remember your name across time immemorial for saving what has been destroyed."

My fur stood up on end like sewing needles, not of excitement, but hope. Euphoric hope.

Time passed. Life continued onward for the librarians and residents of Alexandria, during which a great naval battle on the Nile River ensured Queen Cleopatra and her younger brother Ptolemy XIV's continued reign as the Pharaoh. As Caesar's civil war continued elsewhere, the Great Library's rebuilding began, no doubt in thanks to support and funding provided by the Alexandrine nobility who wished to seek local prestige.

I did not listen to the rumors and political talk regarding the Republic of Rome, not when the Great Library needed to lick its own wounds. So, I started what was believed to be my destiny.

"You shall be given your own working room for privacy," Didymus Caecilius explained to me, "Do not worry, your former duties will be divided among the other librarians and attendants, who will understand the necessary workload alongside everything else that the gods have given us in these tumultuous times. I will expect at least one reconstructed tome or scroll by the night of each full moon."

Thus, I was given my own workplace, the same meeting room in the Great Library that housed many of the damaged or smoke-ruined scrolls in one corner. In the center, set directly to a window facing towards the Alexandrine Harbor, stood a long acacia wooden table repurposed into a writing desk.

The first days of my task, I put a wooden pen to ink, then recalled the very first memories of when I read the book in question. The first text to be saved had been the copied version of the Homeric Hymn. I completed it within two days of uninterrupted scribbling. The second text to be saved was neither an ornate manuscript nor an epic about arcane societies, but a simple notebook on Greek architecture, specifically on columns. I'd read it once throughout a slow evening within the library, browsing each page for mere seconds before returning it to the proper shelf. Little did I know such a bored impulse would guarantee its existence.

Other notable texts did spring forth. I intensely remembered passing days when I'd read through entire literatures and plays such as Dyskolos, Medea, the Plautines, Heauton Timorumenos, as well as other works of entertainment previously consumed by me in fleeting boredom. I particularly reenjoyed the experience of bringing back the fables of Aesop, despite knowing that copies likely existed elsewhere, it still felt rejuvenating to pen it by my own paws in the fabulist's name. I could still feel the dried ink on my pads as I'd read it long ago, each stroke forming words, which turned into extravagant sentences, transforming into descriptive paragraphs.

Scrolls, tomes, entwined texts, books, novels, catalogues, and letters; they all appeared to my eye as bright as the Sun!

Between these bursts of ravenous writing, I did at first take personal breaks, sometimes walking away from the room to either peruse the Great Library or relax as my footpaws wandered the surrounding chrysanthemum gardens walkways outside. I still breathed in the clean air, basked in the subtle warmth of sunlight, marveled at the magnificent view of the city and Mediterranean Sea. Far away on an island within the harbor, I could always make out the Pharos of Alexandria and its eternally burning pyre. All through my tenure, I'd end each receding dusk by watching the sunset until only the lighthouse's faint glow remained, heralding to travelling ships that their journeys had ended.

Tiberius sometimes accompanied me on my walks. He expressed jubilation of my endeavors in the only way lions like him could express, by purring in my presence.

"You act as if I am covered by incensed catnip, my friend," I laughed, following him back inside one of the Great Library's halls, and towards his workstation. "Why do you make these noises whenever you are around me?"

"What is offensive to you about purring, Caius?" He affectionately rubbed one of my shoulders, then held the door open for me to enter first. Back then, I had been too distracted by my task and blinded that I never noticed these actions. "I purr because you are my friend. I purr because I am still in amazement about how you will singlehandedly bring back everything lost."

I sighed as my left paw examined a scroll on his desk. Partially unraveled, a single glance led me to see some passages, and know it to be an account of the First Punic War between an infant Rome and mighty Carthage. "Not all that has been lost," I reminded the lion. "The *Pinakes* is still reduced to ash."

"But the Homeric Hymn is not," he pointed out, "all thanks to you."

"Which is why I must keep working," I said, looking up to the tall feline as my tail wagged. Sheathing my left paw back into my cloak, my right paw emerged to shake his. "It is a dreadful shame you cannot continue your contributions, Tiberius."

"Alas, I must continue Father's work." He cordially gripped my paw, letting his fingers linger on mine, if only for additional seconds. "He has grown quite ill since last month and expects me to take over his trading business. There is an artisan's daughter whom I am willing to bet a silver talent or two my father will want me to marry."

"Who is this artisan's daughter?" I asked. "Do you wish to marry her?"

"She is Proserpine of Crete and Cyrenaica, daughter of Spiridon Perriades," he said with a forced smile. "She fulfills all the requirements of a wonderful wife, but it is her personality I like more than her beauty. She is kind, considerate, attentive in conversation, wonderful with a lyre, yet I worry if she will be happy to be my bride..."

My question needed repeating itself as I asked, "What I meant was...do you wish to marry her?" Tiberius became hesitant to answering my question. "Do you find her attractive?"

"She would make a wonderful wife, but it is not her I am fully attracted to," he admitted seconds later. "However, if our marriage is what's best for my father's business ventures, and if she is willing to be my wife, then I will be the best husband I can ever be for her. It is what is least expected of me as a spouse, after all."

My tail swished. "You are a good man, Tiberius."

"And you are as well," he nodded, still purring until he grew silent. "Truth be told, I will miss the library, but I will not miss Caecilius in the slightest."

An ear of mine perked up in confusion, "What do you mean?"

"Caius, your nose has always been to the ground, if not in papyrus," the lion snickered, if only for a second. "Didymus Caecilius is a senile old avian who favors you. Meanwhile, to the rest of the other librarians and attendants, he's been more frantic and stricter than usual since the fire. Today, he didn't even thank me for my services when I tended my resignation and mentioned my ailing father. He only told me to leave him be!"

"Caecilius is a busy man, Tiberius," I argued in nervous disposition. "He's Head Librarian, after all. I...I think he was merely busy and you came at an inopportune moment."

"Of course, I did..." He scoffed, then stared at nothingness in deep, apparent thought. "Caius?"

"Yes, Tiberius?" I asked.

"Will you promise me not to overwork yourself in your new station, please? You are only a mortal. Yet you sometimes overwork yourself to exhaustion. I've seen this on the busier nights we've worked together, and it worries me."

I laughed at the notion of him needing to worry, but Tiberius wouldn't budge.

"I mean it," he said earnest and truthful as we stood at a corner. "Your mind is extraordinary and rivals a god, but your body does not, so promise me you will not die within these halls. Will you promise me, Caius?"

Mulling it over, I grinned, then bowed to my best friend. "I promise."

We soon parted amicable ways as our personal lives became more condensed in workloads, but I did my best to remain unexhausted and not neglect my health. Although as Caecilius insisted I didn't postpone the rebirths of longer texts, I prioritized a decent sleep over adding yet another paragraph to the book. I still appreciated my hearty meals provided by staff each morning and evening. I even found myself attending the eventual wedding celebration between Tiberius and Proserpine, who immediately welcomed me as a good friend.

A lunar year came and went as I traveled from my dwelling to the Great Library each morning, then vice-versa each night. One dreary dawn near the end of December, a rainstorm wept frigid tears over the Nile River. Severe wind collided with these raindrops, making it difficult to see as people tried crossing between buildings. Despite my memorized familiarity with walking between my home and where I worked, the intense rainfall and punishing winds prevented me from seeing clearly.

I desperately fought against the howling cries. My fingers brushed against solid surfaces such as walls, a fallen cart, a rough acacia tree, trying to traverse the madness. The cloak and chiton I wore beneath was completely drenched, but my concern remained less on how freezing I felt and more on what I could see. I tripped into puddles multiple times, meandering right, and meandering left through the dense rainfall.

"Hello!" My voice carried out in a drowning call, my entire body to and froing like a ship in the open ocean. "Can anyone tell...Can anyone help me, please! I-I'm lost! Can anyone help me I'm—oof!"

I stumbled into a solid object, falling backwards. Instinct made my hind leg kick desperately against the mud until I felt solid ground. Except, it felt so familiar against my toenails. It sounded familiar too. Why, because my ears recognized the clacking noises made whenever I'd danced along the river's stone edge.

One crucial step forward nearly condemned me to the bottom of the Nile.

"By the gods!" Opening an eye in time, I gasped at seeing the waters below my outstretched footpaw. Walking madly backwards until I stayed a safe distance, I realized in my confusion that I almost fell into the Nile River. "By the gods, thank you."

Shivering and grateful for the calmer rainfall, I renavigated in the direction towards the Great Library, forcing my tired frame to rest at the communal fireplace in the center of the building. A few attendants kindly grabbed some replacement clothes as I stared in shocked stupor at the embers. Reminisces of the infamous siege returned to me the longer I let the flames warm my dripping canine body.

At some point in the day, Didymus Caecilius found me half-shaken by the fireplace, shivering and half-asleep. "Caius Benedictus, what is the meaning of this?" He demanded, interrupting without giving me a chance to explain myself. "You stall on bringing me a completed poem six nights ago, you are late to your post, you track rainwater into these halls, and I find you lazing by the fire as if this is a holiday. "

"Head Librarian, I am sorry—"

Already, the disappointed owl went storming off down another corridor. He merely left me to my own devices as I processed the events of the day. Trickling like rainwater, negative emotions swirling inside me turned rigid as stone. The contents of my stomach nearly escaped when a horrid glimpse of what could have been came to mind; imagine if Fate did indeed decide to have been cruel. Imagine if my mortal form did die after falling into the river. Anubis himself would've brought me before the Duat. The Jackal God would not have just escorted my soul to be judged, but the other texts within my memory too!

Such fear intangibly rooted itself into my routine when I'd finished recuperating by the fireplace. I accepted a new cloak and chiton from the attendant, then set to work completing the *Argonautica* by mid-afternoon. Such an accomplishment usually resulted in a congratulatory sip of wine at home later that evening, but then the memory of almost falling into the Nile returned with painful prominence.

Didymus Caecilius voiced such gratitude for the tomes the next day. He quickly apologized for his behavior, masking it as concern regarding another library patrons' interest in reading the *Argonautica* soon after its completion; each restored reading text equaled another silver talent to be donated for the Great Library's maintenance.

Like a beaten puppy, I bought the excuse, feeling grateful for hearing his approval towards me. Over the weeks to come, Caecilius would test my resolve by asking me to rebirth two tomes instead of one within a lunar cycle. When I gave him the result he wanted, the old owl asked for only another if I had the strength. His honeyed words of encouragement only pushed me to reach beyond my own limits.

Whatever inclination I held about holding myself back was slowly abandoned. I learned to think of my comforts as less like necessities and more like obstacles. Could I put another page to paper if I only stayed awake an extra hour? Would I be able to fit an additional tome into the Head Librarian's quotas if I missed one more meal? What did small comforts matter when the sum of knowledge remained at stake?

Thus, I fully commanded myself further into my work. I forged forward without further care for myself. Days fluidly turned into weeks, blending together. Weeks into months. Months into an existence I began to slowly no longer recognize as my own.

For two additional years, my waking days were spent feverishly penning memorized scrolls to papyrus and paper. I only slept four hours each evening. I only ate as a reward for each finished scroll. Every instance of seeing Caecilius' visible approval motivated me to keep going forward. During which, I became lost myself inside that solitary room. The same room within the Great Library that I'd transformed into my current personal quarters, where I slept and worked from dawn until agonizing dusk. It developed into my sanctuary haven from the dangerous world of natural disasters, wars, disease, robbers, and muggers. Nowhere else could I be, if not to bring back what had been stolen through a single man's accident.

At one point, the door leading inside my work room opened.

Harsh torchlight reflecting from the walls made me wince. "What is it?" I asked bitterly. A glance to the window made me realize mid-morning turned into late evening. "Go away—"

"Caius?" Called a deep voice under my room's doorway. "Caius Benedictus?"

My creased face softened at the familiar sound of purring. Slowly turning from my writing desk, I set the wooden pen aside as a large presence stepped inside, tired eyes narrowing and widening at a golden-maned lion in citizens' clothes.

"Tiberius?" I whispered.

His bright smile faltered at the sight of me. "Caius, it…has been too long." He stepped forward again, then guided me into a momentary hug. He thought I didn't notice his wrinkling nose, hiding disgust. "Have you been busy these past several months? Proserpine and I have not received any of your letters since our visiting trip to Antioch."

"You are back already?" I gasped in surprise. "I thought you would return by the month of Mars."

"It is the month of Juno," he exclaimed in utter shock, then glared down at me as his critical eyes wandered to my makeshift bed, followed by my eating table, where a disregarded meal sat decomposed on a plate. "How long have you been inside this place, my friend?"

An ear weakly perked. "I am not sure." I tried giving the lion a reassuring smile, only to stagger when a noise resonated from my stomach. It was a powerful growl, like a feral beast roaring inside my gut. "I-Ignore what you heard, Tiberius. I am—I am almost finished with the next book."

The concern melted into an indignant snarl.

"Your letters never mentioned living inside the Great Library!" He accused me, baring his fangs before hiding them behind his whiskered lips, which formed a saddened smile.

"You never asked," I tried to say, only for it to come out as a hacking cough. Sitting back down at my desk, the lion at least waited for me to calm down.

"I don't know about you, but I think this has gone on for long enough," Tiberius spoke.

"What has?" I absentmindedly grabbed my pen, restarting to write in the scroll. "I am fulfilling my destiny as a librarian. I am preserving history and literature, am I not?"

"Your love for literature and the Great Library has always been admirable." The lion emitted growls as he stepped into my hunched vision, half-focused on the half-blank scroll. "But it is obsession now. Your lust for life used to be strong, Caius! Look at you now! You're nothing but an unwashed bag of jackal bones!"

I fought to keep writing, despite my paw noticeably trembling. Invisible needles clung inward through my wrist, digging and scraping towards the bone with a movement of the thumb or press of the index finger.

Hitching his breath, Tiberius noticed my pained winces. "Your paw is shaking…" he realized, "Caius, how long has this been going on for?"

I tried my best to brush away the agony, which I labeled mere discomfort. "Exactly two lunar cycles and ten days, my friend. It doesn't matter, really. I will have it looked at when I'm finished."

"By the gods, stop torturing yourself!" He stood closer to the desk and frantically tried to lift my head up, "If your writing paw is hurt, then you mustn't work. You need to heal and rest, Caius."

"I can rest when I want to," I scoffed, only to wince again when I felt the tremor worsen and a scribble of ink ruined my writing. Time to start over again. "Maybe it is best we discuss this later. As you can plainly see, I have work to be do—"

A large arm suddenly thrashed at my desk. The ink jar cracked and splashed over the flown papyrus scroll, then crashed to the stone floor. My right paw snapped the wooden pen into two bent pieces, and I growled in flaring pain. Furious, uncontrolled eyes fell on the lion.

The broken pen fell to the floor. I attempted to punch Tiberius, only for the stronger mammal to snatch my wrist, then pull me from my writing chair. The unexpected movement knocked it over as I tried flailing my left arm at him. Again, Tiberius gripped my paw. I struggled to break free while muttering snarls and angry barks.

He pushed me to a wall.

We stayed there.

Our hearts beat in synchronization.

Our panting and heavy breaths slowed.

"Caius," he finally said, "This stubbornness is making it difficult to love you."

"Tiberius…you?" I tried saying, only to fall silent.

Of every action I expected him to take, kissing me wasn't included on the theoretical list.

His whiskers were Eastern silk brushing against my muzzle. His soft lips pressed into mine once they surrendered. Surprised at first, either through longing to feel another's affections again, or because it belonged to Tiberius himself, I parted my maw for him. I let his tongue tenderly caress mine as I embraced the strong lion.

Our muzzles separated. Only then did I look down to my thin, emaciated paw placed on his well-nourished chest. When had I truly begun to let myself fall so far?

"Is this how you want to live the rest of your days, Caius?" Tiberius questioned me in a somber, serious tone of voice, partially obscured by a minor purr. "Locked inside of this room like a prisoner of war? Recalling and recalling unimportant texts from that extraordinary memory of yours until your heart stops beating, and you're returned to dust?"

Momentarily, the dense fog clouded my judgement.

"The-These are not unimportant texts, Tiberius!" I tried arguing. "I-I need to do this—"

He interrupted me to repeat his query, "Is this how you *want* to live the rest of your days?"

A rebuttal never came to mind. Instead, my attention turned to the moonlight glinting from those hazel orbs staring down at me. Such beauty ignored in the past distracted me from the countless writings to be rewritten and retold. For once, I truly began to grasp how handsome the lion looked beyond his past librarian's clothing. The white wool toga he currently wore did more to reveal his defined muscles and exposed pectoral than the librarians' cloak ever did. It also allowed me to appreciate a proper view of his shining auburn eyes, filled completely with nothing but concern for my well-being.

He did not just love me as a friend. His love contained something more potent, I realized.

"N-No..." came my confession, "N...No. No, I don't."

Tiberius released me from his grasp. I almost fell to the floor, but the muscular feline refused to let me. He held me up by a single arm, being sure to stay gentle.

"But countless tomes entombed within me will die out," I tried one final time to stay.

"They already died, Caius. What you've been writing are nothing more than shadows."

The emotions welling inside me burst at those words. I sobbed along his broad shoulder, only for no tears to be shed. They'd already dried out from lonesome nights long since passed.

Consciousness lapsed in and out as I felt fresh evening air in my lungs. My frame felt too weak to walk, let alone continue to be awake afterward, so Tiberius carried me out of that disgusting room, and out of that beautiful mausoleum. Bringing me by chariot to his estate, he called on the physician to examine me as an alarmed Proserpine personally cooked various foods for me to consume. The latter felt more important than the former, so it didn't take until half an hour of coaxing from Tiberius that he compelled me to eat, despite not feeling hungry.

Upon swallowing the last morsel, only then did the physician fully examine me. The overuse of my fingers meant I could no longer write as quickly as I used to. Not only that, but the neglect of my own health required much time away from the Great Library. At first, I protested such an idea, only for Tiberius to bring me a silver-backed handheld mirror. My lithe canine form had become more skeletal over the years, to the point I almost mistook myself for the soul of an undead mammal brought before the Forty-Two Judges. Even the familiar spark of hope in my blue eyes had faded with time.

A day later, with the strong feline's assistance, I moved myself into one of the guest bedrooms of his estate. Temporary at first, or at least in my stubborn mind, Tiberius and his loving family helped nurse me back from the brink of death. They helped feed me, clothe me, bathe me if needed, and guided me from the dark tunnel.

During this time, Tiberius tended my resignation for me to the Head Librarian. It cited to him my failing health, the physician's diagnosis of damage to my writing wrist, how it would take several months of needed rest to fully heal.

Amidst my recovery, I further learned about it from a letter written by him and given the Head Librarian's seal. Didymus Caecilius could never forgive me for 'squandering away' my post. He could not deny my contributions in preserving half an entire building branch of knowledge, but the old owl expressed disappointment in me. The previous friendly promises of wealth and splendor spilled into fury.

As punishment for 'forsaking my blessed gift' and 'condemning texts to forgotten memory', he vowed to turn me into a forgotten memory. By that, he meant stripping my name from the Great Library's records, as well as not crediting me for the preserved archives I had already written. To readers across Egypt and the rest of the known world, they were simply random texts saved from the fire.

Painful tears welled up again as Tiberius and Proserpine's comforting paws patted each of my shoulders. Finally, I saw the curmudgeon owl for what he truly was. Reading the letter over and over despite having it sewn into memory, I vowed to never return to Alexandria's Library. If I ever did, merely seeing the inside walls would have tempted me to stay, and I would have become one part of its infinite collection.

In the years since Tiberius saved me, his family welcomed me as an equal, valued member of the Ectorius household. If not to organize the servants or handle financial records, then to gladly keep the handsome patriarch's bed warm whenever his charming wife desired sleep. I still experienced daydreams and nightmares about putting those lost literatures to ink. I sometimes woke up feeling immense regret no words could ever describe, but with the help of Tiberius, Proserpine, and their wonderful cubs, I eventually learned to seek contentment in my newfound peace. Rather than decompose amongst papyrus scrolls, I could put my knowledge to better use, away from my former job.

Among her genius ideas put to thought, Proserpine suggested, "You can be our cubs' tutor when they come of age, Caius. You can teach Ambrosius the languages and literature you know, as well as Young Evmorfia how to be cunning in this world of men."

Safe to say, I happily told Proserpine it would be my honor to be their future teacher. It excited me to perhaps not only educate the youths, but to pass on my contained knowledge to a less bitter, more hopeful generation.

"Caius?"

"Hmn?"

Tiberius found me in the villa garden one day, thinking and marveling at Antioch's gorgeous coastline. For once, I agreed on the merchant lion's impulse purchase.

He wrapped those great arms around my torso, pulling me closer to huddle against him.

"What is on your mind?" He asked.

My tail swished against his bare stomach as his fingers stroked my elbows; a familiar movement reminiscent of our nights spent together.

"Nothing," I nuzzled into his neck, feeling the gentle sea breeze kiss us under warm rays of sunlight. "Nothing at all. But what of you?"

"It has been a wonderful couple of years for business," he chuckled, "Proserpine desires me to take a leave, if only for a time. She wishes to go beyond the Levant and Egypt, however, and wants to bring the cubs to see the land of our ancestors, in Athens."

"Greece?" I turned to him with wide saucers, as well as a crescent smile.

"She wishes to see the known world as well," he explained with an equally bright grin beneath his whiskers. "There is also Ephesus, Syracuse, the rest of Sicily, the newly founded Carthage, and perhaps

Rome itself. She has suggested that you join us too, since you're a member of our family."

"You mean...?" I stalled with my words.

"She believes that after all of your years spent reading about those places, the years spent locked away writing about them, that you deserve to witness these faraway lands for yourself," Tiberius swerved me around to look directly up into those auburn marbles, shining in the rays of light. "I concurred with it, but we feel it is still your decision."

His rope-like tail wrapped around my hip, pulling us closer. Joyous laughter bubbled forth until I kissed him as my answer. Holding still for long seconds, we reluctantly parted as I licked his cold nose, and Tiberius purred ever so louder.

"Travelling the world? Seeing these lands? This is the greatest gift of my life," I said with a sigh.

Tiberius shook his head with a soft chuckle. "It's too early to say that. After all, your life as a free man has just begun," he held my paw and gave it a gentle squeeze. "And I promise to help you make the most of it."

LATE

TO YOUR OWN DEFENCES

TELEVASSI

They sat in the roundhouse watching the flames, waiting like the ancestors had done centuries before.

"Do you think it's true, Artos?" Gwenhwyer sighed, poking the scrawny fox beside her.

"What?" He grunted, trying to keep his attention on the fire. "That the Romans have gone?"

Despite appearances, Artos wasn't really invested in divining a sign from the flames tonight. His efforts were to draw as much warmth as he could from the hearth. The mountains grew little and tonight he had only a bundle of twigs to feed the fire. Barely worthy of kindling, it seemed a luxury to waste the meagre heat on anything else.

It wasn't like the gods spoke to him anyway.

"Come on, Artos," Gwen thumped her tail behind her. "Even the rocks have an opinion on the recent signs. Do you expect me to believe that you, a fire-touched believer, would not?"

"I'd rather not waste my breath arguing with you."

The fox pulled his cloak over his fur. Most of the mountain tribes' fur was brown, stoney, or grey. But while Artos had not earned the right to daub his fur with woad, the orange hue to his fur was enough to whisper that he might be the first druid in centuries.

"Arguing isn't the worst we could do. Tonight's gathering has already wasted our time, firewood... We've had omens before. They've always never come to anything." Gwen grunted and shuffled closer.

"You never shy away from any opportunity to criticise, do you? Has it ever struck you that for some of us, prophecy is the only fire we have?"

"Do you really think some old tale, supposedly from the dying breath of the last druid on *Ynys Môn*, can keep you warm on a cold night?" She narrowed her eyes, tilting her head to the side. "Is reclaiming the lost lands even possible, nevermind the cost? We might be poor, but at least the only enemy we have up here is the cold. Besides! If the prophecy wasn't true, you wouldn't have to worry about your fur..."

They held their tongues for a moment, ears twitching at every sound from the struggling fire.

While Gwen was the same season as him, the grey-pelted vixen towered above everyone else in the tribe. The whispers about her were less complimentary - that she was wolf-blooded, half-Roman - but no one had the courage to make that charge directly. He didn't know whether to envy her - whether that freed her to choose her destiny in either world, or condemned her to exile in both.

"Hope takes the edge off freezing, even if you've run out of firewood."

"Perhaps I should stick you on the flames then?" Gwen teased.

"One day you'll run out of clever things to say. Maybe then you'll know where I'm coming from."

She scoffed, throwing her head up to the sky, half-laughing, half-howling.

"Shall I trust my faith the next time I come across a false trail then? Will the gods we're cut off from show me the way? I rather think that they'd have me use the nose they gave me, and sniff twice just to make sure," she muttered.

"We wouldn't have to fear the tricks of the mountains if our ancestors had kept their faith."

"Perhaps we wouldn't be stuck in these mountains *because* of their faith? Painting ourselves in woad wasn't armour enough to stop swords then, so why do we still do it?" She snorted, shaking her head. "Artos, please. Lie to the others if you must, but don't lie to yourself. You're far better than all that nonsense."

The fire wheezed. The cold crept further in, forcing them closer, even if this was just to stop their teeth from chattering."

"Myrddin has been talking out there for hours now. Hopefully she'll bring the assembly back inside soon." Artos pulled his cloak closer and tucked his muzzle underneath it.

"Perhaps there is something more to the omens for once?"

Artos shot her a sour look.

"What? I'd rather be kept awake for something," she yawned.

"I'd rather not spend tomorrow scouring the cliffs for firewood, hacking away at gorse." Artos fiddled with his empty paws as he stared at the spluttering fire. He'd used up all the firewood by now.

"At least gorse burns hot."

"Small consolation when you're gathering it."

"Remember to curse old Myrddin's name then, each time you have to pluck a spine from your fur." Gwen instinctively picked at her thick grey fur.

"I thought you didn't feel it?"

"I don't show it, like a lot of things. But I'd take pulling thorns over freezing my tail off here, though" Gwen growled, muttering a curse under her breath.

Artos looked up from the fire and over the faded murals on the roundhouse walls. In the dim light, the splendour of the old songs felt tantalisingly in reach, despite the decay. The figures there were tall, proud and with full, fiery pelts. Woad adorned their fur. Fine torcs of silver and gold hung around their necks. Every paw held a sword, their blades things of equal beauty and terror. He didn't know whether he felt pride, or just wanted it to crumble to dust. In reality those were ghosts, haunting a life that did not belong to them, an unwelcome reminder of something nobody remembered.

Finally the roadhouse door was pulled aside, and the elders filed back in. Their fur was like the leaves of a wet autumn, or dead heather clinging to the mountainside. Few among them possessed even a hint of the colours on the walls.

"They look even worse than earlier," Gwen whispered, nudging Artos with her elbow as they made way for their betters. More had joined since the night had begun, travelling in the dark from the nearby peaks to add their voices. Though some of them wore finer cloaks, their bodies underneath were just as scrawny, while others had fur that was entirely grey, as if the mountains had made them in their likeness. The only thing that seemed to unite them was the fact that none of them were warriors: in body, mind, or even belief.

Finally when all were seated, Myrddin entered. She was ancient, grey-furred through age, with a deep weariness to her eyes. Yet she has a sort of gravity to her every move that made her seem stronger than her frail form.

"We have spoken," Myrddin announced, silencing the room with a lifted paw.

"Signs have been called. Witnesses have spoken. Their words, considered. But we must discover the truth: these whispers of Vortigern, a king of all Pretani, and a land free of the Roman yoke."

Her eyes snapped towards Artos.

"Flame-keeper, what have you seen?"

"Nothing," the fox replied, struggling to swallow the lump in his throat.

A familiar, disappointed sigh rippled through the crowd.

Myrddin waved her paw, silencing them.

"Then our wait must continue, until one who can *see* is spoken too." She dismissed the gathering with another wave of her paw. Their elders drifted away into the night. Like the smoke, their bitterness was equally palpable.

"Don't worry about it," Gwen whispered in his ear. "None of them could do any better."

Though Artos appreciated her sentiment, it still wasn't a relief. Perhaps if he'd tried harder he might have seen something? Maybe if he had more wood to burn? Or - he bit his lip - what if Gwen hadn't been there to distract him?

Something twisted in his chest, hurting until he pushed away that thought. Instead, he quietly cursed his red fur, wondering, at least, what things *could* be like if they were different. It made him feel a little better, so he turned to follow Gwen out the door.

"And where do you two think you are going?" Myrddin snapped. "I'm not done with you yet."

"Sorry, Great Mother," they replied.

"Gwen. Tomorrow, go find more wood for the fire. Artos, remain here with me." She flicked her paw, dismissing Gwen.

Myrddin kept silent as the fire finally died. The shadows flooded in around them, obliterating all trace of the murals surrounding them, even when the darkness gave way to faint starlight.

"I want you to go down from the mountains and see for yourself if the rumours are true."

"But I saw no sign-"

The words tumbled out from his muzzle, unfamiliar enough that it took a moment to realise they were his.

"I'm sorry Mother. Forgive me for speaking out of turn." He quickly ran through a prayer of forgiveness.

"Your prayers do nothing to help dead gods," she snorted, her wrinkled muzzle quivering as she took amusement from the young fox. "Perhaps the loss of the druids severed our link to them forever. Perhaps not. But I have been watching for signs longer than anyone gathered here tonight - and in that time, I've only ever seen silence." She sighed, motioning for him to sit next to her.

"You're still young. You don't remember, but we trusted in omens once - what the flames told us. And what happened?"

"The Romans beat us."

"Well-observed," she smirked. "Our enemies wielded brute and cunning well, so we have learned to be smarter to survive. But for our vengeance, more is required. Our time in the mountains has not helped us rebuild our old strength. You saw the remnants of the tribe tonight - the last of the Ordovices. Survivors of the great conquest, the slaughter of *Ynys Môn*, the burning of the sacred groves..." She sighed and shook her head, her breath rattling out in one long wheeze, as if words failed to express their collective weakness. "We must be careful if we are to reclaim our birthright."

"What signs should I look for then?" Artos asked, seeing how the memory hurt her.

"Real ones," Myrddin snorted. "Go to the great legionary fortress of Deva. If they have truly abandoned these isles, then that fortress should be empty," the old vixen said with steel.

"Must I go alone?"

"It makes sense if you wish to remain hidden."

"Wouldn't two sets of eyes and ears be better than one?"

"Who would you take?"

"Gwen has the best nose among us."

"You only double the chances of getting caught," Myrddin sighed. "But fine, I will allow it."

He flicked his ears, detecting something more in the wordless tongue of fang and fur.

"In the first century of our sorrow, we gave away our gold. In the second century it was our silver. In the third, our steel. Now there is only one thing for us to give. Do not let the burden of this task consume you. I will not give away our people without good cause. Now go, while the night still has strength to lend you her dark cloak."

For the first time in the night, Myrddin sounded old. She narrowed her eyes and dismissed him from her sight with a nod and flick of her wrist.

She would have made a fine warrior-queen centuries ago.

"Why did you drag me into this?" Gwen sighed, whipping her tail behind her. "I should be sleeping in my warm den, not risking a broken leg on old trails."

"Why did you agree to come then? No one can tell a full-pelted tribe member what to do," Artos reminded her.

"Then why did you? Myrddin sure did pour cold water over any hopes the prophecy might be about to unfold."

"There's nothing wrong with checking if the trail ahead is false." He teased, trying to catch Gwen's eye. She shook her head and sighed, but he thought he glimpsed a ghost of a smile in return. "Speaking of..."

The fox bit his tongue as he studied a tricky section of the trail, a rocky outcrop that plunged down vertically. It'd take at least a couple of metres to climb, and the night only made it feel more threatening. Cautiously, Artos shook out his shoulders and scrambled down on all fours, slinking against the rock like one of his wilder kin. After a couple of moments where his paws slipped, Artos composed himself and he reached the bottom. Standing tall as he brushed the dirt off his paws, he called up to Gwen.

"Besides, if we didn't go, someone else would. Who knows what trouble they'd get us all into?"

"I just can't believe you listened to me for once." The vixen cooed. "Perhaps miracles do happen?"

She laughed to herself for a couple of moments, before beginning her own climb. Instead of crouching low, she climbed down the rock face skillfully, hooking her claws on thin cracks that from his lower angle were impossible to see. Her movements were deliberate and graceful in the moonlight, finding a different route made it all look effortless.

"You handled that well," Artos mumbled.

"Thanks." Her fur lifted subtly. "Perhaps you should let me lead then?" She patted him gently on the shoulder and nudged him to continue.

"I think that's the worst of it," he replied, pointing to the trail that snaked down the ridge. "But sure."

They slipped into silence as they descended. In some places, the path was rough and weathered, in others, polished smooth - presumably from the hasty retreat of many feet upon it. And at all times on either side, the mountain's flanks tumbled away into the dark, airy void that seemed to reach out and taunt them.

As exposed as it was, the mountains were more beautiful than during the day. The full moon came out from behind the clouds, shining down on them to light the way. On the sheer faces, invisible crystals in the rock sparkled. Veins of white quartz became bold and luminous in the moonlight, pools of water rippled with a silver sheen, and waterfalls tumbled through the void like liquid metal. Even the shadows' velvet darkness complimented the starlight.

Eventually the flanks of the mountains rose on either side, bringing a sense of security as the trail led away from the ridge.

"You know, you still didn't tell me *why* you really wanted to do this?" Gwen probed.

Artos sighed. Fortunately she wasn't asking the other question.

"Sometimes I think about getting out of these mountains," the fox admitted, ears drooping. "I wonder what things could be like, if things were different."

"What's your plan?"

"I don't know. I need to know what's out there first," Artos sniffed, trying to gather what intelligence he could from the air.

"Surely it's just Romans and faithless Pretani," she teased.

He growled, wanting her to take the moment seriously.

"My entire life has been spent hidden up between these peaks. Don't think I've never dreamed what wonders lie over the horizon - it's easy enough to see from here."

"Well, you'll have to brush up on your Latin then," Gwen sighed. "My master used to tell his guests how big their world was."

"I thought you came from a neighbouring peak?"

"Yeah, Myrddin did say that," Gwen grunted. "I ran from the estate as soon as I was strong enough. Only time I've moved on all fours."

"I'm sorry to hear that."

"Don't be." Gwen shrugged. "It's fortunate for you. Did you really think you'd be able to get to Deva Vitrix without any Latin, or even Cornovii?"

"Nice of you to say you don't want to see me get killed." Artos chuffed. He narrowed his eyes, trying to pick out the tell of Gwen's.

"You're welcome," Gwen shrugged, pushing ahead.

The trail now levelled off slightly into a grassy plateau. Tangled shrubs and stunted trees rustled in the breeze, too high up to grow into anything bigger.

"I reckon we're about halfway down," Gwen called back, scratching her head. "We should make the foothills by dawn if we-"

A bolt of lighting interrupted the vixen. Fearing its touch, they threw themselves to the ground, gasping as the fall knocked out their breath. Panting, they watched as it forked through the sky, arcing slowly through the cloudless sky, illuminating the horizon. It hung there for seconds, making no sound, before suddenly burrowing into the ground.

They counted the seconds, waiting for the ripple of thunder so they could figure out how far away the storm was. Being caught out high up in the mountains was the worst place to experience a thunderstorm. But as the seconds crept by, nothing came.

"Was that... an omen?" Gwen breathed. Her eyes were wide. "I've never seen lightning behave like that before."

"It's no sign of our gods," Artos whispered. "Did you see where it landed?"

"No," Gwen breathed, her hackles bristling. "But I think it was close to Deva, maybe right by the sea."

"Could it be a Roman god?"

"I was but to work, not learn their ways," Gwen snapped. She paused for breath, then relented. "I'm not sure. I never really paid attention to anyone's gods."

"Perhaps it's one of the Brigantes? They're further north, perhaps the rumours of this Vortigern have spurred them to come down from their lands?"

"I wouldn't count on it," she warned. In the moonlight, the narrowed whites of her eyes caught the moonlight, pulled back like twin arrowheads. It was unsettling to see her this way, looking so fierce and wolf-like.

"Well," Artos conceded, "I suppose we'll find out anyway," he said, brushing the dirt from his chest fur. "You coming?"

Gwen nodded. She still seemed troubled, but she kept her doubts to herself as they set off, keeping a brisker pace than early morning warranted.

There was no more lightning. The stars overhead wheeled on their way to their sleep, fading as the light of dawn began to approach. With the loss of the moon and stars, the night briefly deepened, but it did little to hinder their progress as they reached the long, rolling foothills.

Artos felt his hackles rise as the peaks loomed protectively behind him, each step forward bringing a growing uncertainty. His paws itched, longing to break into a run and dash back home. All he had ever known were the mountains - rock underneath his feet and the awning sky all around.

The world ahead was wide, open, rolling, and like a bad memory. As the sky lightened and the sun reared her head, her sight served only to show how much had changed. The oak groves were gone. So too were the ancient yews; the eternal forest replaced by large square fields ringed with wooden fences or stone walls. In enclosures further beyond, cattle and sheep ambled about, growing fat without worry or care. The morning light made it seem beautiful, but Artos did not know how to feel about it.

"We can't keep moving - there's no cover once we enter those fields," Artos hissed.

"We'll camp in that gully away from the first field. That should keep us out of sight for a couple of hours," she sighed, pointing to a dark cleft in the rolling hills ahead. "We'll move again after that," Gwen finished. She seemed unphased by the alien world ahead, her tall grey ears flicking back and forth, understanding the words in each and every sound around them. She stood tall, her tail held high, scanning the horizon as she figured out their next move.

"Sounds like a plan," Artos nodded, following the vixen.

Whatever her reasons for joining, the fox's fur rose at the fact she was here with him. Her familiar scent did much to dispel the fears that came from enemy territory.

Sleep came fitfully.

Though the gurgle of the brook was soothing, the soil underneath him felt wrong. It was indifferent to his presence, as if the nameless ancestors buried within slept deeply.

Such rest was denied to the foxes by a family of particularly cheeky sparrows seeking to line their nests with vulpine fur. Each time they were about to fall asleep, the sharp pinch of their beaks plucked them from sleep, waking to see a blur of brown feathers as they fluttered away, their beaks triumphantly filled with a thick tuft of fur.

Sooner than Artos liked, Gwen was kicking him awake.

"Must we get up now?" Artos grumbled, rubbing his heavy eyes.

"There'll be plenty of time to rest when we're done." She ignored his groans as she climbed up the side of the gully and poked her nose over the ridge. She spent minutes casting about for scents, and finding nothing new, risked poking her head further above ground. There was no one to be seen.

"Let's get going, while it's quiet," Gwen huffed, beginning to lose her patience.

"What's the hurry?" Artos asked, still picking sleep from his eyes.

"We're still in border country. If we can cross these fields and get onto the main road without anyone spotting us, it shouldn't be hard to get to Deva."

"Are you mad?" Artos snapped wide awake.

"You expect travellers dressed like us on the road from Segontium to Deva," Gwen explained. "If anyone gets suspicious, we just tell them we're prospectors for a new lead mine, and we're looking for partners to invest," she shrugged, as if it were common enough. "You're my mountain guide, in case anyone asks why you can't speak a 'civilised' tongue," she smirked.

"And what, on that alone they'll just let us pass?"

"If we act convincingly," she nodded. "You've got to remember, the Romans have been here for at least four-hundred years, and apart from Boudica, most of that time has been at peace," she shrugged. "As much as we'd like to think highly of our efforts, their attention has largely been towards the north anyway."

"I think you're mad."

"Trust me. It'll work. The further we get from the borders, the less they will be on the lookout for potential cattle thieves or raiders. Besides, it's a likely story. The Romans love a good tale about 'civilising' the wastes."

"Explains what they've done with the place," Artos huffed, shaking the remaining dirt off his cloak.

They left the gully and brushed through fields full of wheat and barley, stumbling across a dusty trail that wound a level path between the hills. The orderly, rolling fields stretched on and on, making it hard to imagine that this land had ever belonged to someone else. The old forests had been cut back and tamed, the tangled groves levelled and buried under the plough - even without the druids to divine their will, surely the gods saw such an affront to their works. Why did they do nothing?

Artos chewed his tongue, the question souring his mood as afternoon faded into evening. By now they were deep enough in Roman territory to feel more at ease, but it still seemed odd that they'd bumped into no one all day. For all he'd grown up hearing stories about them, the fox was oddly curious to see what a Roman wolf looked like up close.

"Those are some fancy dwellings," Artos noted, pointing at the whitewashed walls of the villa on the crest of the next hill. It was bigger than any building he'd ever seen before, putting shame on even the tribe's largest roundhouse.

"That's nothing, just wait until you see the bigger estates." Gwen shrugged, tossing her paw through her mane. "Imagine the wealth and power of someone whose lands stretch from one horizon to the other."

"How do they manage that?"

"With a lot of 'help'," the vixen muttered. "The Romans are always looking for greater conquests." She slowed her pace, crooking her head to the side as she strained her senses.

"Everything alright?"

"Let's not linger," she replied cryptically. Artos noticed how her hackles had risen, but he kept walking.

At first it was faint enough that he thought it was a nervous trick of his senses, but as the sun began to skirt the horizon, the smell of smoke was unmistakable. Artos looked over to Gwen anxiously, but the grey pelted fox said nothing. A brisk pace crept into her strides, and he struggled to keep up with her loping gait.

The stench of smoke grew until it overpowered everything else. It was not the pleasant tang of woodsmoke on a crackling fire. It burned each breath; the dry, acrid air stinging and clawing at their throats, born of a fire that came only from hatred and violence.

The source came into view as they turned the next bend in the farm trail. The villa's once proud, immaculate walls were blackened with soot, ruined as the fire had brought the red roof tiles crashing inside. Even though there were no flames, thick black smoke twisted up into the sky from several places, adding to the desolation.

A lump formed in the fox's throat. It proved hard to swallow.

He remembered how he yearned to see such destruction repaid upon the Romans. Now he witnessed a fraction of such violence, he could only think how this was someone's home.

He took a stop off the path, trying to find a trail up the hillside towards the ruined villa.

"Get down from there!" Gwen hissed.

"Why? This must be from the lightning bolt we saw last night."

"And you think that's a good reason to get closer?" She growled, pulling him back by the tail. "We don't know who's responsible for this - they're likely just to blame us!"

"How could that be? I thought you said lightning was a Roman sign!"

"*Thought*." Gwen growled. "I didn't say I was certain. Do you think a Roman god would do this to their own?"

"So it's someone else's god then?"

"Not a Pretani one, that's certain."

"You know what they say..."

"Since when has anyone ever been our friend?" she snapped.

"Fine," Artos mumbled, chewing his lip. "Let's at least stay off the main road from now on, especially if we think something else is afoot."

"Agreed," Gwen nodded. "We're lucky there'll be a thick fog tonight."

"How can you tell?"

"Don't you feel the damp rising underneath your paws?" She called after him, cutting across an empty meadow and heading for the remaining treeline. Unwilling to be caught in the open, the fox dashed after her, an orange spark zipping towards the shadows.

Sure enough, as eventide washed over, a thick grey mist began to rise from the earth, covering first his paws, then his legs in its cool embrace. Perhaps the land didn't sleep so heavily after all.

The night was smothered by the mist. It devoured the moonlight, creating a darkness deep enough to blind sharp vulpine eyes. The fog obliterated scents too; clustering them together in the damp air, turning them into an indecipherable mass that barely shifted on the breeze.

The weather hindered the foxes as much as it helped them. More than once, the loud snap of a branch pierced the silence, forcing them to freeze while they waited for what felt like hours on end. Even when there was no cause to remain still, their hackles still remained raised, as if something drew close, invisible to their senses.

Dawn came as a welcome relief. The first rays ignited the fog, transforming the air into a golden haze before quickly burning off. As it faded it revealed Deva Vitrix, spread out before them.

The fortress-city was nestled in a bend in the river. The rectangular settlement resisted nature's contours. The proud walls jutted out from the green river plain, forming an imposing bastion of red sandstone. High up on the overlooking cliff, Artos quickly lost track of the number of the plumes of smoke rising up from the buildings. There had to be many hundreds of hearths, and they certainly did not lack firewood.

"It just keeps going," Artos breathed, tail twitching. He grabbed it with a paw to keep it still. "Look at all the smoke." He pointed at the rooftops. "I've never seen so many people in one place."

"This is small by their standards, apparently," Gwen grumbled, taking a moment to rest her weary paws.

"Thanks," Artos mumbled, trying to feed his faltering conviction.

"We'll need to get a closer look. Appearances don't mean anything," Gwen replied.

"Stop trying to cheer me up."

"Am I?" She grunted. "None of this explains the empty fields, burning villa, or the lightning."

"I guess so," Artos grumbled.

"Let's not waste the early hour then. Do you see any patrols down there?"

Artos sighed and squinted, trying to make sense of the long shadows cast by the morning sun. Here and there he thought he spotted black scorch marks on the weathered masonry, and spots of green shoots sticking out between the stones. The outlying buildings were in a similar state, leaving it a fair guess whether their disrepair was due to the length of time they'd been there, or the long time since their builders had left.

"Well?" Gwen prompted.

"Apart from the bridge I don't see any."

"That settles it then! You up for an early morning swim then?"

"Can't we just pay the toll?" He yelped, already feeling the cold water. "Surely that's what your trader story is for?"

"That's our fallback if we were to get caught." Gwen shook her head. "Besides, we don't have the coin."

"Great traders we are then…"

"No one will be any wiser once we get into the forum. Besides, we'd be seeking investors, not spending. But enough. We're wasting time!"

"We don't know if it's safe to cross. What if there are currents? Why would they build a bridge if it was safe to just swim across?"

"Because Romans don't like getting their fur wet." Gwen grinned, nudging him with an elbow. Without even waiting the grey vixen dashed down the rocky slope, weaving a nimble path towards the water. Artos scowled and followed her lead.

Soon enough the river lapped away at their feet. The fox wrinkled his muzzle but Gwen pushed past him, and through the reeds before sinking down into deeper water. Artos took a deep breath and bit his lip before taking the plunge.

The water was cold, but not enough to make him gasp. He followed Gwen as she began to swim, feeling the current wash through his fur. Fortunately, the river remained gentle. Clouds of mist hovered above the surface, concealing their movement, but the steady flow made it easy to stay on course. It lessened as the bank loomed in the fog, his feet touching the riverbed as they waded between the reeds. They headed further downstream, searching for where the vegetation was thickest and lingered for a moment, listening to the wary calls of the wading birds, before pushing through to firmer ground.

Suddenly, the reeds disappeared. The foxes stumbled into a large clearing cut into the wetlands. Tall shrubs still hid them from view on all sides, but not from the tall wolf sat in the centre, tending to a small fire he used to smoke his first catch.

"Woah! Easy! Easy!" The wolf whined, holding his big paws up. "Don't start chewing me out - you think I'm up early poaching from the river because I like to save money?" He sighed, pointing at the wicker basket further back, hidden among the reeds. It wiggled from side to side occasionally as the wolf's catch struggled for breath.

"I thought legionaries were paid well enough to go to market," Gwen growled, remaining defensive. Even though there were two of them, the wolf was big enough to easily overpower them both.

The wolf laughed, pressing a paw against his chest. "Do I look like army material to you? They'd clip me at the very least for keeping my mane so long."

The wolf swung his muzzle towards Artos, taking one deep sniff.

"Ah, you're not from around here." He shrugged, muscle rippling under his fur as he waved them over, inviting them to sit in dust next to his small fire. "Please, you look cold."

Artos shot Gwen a look. She dipped her head slightly, enough that the wolf might not notice.

"Thanks for the fire," Gwen grumbled, holding out her paws as her fur still dripped with water. Artos did the same, trying his best not to stare into the leaping flames and lose himself in their dance.

"You're welcome. It's not much, but I do what I can with my kindling."

"Have you tried burning gorse?" Artos muttered.

The wolf's large ears snapped to attention.

"It wouldn't occur to me to do that," the wolf frowned. "Where did you say you're from?"

"Segontium," Gwen snapped, her fur bristling. "We're travelling from that city."

"Right," the wolf nodded, eyeing them both up. He didn't seem convinced by the way his fur ruffled. "If that were true, I suppose you'd know that the place was abandoned when the legion left there years ago."

Artos frowned.

"You know, I get lying about where you're from, but there's not much point lying about it when the truth's plastered all over your muzzle," the wolf sighed. "I don't know whatever rock you've been under, but just about everyone knows the Romans have left."

"What do you mean, *left*?" Artos asked, flicking his ears in disbelief. "When? Who beat them in battle?"

Gwen rolled her eyes, her teeth grinding audibly. "Why didn't you go with them?" She snapped, scowling at Artos for slipping up so soon.

"Do you think I look young enough to follow them to Gallia?" The wolf laughed again. "I heard the Emperor found this miserable, rainy island more bother than it was worth. Apparently he told the Britons to look to their own defences. Can you believe it?" He shook his head and poked at the fire angrily. "Well, some of us didn't feel like moving home all over again."

"So you're some sort of honourable deserter, nevermind a poacher?" Gwen pressed, still holding his sword close. "I suppose it's fortunate that no one will miss you."

"Actually, I declined being called back as an *Evocatus*, despite the honour. Enough blood has been spilled in these lands. I wished to have no more of a part in that."

"Do you really expect me to believe that a soldier like you would suddenly have a change of heart? You Romans *hate* this miserable, rainy, gods-forsaken rock at the edge of the civilised world!"

"You sure know how to swear like one of us," he replied, concealing a low growl.

"You'd best turn your fish," Artos piped up, pointing at the fire. "They're starting to burn."

"Thanks." The wolf grumbled, keeping a wary eye on Gwen.

"What my friend is trying to say," Artos began warily, trying to keep the peace, "is that she's surprised a Roman would choose to stay here. You can surely forgive us for finding it a bit hard to swallow."

"It's fine." The wolf grunted. "There are greater storms out there than just the rain. Against those, being at the edge of the world doesn't sound so bad," he said cryptically, gathering up the last of his catch. "Besides, Rome may have left, but they couldn't take the walls with them."

The wolf smiled proudly, pointing up at the imposing red bastion. Despite the lush grass poking out from cracks in the mortar it seemed resolute, though marked with black scars reminiscent of those at the villa.

"They certainly seem like some refuge," Artos replied, brushing down his fur as it fluffed up from the heat of the fire. Even Gwen, with her thicker grey fur, seemed dry. It was time to make a decision.

"Well, thanks for sharing your fire," Gwen said, trying to disguise the loud gurgle from her stomach. "You can do us one last favour and point us towards the forum? I'd quite fancy digging into a fresh loaf of bread."

"Oh, the forum is long gone. We have a small market in the ruined amphitheatre outside the walls, just over there."

The wolf smiled and pointed between the swaying rushes. When the wind bent them, a dilapidated circular building appeared in view, open to the elements and spared from none of their fury.

"Hengist did that to save the hassle of letting strangers inside the city. Fortunate for you." The wolf laughed, his yellow eyes locking with Gwen's, goading her.

Make a decision.

Gwen grunted and said nothing. She bit her lip and dragged her paws in the mud, her claws digging deep furrows. The leather grip of the sword squeaked as she squeezed it tightly.

"Fine." She cursed and swung the sword. The metal whirred in the wind, before disappearing into the reeds behind them with a wet splash.

"Thanks," the wolf grunted. He did a good job hiding his relief.

"Just in case you think about stabbing us in the back," she snapped back. The wolf sighed and went back to tending to his catch.

Without so much as a goodbye, Gwen stood and started briskly towards the arena, refusing to speak to Artos as they struggled to push through the thick, tall reeds.

"Why didn't you kill him?" Artos hissed. "How do you know he won't betray us?"

"Because he's right about one thing - too much blood has been spilled."

The grey-furred vixen sighed heavily, an invisible weight lifting from her shoulders.

"I came along with you because that night, I dared to hope the future meant something *more*. If your prophecy is true - that the Romans have indeed left - do you really wish to greet it with more blood?"

Artos looked down at his feet. Even here, among the watery banks of the reeds, the earth was dark and red.

"I'm sorry," the fox whispered.

"Don't let your story slip again. Let's get this over with, and get out of here." Gwen turned around and stalked along the narrow trail, disappearing among the swaying reeds.

The fox paused for a moment, poking again at the waterlogged earth with his feet. He didn't know if the bubbles of air popping up from underneath were a sigh of relief, or merely just the natural decay of things buried. But as he listened to the cautious piping of birds hidden in the marshes, he too dared to hope for something more.

Quickening his step, he set off after Gwen, following her large footprints. However her tracks quickly disappeared, swallowed up by the mud. He kept going - she couldn't have gone far.

There was a loud crack that thudded against his head.

The last thing Artos saw was the grey, uncaring sky above. It was filled with dark, roiling clouds of a storm blowing in, and the wolf standing above him, wearing a leering, ugly grin.

When Artos came to, the dying rays of the sun cast a copper sheen across the world. The storm had passed. The air smelled fresh, full of the scent of petrichor. But the brilliant sunset heralded deepening shadows.

It took a moment for Artos to recall his surroundings. The journey to Deva came together in a disordered blur: mountains, lightning, wolves.

Gwen.

He'd made it to the ruined amphitheatre somehow, and was now lying in the remains of some once-fancy box above the rows of ordinary seats. It had suffered from the weather, but, like the faded mural in the roundhouse, it hinted at a brighter past. A broken, dusty mosaic still showed two canine gladiators locked in battle, snarling teeth hidden behind bronze helms. Their names were forgotten, obliterated under the scraps of rotten wood and mouldy cloth littering the floor.

The approaching clatter of hooves against the floor told the fox he was not alone. A tall red deer came to stand ahead of him, leaning against the balcony wall like an emperor surveying his realm. The stag flicked an ear, deciding to acknowledge his charge behind him, before turning around to face his catch. His confidence was evident as he'd chosen to leave the fox's limbs unbound.

The stag had a terrible beauty to him. There was a violence behind his sharp eyes that set Artos's fur on edge. He was dressed for war in a foreign way, not in the Roman style or the wildest of Pretani. A smart red tunic sat underneath a shirt of fine mail, finished with a thick golden thread twisted about the leather hem of his coat of mail like interlocking snakes. His short cropped fur was painted with a strong-smelling mixture of ash, charcoal and lime. The markings swirled about in dizzying, interlocking shapes of beasts and animals he did not recognise. And from his hip, he held the hilt of a long, thick blade - gripping it like the shaft was part of him.

"I don't usually entertain spies. But sometimes I enjoy these simple pleasures." The stag smiled. He spoke with an odd accent. Formal yet informal, his tongue treating words like things he could push around.

"We're here to trade lead... to start a new mine."

It was hard for the fox to speak. Though the rest of his body felt fine, his head throbbed and he felt close to being sick.

"I'm not into that old Roman rubbish," the stag smirked, shaking his head.

"What about the rest of Deva? Do you speak for all of them?"

"Of course. They're mine." The stag laughed, pulling at a golden ring on a hoofed finger.

"Shame. It's quite a marvel. Water running fresh into your home."

"The river is good enough for me. If I need more, I can make someone else fetch it for me." He shrugged. "Perhaps if the Romans were as powerful as they claimed, they wouldn't have needed such silly inventions."

The fox tried to keep his eyes on the stag, but his head was getting worse. The edges of his vision started to swirl.

Sensing the fox's wandering attention, the stag crouched down and held the tip of Artos' muzzle, holding him steady.

"I know you're lying. I've dealt with enough Pretani to know you better than you know yourselves." He tutted, brushing away some of the grime sullying his orange fur.

"Sorry," Artos groaned. "I only came here to seek investors. I'm not interested in whatever it is you're trading," he quipped, trying to get a good one in. But joking didn't lift his spirits like it usually did. The headache didn't help.

"Oh, but you are, little fox. I just won't be peddling lies."

"I'm not a spy!" He coughed, trying to channel his injury to embellish the lie again.

"Come now, fox," the stag said. "I don't need a turncoat wolf to tell me you're no trader."

The stag sighed. He squeezed Artos's jaw harder, pulling him closer.

"You're just the last embers of an old, dying fire. Spluttering away, waiting for someone to kick dust over you and move on." The stag paused, staring into Artos' eyes like how he'd stare into the flames back home. Searching for a sign.

"Fortunately for you, my gods see no glory in killing spies, or raising settlements to make some needless statement. I'll warn you once. Test me, and your mongrel vixen will regret it."

"Where is she?"

He smiled.

"I don't need to hold her here to hurt her. Not when I have you. So... do you want to trade then?"

"What is it?"

"A message," he replied. "Hengist has had enough of you Pretani stirring up trouble wherever a little piece of Vortigern is not. There's not enough bits of his corpse to go around for that, so you'll have to do."

"What happened to the Cornovii?"

"They had some dangerous ideas." Hengist smirked. "My god Thunor made his displeasure known." He imitated a lightning bolt from the heavens. "Whatever tribe you're from would be wise not to make the same mistake as them. The Romans took all the fire from your people centuries ago. I'm just sad they left me these isles without even the honour of a decent battle."

"That's a message... but what are you offering?"

The deer grinned and bit his lip hard enough to draw blood. He sucked it, hard, as if he couldn't get enough of the taste.

"Your lives. In exchange, your people will be grateful and give me the proper payment."

He tossed the fox his gold ring. Artos caught it in a start, glancing between it and the stag quickly.

"Do you really think the Romans left us with anything? They stripped any wealth from us long ago!"

"You survived many years of their occupation though. I'm sure you're resourceful enough to survive me. Perhaps you'll start that new mine after all?" He laughed, and unleashed a swift kick square into Artos' chest, knocking the wind out of him and pushing him back down onto the floor.

He barked something in some harsh tongue, summoning two of his kin. Their antlers were equally as impressive as his, but they obeyed him without hesitation. They pulled Artos out of the arena, through the empty fields, the falling night, and finally across the empty bridge.

"Don't worry foxes!" Hengist bellowed out into the night. "I'll waive the toll for you this time! Just remember to deliver this message!"

He laughed, sucked his lip, and grunted for something from one of his companions. Even in the gloom, it was possible to make out the stag stringing a bow, the white blur of an arrow's fletching kissing his cheek.

"Best get moving. In my experience, word travels faster when you send one messenger."

Artos' heart leapt first. His body followed him, sprinting towards the dark treeline without a second's thought. The sinews in his body burned in a new way, unused to the gait of all fours, but the surge of adrenaline quickly obliterated all other sensation or thought.

His ears snapped taut as somewhere close by, an arrow whistled into the night. It was quiet and distant, but still surprising the thud it made.

He kept running, and soon the dark boughs welcomed him under their embrace. His lungs burned. How was he already out of breath?

The fox risked a look behind him, safe in the cover of the trees. Relief swelled through him as he saw the deer crossing back over the bridge, laughing and joking as they went.

He still yelped in shock when he felt Gwen's paw touch his check - quickly followed by her lips.

"I almost feared the worst," she whispered, running her paws across his body, seeking reassurance that he was indeed all there.

She froze, plucking something below his ribs.

"Stay still!" she hissed, pushing him to the ground.

Artos didn't remember feeling any pain. He was still trembling from the surge of adrenaline. But sure enough it bloomed within him, leeching out in all directions from the shaft protruding through his chest.

He felt cold. His mouth tasted of blood.

"To think I would curse Myrddin's name when plucking a big thorn!" He laughed, but again the joke brought no comfort. He couldn't stop staring at the arrow with a shaking hand. It felt strangely part of him.

"Hold still," she hissed. "I need to break the fletching off before I can pull it out and patch you up-"

"I don't think that'll help," Artos coughed. He could only taste blood now, and feel it trickle from the corners of his muzzle.

"Don't say that! You're stronger than you think." She growled. Then she howled.

"Gwen." Artos shook his head. "Say something clever."

"I can't-"

"Please. I need to hear it."

He whispered, reached out, and squeezed her hand. That was all the strength he had left.

For a second time, Gwen ran to the mountains. This time, she didn't bring a message. A new fire had kindled inside her heart: a spark that she swore would consume Saxon-kind.

GO TO THE ROAD, AND ASK ANY PASSING TRAVELER

ROB MACWOLF

In the fourteenth year after the ascension of Emperor Sumerdismes III to the Ziggurat of the Sacred Fire, and in the same year death released his predecessor Ignominious Balirhan from exile in the Palace of Silence, the Patriarchs of the Atheotokosic Orthodox Church called a universal council in the royal city of Shah Murkhandeh. This was to be, of course, attended only by Atheotokosic patriarchs and prophets, abbots and abbesses. More than a century of formally denouncing each other as heretics and anathema and schismatists had culminated in every sect in this curious faith thoroughly excommunicating every other. Now ecumenical relations were reduced to a mutual-if-unspoken policy of pretending all the other kinds of Messianics did not exist.

While the reasons for calling this conference were doubtless sagacious and theological, they were entirely lost on Narseh the Caravanier and his father Husravah the Merchant. But a gathering of such holy men must require incense, explained the horse, which meant the price of incense in the city of Royal Murkhandeh would be rising faster than a drunken mercenary, and a clever merchant and his dutiful son could make a fortune and a half.

Which was why, in the courtyard of his stepmother's caravanserai, among high glacial valleys and steep pastures, the mule was even now loading the panniers of a line of very disinterested camels with the cheapest incense his father's money and influence combined could secure. Surely mostly sandalwood, Narseh thought, he could smell it clearly. He did not know much about holy men, and even less about Atheotokosic Messianics, but they must be truly desperate for incense if his father thought they would accept any of this.

The sun was not yet risen, though the sun rose late here. The mountains to the east were said to be the highest in the world, though by whom Narseh could not tell you. It was said a proud god once had been determined that the mountain upon which it dwelt must be higher than any other god's mountain, and so it built peak after peak, ever higher, each jealous of the next, until at last it built one so high it could not climb down, and there it remained to this day, howling in frustration at the rising sun.

"Maybe we should check the provisions." Husravah had a smooth, cautious voice, meant for making bad bargains sound less insulting. To a trader or a customer, who did not know the horse, it would sound like a man so used to the game of buying and selling, of bartering and haggling, that he could play it in his sleep. To his son—illegitimate, to be sure, but acknowledged and with the lead-sealed tablet to prove it—it sounded like a man deeply unsure of his course but with no idea save to forge ahead.

"They have been checked," Narseh replied. "We checked them last night, father."

"Well," Husravah stared down the disdainful line of camels as if hoping one of them might interject, "it may be we should check them again."

It would do no good to argue. Many a caravanier would have sharp words for a merchant who had decided to be a busybody as well, but Narseh knew his father well enough. The old workhorse needed to be doing something, to feel practical, or he'd choke on his own nerves.

He had reason enough to be nervous, Narseh would have said to the camels if they had cared, which they didn't. He opened the saddlebags and ran his fingers over the bundles of hard smoked cheese, pouches of dates, twists of dried millet dough waiting for a boiling kettle to wake them up. And he thought all the while: this wasn't the season for this kind of trip. Cold enough for snow, but not cold enough that the snow could be relied on to stay where it belonged instead of blocking the passes. They also said earthquakes were more common as the ground froze. Not to mention how an out of season trip meant being the only caravan on the roads. Imagining bandits was a grievance at the best of times, how much worse was it to know you were the only prize dangling before the noses of every outlaw between here and Satrapidesh?

But maybe the bandits would also have concluded there would be nobody on the roads this time of year. Maybe they would, like sensible people, stay warm at home.

But maybe the money to be made on incense was worth the risk.

But maybe Husravah knew better than a mere caravan driver—his father, after all, was the merchant, while Narseh was none.

Maybe.

Maybe he should check the provisions again.

The sun was nearer, though not yet across, the eastern peaks when they set out.

The rest of the party had at last assembled, yawning with excitement and taciturn with yet-to-be-eroded unfamiliarity. A handful of guards, hired by Husravah, but Narseh knew how to see his father got his money's worth out of this usual handful of yaks and goats and marmots as porters too.

A brown fox, square faced, serious mouth, eyes low and never more than half open like a statue of one of the holy awakened ones in a temple. His clothes were very simple, but very fine, and he had brought no cargo with him. Only a staff and a small satchel. Pilgrim, Narseh guessed, he'd seen the type often enough before. Not likely to be a Messianic, which was a pity—having someone to speak for you to potential buyers never hurt. This pilgrim was making polite conversation with Husravah as they set out, which was only proper. You spoke to the merchant from whom you'd bought escort, not to the caravanier who worked for him, and thus for you.

A sable and a bear, heavily and enviably bundled up in the layers of one-armed woolen longcoats and the immense furry hats of the plateau dwellers. Between them they carried a litter—long poles, bamboo-wood latticework, thick warm curtains. It was some time before Narseh got a glimpse at the passenger—whom the two of them called 'Miss Cepla'—when she leaned out a hinged window in the litter door to wish all sorts of courteous blessings on his father for making her journey possible: A plump old pheasant with a grandmotherly face under feathers long since greyed from gold to brown, huddling in blankets.

Finally, a brindle dog, darker fur on his face. Like he'd stared long into the sun and been burned for it. Plain clothes, long worn and faded, of no place in particular. Boots well broken in. An experienced traveler: Narseh had seen the type before. Though he had even less with him than did the pilgrim. He also did not speak to Narseh, but then he didn't speak to Husravah either. The mule determined to keep an eye on this one. Thieves weren't unheard of. Nor were scouts for bandit tribes, infiltrating, awaiting an opportunity for betrayal. Narseh had seen that type before too.

There were no other merchants.

Not surprising, but not reassuring. A comfortable caravan was four or five troops of camels, each with lookouts and guards, maybe even as many as four score total in the late summer. Not just more eyes, but more hands to deal with blockages and washouts. More camels to share the load of the one that fell sick. More spare provisions in case of spoilage. Better chances of finding a handsome fellow to keep warm nights with in a shared bedroll.

Maybe it would be for the best, thought Narseh as he coaxed the bell-bedecked lead camel down the winding valley where the road followed a gnawing rivulet of snowmelt. No other merchants meant no competition when they reached Shah Murkhandeh.

But that would be his father's concern, as would everything else there was to be glad about. His concern was whether they would reach Murkhandeh at all, and everything else there was to be worried about.

On the first day they made good time and reached the caravanserai well before sunset. Nasreh knew all the innkeepers along their usual route, of course, but the crow here was an old friend of Husravah's. He let the horse and his son, and their hired porters, stay for free. Only those they guided, or other merchants if there had been any, were charged for food and lodging.

He charged for their camels of course, he was not a fool.

While his father and the innkeeper reminisced about the days they'd traveled together over a bowl of heated wine, Narseh took his meal—flatbread folded around a stew of chicken and mutton, leeks and some vegetables stuffed on top—by the fire at the center of the courtyard.

"If one might be permitted to ask?" the square-faced fox took a seat beside Narseh, and waited. His own flatbread was filled solely with vegetables.

"Ask, then." Narseh finally said once he realized the question hadn't been rhetorical.

"Many thanks," the fox bowed gently. "There is yet daylight remaining, even now. Why is it we stopped so early in the day? Could we not have covered more distance, if we had pressed on?"

"You, honored sir," Narseh chewed thoughtfully before finishing the thought, "have not traveled these roads before."

"Indeed no! You are most perceptive, honored sir!" When the fox smiled he somehow left the stony tranquility of his cheeks undisturbed. "And please, if one might be permitted to presume to friendship, I am called Ambhi."

"I am Narseh," no reason not to be friendly with a paying fellow traveler. "We stopped here because here is where there is a stop. Walls, a fire, hot food, a roof over our heads. The next place like this is two days further on, I'd guess, which will mean tomorrow night in the open." The mule shook his head. "Neither restful nor comfortable, honored sir!"

"Ah, you have the wisdom of experience! I thank you for sharing it." Ambhi turned to the old pheasant, approaching on the arm of her bear litter bearer. The dog and the sable bearer followed behind. "If one might presume to ask, please honored madam, honored sirs, be welcome with us! I am called Ambhi, and our wise guide is Narseh!"

"Oh, thank you my dear!" the old bird settled by the fire. "I am Cepla, and it is good to meet you both. Oh yes, and this," she patted the bear's paw, "is Rabga, my other helper is Tsu."

All eyes turned expectantly toward the brindle dog, who stared back just long enough for it to be uncomfortable before he said "Taljhou," and turned away.

"Well!" Cepla decided that was all the remark he deserved, and turned back to Ambhi. "I'm off seeking my son! My husband, my third and the last one to pass—may he be at peace—why, he and our son never had a civil moment between them! The gods know how I tried to put them in agreement, but to no avail! So some five years ago my poor Yonten stormed out of the house! Last I heard he was a saddlemaker in a city called Sha-Mar-Candai? Something like that I'm sure. Now his father's gone, poor soul, so I'm off to bring him home at last! Somebody has to see to the pastures, you know!"

Tsu and Rabga shared the look of men who'd be perfectly content to never hear this story again.

"I myself," Ambhi had finished his flatbread without a single crumb out of place, "must travel further. My family is fortunate enough to enjoy noble birth and some modest wealth, so since my grandmother's days we have been honored to support a monastery. The monks and nuns there contemplate the noble truths and live the noble eight ways of awakening. How fortunate, to make such a life possible!"

The fire popped after a moment of silence, as if to ask what this had to do with the fox's journey, if nobody else intended to.

"According to tradition," Ambhi continued, "my people came with a great conqueror, from a land far to the west. He is said to have been a philosopher king, with a court of wise teachers. But those teachings are lost to us. Rumor says they wrote on Pure Being Untouched by Time or Matter, on the Nature of Virtue, and even taught that the world of the flesh is all illusion, there is a true world of pure spirit, fully real, of which things here are mere shadows!"

"Oh, and you hope," Cepla clasped her wings, "to recover some of these texts to the monastics?"

"Indeed. Initiation to the monastic life is a matter of proving one's serious-mindedness, one's dedication. And I thought, one might hardly presume to do better than journeying to the ends of the earth to bring back lost wisdom?"

"I wish you luck then," Narseh said. "And you, honored sir, what is your journey?"

But when he looked to where Taljhou had been standing, the dog was gone.

Snow threatened for much of the second day, but the sky had cleared as the sun began to descend. Which was a mercy. As Narseh had predicted, they made camp in the open.

While porters saw to lighting a fire, and another filled a kettle to transform their provisions into something edible, Narseh and Husravah saw to it their fellow travelers knew how to be as comfortable as possible.

"If one might presume to assure you, honored sir," insisted Ambhi, "bodily discomforts are a test, and I shall do my best to disregard them."

"Well, all the same," Narseh sighed through his nose, "you should disregard them better with this bedroll laid out and lying on the leeward side of a sleeping camel, if you understand me."

"Ah, yes," Ahmbi and the camel, relaxed on its belly and chewing placidly, regarded eachother, "I do take your point, honored sir."

"Is the old woman well enough?" Narseh was brushing one of the camels later when his father approached.

"She'll sleep more comfortably than any of us," Husravah scoffed. "She's brought enough blankets she could make a whole tent of them. What about Taljhou?"

"Already settled, there was nothing for me to tell him. An experienced traveler, that one."

"Experience is worth more than its weight in gold," Husravah quoted, "for it weighs nothing."

"Only when it is trustworthy." The mule leaned closer to his father and lowered his voice, "He will say nothing about who he is or where he is going. He's barely said anything at all, just watches. Did he tell you anything when he bargained for passage?"

The horse worked his lips and folded his hands into his sleeves. "No, no he didn't. Just said he needed to go west. Didn't try to haggle the price, either, just paid what I asked."

Narseh shot a glance toward the other side of the camp. It was too dark to see by now, but the last he'd seen Taljhou he'd been sitting up on a bedroll, leaning back against a camel, already sleeping the kind of immediately deep sleep, ready to be interrupted any moment, that a long experienced traveler learns.

Or an experienced bandit.

"You think he's fleeing something?" Husravah said.

"Maybe. Or maybe scouting us for an ambush."

"Or maybe he is just a quiet man who keeps to himself and needs to travel west."

"Maybe." the mule sighed. "We should stay alert, at least."

"You cannot do that unless you sleep, son." Husravah patted his shoulder and headed for his own bedroll.

His father was right, of course. But it was longer than usual before Narseh found his way to sleep.

On the third day, they reached a caravanserai kept by the daughter of a priestess, whose small temple sat across the road. They were too late for the day's rites, and would have to leave too early for tomorrow's, but still it was a comfort to stand in the presence of the sacred fire and hear prayers offered for their preservation against evil.

Especially if that evil included one of their fellow travelers.

And what a shock it was, after having thought that, prayed that, for Narseh to spot Taljhou in the temple, behind the porters. He didn't come forward to pray or touch purifying water, but he still left his two coins in the alms bowl, and placed his twig of pomegranate—proper offering for the uninitiated—in the basket beside the sprigs of holy ephedrus from him, his father, and most of the porters.

"I did not know," he might as well take the opportunity, as he left the temple, to find out what he could, "you were a pious man, honored sir."

"I do not know," Taljhou answered, "if I am, myself." The dog read the unasked question on Narseh's face, and continued. "It is well to be courteous, in whatever land one is."

"You have," Narseh tried, "had business in other lands, then?"

Taljhou stopped just within the temple gate. "I was lately far to the east. It is said to be a great empire. I suppose it still is, but it is divided. One branch of the imperial family holds the north, the other holds the south, each says the other is a false pretender to the throne, and between them all is chaos. They say open war could begin at any moment."

"What business brought you so far?"

"I was seeking something. I did not find it there. So I journey to another land to seek there." Taljhou sighed. "I will swear to you I mean neither harm nor theft to you or any of my fellow travelers. Will that ease your suspicions?"

Narseh cringed. He hadn't thought he had been so obvious.

"I bear you no grudge." Taljhou said as he left. "You would hardly be the first to be untrusting. But my business, honored sir, is my own."

The dog kept his solitude the rest of the night. He had promised, Narseh told Husrava, no harm, and within the bounds of the temple no less. But the mule was not so naive as to think men never promised in vain.

On the fourth day, they found the road had been blocked by an avalanche. Though Husravah feared they'd need to take an extra day to descend and go around, Narseh judged the mass of snow and mud had been here at least three or four days, melting and refreezing, and might be solid enough to at least test.

The mule borrowed a pole from Miss Cepla's litter. Carefully probing the snow surface before him as he went, he climbed across with one of the porters. There were a few places the surface broke through, but they were shallow and easily stomped down till they were solid.

There was something eerily elating about seeing a landscape he'd learned through years of familiarity from higher up than he was used to. It made Narseh aware, somehow, of the shape of the land, as if he could run his hands over the mountains and the valleys. The certainty struck him like a blow: the world was far wider than he'd known. How much of the road must there be to see, both west and east, beyond the stretch he'd known back and forth all his life?

In all, it took less than an hour to reach the other side, and even less to walk back.

"I'm still unsure," Husravah blew doubtfully at his son's return. "It may be firm enough for our weight, but what about the camels? The litter?"

So they unloaded one of the camels, and Narseh led it across. Two porters carried the saddle bags, and stayed while Narseh went back alone.

He met Taljhou coming the other way. "I didn't want to wait," the dog shrugged.

Which was understandable, Narseh mused as he led the rest of them across the remains of the avalanche, but didn't make him less suspicious.

All told, the avalanche cost them about four hours. Still better than spending an extra day going around.

They slept in the open that night.

On the fifth day, Ambhi proposed a slight diversion.

"It would be but an hour out of our way, I am told," the fox claimed. "But it would mean shelter for the night. Such places are duty-bound to welcome travelers."

Thunder sounded just then, further up the valley, so Narseh had to admit it would be well not to spend another night in the open if they did not have to. "But what is your interest in this place, honored sir? And why have I never before heard of it, who have traveled this route most of my life?"

"Ah, it is a monastery, older than the one which my family sponsors. I was counseled to visit there, presume to make introductions, if at all possible. Such places do not always announce themselves, you know, or take notice of worldly concerns. It is hardly a wonder if outsiders do not know of the place."

Ambhi had underestimated the distance of this diversion, but not by much. Instead of proceeding down the main road, they cut off onto a narrow path winding up round a shoulder of hills till it reached a brick enclave built in tiers. A hawk in simple robes like Ambhi's, though these were sunset-crimson, stood up attentively by the gate at their approach.

The stables and guest rooms, on the lowest tier, were honestly as good as any caravanserai and better than some. And Narseh would have been grateful for any kind of roof when the rain not only arrived, it quickly turned to sleet, then to driving snow. None of which meant he had to accept Ambhi's enthusiastic invitation to go upstairs for a sermon from the resident teacher, with debate to follow.

Husravah did go. "If I make a good impression," the old merchant explained, "we may be able to rely on this as a stop from now on! And the 'donation' they asked was less than an innkeeper would want!" Taljhou went too.

Narseh spent the evening listening to Miss Cepla talk about her seemingly innumerable nephews and nieces. Which still had to be better than a lecture about the holy awakened ones, or than lying outdoors, cold, wet, and miserable.

As they left the monastery on the sixth morning, Husravah was bursting with confidence about the place.

"They were most polite, and grateful for the donations, and eager to hear the news about the Atheotokosics and their council!" the horse explained. "And listening to some soothing speeches about virtue and unworldliness is worth the price, I say!"

Narseh didn't argue. It wouldn't be him who'd have to listen to the speeches.

Early in the afternoon they were overtaken by a party of cavalry.

Both riders and mounts wore armor with an intricate geometric emblem in red and gold. The leader's helmet had a tuft of bright red feathers. They slowed to look suspiciously at the caravan who shuffled to the side of the road to let them pass.

"Honored sir," Husravah began when the leader, a dog with a fluffy golden mane but lips and tongue the color of sodalite beads, drew up to him, "to what do we owe the honor of–"

"Be thankful, merchant!" snapped the soldier "That the house of the Harmonious South and the Phoenix Throne keeps your wares safe from robbers!"

Which, Narseh thought as they disappeared down the road ahead, if this was what they were doing, it would be the first time.

"Well!" commented Cepla from her litter window, "what a rude young man!"

If anyone other than Narseh noticed Taljhou had disappeared into the scrub brush just before the cavalry rode into view, and did not emerge until they'd passed, then they made no mention of it.

The caravanserai at the close of the seventh day had a public bath, which was by now most necessary. Narseh always looked forward to this stop.

The oils in the bath house were scented with the wild lilies, white and orange, which would bloom here come summer.

This place reminded him of Dionikos.

It had been...how many years ago, now? Four? Five? When he and Dionikos had lain in the rooftop garden of this inn. It had been high summer, and a heavy rainfall had kept them here an extra day. But when it passed the dry valley had come alive with uncountable millions of pale orange and moon-white lilies. The perfume had carved the memory of the otter lying in his arms, warm in the summer night, naked under the stars, into Nasreh's mind like a chisel in granite.

Dionikos was—well, had been—a porter and hired guard, from some place far to the west. At first he had hired on for a single journey, as was usual, but then he offered to stay on for the next. Narseh had wondered why.

The otter had slipped up to Narseh's bed above the stables, at Stepmother's inn back home, the night before they were to set out again. And Narseh ceased to wonder why.

"No, I won't ever take over from Father," Narseh remembered explaining, "He doesn't mean me to be less than my brother or sisters, but they are his wife's children and I'm not, and that's the end of it. It's the law. And I can have no heir myself, I am as I am."

"As much as I'd like to keep you all for myself," Dionikos had chuckled, "I've known men like us who still did what was required when they needed an heir."

"No, I mean…" Narseh had blushed, "I remain a mule. I truly cannot."

"Oh." Dionikos had stroked his flank in silence a while, then asked, "what are you supposed to do, then?"

"I'll have the caravan," Narseh had resisted the urge to shrug, careful to avoid unbalancing the man cradled on his chest. "When Gudarz is of age, when Father's merchantship passes to him, he'll need me just as much as Father does."

"Is it enough?" the otter's paw on the side of Narseh's face had been soft. "To go back and forth, over the same stretch of road, all your life, for someone else?"

Dionikos had been about to say more. Narseh had kissed him so he wouldn't, and held the kiss until he stopped trying.

After a year and half more, Dionikos had saved up enough to clear his family's debts, back at the western edge of the world. Narseh wished he'd had it in himself to ask him to stay.

At least there were memories, and the smell of lilies.

On the eighth day, a camel shied at a snake beside the road, but a porter was beside it to prevent it bolting, and Narseh had time to run back and calm the beast. The snake hadn't been venomous, anyway.

On the ninth day they made camp in the shelter of a narrow canyon where a long ago rockslide had formed walls. A cold wind had come up and strengthened all day, eliciting no end of complaints from Miss Cepla, so all were glad to be sleeping behind a windbreak.

"Why, it was as if it blew right through the blankets and robes to my very bones!" she was saying somewhere to Narseh's left. Probably to Tsu, Rabga seemed to have much less patience with the old pheasant's rambling.

Narseh paid but little attention. Her complaints had reminded him of Naramora.

The man had been beautiful, some kind of bird unheard of. Blue and green feathers shimmering like silk when he moved. Long, long ornate tail held carefully above the dust of a caravansarai outside Shah Murkhandeh.

"I need to get to the Eastern Empire," he'd called to every passing merchant, "please!" He clearly couldn't pay, or he wouldn't be doing this, in a place like this.

"I may be poor," he'd said, in tones unambiguous, when Husravah passed, "but I can pay my way in other ways, noble sir!"

The horse had frozen, shoulders up, ready to bolt from the brazen impropriety. But then he'd stopped. His glower softened into what Narseh recognized as the face his father kept for considering a bargain. And then he'd met Narseh's eyes, brows questioning.

The young mule had risked a glance at the bird, blushed, and nodded.

For the trip back, Naramora had stayed close by his side.

"They say at the eastmost edge of the world, a musician can find careers and audiences and rich patrons aplenty," he'd explained, "if I can make it there! The pleasure houses pay very well, I am told. They say even the tea shops, wine sellers, and gambling pavilions require an artist like myself, for ambiance and tranquility!"

"And if I can't impress with music, why," he would grin wickedly and rustle his impossibly ornate tail of feathers, "there'll be some wealthy, wicked, old courtier to seduce, I'm sure."

He had played a flute of resin-finished bamboo, rich and warm and smooth-sounding, every night when they stopped. The whole caravan, five companies of merchants with all their porters and mercenaries, would be rapt in silence until he finished. Only the camels were unmoved.

Naramora had another instrument, too, but it remained in a case over his shoulder from which the bird would not remove it. "Too precious, I'm afraid," he had explained when Narseh asked one night: the bird was unused to the cold mountain air, and would huddle tight against the mule for warmth even after neither had any need left to spend. "If it were to be damaged, out here, with none to fix it for a hundred leagues? I'd be finished! Once my mother heard of it—and she would, somehow—I'd be better off dead!"

Narseh made sure it was securely fastened on one of the camels, the next morning.

Only when they reached home, back to Stepmother's inn, had Naramora unpacked what proved to be a strange, large, deep-bellied lute, with too many strings running up a long narrow neck. It was so large it couldn't be held properly level: Naramora had sat behind it and rested the base on the side of his foot.

"Now, noble sir," the bird had grinned at Husravah, "you will discover a treasure unlooked-for, when you bargained only for me to warm your son's nights!"

And if Stepmother had looked scandalized, she soon forgot it entirely. They all did, under an avalanche of music, more wild and intricate and heartbreakingly beautiful than any Narseh had heard before.

Or since.

He'd escorted Naramora to the next caravanserai eastward the next day, made sure he was with a trustworthy caravanier.

"I will sing to the drunken scholars, the courtesans, and all the bitter, frumpy old poets," the bird had whispered at their last kiss, "of the strong, quiet, rugged caravan boy, who held me so gently and stole my heart. Only to give it back, undamaged, when our journey together was done. That kind of bittersweet love story plays very well."

Narseh had no idea, now, if Naramora had won the success he'd seemed so sure of. Or even if he had reached the distant east.

But he dreamed of the sound of his flute.

On the tenth day they reached Kentbesch.

Husravah was quietly pleased, though it was unlikely anyone but his son could tell. The old workhorse thought of this town as the halfway point on the accustomed journey, and they'd made it without delay.

Narseh was less excited. This was the largest and most comfortable caravansarai they knew—save for outside Royal Murkhandeh but you could never count on getting space in one of the good ones there—and he had never stayed here without sharing it with three or four other groups. It was unnerving to be the only ones here, among so much empty, echoing room, which should have been filled with other travelers.

Perhaps that was why he went to seek companionship. Or maybe his body wanted something to do with the tension clawing within it. Or maybe he was simply cold, weary, and frustrated with a solitary bed.

"Of course, honored sir," said the innkeeper when he asked, "it is not a busy time for us, but there is always a hospitable lady here to welcome a hardworking merchant!"

"Uh," Narseh felt his ears heating and wished they weren't so prominent, "...there are only, uh, the ladies?"

The shaggy yak looked perplexed for a moment, then apologetic. "Ah, I see, I must apologize sir. Ordinarily, yes, but, well...it is the height of harvest season with us. All the men are needed in the fields.

To be honest, most of the women have gone too. This is the first time it has ever...caused this problem, honored sir, but the caravans, they–"

"–they do not usually run this time of year, I can attest to it. Ah well. I thank you for your courtesy, honored sir, but you need concern yourself no further. I will sleep alone."

He was proved wrong in this: not only in saying he would be alone, but in saying he would sleep. He sat by the fire, with only Ambhi, lost in silent prayer, for company, as flames faltered and turned to ember.

"It is a misfortune, my friend," said a voice in the darkness, "to have neither reason to stay, nor reason to go." Taljhou took a seat on the opposite side of the fire.

"What do you mean?"

"I have observed men's souls these long years," Taljhou stared back through the fire, "I know quiet despair when I see it."

"If there is aught I can do," Ambhi opened his serious eyes, "then might I presume to compassionately advise?"

The mule's back tensed, ready to rise in indignation, "Very well!" but some determination within Narseh collapsed. Maybe he was weary of pretending he was not weary. "I begin to wonder, impiously," he confessed, "if there is anything in life for me. I go on journeys I don't wish to, carrying luxuries I will never taste, for my father's profit and none of mine. Others proceed onward to behold all the glories of the empires of the world, while I journey to nowhere but the same handful of rough places over and over again. Where I cannot even pay a man to pretend to love me! When I grow old and die, having done nothing but this, there will be no descendants to pray for my soul. Finally, and very soon, none will remember that I lived at all."

Ambhi and Taljhou very kindly turned away, to spare Narseh from having to say they had seen him weep.

"I have presumed to consider," Ambhi said at the end of the tenth day, "your predicament, honored sir."

Once they began to climb over the final shoulder of mountains the caravanserai were smaller and plainer. But at this one they finally met another mercantile party. Just as small and unseasonal as theirs, headed the opposite way and with every intention of turning south, away from the mountainous winter, when they reached Kentbesch.

They had news, though, beside which nothing else mattered.

The news which sent Husravah into elations was of the price of incense in Shah Murkhandeh, for it had soared beyond the horse's wildest hopes.

But the news which lowered Narseh's brows with worry was that this party too had encountered cavalrymen, red insignias on armor, from the dynasties to the east. They had been very rudely threatened, and some of the soldiers had even dared search both person and cargo of the youngest merchant.

The same ones they had met? Impossible to say.

So now the mule struggled to dismiss anxiety long enough to hear the square-faced fox out.

"The first of the noble truths, my friend," Ambhi explained, "teaches us suffering arises from desire. You yearn for what the world has not vouchsafed you, and this is natural. But would you not only find new things to yearn for, if you had them? Far better to pursue contentment—one of the noble eight ways of awakening—and cultivate happiness in the things beyond this world, and beyond this life, which can never be out of reach. And with good works, with dutifulness and piety, and with harm to none, surely divine balance will, in the next life, place you far from the fields of loneliness in which you find yourself."

Narseh gazed into his cup of spiced wine, warm at least even if it was severely watered. "Does this sort of counsel," he finally asked, "often work?"

"Ah, well…" Ambhi rubbed the scruff of his neck. "It is said, one never hears the call to awakening until fate finds one ready. Perhaps this is why? If I have presumed too much, honored sir, I sincerely ask your pardon."

Narseh assured him all was well, no insult taken. "Here, my friend, let me buy you a cup of wine."

"Oh, my thanks, but monks are supposed to abstain from all that intoxicates."

"That's all right then," Narseh laughed, "they've watered this down so much I doubt a whole barrel could intoxicate anyone. And anyway, you're not a monk yet, are you?"

In the end, Ambhi decided the greater error lay in a failure of compassion by abstaining, rather than in indulgence.

A slick mountain fog arose on the eleventh day. The kind which flows up the slopes like water poured backwards.

Usually they would have stopped at the caravanserai they reached at noon, but if there were aggressive parties of soldiers about, then Husravah and Narseh agreed they should make good time while they could, even if it meant a night in the open.

By the time the sun began to set in earnest, the fog had settled thick and level in the valley. The mountains, and any travelers unlucky enough to be out upon them, towered above clouds the color of moth wings and luminous with moonlight. Above, the night air was clear enough to conceal not a single star. It was a sight to fill the breast of even the most jaded and world-weary caravanier with a wild, cold elation. Like a carved puppet before a lantern screen, when beheld before this sight Narseh's loneliness was transformed into something noble, and deep, and sweet to feel.

"It reminds me of the sea," Taljhou remarked, when Narseh found him looking out over the fog. "I suppose you have never seen the sea, though?"

"I have heard tales of it, honored sir."

"I thought not." The dog rose and stretched. "You ought."

"I ought what?" Narseh flicked his ear impatiently.

"Go to the sea. See it yourself. See the whitewash-walled gardens, and the little forgotten islands, and the ruins of the ancient temples, and everything in between. One can be happy in one place, in one life, content to leave the rest of the world to itself. Aye, it can be done. But such a happiness is a fragile thing, easily broken, and it does not heal. Some, fortunate few, may repair it, but most must seek for a new happiness to replace it."

"As you are doing?" Narseh whispered to the fog.

Taljhou pretended not to have heard him. "You will say duty, or filial piety, or loyalty mean you cannot leave. I will not hear it, sir. Those are merely ways to vainly deny it is you, and only you, who makes the choice to go or stay. When we reach Shah Murkandeh will duty block the road? Will loyalty bar the gates? Will filial piety tie you to this caravan? What walls will there be, what chains, to stop you from continuing west or east or any direction in the world without breaking stride? Only yourself."

The world felt strangely fragile, like Narseh had stumbled into a temple he couldn't see, before unknown gods waiting on him to speak. Perhaps the entire world had always been such a temple, and he had not guessed it until now. "How would I know that it is time to leave? To decide, if you say deciding is all there is to it?" he asked.

"When I decided, very long ago, to leave my home, now very far from here, I did not know I could decide, nor would, till after I decided and was gone." Taljhou pronounced.

Nasreh was afraid of what he might say if he spoke again, so he remained silent.

"It remains to be seen, my friend," Taljhou said, "whether we will make that royal city in safety. I mislike the thought of these soldiers: I am no oracle, but what I saw, before I left the east, was no reassurance. But if we do, I will hope to see you discover for yourself how it feels to set foot on a road never before trodden." The dog slipped into the darkness as if it were a blanket. "Goodnight to you, honored sir."

There was rain on the twelfth day. It made for dismal traveling, but not enough to cool desire for as much progress as could be made.

It was some encouragement when, as the rains began to pass, a porter sighted the first of the Emperors' Pillars: a column of stone standing by the roadside, bearing the image and name of an ancient king of Murkhandeh in carved relief. They had crossed, then, the highest point of the pass, and into lands claimed—or had been claimed, once, for the pillar was very old—by the Ziggurat of the Sacred Fire.

They made camp in an empty courtyard. "I remember when this was an inn," Husravah twisted his fingers a moment into the sign of the setting sun, to appease against the spirits of abandoned places, "when I was a boy."

"What happened?" said Miss Cepla, suddenly hesitant to descend from her litter.

"There was a war. A little affair, some noble's grudge against some other, but war nonetheless. My father said the place burned, and none have yet dared reopen it."

They were not the only ones to see this place could still serve as shelter, even abandoned. In the fresh mud of the morning's rain were hoofprints, plain to see, of a good many cavalry horses.

On the thirteenth day they were obliged to negotiate a winding road above a steep canyon. The cleft was narrow enough, porter's tales said, for a man to shout a greeting to the sister road on the other side.

"If one might presume to ask, why a second road?" Ambhi wondered, in an apparent attempt to ease Miss Cepla's agitation, for she did not care to be this near the chasm. "Surely one is sufficient to go to the same place?"

"Because they don't go to the same place," Narseh answered.

"Where does the other go?" Miss Cepla did her best to join in, and not to look down.

"It turns north at the mouth of this canyon, honored madam, toward Aulmhatau and the Apple-lands," explained Husravah, "But the only bridge which reaches it lies at least a day, more likely a day and a half, behind us now. I did once travel–"

His tale was cut off by a warning whistle from one of the porters.

Around the bend of the hills, heading the other direction, came cavalry wearing red and gold badges.

Up the opposite side of the canyon.

The caravan stopped as the soldiers in single file passed slowly by. Their captain was a tiger with cold and arrogant eyes.

If the other side was close enough to shout a greeting, nobody did.

"How far behind us," Taljhou growled, when the last cavalryman had passed, "did you say the bridge was?"

"A day and a half," answered Husravah. "Maybe less for riders."

There was serious talk, come evening, of pressing on after sundown. But Husravah, Narseh, and to Narseh's surprise Taljhou, all agreed it was too steep, too dangerous.

They made camp in the open again.

The sun was not yet risen on the fourteenth day when the camp was awakened by shouts.

When Narseh struggled out of his bedroll it was to find Tsu, the sable litter bearer, snarling curses as he tried to wrestle out of Rabga's grip. The bear held him back from Taljhou, who was holding aloft a folded paper with a seal in emerald wax. Miss Cepla stood behind, feathers unbound on her head and dismay, though not her usual flustered kind, on her face.

"What is this?" shouted Nasreh, interposing himself.

"The dog is a thief!" shouted Tsu, "I suspected it this whole trip! He has stolen from Miss Cepla's luggage!"

"I have not," Taljhou beckoned to Husravah, "because if these papers, messages I'd deem, are hers, then she is not Miss Cepla. According to this," he brandished the document at the gathered caravan, "her name is Āyí Lǎo Lì!"

Husravah moved toward the struggle, but froze.

"You will," Tsu growled, "return Mistress Lǎo Lì's property to her."

"Tsu, no!" cried Cepla.

Where the sable had been hiding the long thin sword whose tip was now less than an inch from Taljhou's throat, none could say.

"What do you think is going to happen if I don't?" the dog spared not a glance for the weapon, kept his eyes fixed on Tsu. "There are nine other men around you, most of them armed. If you strike me, you will die, and they will read it anyway." The sword tip wavered. "Then she will have nobody to help her when the horsemen find her alone in the wilderness. It is her they are seeking, is it not?"

"Let them see it," Cepla's voice was far steadier than Narseh had heard it before.

"Mistress, but–"

"Secrecy is no longer a fitting instrument, Tsu."

Taljhou handed the paper to Husravah, who unfolded it carefully. "The Firstborn of Heaven, the Elder Brother of all Kings and Princes, Guardian of the Centremost Realm of Earth, the Lord of the House of the August North and Master of the Dragon Throne sends thee greetings!" Husravah read incredulously. "Inasmuch as it is Our task to order all things for the blossoming of peace in all places,

We would propose to thee a treaty of alliance and of friendship between Us and thy noble city. As token of this, We ask of thee neither taxes nor tribute, but only thy amity. And in the spirit of such amity, We thus propose and advise thee to have no business with traders and merchants who claim false allegiance the recusant Southern Dynasty and the Phoenix Throne, and forbid their custom–," the stallion raised narrowed eyes to glare at the pheasant. "Woman, what business is this?!"

"This," the old woman who clearly was not named Cepla at all lifted her chin proudly, "is how peace is made."

"The north dynasty," Taljhou spoke up, because that hadn't explained anything, "wants the south dynasty cut off from trade, and is asking Murkhandeh to turn away their merchants."

"Can they do such a thing? Would it work?" Ambhi said.

"It…it might." Husravah's gaze went distant, eyes on some invisible internal abacus, racking back and forth all the fortunesworth of silk, perhaps no longer able to travel the roads if half the merchants were turned back.

"It will," insisted Mistress Āyí Lǎo Lì. "Without the silk trade, they have no treasury. Without the treasury they have no army. Without their army," she took a deep breath, "my homeland is whole again at last."

"What do we do?" Narseh looked over his father's shoulder. He couldn't read whatever was on the paper.

"I think we must presume," Ambhi said, "this is what the soldiers are looking for."

"My wife said she wasn't to be trusted," Rabga wailed, "when she was hiring porters, Pema warned me! I didn't listen!"

"Father! What do we do?"

"Turning it over to them won't accomplish anything," Taljhou said darkly, "there will be no reasoning with them once they have what they want."

"What do we *do*?!"

"Silence!" Husravah bellowed. He approached Lǎo Lì with narrowed eyes as the echoes faded. The silence he had called waited for him to act. "It was an impoliteness, honored madam," Husravah said as he carefully refolded the stiff paper, "not to tell us you carried such risky cargo."

"A necessary one, honored sir," she accepted the letter back, "but an impoliteness nonetheless. And regrettable."

Husravah turned back to Narseh. "She bargained for passage. We accepted her money. I will not have it said my son dishonored a bargain made, even if it is now you, as caravanier, who must see us to safety because of a choice your father made for you." The horse seemed to be talking only to him. "It is not for me, it is not for any of us, to say why another may or may not journey."

Now the silence waited on Narseh. "Very well," the mule finally said, "we waste no more time."

All the fifteenth day, they made the best pace they could.

Narseh had two additional porters help carry the litter, as with only Tsu and Rabga it had consistently been the slowest part of the caravan.

Three times Narseh thought he heard galloping hooves behind them, but it proved to be only his nerves.

It began to snow.

Camping that night was miserable.

Just before noon on the sixteenth day, the cavalry was sighted behind them at last.

They had come to the end of a long flat stretch, under a sheer slope smooth with fresh autumn snow. It was fortunate they had not gone even twelve paces more, or they would have been around a bend, and any warning would have been hidden by the mass of the mountain.

"Will they not listen to reason?" Ambhi said, hopefully. He gripped his staff in such a way as to make clear his dedication to doing harm to none, for it left no doubt he had never once held a weapon.

"Warriors of the Southern Dynasty," answered Lǎo Lì, "win no promotions for listening to reason."

Tsu drew his sword, turned to Narseh. "Take them and go. I will buy you time."

Narseh knew immediately that wouldn't work, but his mind was racing too fast to find the words to say so.

"There are more than a score," Taljhou snapped, "mounted, with spears. Your sword will not buy much time."

By all the gods, if only he had never come on this cursed trip, cold and lonely and unseasonal, plagued with rain, and fog, and snow…

"With my life, then." Tsu intoned.

"Which will buy little more!"

The snow.

"Get around the bend!" Narseh shouted. "Go! Now!" He did not wait to see if they obeyed, but scrambled up the slope toward the ridge at the top. If the gods were just the snow would be loose, un-firm. Snows often were, in the worst season for caravans.

"Yes!" Narseh heard Taljhou bark behind him, but he had no time to look. He forced himself to trudge higher.

The cavalry were well into the flat stretch below him now.

The further up the disturbance, the better.

In later years, Narseh would say it felt like the ground shifted below him, as if he were a dumpling on a shaken skillet. In the moment, though, his feelings were simpler and less fanciful: a sheet of ice, the top of the last snowfall, now straining under the weight of yesterday's further bounty, had cracked under his hoof and slid, and that is a feeling which hits the heart and the back of the throat in a most prosaic, unmistakable way.

Something like a ripple passed across the snowface, all the way up the mountainside. And it was no longer a snowface, but an avalanche.

There was just time to look down and see the face of the cavalry captain, the tiger, furious in disappointment, before a roaring cloud of snow was drawn over him and all his men like a veil. Which was well. Narseh had no wish to see such a thing.

"Did we escape?" he asked the sound of approaching footsteps crunching through the snow, didn't matter who they were.

"They got safely around the bend," said Taljhou.

"And the soldiers?"

"Perhaps buried, perhaps swept away. Even if not, the road is entirely blocked." Taljhou held out a hand to help the victorious caravanier to his feet. "How did you know you could bring down the snow?"

"I didn't," Narseh picked his way back down the denuded slope, "until after it was done. But someone had to do something."

Taljhou sounded as if he'd meant to say more, but if so, he thought better of it. They rejoined the caravan and Narseh's father, both sick with worry, both safe, both amazed to be safe.

Around the corner they had turned the plains spread below. At the horizon, at last, lay the royal city of Shah Murkhandeh, though they had all been too preoccupied to notice until now.

They arrived on the seventeenth day.

The city gates were already shut for the night, but it mattered little. There was no shortage of caravanserai outside the walls, and given the lateness of the season—though about the knees of Great Shah Murkhandeh of Royal History there would always be trade coming and going, no matter the season—Narseh was able to find space for them at one of the better ones, and at a reasonable price at that.

Which was his last duty. Now his father was responsible for whatever happened.

So Narseh sat by a fountain in the courtyard, nursed a flagon of wine, and wondered about the advice he had been given.

"Though I have already presumed to thank you, my friend," said the square-faced fox beside him, "I am tempted to excess. Truly, you have saved not only my self, but the goal of my journey as well. When one day I bring back lost volumes of the ancestral philosophers to my monastery, it will be thanks to you."

"Talking of goals," Narseh turned to the brindle dog on his other side, "you never did say what it is you seek."

"No," Taljhou shot them both a sidelong glance, "I did not."

"Most respected gentlemen!" Lǎo Lì appeared through the archway from the upper rooms. Tsu came behind her at a proprietous distance. They had both abandoned their disguises, and were clearly the more comfortable for it in smooth silk of somber hue and serious cut, emblazoned with a serpent-like insignia of blue and green. "I must express my gratitude. Once my people learn how much they soon will owe you, there will be neither words nor time to thank you enough. So it is better for us all, I think, if I thank you now."

"I presume to imagine, Madam...Ambassador?" Ambhi ventured, and Lǎo Lì swallowed a laugh, "you will be very busy on the morrow?"

"Oh! Ever so much! I must present my credentials at the palace, beseech an audience, take housing of sufficient dignity in the meantime. I must make introductions and spread favorable rumors among the nobles. Oh, and dear Rabga has agreed to remain with me, for increased pay I might add! Which means I must send word back to his honored madam wife, and find a market and a tailor, he'll need something more suitable to wear. I do think he'd look dashing in a good dark green, wouldn't you agree?" She sounded very much like Miss Cepla before fluttering her wings to bring her words to a stop. "But! I shall not forget to tell the good Emperor Sumerdismes of your bravery, whenever I do come before him on more urgent business." She turned when Husravah entered the courtyard, "Oh, most respected sir, please, I must have some words with you!"

"What am I to do?" Narseh asked, unsure of which, fox or dog, he was asking. His father, in animated conversation with the covert ambassador, was a picture of the archetypical merchant: prosperous, charismatic, jovial, cunning, and weary. This trip was likely to prove the old horse's greatest triumph. A triumph Narseh would never be allowed to have himself.

Perhaps one he no longer wanted to.

"It has been said the purpose of the cycle of death and rebirth," Ambhi mused, "is that the soul might learn, over many lifetimes, all ways of being ere it ascends into awakening. If a man is unable to find contentment, then it may be a sign he has not yet learned what this life was meant to teach him, and must seek learning elsewhere?"

"I don't know about that," Taljhou shrugged, "but nobody finds what they want if they do not go and look."

Narseh came to a decision.

"Father," he stood once Lǎo Lì had at last run out of things to say, "the cargo is safe?"

"It may be I should check it again...but you, my brave son, need not worry yourself!" the horse embraced the mule. "Oh, it's beautiful! All these other merchants? Are leaving the city, going southwest! You know why? To try to buy incense!"

Narseh didn't realize he was going to say "I am leaving too" until he had said it.

"...what? What do you mean?" Husravah looked as if he'd been struck.

"I must see more of the road, Father. You traveled further than this, in your youth, and for your own sake. I cannot be whole, cannot be content, with traveling only the same path all my life, even if it is for my family. Our lives nearly ended yesterday. Yours would have ended full—the world seen, a family and home, a livelihood established, an heir to pass it on. My life would have ended empty."

"How can you be sure you are ready?"

"I didn't know I was, Father," Narseh admitted, "I only now found I was determined, and that must needs be readiness enough."

"When the rain falls," Husravah quoted quietly, "it does not stop to ask if the river is prepared. I...should have expected this, one day." The old workhorse's face was like unto that of a bereaved child, "But why? Where will you go?"

"West, I suppose. You remember Dionikos? I think I would like to see his homeland. Maybe east, then, and perhaps hear Naramora's music again." The mule shrugged. "But why? Because it is not for any of us to say why another may or may not journey."

"Oh my son. What am I to do, without you?"

"Isn't it about time Gudarz began to learn the things you taught me? He has never yet traveled! How can he succeed you if he doesn't learn the route? How to haggle? How to make camp? How to manage a camel?" Narseh felt his ears heating and ignored them. "Besides, you will not be able to go back until spring. The pass leading home was blocked by an avalanche yesterday, remember? Take the winter, sell your incense, buy other goods to take back to Stepmother. And then, one day, when Gudarz is a young merchant, why, I will know where to return. I don't doubt he will need an experienced caravanier."

Husravah hung his head for a moment, closed his eyes, then straightened up. "It may be you are talking sense after all, my boy," he exhaled sharply. "If the price of incense is half what rumor says, I'll have more wealth than could be safely carried back, I think. Perhaps...perhaps I ought to invest in a cargo or two of silk? There's reason to believe the price may be about to rise, you know!"

And so it was that, in the twenty seventh year since his birth, Narseh the Caravanier, son of Husravah the Merchant, set out westward from the Royal City of Shah Murkhandeh, with a single camel bearing a small cargo of semi-precious stones, purchased in the gem market at sunrise with only the first of the enormous profits reaped in selling shoddy incense to Atheotokosic clergy as they arrived for council. His father had insisted he take the same in payment for years of loyal and diligent work, saying, "Gems are a good business!

Light, easy to hide from thieves, and very stable value! A better start, for a merchant, than I had!"

He had not spent more than a day among the delights of Royal Murkhandeh, but he had every intention of returning.

"If one might presume to ask," said the fox who met him at the western gates, "to continue in the company of an honored friend? I would welcome your experience and wisdom on my further journeys, and would be honored if, when I recover the texts I seek, you were there to witness."

"He's hardly going to refuse, you know," the taciturn dog leaning against the gate rolled his eyes, "we're all going the same way anyway."

"I would, honored sirs, be pleased to be your fellow traveler," said Narseh.

The road stretched before them, inviting, beckoning toward the sunset.

"Maybe you ought to check the provisions?" Ambhi asked as they set out upon, for the first time in his memory, a road Narseh had not yet traveled.

"He already did," answered Taljhou.

Narseh did, however, check them again when he got the chance, as his father before him would have.

THE TRACES OF THOMAS ANTIOCHUS MACROTIS

ROSE LACROIX

Author's note: The further back in time you go, the harder it is to reconstruct the life of someone who lived in the past. Entire lives of people with illustrious careers as successful officials in the Roman Empire, for example, have been overlooked by ancient historians and remain known only from fragments. Sometimes we have little more than a name. Sometimes pieces of information take decades or centuries to piece together, and are found in archives or in someone's sock drawer. While a story preserved in as many fragments as the one presented here may be highly unlikely, it gives one pause to consider how scattered these traces of a once-living person can be.

(Excerpt from the first English printing of Marc Roenel's book "Creatures And Traditions Of Roman Britain," Hayworth & Sons, London, 1978):
At its height, the Roman Empire was extremely diverse; particularly in the Roman Army, that often saw recruits travel very far afield from the provinces they came from, all for a chance at Roman citizenship after twenty-five years of service. Soldiers from as far away as Syria and Dalmatia came to the sodden frontiers of Gaul and Britannia; some of them we know only from fragments of text or tombstones. Others have been erased from time forever.

(From The Vienna Letters, a series of letters found preserved in a library in Palmyra by a Venetian antiquarian in 1529 and kept in Vienna since 1703):

My dearest mother whom I have not seen in so long, a heartfelt *salve* to you. As you know, in a year I will have served my obligation as a soldier, and gained for myself and my future children the honor of Roman citizenship. And if I am fortunate I will serve in some exalted position and become *nova bestia.* The Empire needs good creatures in civil service in beloved Antioch or perhaps Palmyra; but no further from home. I wish to serve in the land where I was born.

How I have missed the sunny courtyard of our home, with its palm tree garden! This frigid, sodden, bleak land where wild beasts lurk in wooded glades, with barbarians at our back and curious, scruffy, surly natives for neighbors leaves me homesick.

The natives here, these British, are the worst of all Celts. Even the peatiest Hibernians are ashamed of them. They are possessed of all the worst traits of every creature born of cold, hostile lands and though some will try to become Romans, they do so poorly at it!

We had one fellow, a long fellow, a creature called a stoat I think. You may have seen his like in Seleucia Pieria for they are more often tin merchants than soldiers. This particular stoat was wormy and mangy and had to be taught how his helmet ought to be worn! Imagine, mother, not knowing how to wear a helmet!

Even the foxes here do not look right; their ears are far too small, smaller even than the foxes of Rome. And their fur is far too long, with their hocks blackened as though they had walked ten thousand miles in soot. At least Roman foxes are leaner and more colored like the earth; these British foxes are a miserable dark red and gray. They look filthy, even when they take to bathing!

[The upper portion of the second page exists as a series of vellum fragments from which can be recovered only the following]...

stomach was on fire... food not fit to be eaten... best not to stay at an inn at the border...

In matters of religion they are reluctant to give up their old gods to the gods of our Emperor, yet they have all too gladly become Christians given half a chance. Already there is talk that these Christians are plotting against the Emperor though we have of late seen nothing of the sort. Nonetheless we remain cautious; these British do not care one miserable bit about being a part of the empire. They only want our nice cloth, our good wine, our streets and sewers and our baths, or oil to fry their beet roots in. But they do not want us or our emperor and I for one do not want them!

Marcus, you remember, the hyena centurion I serve under, has assured me that if I so wish I may have soldiers under my command and an officer's post at Vindolanda when I have finished my obligation. I have been most fortunate to have a commander who thinks so highly of me. But I do not wish to remain a soldier. I wish only for the life of a respectable Roman citizen and for my swift return to the city of my birth, for a wife and a home and a family and a grove of date palms that I might make wine from their dates til I am too old to work.

Send father my greetings as well, and to Philip and Aristomache. It is my hope that this letter should reach you around Saturnalia and find you well and safe.

(Excerpt: "From Vestal Virgins to Mary Magdalen: The Art And Iconography of Holy Harlots In Late Antiquity" by Lilith Vickson, Her Voice Publishing, Philadelphia, 1994):

One of the attributes you see most often associated with Mary Magdalen is a jar of spikenard. An aromatic plant of the honeysuckle family, oil of spikenard was used both for flavoring wine and as a main ingredient in perfume. It had a rather sinister reputation as a cheap perfume used by females of various species (but especially foxes) in the sex trade, much the same reputation rose water would develop in Victorian times.

(From a scrap of lead found in a field where a Roman forum once stood):
Exuperata Lovernisca paid Horacius Hippolytus seven sesterces for a vial of spikenard.

(From "Sexo In Urbe: Sex And Scandal In the Roman City," by Franklin Wolfe, Banner Editions, New York, 2002):
The public latrines, used by male and female alike, were a space we would find both familiar in its basic utility, and baffling in its role in the community. For these were as much a communal space as the bathhouses; creatures of all ages and species gathered in one place to do their business. But it was also a place to socialize, to gossip; latrine rumors were a frequent way to ease the awkwardness of lifting one's toga in front of a complete stranger. And when there was no one to exchange gossip with, either late at night or when few others were present, it was not unusual for males to brag about their sexual exploits by carving their deeds—many of them no doubt exaggerated or made up altogether—into the wall. Here and there, in places like Pompeii, these rare graffiti have been found preserved against all odds. They give us a glimpse into both what Romans did sexually, and what they aspired to do. A common brag was having penetrated every hole on some desirable creature.

(From a fragment of the walls of a public latrine in a public bath near what is now Hexham, found in 1930 by a local farmer's son unaware of its meaning, gifted to his grandson in 1991, sitting in a drawer of things unknown to archaeology in an English attic):

Hand 1: What vixen wears spikenard and isn't a whore?

Hand 2: We're not sure about Exuperata...

Hand 3: I have fucked Exuperata in every hole!

(Two letters from a small collection of surviving correspondences and bureaucratic documents of the old Roman empire, tucked away in a forgotten corner of the Vatican library):

Ave, my most glorious Emperor! Marcus Terence Africanus begs your attention.

I began this tour of Britannia with ninety-six capable soldiers; but the harlots of this damp, cold wasteland have proved all too tempting to my best soldiers and as we near the end of this post and the discharge of twenty-five more soldiers who have served their obligation for citizenship, my ranks are depleted.

I am especially concerned that even my finest soldiers are not immune. There is one, a desert red fox called Thomas Antiochus. He comes from a good family of olive merchants in Antioch and Palmyra and I have seen much promise for civil service in him, either in Rome or in Antioch as you wish. But already I see him in the company of a most notorious lady, a dirty camp follower, a vixen who reeks of spikenard. They were in the tavern together, coy at first but they began conversing, first in terse words, then in lighthearted jokes, and next I knew they had left the tavern, arm in arm! Now he spends all of his spare time with her, no longer playing at games of dice or boxing with his comrades. I have seen this before; this is how good soldiers go bad, turning away from the service of Mars and into the decadent arms of Venus far too soon.

I beg you, if you cannot help me retain any of my other soldiers, please help me retain Thomas! He desires a position in civil service in Antioch or Palmyra, to be near his family. Please, offer him something prestigious with generous pay. If I lose him, once my best soldier, I have no hope to avoid the rest of my century disintegrating.

I will have everyone know that I, Marcus Terence Africanus, am sincere and honorable in every word and deed. Ave!

Thomas' Rebuttal:

Ave, most exalted son of Jupiter! Please forgive me, a humble soldier, this intrusion. For I have served honorably; in this my commander has spoken well. However it has reached my ear that my commander has spoken dishonorably of a girl from an honorable family fallen upon hard times whom I have given comfort to, and a few sesterces when I can spare them. Exuperata Lovernisca is not a harlot, nor do I have any intention of leaving the army before my tour of service is over. I intend to return to Antioch and enter the civil service there and mind my family's business.

However, what Marcus Terence Africanus said of Exuperata and of my friendship with her has done great damage to my reputation that may ruin my ambitions before they have even begun. And though I am not yet a citizen I am so close to earning that honor that to have this insult done to me before I can see the justice due a Roman citizen is especially cruel. Please, intervene in this matter if you see fit. I would be satisfied with a remedy of a public apology and a settlement of four gold Solidi. Please forgive me if I have asked for too much. But the dishonor these words have brought to me is great.

Happily I do not need to ask for any justice on behalf of Exuperata. Her father is already a citizen and is litigating this matter separately on her behalf. But be assured that Marcus' words have done great harm to her as well.

I treasure the honor of Roman citizenship guaranteed me by my full term of service. Please, Your Radiance, do not allow this honor to be stolen from me before I can even have it.

(From "Just Like Us: The Familiar World of Ancient Rome" by Dave Collier, University of California Eureka, 2004):
Someone who isn't obsessed with legal history might be forgiven for thinking the lawsuit a modern invention; however, the ancient Romans were every bit as litigious as the people of the present day.

(From a pay chit cut into a scrap of leather, found miraculously preserved in thick mud near Corbridge on a 2001 episode of the UK television show "The Excavators" that aired only once, now considered lost media):
Marcus Terrence paid Thomas Antiochus
60 Sesterces for 60 days service
And 4 solidi settlement

(From a fragment of a wall found at Corbridge Roman Town, probably from a soldiers' latrine, during an archaeological survey in 1961):
Hand 1: I hear Exuperata eats cock and pussy both
Hand 2: She has the best tongue. I came so hard!
Hand 3: Too bad she only sucks Thomas' cock now.
(The final remark is illustrated by a crude drawing of a sad wolf with a comically oversized phallus).

(From "Creatures And Traditions Of Roman Britain," Marc Roenel, Hayworth & Sons, London, 1978):

York—or more properly, Eboracum as it was called—was the great city of the north. So important was this fort city, perched on the northern edge of an empire, that even when Londinium lay an abandoned ruin, Eboracum remained inhabited continuously. The city was a nexus of both military power and trade, and boasted a large garrison, the foundations of which are now buried partly under York Minster.

(From the Vienna Letters)

Salve, mother,

The day has come. I have completed my service and I am soon to be made a citizen of Rome. I am extremely proud of my achievement, as you are no doubt proud of me.

I have some important news for you, however. I may have to delay my return to Antioch. I have of late been helping another fox family down on their luck. I am great friends with their daughter, Exuperata Lovernisca.

They have asked me to help them with their business for a while. I have also been offered a post as a civil servant in Eboracum in the future, if I wish. Let us say in a year or two I will make my decision, but I am still homesick for Antioch.

Send all my love to everyone back home. I hope this letter finds you well. I am forever your loving son, Thomas.

(From a wax tablet, preserved in river mud at York):

Thomas Antiochus, called Macrotis... magistrate of...

(From a receipt scratched into lead, found under the foundations of a medieval butcher's shop in York, razed in 1902 to build a telephone office):

For Thomas: two barrels of fine wine from Hispania, one jar of garum from Ostia, one bushel of dates from Antioch, one jar of olives from Tuscany, and a tunic cord of gold thread.

For Exuperata, as a gift from Thomas: a fine mantle of byssus, one pair of Egyptian sandals accented with lapis lazuli, a bushel of Corinthian raisins, a comb made of abalone, a vial of two measures of spikenard, and a ring of gold with letters beneath the band.

(From inside the band of a gold late Roman ring found in a cache of Roman, Saxon, and Viking-Age coins and trinkets in Selby, a few miles south of York):

Thomas Loves Exuperata

(From a gravestone found in York, inscribed in Attic Greek):

Here rests Thomas Antiochus Macrotis, Aedile long-serving in Eboracum, who died age seventy-one years;

And his wife, Exuperata Lovernisca, also entombed here, having died age seventy-nine.

Love followed them always and everywhere.

Their son, Horatius Lovernios Nero, has placed this stone.

Utunu

Utunu has been a video game developer since the mythical early '90s, and is fond of worldbuilding, linguistics, ancient history, fantasy, and Oxford commas. He's written a few short stories, and has received both a Cóyotl and Leo Award. His recently published first novel, *Rafts*, is now available at his website, *mapakuvillage.com*.

Gar "Sahoni" Atkins

Sahoni is an indigenous author of comics, radio, games, and more in the pursuit of continuing a storytelling tradition. You can find most of his games at bramblewolfgames.itch.io including the critically-acclaimed Exceptionals, a game inspired by X-Men about the community and spaces marginalized folks make for themselves as well as the lenses through we experience the mutant metaphor.

NightEyes DaySpring

NightEyes DaySpring is a known troublemaker who is rumored to have a penchant for coffee and an interest in dead, ancient civilizations. He has been writing furry fiction for over twenty years, and over thirty-five of his short stories have been published. His work has appeared in various anthologies, including *Werewolves vs. Fascism*, *Heat*, and *FANG*. He also has contributed multiple stories to The Voice of Dog podcast, and he recently published his first novel, *Scars of the Golden Dancer*. Currently, NightEyes resides in Florida with his fiancé, where in his spare time he masquerades as an IT professional, plays board games, and doodles.

Visit his website, *nighteyes-dayspring.com*, for more about his writing, or find out where he is on social media at *nighteyes.carrd.co*.

Casterway

Casterway is a writer with an obsession with history, mustelids and random pieces of trivia. While not busy with his long collection of quiz competitions or his not-as-long series of Redwall fanfictions, he is currently studying Chemistry in England, though he lives with his family in Canada.

Faolan

Faolan is a writer and dancer living in the Netherlands. He spends his days trying to teach kids the beautiful English language, and his nights gaming, watching series or films, writing, reading, buying things he absolutely doesn't need, and hoarding gems and jewelry. You can read more of his work in publications by Thurston Howl Publications and Weasel Press, such as *Infurno*, *Purrgatorio*, *Slashers*, *Dogpile*, *BEAST*, and *The Howling Dead*.

Fopfox

Fop is a furry writer and IT worker from Vancouver, Canada. Most of his stories deal with fantasy or science fiction and can be found on *fopfox.sofurry.com*.

Huskyteer

Alice "Huskyteer" Dryden's short stories have been published in and out of the furry fandom, and have won two Cóyotl Awards, two Ursa Major Awards and one Leo Award. She edited *The Furry Megapack* for Wildside Press, and in 2019 she was Guest of Honor at Fur the 'More 007: Furry Never Dies.

Thomas "Faux" Steele

Thomas "Faux" Steele is an author and attorney who has been creating short stories since 2015. He enjoys writing in many genres, including horror, science-fiction, fantasy, and adult contemporary. He specializes in descriptive stories with rich world-building whose written words render a painting in the reader's mind. His work has been printed in many anthologies, including *FANG Vol. 7*, *Exploring*

New Places, and *Beast Vol. 1* as well as many 'zines including #OhMurr. In his free time, he's an avid coin collector and fancier of antiquities and fine art, almost all thrifted or picked from estate sales.

Kayodé Lycaon

Kayodé Lycaon is a gregarious painted wolf living in the questionable habitat of southwestern Ohio. By day, he pretends to be a human, writing software. At night, his paws weave character-driven stories inspired from his own life. When not writing, he can be found dabbling in the dark arts of Linux, D&D, and home automation. You can find out more on his website, *kayode.co.*

J.S. Hawthorne

J.S. Hawthorne was raised in New England, but now lives in exile on Long Island, where she pretends to be a lawyer by day. When she isn't writing either fiction or law, she mostly enjoys running more Dungeons and Dragons games than is strictly necessary and collecting books written by her friends. She promises she'll get around to reading them eventually, honest.

Casimir Laski

Casimir Laski is a writer, YouTuber, and literary critic from Virginia. He is the author of *Winter Without End*, a post-apocalyptic survival story told from the perspective of a dog, inspired by the animal stories he grew up reading. Additionally, he writes for Furry Book Review, and operates the YouTube channel Cardinal West, primarily devoted to discussion of literary xenofiction and western animation.

J.F.R. Coates

J.F.R. Coates is a speculative fiction author living in Australia, though originally from the picturesque West Country of England. His stories tend to focus away from human characters, instead giving life to the creatures that dwell alongside the familiar. He has been the Furry Writers' Guild president since 2021.

Pascal Farful

Pascal Farful is an author, musician, fursuiter, railway enthusiast, and photographer. At one point almost all of these occurred at once. He lives in a hollowed out volcano on the outskirts of the UK where Angels Pizza Company fear to tread.

Ziegenbock

Ziegenbock is a long-time creator of furry literature who lives in the United Kingdom. He is a goat who wields both pen and sword (though rarely at the same time). He was the winner of the 2021 Sofurry Short Story Contest, and his work has been featured by Thurston Howl Publications and The Voice of Dog podcast.

Domus Vocis

Nathan "Domus Vocis" Hopp is an author, writer, storyteller, and dedicated lover of literature and learning history. His debut novel is a historic coming-of-age fantasy set in 1890s New York titled *The Adventures of Peter Gray*, and he's been published in anthologies such as *Furries Hate Nazis*, *The Haunted Den*, and others. If you can't find him writing in a quiet café or reading in a library, he can be found on *domus-vocis.sofurry.com*, as well as on Twitter @HoppNate.

Televassi

Televassi's stories have been previously published in a number of anthologies and publications in the furry fandom. They write in a number of genres, but mostly fantasy, science fiction, and speculative fiction. You can find more about them and their writing on the usual furry places, including *televassi.sofurry.com*.

Rob MacWolf

Rob MacWolf lives somewhere in North America waiting for the world to end. In the meantime he practices neo-paganism, writes poetry, and co-hosts the audiofiction podcast The Voice of Dog, at *thevoice.dog*.

Rose LaCroix

What Rose LaCroix lacks in recognition she makes up for in versatility and staying power. Her first published novel, *Basecraft Cirrostratus*, has been in print since 2010. She writes both fiction and non-fiction, speculative and historical. Some of her medieval history research has been published on *Britannica.com*, and her short stories and poetry can be read on *Spillwords.com*. She lives in the Portland area with her husband Kobi and their cat Venus.

www.ingramcontent.com/pod-product-compliance
Lightning Source LLC
Chambersburg PA
CBHW070231200726
48293CB00005B/1572